DEVIL'S
DEN

Happy Reading!

Jeff Altabef

Jeff Altabef

FIRST EDITION SOFTCOVER
ISBN: 1622531388
ISBN-13: 978-1-62253-138-7

Editor: Kimberly Goebel
Senior Editor: Robb Grindstaff
Interior Designer: Lane Diamond

EVOLVED PUBLISHING™

www.EvolvedPub.com
Evolved Publishing LLC
Butler, Wisconsin, USA

Printed in Book Antiqua font.

What Others Are Saying
about DEVIL'S DEN

"[A] vivid, winning tale of a former couple's confrontation with themselves, each other, and a wider-ranging threat that grabs the reader from the beginning and proves nearly impossible to put down. Thriller audiences will find Devil's Den more than a notch above others in the genre."
~ *D. Donovan, Senior Reviewer, Midwest Book Review*

"Altabef's engaging tale is both wild and wholly believable. His carefully developed plot is high with tension and intrigue. ... Overall, it's an entertaining yarn for lovers of detective mysteries crossed with supernatural suspense."
~ *Dylan Ward, US Review of Books*

"Non-stop action and chills abound in the astounding speculative novel... This book has a thrilling plot, complete with formidable characters, magnificently blended with heart-pounding scenes filled with blood and guts. It starts with a bang and continues to build to an explosive finish."
~ *Susan Sewell, Readers' Favorite Book Reviews (5 Stars)*

"...intensely gripping narrative with vivid descriptions, striking characters, and a plot that sinks its claws in so deep you may end up scarred for life. It is impossible to put down; you just have to know what is happening, you need to see the bigger picture, and when you do see it ... you may wish you'd had the foresight to avert your gaze."
~ *K.J. Simmill, Readers' Favorite Book Reviews (5 STARS)*

"Exciting action makes this thriller move quickly and the added spice of supernatural elements increases the appeal. ... Intense with a love story thrown in, *Devil's Den* is a great book and the perfect beginning to what should be a wonderful series."
~ *Melinda Hills, Readers' Favorite Book Reviews (5 STARS)*

Books by Jeff Altabef

A NEPHILIM THRILLER
Book 1: *Devil's Den*

A POINT THRILLER
Book 1: *Fracture Point*
Book 2: *Shatter Point*

RED DEATH
Book 1: *Red Death*
Book 2: *The Ghost King*

CHOSEN
(By Jeff Altabef and Erynn Altabef)
Book 1: *Wind Catcher*
Book 2: *Brink of Dawn*
Book 3: *Scorched Souls*

Dedication

For all the angels who walk among us.

Devil's Den

A Nephilim Thriller

Jeff Altabef

CHAPTER 1

December 5th, 2041, 3:23 PM

The clouds break, transforming a dreary, drab day into a bright, brilliant one. The warm sun caresses Megan's face, and she smiles. She'd love to spend the rest of the day outside and enjoy the unexpected summer weather, but she's way too busy.

When she crosses a street, a glimmer shines in the distance, and she pauses, a queasy feeling twisting her stomach. The burst of sunlight sparkles off a new, white van parked along the curb in front of Peterson's small grocery store.

That's weird. When was the last time a new car parked in this neighborhood?

Perhaps Mr. Peterson is getting a delivery, but where's the logo or some other identifying marks? And usually delivery vans are old and beaten up.

A small chill knifes through her back, and her heart hammers. The van creates an alley of sorts with the glass wall of the small grocery on one side and the vehicle on the other, and the blackened windows prevents her from seeing inside.

I'm being silly. It's just a van. Standing on the street watching it is stupid. She has schoolwork to finish and offices to clean. There's no time to be childish. A new van can't hurt her, and her apartment building is only a half-block away, so she shifts her backpack on her shoulders and marches forward.

Once she reaches the front of the van, a man stalks out from behind the vehicle directly in her path.

CHAPTER 2

December 6th, 2041, 5:17 AM

I take in the city, all of it—the smell, the taste, the fear—and instantly regret it. Twenty years ago, I last called this city home and returning dredges up toxic memories I've tried to bury. Back then I joined the Army to escape this place, but I should have known better. It's a part of me like an arm or a leg. As hard as I try, I can't just cut it off and drop it into the sewer.

The ghetto streets haven't changed much. They're empty and exhausted. The air smells foul, a toxic stew of anger and desperation held together by the will to survive at the expense of anyone and anything. If I breathe deeply and concentrate, I can still catch the faintest trace of hope. When that dies off, the country will go completely to hell. As far as I can tell, it's a race to see who gets there first—it or me. I'm betting on me.

An almost-full moon takes the sting from the darkness. The moon reminds me of an old story a fellow soldier once told me. The story isn't particularly remarkable, but it's stuck to me.

Charlie was soldiering for a stretch, maybe three years, two and a half more than me. He believed in a future. He believed good things waited for him when he finished his tour. He even believed one day he'd get out of the Army. Basically, he was an idiot who had no more sense than a pile of rocks.

He liked to tell stories. Most of them utterly nonsensical, but one night, under the silvery light of a moon like this one, he told me a tale about three witches who control everyone's future. These witches weave strings that determine our destiny on a vast loom. Pull on one string and romance blooms; tug on another and illness strikes; cut the heartstring, and death takes you.

He told me these witches' names, but my memory isn't as good as it used to be and that's not important. He called them "the Fates." He said prayers to them every night, begging them to be good to him, to pull on the right strings. The next day a sniper blew a hole in his head. Parts of his skull and brain splattered on my uniform. I still remember the sound the high-caliber bullet made as it ripped through his helmet and into his skull. A sickening thud—the sound of death.

Maybe the Fates let him live just long enough to tell me their story. This way I'll know they're responsible for my predicament. It seems like something they'd do, like a poke in the eye.

I think Charlie was right about the Fates, but he was wrong about one thing. Sucking up doesn't do much good with them. They'll weave the tapestries any which way they damn well please. Still, in an odd way, the story offers me hope, a touch of solace. If these witches exist, they can change my fate, alter my path, add a new string to my tapestry. That would be good, because there's nothing but choppy water around me. It might be flimsy—this idea that the Fates can save me—but a drowning man will grab onto anything if he thinks it might keep him afloat, and I feel the water lapping against my face.

Witches or not, I've returned to the city of my birth. North Philly looks only slightly different from the last time I was here. Most of the stores look the same: small bodegas, a few bars, liquor stores, massage parlors, and check-cashing places. One apartment building is newish, while the others look in worse shape. All the stores are locked up with heavy metal gates except for a few of the seediest bars and the random massage parlor with a red neon "Open" sign still lit in a window.

Down an alley, the moonlight reveals glimpses of the path before me: a rat scurries out of my way, a dumpster overflows to my right, a half-dozen empty bottles stacked against a wall on my left. Deep shadows like wells live in the nooks and doorways here.

I'm no more than three blocks from my destination, the apartment building where I spent what passed as a childhood.

A shoe scrapes against the pavement behind me. Someone is sneaking up on me—a man, thin, cautious. He walks quietly, which is not easy to do in an alley.

I turn a few inches so the duffel over my shoulder blocks the stalker's view as I slip my hand into the pocket of my old army jacket and remove a four-inch blade.

A step moves him closer and then one more. He's within arm's length now. If he wanted to kill me, he should have done it already.

I spin and press the tip of the knife against the stranger's throat.

An old man freezes and lifts his hands in the air in surrender. Deep canyons carve into the stranger's ashen face. Stringy, gray hair hangs to his shoulders, his cheeks gaunt, as if his skin has been stretched tight against his skull. He wears a black trench coat, black pants, and black shoes. His thin body hunches forward, bent on stooped shoulders. He looks sickly and smells awful, a combination of body odor, booze, and something even worse I try to block out. Still, light shines in his almond-colored eyes. He wants to live, which is something. Maybe everything.

"Who sent you, old man?"

"No one's sent me anywhere. I live on these streets."

I press the blade against his flesh. "Human or demon? Don't lie to me."

"Human...I guess. I've been called many things before, but never a demon."

Paranoid? More than a tad, but that's better than a demon ripping out my heart and dragging me to hell, so I check him for signs of being a fiend. No hellfire burns in his eyes, and I don't see any other obvious signs. In my experience, though, demons are tricky. I've never met one with wings, horns, or a tail. I killed one in an alley in New York City a while back that shifted its form. Hands turned to claws and teeth transformed into fangs. He almost killed me, that one did. He tried to rip out my heart with his bare hands. I have the scars to prove it. At least that's how I remember it. It was dark, and after I stabbed him in the eye, he returned to his normal form.

I nick the old-timer just to be certain in the uncertain light. A crimson trickle rolls down his neck.

"Hey, that hurts." He rubs the blood from his neck. "Why'd you go and do a thing like that?"

"Just to be sure. Demon blood oozes like black sludge, and it stinks like sulfur." His blood smells oddly sweet.

I slip the knife back into my pocket. "It's not safe to sneak up on people, old-timer."

The man lowers his arms. "Who, me? I wasn't sneaking up on anyone. I walk quietly, that's all. It's good to blend into the shadows here. It keeps me alive, lets me know things."

"Right."

The old-timer is my welcome home committee, and he's more than I deserve. I continue my trek down the alley, and he keeps pace besides me.

"I haven't seen you around here before," he says.

"I didn't realize I needed to check in with you. Is there a booth somewhere?"

"I've lived here a long time, that's all. Not much goes on that I don't know. I know just about everyone."

I pause for a second. Maybe the old-timer can help me. I remove my phone from my pocket and retrieve a picture a street artist created on a tablet for me. He was no Rembrandt, but he did a decent enough job creating a face I remembered from a lifetime ago back. Aging software added the years on, so it should look like her now.

I show him the artist's rendering. "Do you know this person? Ever see her around?"

He shrugs. "She looks sickly. I can't say I've seen her."

"She used to sell drugs for the Monarch gang twenty years ago. She lived in a building around here with her son. Look again."

He shakes his head. "So many people come and go. Besides, the Monarchs vanished some time ago. Maybe five years? My sense of time isn't what it used to be, so I can't say for certain. She has a wicked look to her though. Downright nasty."

"You can't even imagine. She's stolen more from me then I can tell you."

"Are you sure you want to find her? Some people are better left buried in the past."

"She's probably dead anyway, but she's the only person who might have answers for me."

"Who is she?"

"My mother."

My mother saw demons, and she worried they'd drag her to hell. When I was thirteen, she killed my father in a fit of rage, stabbing him to death with a pair of scissors, claiming he was a demon. When she started in on me, I fled and joined the Army. I was fifteen. I thought she was crazy, but that was before I started seeing demons myself. Now I don't know. I try to remember what my father's blood looked like and can't. Although, I recall the smell and that turns my stomach and worries me. If my mother was right about my father being a demon, what does that make me? Am I fated to the same destiny?

I hear my old training instructor's voice in my head. "Look alive, Cupcake. You've got company."

"I know. I'm not a trainee anymore, Caesar," I say.

"Are you talking to me?" asks the old-timer, understandably confused.

"Just a ghost from my past who won't keep his big mouth shut and leave me alone." I hand the old-timer a twenty-dollar bill. "You'd best scram. Some hostiles are approaching."

The old-timer takes the bill and looks down the alley, squinting. The group passes under a light from an apartment building window. "Those are Red Dragons. They're a mean bunch. You'd best run for it."

"I haven't brought my running shoes."

"There are four of them and they're nasty."

"Doesn't seem fair, does it? They'll need another four to have a chance."

The old-timer fades into the shadows where it would take a spotlight to find him.

I glance at the time on my phone. It's been two weeks, six days, and seven hours since I last killed someone.

Pity, I really wanted to reach three weeks.

CHAPTER 3

I check to make sure my Smith and Wesson is firmly holstered to the small of my back and march toward the four young men, who haven't seen me yet. One is totally wasted, while a second staggers a bit less than the first, but he's still compromised. The other two walk confidently, as if they own this alley, which is probably true. All four wear leather boots with steel tips meant for kicking defenseless people. These guys are exactly the type to do just that—kick defenseless people.

The group strolls under another light less than a block away. They wear black jackets with Red Dragon patches on their chests. I scan them from left to right: the drunk, a steroid-induced hulk, a thin sneaky-looking guy with a nervous gait, and a tall fellow who swings a baseball bat like a nightstick.

The sneaky-looking guy stops under the light and taps the hulk next to him. "Look, George. We have a visitor."

I pause ten paces before the gang. I could turn and run like the old-timer suggested. Still can, but I won't. Caesar's voice rumbles inside my head. He wants me to punish, to cause pain, to hurt these thugs. The sound escalates with other voices that join his.

It starts to get crowded in my mind, but I fight hard against the noise and the building pressure and offer the four a chance. They deserve that, and I can still offer it. Maybe the Fates will shine on them.

"I'm just passing through. It would be best if you step aside. I have no beef with you fellas, and I'm in a hurry."

Sneaky grins and pulls a Glock from under his jacket. Hulk grabs a six-inch blade from a sheath on his belt, and the slugger with the bat taps the barrel menacingly in his hand. The drunk, too wasted to do anything, shakes his head and sways from side to side.

My training kicks in. I need to disarm the leader with the gun first, then the hulk and finally the guy with the bat. I can ignore drunk guy until later. The worst he can do is vomit on me. My only problem: the distance that separates us. Ten steps are seven too many. Three would be ideal.

I stumble a bit forward on purpose to act like an uncoordinated buffoon. I lift my hands in the air to put them at ease and offer one final chance for them to save themselves. "I really don't think you appreciate what's going to happen next."

The leader points the gun at my chest horizontally, gangster style. The barrel shakes a bit and his stance is all wrong. He'd be lucky to hit the side of a barn at thirty yards, but I'm only five paces away now, which makes me a hell of a lot easier to hit than a barn.

He waves the gun at me. "Stop right there, asshole. I know exactly what's going to happen. You're going to hand me that duffel and then we're going to search you for anything else we might want. And if you're lucky, you'll survive with just a beating. Otherwise..."

The slugger grins and swings the bat in a looping arc. His eyes twinkle. He likes to cause pain; dried blood streaks the barrel of the bat as a warning. At least it's an old-school wooden one. He deserves points for that. I hate the new titanium ones. They don't sound right when they hit someone.

I adjust the strap on my duffel so it won't swing too much and get in my way, take two steps forward, and stare at the leader. I know what he's thinking. He sees an easy mark, an unarmed man, not particularly tall at just under six feet and not particularly wide. Sometimes appearances can be deceiving unless you look closely enough.

There's an easy way out of this mess for me. Even though the leader has his Glock aimed at my chest, I'm still too fast a draw for him. I can pull out my Smith and Wesson and blast him in the chest before he'd squeeze the trigger. After he goes down, the other three would likely run, or in the case of the wasted guy, stumble away. I'd take one step to my left just in case the leader is quicker than I think he is. That way, he'd miss me, even if he manages to fire a round. My chance at success is so close to 100 percent, it's not even worth doing the math in my head.

There's only one problem with the easy way out. I don't want it. Not tonight. Not in my old neighborhood looking for my mother, so I work out a different plan. My only question—will the Glock actually work? I create two scenarios to overcome the uncertainty, both equally effective. My chance at success drops from nearly 100 percent to a manageable 96.

I smile a goofy grin to put the leader at ease. "This is your last chance. I don't have a problem with you guys. Move aside or you'll regret it. I'm wasting too much time already."

The leader laughs, but it sounds forced. The gun barrel shakes a little more than a moment earlier.

My confidence unnerves him. Deep down, he knows he's in trouble. His intuition is barking at him. It's not his fault he doesn't understand what it's trying to tell him. He's only a product of his experience, and he's never met anyone like me before. If he has any sense, he'd pull the trigger — but he won't. He's the type who needs the last word. A thin guy like that uses his tongue as a weapon to move up the ladder.

So, he throws out a barb. "Can't you count, or are you simple-minded? There's four of us and only one of you."

I point to the drunk on the far left, whose head sags against his chest. "You can't count the lush. Look at him. He's about to fall down."

The leader flashes his gaze at his friend. An easy-to-predict involuntary response. It takes no longer than a heartbeat, but that's enough.

I dart forward, grab the Glock, twist, and yank. The gun comes free, and in one smooth motion, I shoot the hulk in the thigh. In the alley, the gunshot sounds like an explosion. The other three guys freeze for a precious second.

I chop the leader in the throat, which drops the thin man to his knees. A knee to the forehead knocks him out.

The slugger grins at me. The twinkle in his eyes turns crimson and blazes with hellfire. "Welcome home, Stevie," he says in a deep voice that sounds like it's risen from hell itself.

He flies forward, moving faster than he should for his size, and jams the end of the bat into my stomach. The shot bends me over, and I drop the Glock. He hits me with a right cross that staggers me backward.

My head swims. I didn't count on fighting a demon. This throws off the math and not in a good way.

"Why are you fighting us?" he growls. "Join us, Stevie. You're so close to turning into one of us now."

"Never."

"Too bad. He has big plans for you."

The demon swings the bat in a vicious swipe at my head. I duck under and kick his knee. His leg buckles. I grab him by the shoulders, and ram him into a wall, head first. Brick chips flake off and fall to the ground.

He drops the bat.

I roll my shoulder and smash a fist into his kidney. The punch would have crippled a linebacker, but it barely registers on him.

He grabs my neck with both hands and squeezes.

I try to pull his arms off, but he's too strong.

Lights flash in front of me. His face changes, his nose turning into a snout and teeth extending into fangs. Another minute and I'm dead.

I reach for my handgun. My fingers slip off the grip and my lungs ache. I try again, close my hand on the handle, pull it free from the holster, and shoot him in the chest.

His face goes taut, and he reels backward. Blood, as black as night, seeps from his chest, and the sulfur stench burns my nose.

He scowls at me. "You've ruined my jacket. Now I'm going to play with you before I send you to hell."

"Man, you stink." I grab the bat from the ground, spin, and crack him in the head. The blow knocks him to his knees, and I start swinging. Four swings later and there's nothing left of his head but bone fragments and tar-like sludge.

I check my phone to note when I ended my streak and freeze. Does killing a demon count? After all, he wasn't human. No, demons don't count, so I put my phone away.

Wasted guy vomits. "What the fuck just happened?"

"You've got to upgrade the people you're hanging out with. Demons are not good company."

"You killed Doug." He wobbles backward. "Who the hell are you?"

"Good question. I'm having problems with that one myself. How did he know my name?" I step toward him, bat still in my hand.

"I don't know, man. I didn't hear him say nothing."

"He called me by my name. Explain." I take another step.

He starts to cry. "I don't know. We were just coming back from a party. No big deal."

He looks honest, and he's too wasted to put on a convincing show. I think about killing them all anyway. I'd snap his neck (three seconds), shoot the sneaky-faced leader in the head (two more seconds) and finish off the hulk with my knife (ten seconds). I prefer using my knife. It's more personal than shooting someone and lets me be creative. It's important to be imaginative. I have so few outlets to express myself otherwise.

Murdering the trio would take me a total of fifteen seconds, but killing the demon has satisfied the voices in my head for now. Only Caesar's voice barks at me, and he's not insisting I kill them. He's intent on making fun of me for hesitating. I focus my energy, clear my mind, and his voice fades away.

The muscle-bound thug moans. "I'm bleeding. You shot me. It really hurts."

He sounds a bit like a bleating sheep, and I rethink my decision as I step over to him.

"No kidding." I stomp on his head to shut him up. The giant bends backward to the ground, unconscious.

"What's your name?" I ask the drunk.

"Griffin."

"Like the magical creature?"

"Huh?"

"I've got to be honest with you, I don't see it, Griff. You're young still and admittedly not at your best, but I think your parents placed unreasonable expectations on you." I point at the hulk. "He'll bleed out if you don't take him to a doctor."

"Fuck him. Listen man. Just don't kill me."

"You see, that's not exactly magical thinking, Griff." I point the Smith and Wesson at his chest. "What type of gang are you guys running anyway? Aren't you supposed to be a brotherhood? All for one and one for all. That type of shit. You're giving gangs a bad name."

"You're a fucking maniac. You caved in Doug's face."

"He left me no choice." I holster the Smith and Wesson, retrieve the Glock from the pavement and slip it into a jacket pocket. "You saw what he became?"

Griffin shakes his head. "I don't know what I saw."

"Well, that's what drinking and drugs will do to you. I hope you've learned a valuable lesson here."

"All I saw was you swinging that bat."

Griff must have grabbed the knife the hulk dropped. He waves the blade in uncertain swipes, tottering back and forth on his heels. "Stay away from me."

Whichever Fate is governing his future is closing the shears on his heartstring.

"Seriously. Okay, Griff. Put it down, and I won't hurt you. You haven't pissed me off yet, but you're starting to annoy me. Besides," I slip the Glock out from my pocket and point it at him, "my gun outranks your knife, Sparky. You have three seconds to drop the knife, and I'm not doing any cheesy countdowns. The decision is yours."

He drops the knife.

"Good decision," I say. "Frankly, I was a little worried you were going to make the wrong choice. Can you get him some help before he bleeds to death?"

He nods, and it looks like some light has returned to his eyes. I doubt there's too much wattage when he's stone-cold sober. I'm not working with Einstein here.

"Good, give me your belt."

He fumbles with the buckle and can't seem to yank the belt through the loops in his jeans.

"Come on, Griff. You don't need a master's degree in engineering to remove a belt. Just pull on it. I've got somewhere to go."

He finally pulls it free and hands it to me.

After I've fastened it to the hulk's leg to slow the bleeding, I say, "That'll buy you a little more time. Try to be a little smarter. You've got to make better choices, Griff. You're not representing the Red Dragons well. And keep the demons out of the gang. It should be a simple rule. No demons allowed."

My phone pings a special tone I set up for exactly four people. If any of them needs me, they can message me, and my phone sounds with three distinctive chimes.

A one-word message flashes across the screen: *Help.*

I send a simple reply: *Where are you?*

202 Elm St, Apt 322B. Near Maloney's Pub. Do you remember where that is?

Be there in 20.

Mother will have to wait. Of the four people who can summon me with that special tone, this one hits me in the gut harder than Doug's bat.

Kate! Sixteen years of silence and she has no way of knowing I was back in town. She must be desperate.

I shift the duffel to a comfortable spot on my shoulder and jog away. By the time I reach the side street, dawn has announced itself with a sliver of blue and purple that burns away the darkness.

How much trouble is Kate in?

I run faster.

CHAPTER 4

The air feels greasy, like the inside of KFC at lunchtime, and it smells like an unhappy marriage between a dumpster and a toilet. It's probably coating my lungs as I run through the mostly empty ghetto streets. Those who can afford them use air filters in big cities. Not me. I don't imagine I'll live long enough that it'll make a whole lot of difference.

A few hopeless prostitutes walk the streets, looking for their last john of the night, and a couple of drug dealers lounge against cars, hoping for one last deal. They're both selling a brief escape from a bad situation. I can't blame them. Everyone needs a way to survive.

No one pays attention to me. The only real sign of life comes from one of those new virtual reality life centers. This one's called Otherworldly Experiences. I slow my pace and glance at the well-lit storefront. It's crowded with customers. An armed guard stands outside and another just inside the door—a lot of security for a virtual reality joint.

The new craze, these VR places are popping up everywhere. According to a screen out front, this one promises experiences that are "Better than the Real Thing." I'll never go into a place like that. I wouldn't mind dialing reality back a few notches. But I understand why they're popular. They're selling the same things as the ladies and the drug dealers—escapism.

I show my identification card to the armed Homeland Security trooper at a checkpoint who has a long, sad face. He must have pissed off someone important to get such a shitty detail. He mans the gate between the ghetto and the better district, District 12. During the day, this checkpoint is open. At night, a guard with an M18 protects it. He scans my ID through the reader and logs me in. Everyone needs to be logged in or face jail time if they're caught in the wrong district. Red posters with white block writing litter the place. They tell us to report "Un-American" behavior—it's our duty and the government will pay monetary rewards.

Thanks to my prior employer, my identification card permits me access to all the districts in the country. I'll get some strange looks at the top tier ones, but none of the Homeland goons will turn me away because I don't *belong*. I find Elm Street and check the building numbers until I locate my destination mid-block, a ten-story apartment building, made with new, steel construction.

It's been twenty-three minutes and twenty seconds since Kate called. I'm late and, for some ridiculous reason, I think about bringing her flowers. She likes red carnations best. Once I gave her a dozen roses, and they all died two days later. She banned me from ever bringing her roses again. Said it was a tragedy for something so beautiful to die so quickly, and she wanted no part of such pointless waste.

It's a stupid idea, this idea to bring Kate flowers. First, there's no place open to buy them and second, boyfriends bring flowers. I'm not her boyfriend and this is not a date. She needs help and contacted me out of desperation. That's all this is, a plea for help. I need to keep that in mind or I'll make a fool of myself.

The directory lists a dizzying number of apartments for the size of the building. I trace my finger to Apartment 322B, press the buzzer, and look into the security camera.

The door clicks open. The lobby is clean with a gray-tiled floor, plain steel walls, post office boxes to the left, mirrors to the right that add light and make the space appear bigger. Video cameras record everything. An elevator and a staircase are off to my right. I take the stairs two at time and enter the third-floor hallway.

Designed as a new "communal" living space, the floor holds one large kitchen and two bathrooms for tenants to share. The owners bill it as the latest in "enhanced living," the old-fashioned community center in one building. Total crap. The new design adds to the number of rentable apartments in the building, which adds to their profit.

I've seen places like this one before, massive apartment complexes in the manufacturing districts in upstate New York—vast structures, crammed with people. The factories own the buildings and deduct wages directly from paychecks. They attach or subtract boxes to floors as needed with giant cranes. The residents call the places Meat Packers. The name fits.

At least this place looks better than those—not so many apartments crammed together and the air smells clean—none of the rotten stench from the Meat Packers. I reach Kate's apartment and stare at the door with my knuckles poised to knock.

Even though I returned to Philly, I didn't intend to see Kate. It's not fair to her. I made my decision a long time ago, and we've lived separate lives since. I can't go back and change it now, but here I am. She reached out to me, so what happens is on her. I steady myself, rifle my hand through my short black hair in a failed attempt to smooth it down, and knock softly against the metal door.

The door swings open a heartbeat later. Kate looks almost the same as when I'd seen her last. A little heavier perhaps, but in a good way, muscle added over time.

Long, straight, blonde hair frames her pretty, oval face. A few fine lines around her eyes and on her forehead are new. A couple of freckles dot her nose and cheeks. She used to have more. A small, diamond-shaped scar marks her left cheek near her ear. The toll the years have taken on her do nothing to take away from her good looks, and her eyes smolder as intense as ever, a deeper blue than the Caribbean.

She wears a long-sleeved, plain, white T-shirt that fits loosely over her athletic frame, and faded blue jeans. She waves me inside without uttering a word.

All things considered, she looks damn good. Better than I would've imagined except for the fear and anger that weigh down her eyes.

She shuts the door behind me. I don't know what to say, so I settle for the simple. Better to stick with simple than say something totally stupid. "Hi, Kate. Sorry I'm late. I got here as soon as I could."

She lifts her hand as if to slap me.

I'll take the blow if she delivers it. It's the least I can do, and if it'll make her feel better, I'm game.

She freezes her hand in place and lowers it. "*Hi*? It's been over sixteen years. I thought you were dead and that's all you have to say. When I texted, I figured it would go into a digital black hole somewhere. I don't know whether to hug you or kick you in the balls."

"I wouldn't blame you either way, but the hug sounds better. You kick like a soccer player."

"Tough. I'll decide later."

It's stupid. I feel the need to defend myself, even though nothing I say will make a difference, and in fact, I'm defenseless. I should keep my mouth shut, but it opens and words blather out of it. "I told you I was leaving for good. I told you, you wouldn't hear from me again. I never lied to you."

"No, you never lied to me." She offers a half-grin, which probably means she isn't going to haul off and kick me in the nuts, although I can't be totally sure. She's unpredictable. It's one of the things I love about her—or used to love about her. My feelings jumble together, and I'm not sure what's real or just echoes from the past.

"You've always been an honest asshole," she says. "I don't care about the past. It's long dead. I need help finding my daughter, Megan. Someone took her yesterday. Can you help me?"

I never lie to Kate. We used to fight fiercely from time to time, but never because I lied to her. Even now I can't and won't. She'd see through me if I tried.

"I know how to investigate. I can get people to talk to me. It won't be pretty, but I won't stop until I find out what's happened to her. I won't be hampered by any...rules."

"Good, fuck the rules. No one lives by rules anymore anyway. This is my daughter. I need her safe."

I nod, although she's not being truthful. Most people have limits, even to save their own. Kate has them—I don't.

"Do you have a picture of Megan?" I want a visual image of the girl before delving into the particulars. Images help me sort things through. I can tell a lot about people by looking at them. In person is better, but a good photo will do.

She hands me a photo disk. "This is my Megan."

I press the button, and my heart stops. The girl in the three-dimensional holographic image is beautiful, almost a carbon copy of Kate herself, but that's not what freezes my heart. She looks at least fifteen years old. The math troubles me. I last saw Kate sixteen years and six months ago. "She's beautiful." I want to ask Kate who the girl's father is, but I can't find those words yet, so I settle on something easier. "Did you report her missing to the cops?"

"Right," Kate huffs. "They want a thousand dollars just to list her in the missing persons' registry. To investigate, they demanded five thousand! I don't have it. If I sold everything I'd be lucky to pull together two thousand. Besides, they take the money and never find anyone."

She's right. The police are for suckers. Even the wealthy use private security when they want something done. "Okay. Tell me what you know. Start at the beginning and include as many details as possible.

She sits on one of two chairs in the small living room. In reality, the living room is a simple hallway, a tidy ten-foot strip that connects the two bedrooms together. A small metal table separates the two chairs and a worn couch bumps against a wall.

The couch and chairs are made from black, fake leather. Only a few dashes of color add life to the room: three small throw pillows, two pink and one blue, a white shag rug underneath the cocktail table, and one framed poster of a Monet print on the wall behind the couch.

A flat screen hangs on the wall opposite the couch, but Kate's draped a white sheet over it. The fuzzy outline of the Originalist's logo rotates slowly on the screen behind the sheet.

"You know they can still listen in on our conversation," I say.

"Better that then them seeing us. I'd shut the damn thing off, but one of my neighbors did that, and they carted her off last week. Conduct that's Un-American. That's what they said."

"There's a lot of that going around lately." I drop my duffel by the door and sit in the other chair. I can smell her perfume. It's the same fragrance she wore when we dated: lilac with a trace of honey. It brings back memories of passionate nights, long walks, fiery arguments. The passionate nights bully the rest of the memories to the side.

I don't want to fall down that slide now. Her daughter's missing, so I purge thoughts of her body from my mind and study the image of Megan instead. I'm usually good with ages, but teenage girls can be tricky. Sometimes they look older than they should. Maybe she just turned fifteen or maybe she's closer to sixteen. Closer to sixteen would be trouble.

Intelligence and even a bit of courage flash around the edges of the girl's eyes. Her posture is strong. Her hands are on her hips and a stop-taking-my-picture grin on her face. I immediately like her. She reminds me of a young Kate, but that might be my imagination. I can't fully trust my intuition with Kate so close, smelling of lilac and honey, and looking so good.

After a few minutes, I look up, and Kate begins. "She left school yesterday at the regular time with her two best friends. They walked her usual route, and they separated two blocks away from here. Just two lousy blocks and she never made it home. I came home around seven and asked everyone along the way, but no one's seen anything. If they did, they didn't tell me about it."

"You sure she didn't come home, even for a short bit?"

"She never made it here. All her stuff from school is missing. She always leaves her backpack in the living room by the door. I've asked her a thousand times to put it in her room, but she never does. It's our running joke."

I nod. "Okay, does she have any boyfriends? Most of the time these random events turn out not to be so random."

"She's a good kid. She hasn't started dating anyone yet. She's never been in trouble. She's a straight A student. Too good to be my daughter really. Everyone loves her. No enemies. I asked her friends already. No..."

She doesn't cry; she just pauses with her hand over her mouth, her fingers trembling. She's fallen into some horrifying pit of what ifs that all parents must succumb to under these circumstances. If Dante's right and hell has nine circles, she's slipped into the ninth.

I can't see her like this, so I stand and engage her, forcing her to snap back into the present and out of the pit. "Which room is hers?"

She climbs out of her sadness, walks to the door on the left and opens it. The ten by ten-foot square has barely enough room for a bed, a dresser, a tiny closet, one mirror, a small desk and a chair. One hundred square feet, and that's it. Some prison cells have more space.

It's hard to find much of Megan inside. She's taped several photos of her friends on one of the walls: four different faces, a close group, everyone smiling. She's also taped a poster of Earth to the wall behind her bed.

Kate presses a button on a small device on the desk, and a holographic image of the universe, flickers to life in the center of her room.

This isn't what I expect from a teenager's room.

Kate shrugs. "Megan's into space. She wants to be a physicist, break the speed of light barrier, and travel the universe someday. She won the holographic projector in a science fair at her school. One day she might just..."

Her mouth hangs open, and the grief acts like a roadblock that prevents any words from skirting around it.

The room surprises me. I don't have a ton of experience with teenagers, but they're supposed to be messy. Megan keeps her room military-style neat. I close my eyes for a second and try to imagine who she is: smart, close friends, adventurous, strong. She wants to be an astronaut.

I sweep my hand over the surface of her white, plastic desk. It's clean and clear, except for a yellow post-it note. In a neat, block handwriting, it says, "The truth is hard to find, but it's always worth the effort."

I'm not so sure. Some truths should remain hidden. Teenagers can afford that level of naiveté, but soldiers can't. It'll get them killed.

The color has drained from Kate's face and her eyes look distant. She's sunk to a new ring of hell, the land of what ifs again. I can't leave her there, and I have to ask. If I don't, the question will fester and swallow me whole.

"How old is Megan exactly?"

CHAPTER 5

Megan tosses onto her left side and then flips back to her right, stuck between sleep and consciousness. Eyes still closed, she struggles to recall a dream, which is unusual for her, to say the least. She rarely dreams, and even when she does, they usually flee from her mind and quickly recede to her subconscious where they belong. She finds them useless, annoying, and their meanings rarely clear or helpful.

Life follows a set of scientific rules, the laws of nature. Dreaming about an alternative world where the normal rules don't apply is pointless and counterproductive. Better to understand and fix the real world than be distracted over a fake, dream one.

Still, this dream feels different; it was vivid, the details bold and important. Flashes come to her: a doctor peeling off her clothes with gentle hands, her body reluctantly complying with the doctor's requests, an uncomfortable examining table, and one of those disposable patient gowns that never quite close when you try to tie them. The coarse cotton scratches her skin and a cool breeze sweeps against her naked back, leaving an army of goose bumps in its wake.

The female doctor smiled. Megan tries to recall her face, but all she remembers is a purple birthmark, the shape of a football, on the woman's cheek, and a flash of purple. The doctor assured her the examination wouldn't hurt. She wanted to see how much Megan had sinned before she arrived on The Farm — had sinned!

Megan bolts upright, her breath catching in her throat in frantic gasps. That wasn't a dream. *I did see a doctor.* Her head aches, and her tongue feels fat and leathery. She wades through fuzzy thoughts. *Where am I? How did I get here?* Slowly, she forces her mind to focus, and she conjures memories from the prior day.

A white van was parked on her street. The new paint job shimmered in the afternoon sun. She should've never walked past it. She should have listened to that queasy feeling in her stomach and went around the block. Then the asshole stepped in her way, followed by the two other kidnappers who punched her in the stomach and dragged her into the back of the van.

Someone was already in the van. *Amy!* Amy was in the van, a little older than her with short black hair, and a pretty round face. She was so scared. Her lips kept trembling.

Where's Amy?

Megan's heart jumps and, for the first time, she looks outward. Rich morning light streams through windows. Five beds plus the one she's in fill the room. They're empty. The only other piece of furniture, a large wooden dresser with six drawers — one for each bed.

What happened after I saw Amy in the van? She recalls random events as if she fell asleep watching a movie and can't quite remember what happened clearly: her head crashed against the side of the van, a long-cramped trip, the air smelled clean when they opened the back doors, cows mooing in the distance. *Cows?*

The door opens, and a young man strides inside. In his twenties, he's handsome in a rugged way. Her mom likes old-fashioned cowboy movies, and this guy would fit comfortably in one. His deep-set almond eyes sparkle, and he has a strong jaw and athletic build. He wears a red jumpsuit and a light green beret tilted to one side. Three lime green crosses, each enclosed in a star, have been sewn onto his jumpsuit at his right shoulder. A symbol of some kind, maybe even a rank that indicates he's important.

Megan's voice sounds higher pitched than usual, which pisses her off. "Who the fuck are you, and where am I?"

He smiles. It looks kindly, and not at all sinister, which slows Megan's racing heart. He doesn't look like a monster, and he speaks in a soothing, tenor voice. A movie star's voice.

"I'm Buck. You're at The Farm. Your memories are a little...uncertain because the doctor gave you a drug before she examined you to make that process...easier. I know nothing makes sense now, but everything will fall in place. We'll explain it all to you. If — "

"What happened to Amy? What did you do with her?"

He shrugs. "She woke before you and has already started her transition. She hasn't been harmed in any way. I'm sure you'll see her later in the day. Now it's time for you to start your transition. If—"

"I want to go home. I don't want to transition to anything."

"You're going to be an Angel. You'll find salvation here. But it would be best if you stop interrupting me and do exactly as I say. That way, you can start to find answers to your questions. Come on. Time to get up."

Megan steps out of the bed on rubbery legs. She wobbles and almost falls, but he grabs her arm and steadies her.

When she figures she can stand on her own, she shakes him off. "I don't want salvation. I want to go home. My mom will be worrying about me. Just tell me where I can find Amy, and we'll be on our way."

Buck smiles a friendly, kindly grin that pulls light from his brown eyes. "You'll change your mind soon enough." He removes and then unfolds a long thin stick from a pocket on the leg of his jumpsuit. "These sticks are electrified. A simple touch will cause terrific pain. Don't give me a reason to use it. I'd rather not hurt you. But the choice is yours."

"Sure." Megan touches the side of her face and winces. "Tell that to the jackass who hit me. He seemed to enjoy it."

"Frankie has been disciplined for that sin. Come, you have much to learn." He waves his arm toward the open door in an *after you* gesture. Under other circumstances, she might even consider it polite.

At least that's in the right direction. She isn't going to escape from inside this room, so she takes him up on his offer and steps outside into the sun. The building where she had been sleeping is a small, white, wooden, single-story structure. Three other similar buildings are nearby, all larger than the one she just left. They form a well-maintained courtyard with neatly cut grass in the center and flowers lining the buildings. Used to the city, the courtyard looks odd and disorienting, as if she's woken in a movie.

When she breathes in, the air smells fresh, different from city air. It smells like a trip she took with her mom to a strawberry farm outside of the city. Her mom wanted her to see "where things grow." It seemed stupid at the time, but it wasn't. The sounds of cows, or what she assumes are cows, carry to her on a slight breeze. She's never seen or heard a cow in person before.

The chilly air bites through the long-sleeved T-shirt she still wears from the prior day. She looks for other people and finds two men in red jumpsuits in the distance down a dirt road. They both have two green cross-symbols on their shoulders, one less than Buck. One woman, who wears a lilac-colored jumpsuit, leans against the side of another white building across the courtyard. She looks familiar, and then Megan sees the mole on her cheek—the doctor who examined her.

Buck points to the nearest building with his electric prod. "Mother is waiting for you. Come with me."

"I'm not going anywhere with you. I thought we talked about that already. I'm going home."

Buck grins a half-smile and nods approvingly. "You are a tester. You need proof to become a true believer. Don't worry, you'll find your proof here. This is your new home. Your life has just begun."

She's not going to wait for him to drag her off. Unpredictability is important. At least that's what the self-defense expert her mom forced her to train with used to tell her. She darts forward and aims a front kick at Buck's groin.

He sidesteps her foot, swipes it aside with his elbow, and taps her leg with the electric prod.

Pain explodes up her body. She screams and falls to the ground. It feels as if he's chopped off her leg with a machete. Stars burst in front of her eyes.

God, she wants to cry, but she won't give him the satisfaction. Besides, crying is pointless and silly. It won't change anything, and will only grant him power over her, and she won't do that. He has enough already.

When the pain subsides to a manageable level, she glares at him. "You get off on hurting girls? Is that what happens here?"

He shakes his head and his voice sounds deflated. "I warned you, and I used the lowest setting. I don't want to hurt you. Now get up, dust yourself off, and come with me. Mother is waiting."

Megan struggles to her feet and grits her teeth. "You probably not that tough without your stick."

Buck rolls his eyes and points toward the door to the nearest building. "Keeping Mother waiting is not a good idea. She's a busy woman. She won't like that."

"She's not *my* mother," Megan spits the words angrily, but she'll comply for now. She needs to be smart; she needs a plan to escape.

Buck opens the plain black door.

Megan stumbles up the small stoop and inside. Her leg only partially responds to her commands. The building looks clean and well maintained: white walls, white tiled floor, and black wooden doors.

Buck knocks on the first door to his left and a female voice calls out, "Enter."

He opens the door and waves for Megan to go inside. She doesn't want to walk through that doorway. Whatever's on the other side frightens her. She can't imagine anything good in that room. Her body trembles even though she tries hard not to show any reaction.

Buck encourages her with a small sincere grin.

"Don't worry. She's not going to hurt you. She's going to save you."

CHAPTER 6

Kate rolls her eyes and turns her back on me, knowing how much that infuriates me. Even after all these years, the effect is the same. My blood turns from liquid to steam, but I can't lose control, so I dial down the temperature just enough.

I touch her arm and do my best to keep my voice level. "How old is she, exactly? It's a fair question."

She spins, her face twisted with fury. "You haven't changed at all! Everything is still about you!"

That's not an answer, and it's not true. "I have a right to know."

"What right do you have? You left me and told me you never wanted to see me again. You were joining some secret special operations group and I'd be better off without you. As if you had the right to make that decision for me. I thought you were dead!"

"I *have* changed, and you *were* better off without me. You *are* better off without me. Answer the question, Kate. How old is Megan?"

She narrows her eyes and shoves me in the chest. "She's not your daughter. Okay, I said it. Are you happy? You're off the hook."

The answer doesn't make me happy. More like oddly hollow, as if something special has been robbed from me. "Where's her father?"

"I met Megan's father a month after you left me. Ethan was a good man."

She turns that last part into an accusation, as if I'm not a good man. I can't blame her. She's right.

She lifts her hand and spins a simple gold wedding ring around her finger. It's strange that I didn't notice that before. I never miss details like that. People have a way of skipping over the obvious if they don't want to see it. I'm no different.

"Ethan and I got married before Megan was born," she says.

"What happened to him?" She used the past tense when describing Ethan, which either means he's dead or she wishes he was.

She glances at the floor and bites her lip. "Ethan died three years ago in a robbery. One of the gangs jumped him. I never found out which one."

"I'm sorry." And I am. She deserves happiness. At least she had thirteen years with this Ethan. Thirteen years can last a lifetime. It's more than some people get. It's more than I've had. It's ridiculous, but I'm jealous of him, this dead man, who died in a robbery three years ago. He had thirteen years with Kate. Thirteen years of passion, of life, of sharing Megan, the daughter who isn't mine.

"So am I," says Kate. "If you don't want to help because Megan isn't your daughter, I understand. You can go. You don't owe me anything. Not anymore."

I squeeze her hand. "Megan's your child and that's good enough for me. I'll see this through to the end."

She collapses against my chest, tears flooding down her cheeks. "She's all I have, Steven. I can't bear to think what..."

Even though she can't bear to think about what's happening to Megan, that's exactly what she's doing, and it rocks her. I hold her tight, and for the first time in a long while, I wonder what could have been. What if I didn't join the special operations unit? What if I had left the intelligence agency earlier? Would I be a better person? Would the demons have left me alone? Could we have been happy together?

Megan looks like a good kid. Would it have been so bad if I were her father? She's at least half Kate. She'd be special just because of Kate, but it's best I'm not her father. My genes are bad. They'd probably end up poisoning the good ones from Kate.

Kate's still crying, so I breathed her in for a few seconds more until she pushes against me and turns away.

Worrying about the past is a sucker's game. All I can do is make sure Megan returns home safely. Make sure she has a future with her mom.

"Okay, there are four explanations for Megan's disappearance." I carefully avoid mentioning kidnapping. Disappearance is a neutral term, and I start ticking them off with my fingers. "One, she could have run away, but from what you've told me that seems unlikely.

Two, it could be personal like a boyfriend, or someone else who knows her, and has become obsessed with her. Three, someone who didn't know her could have targeted her for some reason. Or, four, it's totally random."

She wipes her eyes with the bottom of her shirt. For a second, the shirt lifts and reveals her flat stomach and a piercing through her bellybutton. Damn, I used to love playing with that ring, taking it in my mouth, tugging on it when we were naked.

She lets go of her shirt and looks up at me with watery eyes. Luckily, she can't read minds.

"I don't think it's personal either," she says. "She would have told me if someone was bothering her and she doesn't have a boyfriend. We don't keep secrets like that from each other."

"Okay, let's focus on the other two possibilities then. Someone targeted her, or it's a random thing."

I take one last look around Megan's room and nothing stands out. I'm itchy to start investigating. The walls are closing in. If the kidnapping is personal, I have time to find leads and pull on strings. If it's random, I don't have time. We need to find a witness right away. Every minute reduces my chance of finding Megan alive.

"We need to start moving. I want to see the last place Megan's friends saw her and the two blocks she had left to come home."

I return to the living room and open the duffel. I add another bullet to the clip of my Smith and Wesson and then holster it at the small of my back. I stuff the Glock I took from the gang members into the bag. It isn't a bad weapon, but I need to spend time with it to make sure it's reliable. A small, ceramic throwing knife is secreted inside my belt, a thumb-sized explosive device snuck inside the heel of my right boot, and my four-inch blade is tucked inside the pocket of my jacket. I never go anywhere without those. It's sad really, but I think of them like they're almost friends.

Kate's eyes widen a bit when I put the Glock in the duffel. "What else do you have in that bag?"

"Enough. You lead the way."

She grabs a plain brown jacket from a hook by the door and leaves the apartment, with me a step behind her.

"Still afraid of elevators?" she asks.

"Not afraid, but I avoid them if possible. I like choices."

"Right. I forgot. You're not afraid of anything. How silly of me to have forgotten." She walks past the elevator and down the stairs.

A minute later we step outside. "Megan's school is a half-dozen blocks that way."

She stops two blocks later. "This is where her two best friends, Eddie and Denise, left her." She points down a side street. "They live down that street."

The neighborhood is quiet. We passed only one bodega and a handful of large apartment buildings like the one where Kate lives.

"This stretch is perfect to abduct someone," I say. "What time was she here?"

"Around three?"

Interesting. "Few people would be out then. That means fewer witnesses. Easy escape down the main street. Plenty of parking."

"So, what does that mean?"

I shrug. It's never good to jump to conclusions but my intuition starts buzzing. "It's too early to tell for sure. But if we assume this thing isn't personal, whoever took Megan knew what they were doing, and they picked an ideal location for the abduction."

"That's bad then...right?"

"No. It means Megan isn't their first abduction. They probably do it for a living, which will make it easier for us to find a trail. The more abductions, the more obvious the trail they'll have left behind."

Kate shudders. "That's cold. I wouldn't wish this on anyone else."

I retrace our steps down the block, scanning the neighborhood with a keen eye. Where would I abduct someone? Almost any place would work. I'd avoid the entrance to any of the apartment buildings. No need to take the chance that a Good Samaritan would intercede.

If I knew Megan's routine, I'd stay away from the end of the street where she'd leave her friends. They might linger for a bit to watch her walk away. I stop at the edge of a bodega about half a block from Kate's building, and a block and a half from where Megan left her friends. The store is long enough that a kidnapper could use the front section to take her. He'd have clearance from the door, and at three, this place would be empty. It would be a good location, the best in the two blocks. This is where I'd do it.

I study the glass storefront and smile. "Did you talk to the owner of this place?"

"I talked to everyone. He said he didn't see anything. He's a nice man, works hard, and keeps the store clean. He charges too much, but there's not a lot of choices around here."

"Did he tell you about the video camera?"

"What camera?"

"See that box of corn flakes facing the street. There's a tiny camera in that box. It's almost impossible to see, but it's there. Trust me. He probably needs it to get insurance against robberies."

"Son of a bitch! He didn't say anything about a video."

"The store opens at seven." I check my watch. "That's only fifteen minutes from now. Let's see if he'll open a little early for us."

She should be prepared for what might happen next, so I touch her arm and warn her. "Things might get rough. You can wait outside if you'd like."

She shakes her arm free. "Damn right it might get rough. If that prick held out on me, I'll kill him myself."

That's the Kate I know — full of fire and strength. Strange how people never really change. I rap against the glass door. No one comes, so I add more urgency the second time.

A middle-aged man totters into view. Mostly bald, his frame holds twenty pounds he could do without. The excess weight has settled around his stomach, an occupational hazard for a job that involves so much sitting.

Standing a few feet away from the door, he shouts, "Come back in fifteen minutes! We open then."

I remove the photo disk Kate gave me, press the button, and point at the girl's face in the holographic image.

Kate catches on and makes a pleading motion with her hands. "Please, Mister Peterson. It will only take a second."

Peterson sighs heavily, glances at the floor, and hesitates before he strides forward. Signs of guilt sprout across his body like weeds: downcast eyes, the slope of his shoulders, the frown. He knows more than he told Kate and now he's going to spill it.

He opens the door and speaks with a midwestern accent. "I told you yesterday that I didn't see anything. I don't know what else I can add." His eyes jump to the right, a clear sign he's lying. Why people look to their right beats me, but they usually do.

We step inside, and I don't bother looking at Peterson yet. Instead, I shut the door, and turn the lock until it clicks into place.

Peterson's eyes grow as wide as plates. He reaches for a gun holstered on his hip, but he moves at glacial speed.

I grab his throat and slam him against a wall before he ever touches the grip on his weapon. He forgets about the gun and tries to pry my hand from his neck. He'd have a better chance wrestling a bear. His pasty complexion turns crimson.

I grumble, "We'll need to see the video."

When I relax my hand, he gulps in a breath.

I remove my knife from my jacket pocket. Most people are more afraid of a well-placed knife than a gun, especially if the knife flutters near their eyes, as this one now does to Peterson.

"If you grab that gun, I'm going to take it away from you and shoot your dick off. One shot and you'll sing an octave higher in the choir, understand?"

He nods.

I don't take the gun from him. It's better this way. It reminds him how powerless he is against me, and I'm sure he won't reach for it again. "Now about that video."

He rubs his throat, and his voice sounds coarse. "I don't know what you're talking about."

Some people don't know when they've been caught in a lie. They'd rather continue with the deception even though they're caught red-handed. Peterson's one of those guys. We don't have time to screw around, so I grab his wrist and yank it behind his back.

"The video from the camera in the cereal box." I place the tip of the knife close to his left eye. So close the blade nearly shaves off his eyelashes. "If your memory doesn't suddenly improve, they're going to call you One-Eyed Jack. Do you remember now?"

He groans. "Okay, okay. I don't want any trouble. The feed is hooked up to the computer in front."

I shove him toward the counter. "Pull up the video. Now."

He stumbles, but rights himself before he crashes into a rack of cans. He's more agile than I expected. Pity. I wanted to see him crash into the cans and send them rolling around the store.

Kate slaps him across the face. "Last night, you said you didn't see anything. You said you couldn't help me. How could you lie to me like that? You know Megan."

He touches the new red bruise on his cheek. "I told you the truth. I didn't *see* anything."

"But you didn't check the video either," I say.

He glances at the floor. "I don't want to get involved. I'm just a shop owner. If I cross the wrong people, they'll put me out of business, or worse."

The world is filled with people like Peterson, the it's-not-any-of-my-business people. If they could just overcome their fear, the world would be a way better place, but the fear becomes too large an obstacle for them. It's hard to blame them. They're just not hard-wired to be brave.

I shove him forward again. "If you cross me, I'll do things to you they couldn't even imagine. When I put my mind to it, I have a vivid imagination. It goes back to my mother. She used to tell me stories when I was little. Stories you'd rather not hear."

He half stumbles and half marches behind the counter. I stand beside him and watch as he types on his keyboard. It's an old model, at least five years old. After a few keystrokes, the monitor jumps to life, and the view outside of the store appears on the screen.

"Go back to three o'clock yesterday afternoon," I order.

A few more keystrokes and the time on the lower right of the screen shows three o'clock. A new white van is parked on the street in front of the store.

"All right, fast forward."

Time jerks forward until a young man steps from behind the vehicle.

"Stop and play from here."

The man wears an army surplus jacket, camouflage pants, and has short black hair that peeks through a green beret. He moves with a military bearing, looks powerfully built and serious.

I know what's going to happen next. I want to be wrong, but there's no chance.

Megan steps alongside the van and into view.

Kate gasps, lifts her fingers to her face, and watches the video through a web of fingers.

Megan pauses two steps away from the beret guy and they speak for two seconds. From her demeanor it's obvious she doesn't know the stranger. She glances over her shoulder for a heartbeat and charges forward. She kicks the big man in the knee, which bends him over, and punches him in the throat.

I admire the young woman. She looks fearless. I root for her to keep running, even though I know she won't. She loses her balance and hesitates. Two other young men, similarly dressed, come into view. One grabs her by the shoulders and tosses her against the side of the van, and the other punches her in the stomach. She falls to her knees, gasping for air.

I clench my hands into fists. I'll find those two and make them regret what they did. Both men lift her by the shoulders and carry her to the back of the van. One of the guys walks with a limp.

Beret guy stalks to the back of the van, rubbing his throat. His angry footsteps tell me he wants payback. A few seconds later, the van takes off with Megan inside. The entire abduction took less than two minutes. They looked as if they've done this before. Certainly, Beret guy didn't expect Megan to attack him. Good for her. She has grit.

I make Peterson replay the recording a second time. Nothing changes.

Kate stares at the images silently, a detached look on her face, as if some part of her can't process what she's watching.

I've seen it before — denial. Soon it'll wear off and anger will replace it. She'll be so mad she'll have no room for denial.

I grab Peterson by the back of the neck and dig my fingers into his flesh. "I need a copy of that video."

"How much time do you want?"

"The whole day."

He copies the file on a flash drive and hands it to me.

"Let me explain something, Mr. Peterson." I lean close to his ear and speak softly so he has to focus to hear me. "You're now on Team Megan. If I can't find her, I'll make sure no one will ever find you. If she's hurt, I'm going to hurt you ten times as much. Do you understand me?"

He nods but refuses to look at me.

I squeeze his face in my hand and twist it until he sees my eyes. "Have you seen that van around here before?"

He shakes his head. "Never, and I would have noticed a new van like that one. No one drives anything new around here. It must come from one of the Upper Districts."

"How about these three thugs? They remind you of anyone?"

"No one."

"Stand up," I tell him.

He stands, and I punch him in the gut with a short right hook that cracks at least one of his ribs. He bends over and gulps for air.

"You see, Mr. Peterson, this is how it works. One of those thugs punched Megan in the stomach, which forced me to break one of your ribs. I sure hope that's the worst of it. Don't tell anyone we were here. I'm letting you off easy for now." And I am.

Caesar barks at me. "When did you become such a pussy? You're better off killing fatso. What if he tells the kidnappers you're after them? Eliminate the threat, you lily-livered loser. I'm embarrassed to have trained you.... Oh, I see. You want to impress the broad. My bad."

I push Caesar from my mind. He's not totally wrong. He usually isn't, but I can't kill Peterson with Kate here. Peterson should have been honest with her, but he didn't hold back the information about the video because he's a bad person. Fear held him back. I know a bit about fear from when I was young, so I give him this one break.

I hand him a five-dollar bill from my pocket, and he shoots me a quizzical look.

"I'm getting a coffee on the way out. That should cover it. I'm not a thief. I'll be back in case you think of anything new. Remember, you're on Team Megan now. Oh, and everything is on sale today—20 percent off. Don't look so upset. You'll feel better about yourself in the morning."

The sale will probably hurt a guy like Peterson more than the broken rib. I gently grab Kate's hand. Her fingers are icicles.

"Time to go. It's opening time for the store and we don't want to inconvenience Mr. Peterson."

I pour a cup of coffee, add three sugars and a healthy amount of half and half. "Do you want one? It's going to be a long day."

Kate just shakes her head.

I unlock the door, switch the sign to open, and tug Kate outside. When my feet hit the pavement, I make a silent promise to myself. That won't be the last time Kate will see her daughter alive. For a time, Kate saved my life. Hell, she was my whole life, and I owe her.

The kidnappers were careless. They should have known about the video camera. Now they've left me a thread, maybe even a few. I'll pull on them until the truth unravels and it leads to Megan.

CHAPTER 7

Megan summons her courage, straightens her back, and steps inside the office. Even though she's scared, she doesn't want them to know.

An attractive woman sits behind a plain oak desk, facing the door. Curly, short, black hair streaked with gray falls to her shoulders. Her eyes shine a brilliant gray color, like smoldering charcoal.

Unlike the jumpsuits Megan has seen so far, which are all a single color, this woman wears a multicolor suit. It shimmers in the morning light that pours through a window behind her. All the colors of the rainbow blend together in a seamless pattern across the suit. It's quite beautiful.

The woman remains seated and beams a motherly smile at Megan. Her face glows as if lit by an otherworldly light. Megan has never met anyone who looks so supremely confident and sure of herself before.

She nods at Megan to sit in one of the two plain wooden chairs opposite her desk.

When Megan touches the chair, she's not sure how she got there. The woman's magnetic personality must have pulled her forward without her realizing what she was doing.

"Please sit."

Megan looks at the chair, and although she wants to obey, she retains an ounce of free will. "I'd rather stand."

The woman shrugs one shoulder as if she anticipated her answer. "Of course. The choice is yours. My name is Ivy, but people here call me Mother. I think you should do that also."

"I already have a mother, thank you."

"I'm not here to replace your biological mother. I have a different role. I'm sure you're a bit disoriented. Much has happened in one day's time. Your new and true life starts today. You can relax. You've been freed from your old, oppressive life."

"I'm happy with my old life, thank you."

"Really?" Ivy arches one eyebrow. "You're not fooling me. You're smart. You know life has lost its meaning out there," she waves one hand and her slender fingers flicker toward the window, "in the vast ghettos and poor districts where crime runs rampant. No one looks out for each other. People feed on their neighbors. It seems as if God has left us to our own devices, but that's not right. God hasn't left us. We've left Him. He is here with us now, as He has always been. He has plans for you. He wants to be relevant again. Relevant in your life and your world. His time has come, and so has yours."

Ivy's voice bewitches Megan. It has a musical quality, and she speaks eloquently with complete and total authority. Megan has never met anyone who remotely compares to this Ivy, and she struggles to understand what to make of her.

"God?" The word scrapes by Megan's mouth in a whisper.

Ivy tents her fingers on the desk and presses the tips to her lips. "Yes. A fine place to start. What do you know of God?"

Megan shrugs. "I've been to church on holidays. I know the Bible." While technically true, she only possesses a passing acquaintance with the Bible, and doesn't really know much about God. Her mom took her to church a handful of times, and sometimes they even talk about God, but all those conversations were abstract. She never gave it real thought. Never thought about God in a personal sense, like He impacted her life. Not really. No one does.

Ivy smiles knowingly, as if she's reading Megan's thoughts. "Going to a place of worship is not the same thing as knowing God. Those places function as barriers that interfere with our relationship with God. All that's gone now. I've wiped it away."

Megan whispers, "How?"

"God speaks to me personally. He always has, and I've created a way for you to speak with Him directly without interference from others. When you're ready, He will talk directly to you. Tell you what He wants. How you can serve Him. You will become one of his Angels. You have an important role to play before the End of Days is upon us. Critical, really."

CHAPTER 8

Megan feels as if it's hard for her to breathe like she's been sucker punched. Unsure what to believe, she leans against the top of the chair and shakes her head to clear it. On one hand, this talk about God and angels sounds crazy. Only nutters, who wander the streets mumbling to themselves, talk directly to God. On the other hand, Ivy looks sure of herself and completely sane. She almost glows with an ethereal light, her gray eyes blazing with knowledge.

What secrets does she know?

If anyone speaks directly to God, it could be this Ivy. And certainly, some people must have spoken to God in the past. The Bible made that clear. She tries to remember all the people who spoke with God from the Bible but can't recall any besides Jesus and maybe Moses, but others must have. And if others talked to God back then, technically Ivy could now. *Right?* There shouldn't be a time limit on something like that. If no one talks to God for two thousand years, then the connection is lost forever? That wouldn't make sense.

Ivy intrudes upon her thoughts, "I know this is a lot for you to take in right away. I get it. You don't know what to believe, but I assure you, you will be a believer in the end. Everyone does, so long as we can protect them from the Devil and his trickery." She shifts back in her chair. "Let's talk about more practical matters. I know you are a pragmatic person. First, your name."

"My name? My name's Megan."

"I have good news and bad news to share with you. I always start with the bad to get that out of the way. Megan is dead. Gone, vanished, never to be seen again. Spring has replaced her. Your new name is Spring. Spring will be happier and more fulfilled with a higher purpose than Megan could ever have been. That's the good news."

"Spring is a season."

"Yes, and my favorite season at that." She makes it sound important as if she'd done her a favor. She motions to Buck, and he slips a necklace around Megan's throat before she can turn or object. "More good and bad news for you."

"Great," mutters Megan. "Let me guess. You're going to start with the bad news."

"This necklace marks you as one of God's true children from this day forth. We can use it to track your location and it sends us information about you. We'll know about your well-being. Things like heart rate and health stats. This way, we can care for you more efficiently and understand your needs in a way we never could otherwise."

Megan's face heats. "You'll also know exactly where I am at any moment."

"Yes, of course." Ivy swipes the screen on a tablet and Megan feels a shock like a bee sting.

"Hey!"

"There's also a small tab of plastic explosives in the clasp. If you snap the chain, the circuit will break, and the explosive will detonate. In time, you won't even think about the chain. You'll see this necklace for what it is—a way to bring you closer to God and your true calling. Buck wears his necklace, as does everyone here at The Farm."

"So, God wants my head to explode if the chain breaks?"

Ivy smirks. "Only if you're under the Devil's control will you try to snap the chain. No one has done it for some time. It's really not much of a concern."

"Maybe not for you. What if the necklace breaks accidently?"

"No need to worry about accidents. The necklace looks like silver, but it's really a new metal alloy. It's almost impossible to break. We use diamond tipped cutters to break these chains. And only I have those." Ivy lifts her pendant and shows it to Megan, a cross inside a star. "You see, I also wear one. It's pretty, don't you think?"

"It's not my style."

Ivy points to a lemon-colored jumpsuit hanging on a coat rack in the corner. "That's for you. We all wear jumpsuits. We don't want clothing to get in our way. We like to keep things simple and conventional clothing hampers the spirit."

"Why yellow? Buck's got red, and you have one with many colors."

"I am the Mother to everyone, so my jumpsuit blends every color. The colors represent different functions. Red for security. Lilac for medical. Yellow for Angels. Of course, you'll find others."

"And the symbols on the chest?"

"Different levels of enlightenment. You'll recognize them over time and realize what they mean."

"How come mine has a green armband?"

"So many questions. That's good." Ivy leans forward. "That's because you're still pure."

Megan glares at her. "That's why you had that witch doctor examine me? To see if I'm a virgin?"

"Of course. We needed to know if you're pure. There are separate places for the pure and impure among us." Ivy glances at Buck. "Take her to the bathroom to get dressed and then to get a haircut before she starts her transition."

"A haircut?" Megan runs her hand through her blonde locks. She's never cut it more than a few inches to remove split ends. She can't imagine what she'd look like with short hair, but she's sure she won't like it.

Ivy sighs impatiently. "Hair, clothes, names, and the like, are barriers between Him and you. Here, we do away with those things, with the vanity and pride. Everyone is treated fairly."

"Right." Megan looks over her shoulder at Buck. "Am I going to get an electric stick like him?"

"I said fairly, not equally."

"Why would God want you to hurt us?"

"My dear, who told you that God doesn't punish the wicked?" Ivy walks to the side of her desk, an arm's distance away. "You will be transformed. And then you will remember today as your true birthday. You will thank me, and after you talk to Him, you will call me Mother and know that I'm His agent on Earth. We will talk again soon, Spring. I teach a class for the Angels later in the day. You will attend and learn."

Megan touches the pendant. The necklace complicates her plan to escape. Now she'll have to figure a way to disarm it before she runs.

There must be a way.

She eyes Ivy's tablet before leaving.

CHAPTER 9

Kate hands me a tablet, an old one with an annoying dime-sized dead spot in the middle of the screen. She says Megan's is newer, that Megan cleaned offices on the weekends to buy it, but that one is...unavailable.

Old and imperfect is still way better than nothing, which is what I have. Useful tools in my business, I'm pretty good with computers, but I'm wary of them.

Some people start sweating just because they don't have their phone or tablet with them. Suddenly, the devices have become almost as essential as clean air or water. Why need something that bad if you can avoid it? Soon we'll start making humanoid robots, and we all know where that will lead. We'll become lazy and eventually they won't need us anymore. Evolution will continue, and the planet will probably be better off without us.

I settle on Kate's couch, plug Peterson's flash drive into a port on the tablet, and replay the video. Each time I watch it, I marvel at Megan's courage. Fifteen and she has more guts than most trained soldiers I've known. The Army drills behaviors into recruits to get them to react in set ways to avoid making decisions. That way, when faced with life and death situations, they react, without thinking. The Army knows they can't teach courage, so they don't try. Either you have it or you don't, and Megan has it in abundance.

Kate silently sits next to me, looking lost and mired in that horror world of what ifs again. She's breathing heavily as if each breath takes a concerted effort. Maybe it does? Perhaps actually seeing Megan's abduction has so wounded her, she can barely breathe. I'd take that pain away if I could. Absorb it so she wouldn't have to feel it any longer. It would be the least I could do, and maybe it would make up for some of the hurt I've inflicted on others. But I don't know how, and my focus has to be on Megan right now. I need threads to pull. The kidnappers made mistakes. No operation goes off perfectly. I just need to recognize them when I see them.

Halfway through my third time watching the video, my attention level peaks. Megan kicks the lead assailant in the knee, he bends over and a flash of silver sparkles on his chest. I freeze the video, rewind a few frames, and restart it in ultra slow motion. A chain flips out from underneath the scumbag's shirt when he bends over.

I zoom in on the chain until it turns grainy. There's a pendant on the chain. "Look at that symbol. It looks like a cross in a star. Have you seen anything like it before?"

Kate leans forward and shakes her head. "Do you think it's important?"

"Could be." I send a picture of the screen to my phone. "Simple pendants like that are usually significant to the people wearing them. And anything significant to this guy can turn into a lead for us. It doesn't look like a gang symbol. With a little luck, it might help us identify the group we're dealing with, or the guy who's wearing it."

Definitely a thread.

I take a few more screen shots: the best glimpses of the three assailants faces, the license plate on the van, close ups of the clothes worn by the attackers. I'll spend a few more hours pouring over the video on a frame-by-frame basis later, but my eyes sting.

Kate sits lifeless beside me. Her body melts into the couch, but her eyes look eager. They're hoping I've found a miracle that'll bring her daughter home. I wish I had. At least we have a few leads.

"Here's what I think. This isn't the first time this group has kidnapped someone. They're not experts, but they've done this before and have some military training. You can tell by the formation. One in front and two behind to make sure the target doesn't turn and run. The van blocked any chance Megan had of crossing the street. The guy in front moved with a certain confident swagger I've seen before, and they parked the van thirty minutes before Megan arrived at an ideal location to snatch her. Either that's a coincidence, or Megan was their target all along. And I don't believe in coincidences."

"Why would someone target Megan? She'd never been in trouble or..."

Kate pauses and when I realize she won't verbalize her thoughts because they're too terrible for her to put into words, I rub my hands over my face and feel the stubble on my cheeks and chin. It's obvious why someone would want Megan. Kate knows this deep down, but she doesn't want to admit it. I try to be sensitive, but I suck at sensitive.

"I've only known about Megan for a few hours, and it's obvious she's special. You said she's an A student and she looks a lot like you. I don't know what these people want yet, but there's plenty of reasons to target a young, smart woman as pretty as Megan."

Kate shivers. "You think someone wants her because she's pretty? She's only fifteen."

"We shouldn't jump to conclusions, but I've heard of other cases involving young women."

Kate balls her hands into fists. "I'm going to kill whoever's done this."

Anger is way better than the world of what ifs. We can use anger, but Kate's will fade over time. Generally, there are two types of people. Those who can't let go of their anger unless they unleash it at the rightful targets. If they never act on it, they become spiteful, petty people full of hatred. And the second type, the lucky few who can let their anger burn off over time. Kate's a lucky one. I've seen it dozens of times. She can forgive people. Maybe not me. I don't deserve forgiveness, but if we get Megan back safely, she'll focus on her daughter and thoughts of revenge will fade.

That's not how it works for me. The demons rumble in my head. They want blood, and they will not quiet over time. Either I'll satisfy them, or they'll drive me crazy.

"Don't worry about vengeance. Leave that to me. Now we need to follow the clues and bring Megan home."

I tick the threads off with my fingers. It makes me feel better to do it this way. They sound more substantial than they really are, as if we're close to finding Megan, even though we're not.

"First, we have the license plate for the van. It's probably stolen, but we could get lucky. Second, the funky star symbol with the cross inside might lead us somewhere. And third, we've got three partial photos of these guys' faces. Two are decent. They might be in the system. If they're ex-military, we should find at least one of them. We have the best chance with the leader, the one Megan chopped in the throat. His photo looks the cleanest."

"How do we follow up on this stuff?" asks Kate. "I don't know anyone who can help. You're talking about government databases."

I stand, swing my arms behind my body, and stretch. It's been two days since I've washed. I need to clean up and carefully consider what to do next. "I have some friends who can help. Can I use the shower? I 've got to wash away some of this grime before my skin turns green."

"The showers are in the center of the hallway." Kate hands me an identification card and a towel. "We only get five minutes of hot water, so be quick. You'll need to buy it on my account with my identification card."

I take the card and towel, and grab a gray, long-sleeved T-shirt and a pair of socks and underwear from my duffel. I'll wear the pants I have on for a few more days before changing them. They'll do for now. Laundry can wait.

"I'll be right back." I remove a toothbrush and toothpaste from an outside pocket in my bag.

Kate opens the door, and whispers, "Thanks." Tears brim her eyes.

She wants me to tell her that everything will be all right, but I won't. They'd be hollow words. We don't know what we're up against yet, so I walk out without saying anything. If that makes me an asshole, so be it. I've been called worse. A lot worse.

I promised myself I wouldn't go back to my old life. I'd find myself first, find a way to change, but this is Kate and her daughter. How can I turn my back on them? To help Megan, I'll have to reach back into my past, and that will cost me.

"Fuck." I mean it. I'm fucked.

I trudge to the bathroom in the center of the hallway. There are two, both gender neutral, which is fine with me. I'm not shy, and I choose the first door. Inside, the place is crowded. It has six shower stalls and six toilets, and eight people waiting in line. I take my place in the back and the line moves quickly, probably because of the time restrictions. I walk into one of the newly vacated shower stalls on the end. After undressing I look at the options: a card reader placed near the controls for the shower and another one next to the soap dispenser.

I tap Kate's card against the card reader and turn the water to hot. It feels good splashing against my head and running down my body. At least it's hot and not some tepid lukewarm crap. I tap the card against the soap dispenser and buy a squirt of soap. I don't know how much it costs, but Kate will appreciate it in the end.

I wash efficiently, a byproduct of my military training. Running my hands over my shoulders and back, my fingers trip against the scars left behind by a steel-tipped whip an overweight toad used to torture me.

Caught in a desert I'd rather forget, the plump extremist tried to force me to talk. Bad choice.

The demons helped me back then. They might be bad, but they have a will to live, and sometimes that makes them useful. They helped me work my hands free from the restraints, adding strength and dexterity, overcoming my exhaustion. When the toad laughed and reared the whip back for the tenth time, I jumped to my feet. I'll never forget the look on his face. His eyes almost bulged from his head and his mouth opened, forming a perfect "O." He knew at that moment, he was done, and it would be messy. He was right. I rewarded the demons, and he regretted the shabby treatment he showed me.

In the end, the portly extremist and his three friends begged me to kill them. They eventually got their wish. I'm a people pleaser. I guess I just want to be liked.

The scar on my stomach reflects my closest encounter with death. That one almost killed me, but a quick-thinking medic named Wilky saved me. He stopped the bleeding before I bled out. If the bullet had hit me another inch or two higher, it would have pierced my heart, and death would have come quickly. The Fates spared me, or maybe it was just blind luck. The thing about luck is that it has a way of leveling out over time. And there's the scar on my chest where the demon tried to rip out my heart with his claws — two faint lines where the nails slashed into my flesh.

I wash my face. A short, gruff-looking beard covers an angry line along my jaw. A Belgian assassin had a quick wrist, but a glass jaw. He managed to cut me, but when I punched him in the face, he went down, and should have stayed down. That scar bothers me the most. Not because it's on my face, but because I could have prevented it. I should have anticipated his swipe with the knife, but he looked scared, and that fooled me into thinking he would run. He should have. He was alive when I left him, but even his mother wouldn't recognize him. Sometimes the demons don't want me to kill; sometimes they want a different type of punishment, a more apt one under the circumstances. They can be creative when called upon.

The scars are part of me now as much as my blue eyes or the six toes on my right foot. Don't ask. They're living lessons about luck and preparation and, most importantly, what I'm capable of doing. The water turns to ice, so I shut if off. After toweling off and quickly dressing I return to the rest of the bathroom. The line has grown to ten deep, and some throw nasty glares my way. No one wants a stranger to add to the burden.

I study them with a wary eye, looking for demons. They're all harmless, just normal people getting ready for work. I could kill all ten in a few minutes if necessary. I imagine each move, each shot of my gun, each twist of the neck, or chop to the throat, and it's as real to me as if it happened.

Back at Kate's door, my mental wrestling match finishes the way I knew it would, with me being pinned. A few contacts can help me, but only one is the best and the fastest. I'll call the Fourteenth Colony, but it'll cost me the most in the end.

CHAPTER 10

No one answers Kate's door when I knock. I open it and call out for Kate, but she doesn't respond.

I draw the Smith and Wesson from my holster and click off the safety. Kate could be in one of the bedrooms, but my intuition tells me she's not here.

A footstep sounds in the hallway behind me, and I spin, the Smith and Wesson held at chest level.

Kate holds two mugs of coffee. She spills a bit from one as I startle her, and she rolls her eyes. "A little dramatic, don't you think?"

There she goes again with the annoying eye roll. I tighten my grip on the gun before I lower it, flip the safety on, and holster the weapon. When she enters the apartment, I close the door and take a mug from her. "I didn't know where you were, so I was concerned. Sue me."

"Yes, I know. Always prepare for the worst. How many times did I try to sneak up on you and not once did I get the better of you?"

The question sounds like a trap.

"Too many times," she says with more than a little trace of anger. "I should have gotten a cup back at the store, and I know how addicted you are to caffeine. I made it light and sweet, the way you like it."

"You remembered."

"Of course, I remembered. You were always so particular about your coffee." She shoots me a half-smile.

I don't know what that means. Has she forgiven me? Or has she granted me a temporary truce while we search for Megan? Could it mean something more? Things are always complicated between Kate and me. I'm supposed to know what she's thinking without asking. Asking is always bad. She hates that. It means I don't care, which is stupid. Why would I ask if I don't care?

Either way, it's best to lock down my feelings for her out of the way. Better to focus on the coffee. I take a sip.

"This is perfect. Coffee's too bitter black." I feel a little stupid talking about coffee, but it's safe. If I say something about us, it's bound to be wrong. She expects me to know what to say, and I'm totally clueless. Better to feel stupid than get in a row with her right now.

She turns her back on me. At least she didn't roll her eyes this time. That's progress.

I remove my phone from my front pocket and dial my friend, Mary. Only a little older than Megan, she's at the heart of the Fourteenth Colony's operations. She has a photographic memory, a talent for hacking, and believes deeply that the country can still change and avoid a bloody civil war. I doubt she's right, but I'm hopeful.

She answers on the second ring. "Steven, is that you?"

"In the flesh."

"We hadn't heard from you in over three months. We were starting to get a little worried. Are you ready to come back?"

"Doesn't the Fourteenth Colony believe in non-violent change? Non-violence is a foreign language to me."

Mary chuckles. "I noticed, and you know we *favor* a peaceful approach. But when everything breaks down, a little ass-kicking comes in handy. That's why we need you. You're our ass-kicker."

"I'm not ready to come back yet, but I have a problem you might be able to help me with. If you're willing."

"Go ahead. I'm listening."

"A daughter of a friend of mine has been abducted..."

I explain the situation, keeping the descriptions short and focusing on the most important elements. "I have a photo of the van and license number, good shots of the assailant's faces, and a close-up of the symbol on the chain."

She doesn't hesitate. "I'll jump on this right away. It'll take me a few days to hack into the government databases. With Rachel's help, I'd get immediate access and you'd get answers sooner. But if I—"

"If you tell Rachel, Sheppard will know, and I'll owe him. I know how it works. It's okay. Go through Rachel. We don't have time to waste."

"You've got it. I'll call you back when I know something useful."

"I owe you."

Mary's voice deepens with emotion, which surprises me. Everything is logical with her, but this time, she speaks from her heart. "You're family to me, Steven. I don't keep score with family." She disconnects the call.

She doesn't keep score, but others will. I'll have to add her to my list of people who can text me for help at any time. That'll make five.

Kate stares at me, her arms crossed over her chest.

"So, what's this Fourteenth Colony?"

CHAPTER 11

The Fourteenth Colony is a covert rebel faction that puts their lives in danger for their collective principles. I don't always agree with their methods, and I'm not sure they'll succeed, but they have courage. I'm sworn to keep them secret, so I can't discuss them with anyone, even Kate, which is sure to piss her off.

I tiptoe on a balance beam, keeping my description short and vague. "They want to change the country to become more balanced. They believe everyone deserves a chance at success, not just those born wealthy. They'd like to end the Originalist rule."

"Do they want to start a revolution? I've heard talk of such groups. The ghettos are arming themselves and many of the lower districts too. It won't take much to start a war."

"They want to bring about change through nonviolent means. You'd like them."

She huffs, and it's clear she doesn't believe me. "If they're nonviolent, what do they want with you?"

"Nonviolence has limits. I'm the person they turn to when they reach those limits."

"It sounds like you don't want to work for them again. Why not?" She shoots me a piercing gaze. She sees through my bullshit. Probably because she knew me so well before I learned to lie, so it's useless to spin a story now.

"I'd like to make my own decisions for once. Decide who I am before I work for someone else. They're the best and the fastest at hacking and they have useful government connections. If anyone can track down these leads, Mary will do it for us."

I'm not going to mention my growing demon problems. Finding Megan is more than enough for Kate to focus on. She doesn't need my problems weighing her down. Heck, I don't need my problems weighing me down either.

She locks her gaze onto me. "Are you going to say anything else about them or is it all a secret? Just like your super-secret work for the government that no one's supposed to know about. So secret you can't tell me, for my own good. As if spies would march into the apartment and shoot me dead if I knew whatever secret you can't tell me."

"All you need to know is that they'll help. The rest doesn't involve you."

"Right. I know how important your work is to you. I'm not..."

For a moment, I'm worried she'll re-fight our last argument. It was a whopper; she started yelling and throwing things at me. The glass vase almost brained me, but the storm that's building in her voice breaks suddenly and she looks different, caring. She sounds softer than before.

"It's all bullshit, you know. If you want to change, you change. They can't make you do something you don't want. You've always been too easily manipulated by a call to duty. You like to be the hero. You have a desperate need to be part of something bigger. But to change, you have to want to change. I don't think you're ready to be nonviolent. Fire still burns in your eyes."

My heart skips a beat. Does she see hellfire in my eyes? Is it too late for me already? "What type of fire?" I hold my breath and wait for her answer.

"Intensity and a white-hot anger. It's hotter than before. You looked like you wanted to kill Peterson when you grabbed him in the store."

I breathe easy. Hellfire would be trouble, intensity is manageable. "Honestly, I don't know, Kate. I'm not sure who I am anymore."

I take a long, slow drink from my mug, mostly to end the conversation, but also for time to think. Kate used to know me better than I knew myself. Does she still see the true person inside, or have I changed so much she can't recognize me anymore? Have I already turned into one of the demons I fear so much? Would she see the signs?

Kate's gaze is still assessing me, studying me as if she's a psychologist and I'm her patient. It unnerves me, and suddenly the small apartment feels claustrophobic. Small spaces bother me. Not as an irrational phobia, but they squeeze me after a while. I can't stay here alone with Kate and her piercing eyes any longer. My chest tightens.

"Let's get moving. I'm not waiting around for Mary. I'd like to talk to Megan's friends. The two you mentioned that walked with her from school yesterday. They might have seen something useful or noticed something odd."

Kate finishes her coffee. "Eddie and Denise are twins. They live only a few blocks from here. They should still be home before school starts. I called them first last night, so they know Megan's missing."

We escape the small apartment before it crushes me into powder, walk past Peterson's store and turn right onto the twin's street. Two blocks later, we stop outside of a traditional apartment building: brick façade, ten stories tall, decent-sized windows facing the street. It's better looking from the outside than Kate's. She presses a button on the directory and a buzzer unlocks the door for us.

"They live on the fifth floor." Kate glances at me. "Elevator or stairs?"

"Stairs for me. I can use the exercise. You take the elevator if you want."

She opens the door to the staircase and we march up together. This is not one of the new communal buildings. Each apartment has its own bathroom and kitchen, and the doors look spaced reasonably apart.

The door to apartment 51 opens before we reach it and two young faces, one male and the other female, appear. They look stressed. Both have puffy, red eyes and disheveled hair.

I recognize them—two of the four faces from the photos in Megan's room. The boy stands taller than me, but he weighs a good deal less. He's reed thin, while the girl is average height and stockier. Though they're built differently, their faces look similar: the same brown eyes, high cheekbones, and oval shape.

"Come in," says the girl.

We step inside and the boy hugs Kate before the door closes. "We can't believe this is happening."

The girl pulls her brother away from Kate and says, "Megan's going to be fine. She's as tough as they come." She speaks softly, more for her brother's sake than for Kate's.

Kate introduces me as a friend who's helping get Megan back. She calls the two Megan's best friends.

"Are your parents home?" I ask, even though the apartment feels otherwise empty.

"No," says Denise. "They start work early."

She's the stronger of the two. Eddie looks dazed and teary eyed. She walks us to the living room with a purposeful stride. There's a couch and a few chairs, but no one sits.

"Tell me about the last time you saw Megan," I say.

Denise answers, "We walked home from school as usual. We stopped where our street connects with hers. We checked to make sure no gangs were hanging around, and then we separated, and that's the last time we saw her. We were supposed to study for the Assessment Test later, but she never answered her phone."

"Does she have any boyfriends or anyone who wants to harm her?"

"No," says Denise. "Ryan asked her out last month, but Megan wants to focus on the Assessment Test before she starts dating anyone. Everyone loves Megan. No one wants to hurt her."

Eddie blurts, "It's our fault."

Denise glares at him. "Get a grip."

"I'm serious. We shouldn't have left her alone." Tears run down his cheeks. "So many kids go missing. She's so stubborn. She said she'd be fine and I was silly. Now..."

"Megan's strong-willed," Denise explains to me. "We've argued about leaving her alone in the past. We've tried to walk her to her door before, but she wouldn't have it. No one can force her to do anything she doesn't want to do." She turns to Eddy. "It's not your fault. Stop being dramatic."

"How many other kids have gone missing?" I ask.

Denise shrugs. "Five from our school this year."

"Five?" says Kate. "Megan never told me anything about that."

"She didn't want to worry you," says Denise.

Five kids is a lot in three months—too many to be a coincidence. I glance at Kate. "I take it the school hasn't said anything."

Her eyes burn. "No."

"What are these other missing students like?" I ask Denise. "Can you describe them?"

Eddie jumps in. "I can do better than that. I have the flyers." He bounces from the living room and into one of the bedrooms.

"Flyers?" I ask.

Denise frowns. "Every time someone goes missing we make flyers and post them around the neighborhood. We're making them for Megan."

"Have any of the others been found?" asks Kate.

"No."

Eddie returns with five flyers. He shows them to me—four young women and one man. All five are knockouts, even the guy. The hair on the back of my neck stands on end. There's no way this is a coincidence. I hand the flyers to Kate.

"All five go to your school?" I ask.

"Yes," says Eddie. "And they're all good people and good students. Everyone was on the honor roll."

When Kate hands the flyers back to me, I take a picture of each one with my phone and show Eddie and Denise the screenshots of the van and the three assailants' faces.

Eddie gasps. "These guys kidnapped our Megan?"

"It seems that way. Does anyone or anything look familiar?"

He scrolls through the photos, Denise hovering over his shoulder. "No," he says but he hesitates and his face squeezes together as if he's stuck on something. "What's this?" he asks as he shows me the phone.

"That's a pendant one of them was wearing. We don't know what it means yet."

Eddie shows it to Denise. "I've seen that before," he says.

"Where?" asks Kate.

Eddie taps his knuckle against his forehead three times, each one progressively harder. "It's in here somewhere. I can't think when I'm nervous. I'm no good under pressure."

I take the phone back and give them my number. "Call me when you remember and be careful with those flyers. If anyone calls you with a lead, let us know right away. Don't start investigating on your own."

They promise to be careful and Kate and I leave. When we enter the hallway, Kate's pissed. "I can't believe that school hasn't said anything about all those missing students."

"It's worse than that. Someone at the school is selling these kids. Five missing students are too many, and did you see them? They're all beautiful and smart. Someone wants the best and they're getting tipped off. We're going back to school."

CHAPTER 12

The day has ripened into a good one, clear skies and warm air. Busy people hustle along the streets. I set a leisurely pace on our walk to the school, unsure what we'll do when we reach it.

The walk frees my mind to sort through this insanity. Moving helps me organize things, put puzzle pieces in their rightful places. But I'm struggling. How could a teacher sell out his or her students? Have we fallen so far that such a thing is even possible? Or is this simply the case of a bad apple, a leech who sucks the goodness from humanity? Just another parasite like so many we've been afflicted with from the beginning of time.

We cross a busy street and the school appears on the next block. School was an empty place for me. The classes and subjects bored me, and the teachers showed no interest in me. The only positive thing about school—it provided some respite from my mother, but to be honest, she spent most of her days making and selling drugs with the Monarch gang. And nights, when school was out, were the bad times when the demons came back. I used school mostly as a place to pass time and sneak moments with Kate.

"What's the plan?" asks Kate.

"A good question. We can start with the principal and try to wring the truth out of anyone we find. But they'll call security in no time and chase us away. We might get lucky, but all we'll likely accomplish is to tip off the scumbag."

We're less than a block from the parking lot. Time is running out, but I finally get an idea and make it sound like I knew it all along. "We should start here."

Kate pauses. "Here?"

"Sure. Whoever's selling out those kids must be getting cash to do it. What do people spend extra money on?"

"Cars. Guys like fancy cars."

"True, and this seems like something a guy would do. I don't see a woman selling out these kids, but you never know. I'm a feminist at heart, so I'm open to all types of bad guys even if they turn out to be bad women. Let's check out the staff parking lot and see if anything stands out."

School has already started. A bored guard sits in the hut by the entrance. Kate shows him her identification card and makes up a story about having a meeting with the guidance counselor about Megan.

The guard looks like a banana with arms and legs. His pointy head practically hits the top of the hut and his skin is even tinted yellow. I immediately dislike him. He earns a particularly nasty place in my heart when he leers at Kate. He hesitates to take the identification card from her hand, so he has more time to check her out while running his eyes slowly up and down her body.

I can kill him. Literally, in ten seconds. I want to snap his scrawny banana-like neck. The cretin wouldn't even realize what's happening until after he's in hell, where I'll eventually find him. Then I'd take my time with him.

Caesar appears next to the hut. Usually, he's just a voice in my head, but sometimes he shows himself. His fatigues fit tightly over his barrel chest and strong build. A mischievous smile sparkles in his black eyes. He splashes gasoline all over the hut from an orange can. When it's empty, he tosses it to the side and strikes a match. He looks at me with a devilish grin and says, "Banana Flambé," before he flicks the match onto the gasoline. The hut instantly blazes, and banana boy erupts in flames.

"Steven." Kate breaks me from the daydream.

The guard has already scanned the card and handed it back to Kate. He waves us in without a word. He doesn't ask about me or even look at me. I might as well be invisible, which, under the circumstances, is good. He also doesn't think it's weird that we're walking in the parking lot instead of the front door. He's that tuned out. He'd be useless if a terrorist attacked the school or if a disgruntled shooter showed up. Most of these security guards end up useless when they're actually needed. They barely go through any training at all.

Maybe I'll visit him later. Explain simple decency and persuade him to find a job closer to his own skill set—something involving sewers or waste disposal. Or maybe Caesar has it right and I'll douse the hut with gasoline and light it up with him inside. That sounds about right.

We walk into the parking lot and toward the school, which gives me enough time to shake the guard from my mind. The school, a standard government building built fifty years ago, has a brick facade that's crumbling in places. Holes and cracks dot the pavement. The half-filled lot was built to accommodate students and teachers. Now only teachers and visitors use it.

When I went to school, high school lasted until twelfth grade. The Originalists' government passed the Better Education Act a decade ago, capping public education at tenth grade. All those who move on have to pay their way. Most drop out. Some continue to vocational school, while others eventually attend colleges by way of corporate sponsorships. They sacrifice a decade of earning, but at least they have a chance at making it out of the lower districts. A chance, even if it's only a slim one, is better than no chance at all.

I scan the parking lot. Teachers don't make much. Aging American economy cars fill the lot. Nothing catches my eye.

Kate points toward the main entrance. "That's where the principal parks."

We head in that direction. A third of the cars have dents. Every vehicle has to be five years or older. A handful of electric ones catch my interest, but they look like relics handed down from prior generations. When we reach the first row, two cars stand out: a silver German sedan and a blue Japanese model. Both look remarkably better than the others in the lot.

The sign in front of the silver one reads "Principal" and the one in front of the blue one, "Vice Principal." I examine the silver one first. It's older than it looks, probably five years old. It's been freshly washed and well taken care of.

I run my finger along one side. "What do you know about the principal?"

"Not much. I think he's relatively new. He has a family, a wife and two young kids. His wife is an accountant or something like that. I saw them at the science fair. He looked happy."

The front seat of the car looks neat, but the back seat is messy. Food wrappers litter the floor and a drawing of the family that must have been sketched by one of the principal's small children lies on the seat: four people all smiles; the dad is the tallest and they all hold hands. Nothing about the sedan tickles my intuition, so I move to the blue coupe.

Newer than the German car, the Japanese one looks to be three years old and not well used. Probably just coming off a lease, which would be the best time for someone to buy a newish car if they had recently come into money and didn't want anyone to notice.

I imagine the conversation. "Nice ride. How can you afford something so new on our salary?"

The response would be halted and hurried. "I got this great deal because the car was coming off lease. My uncle owns this dealership and I just received an inheritance from my great aunt, so..."

"What do you know about the vice principal?"

"Nothing. Never met him."

A yellow legal pad sits on the front passenger seat. I can't make out the notes, so I use the camera on my phone and zoom in. He's written "Eros" and beneath it a username, "Sam Steele." The username sounds fake. I Google "Eros" on my phone and a hundred different choices pop on my screen. I scroll through them until something clicks—a website for single men. The website appears exclusive, like you'd have to pay a substantial amount to join. My intuition screams at me as I show the website to Kate.

"I've never heard of it." She pulls a picture of the vice principal from the school website on her phone: a middle-aged man with a flabby face, thinning straw-colored hair, shifty eyes. Underneath the picture is the name, "Brad Drudge."

I speed dial Mary.

She answers on the first ring. "I don't have much yet, Steven. The van's registered to a shell company that's owned by another shell company. Someone's gone to a lot of trouble to hide who owns it, but I'll find out. I've got facial recognition running on the kidnappers, and I'm searching the symbol through some databases."

"I'm sure you're zipping through it, but that's not why I called. I've got another favor."

"Shoot."

"Five students have gone missing from Megan's school this year. I don't think it's a coincidence. Can you check out the vice principal? See if he's walked into any money recently. His name is Brad Drudge."

"Sure, that's easy. What's the school district?"

I tell her and hang up.

Kate asks, "So you think this guy sold out my Megan?"

"Maybe."

"Looks like you're a little more sure than just maybe."

Without thinking about it, I've carved a line along the side of the fancy blue coupe with my knife. The demons start grumbling and it's best if I give them something, even if they're not fully satisfied.

I shrug, bend low and slash the rear passenger tire. This will have to do for now. Once Mary gets back to me, the demons will want more, much more.

"Want to get something to eat?" I ask Kate. "I'm famished."

CHAPTER 13

Megan's body aches. Sweat slicks her face and shoulders. She bends down and digs out another rock and tosses it onto the ever-growing pile. Used to a cityscape, the open space disorients her. Working in the middle of a vast field, among freshly plowed rows of soil, she can't fix her bearings. Off to her left in the distance, a wooden fence pens cows in a pasture. To her right, green swaths filled with verdant plants line up neatly in rows. She has no idea what plants. Unlike astronomy, horticulture never interested her.

She sees no buildings, street signs, food stalls, or anything familiar. Only dirt, plants, cows, and space — lots of empty space. She feels insignificant in all this open space, like she's no more than a kernel in a vast cob of corn. She doesn't like it.

Six other Angels dig rocks out of the field with her. She knows they're Angels because they all wear yellow jumpsuits. Two have green armbands like her, while the other three have purple ones. Everyone's hair is cut short, and all six young women are beautiful in their own way. They all seem about the same age as her, and they all toil in the field, clearing rocks from the dirt. None of them looks surprised or even put off by the work. In fact, they seem oddly content.

At least Amy, who is now called Autumn, is working in the field with her. Her jumpsuit has a purple armband. Megan doesn't ask her what that means because she suspects the truth and doesn't care whether Amy is a virgin or not.

Two men in crimson jumpsuits stand nearby. She recognizes one of them — Frankie, the leader of the group who abducted her. As she watches him, he taps a long electric prod against his hand. As if he senses her eyes on him, he turns and glares at her, sending a shiver up her spine. There's more than anger in that look. He wants her, and he's not afraid to show it. He even blows her a kiss when no one else is looking.

Amy, now called Autumn, whispers to her. "I don't like the looks of that one. He keeps staring at you."

A different Angel named Petal joins the conversation. She's tall, dark-skinned and has beautiful emerald eyes. "Frankie's a sinner. You'd do best to avoid him. I heard he spent last night in a confessional."

"A confessional?" asks Megan.

"It's where people go who sin. You don't want to spend a night in there. He bothers other girls. Some don't mind, but I think he's a creep. You shouldn't worry about him though. He won't touch you. You've got a green armband. That would make Mother angry and no one wants to make her angry. Some of us aren't as lucky." Petal pulls a rock the size of her hand from the dirt and throws it on the pile.

Petal's jumpsuit has a purple armband and Megan wonders if Frankie has tried something with her. From the angry look on her face and the force in which she threw the rock, it appears likely.

Megan joined this group four hours ago and, in that time, they've barely made progress in the field. The recently upturned dirt looks ready for planting, but there must be a better way to remove rocks. Surely there's a machine that could finish this task in no time.

She tried to talk to the other Angels when she joined the group. Amy hugged her but no one else wanted to chat. Now that Petal has warned her of Frankie, maybe she's opened a door Megan can walk through. "So, why are we digging for rocks anyway?"

Petal shrugs. "Mother wants us to."

A different Angel joins them. She introduces herself as May. "What Petal should have said is that we're called upon to do chores and sacrifice for Mother and for God. That way He'll talk to us and we'll be fulfilled. And we can have visions." May's face lights up. "You'll see. Nothing is better than when we get to speak directly to Him. It's impossible to describe."

Talk to Him?

Megan can't be sure, but she thinks Petal rolls her eyes and huffs.

An electric truck motors through the field toward them. When it stops, Buck jumps from the driver's seat and waves at the Angels. "Come on. Mother waits for us with lunch and a prayer session."

All the Angels but Amy and Megan raise their faces to the sky and chant, "Praise be to Mother," and head for the truck.

Megan and Amy follow along. Megan's the last to enter the open bed of the pickup, which is a mistake because Frankie sits next to her, electric prod in his hand, a hair's breadth away from her leg.

When the truck moves, Frankie leans close to her. His breath smells of onions. "I'm not done with you yet, bitch. We're going to have lots of fun, you and me. You'll see."

One of the symbols on his suit has been stripped away. He used to have three crosses like Buck, and now he has two.

Megan tries to scoot away from him, but she has nowhere to go.

He snickers.

CHAPTER 14

The truck stops in front of a white, wooden church, a short distance from where Megan had met Mother earlier that morning. Apparently, The Farm is organized around a small village of buildings. Beyond the village, fields, cows, an apple orchard, and more tracts of green stretch into the distance.

The simple church has a steeped roof and a large cross cut into the front in thin slits. They remind Megan of slits used in castle towers so archers could protect the castle from angry hordes of invaders. Are they afraid of invaders? Doesn't seem likely.

Buck appears at the back of the truck, and everyone jumps out. Frankie leads the group inside, while Buck lingers in the back. The dirt road leading out of The Farm is a good half-mile away, and the road stretches another half-mile before it intersects with a small country road, and freedom. Two guards in red jumpsuits man a gate that blocks the country road from the dirt path. She could skirt the gate on foot if she ran fast enough, or she could sneak over it if the guards weren't looking.

Buck steps close to her. His voice sounds sincere. "I know what you're thinking, and you'll never escape that way. Besides, in a day or two, you won't want to leave. I know it's hard to adjust to a true reality, but give this place a chance."

"I'm not staying a day or two. I'll find a way out of this place, and you won't stop me."

He grins. "I like you, Stubborn Spring. That's what I'll call you. I suggest you have lunch first. Hard to run without food in your belly. You won't get far."

"Wow, aren't you Mr. Helpful?" Megan smirks and follows the others inside the church.

The building is empty—nothing but a large room with oak floors and a steeple ceiling. Tall rectangular windows are spaced out evenly on both long sides of the building. Where the altar would normally sit, a massive, oak cross hangs from the ceiling, suspended by white rope.

The Angels have already assembled in a rough circle in the center of the church. Megan counts eighteen. Eighteen girls taken from their homes. She follows Amy and sits beside her, completing the circle. An odd silence fills the church, only distant footsteps of the men in red jumpsuits patrolling around the circle interrupts the quiet.

Megan catches Petal's eye and asks, "So what are we supposed to do?"

Petal whispers, "Stay quiet until Mother joins us. Then follow along. You don't want to stand out."

Megan glances at Amy, but the girl doesn't look her way. She keeps her eyes cast downward and twists her hands into knots.

Time slips past slowly. Candles burn around the edge of the circle that add a pleasant fragrance to the air. Lilac blends with the smell of oak from the floors and ceiling beams.

A door opens behind the cross. Mother enters. She strolls casually through the circle and stands in the center. Light beams through one of the windows and shimmers off her multi-colored robe. The faces on the Angels look at her with a combination of reverence and fear.

Mother smiles and lifts her arms to her sides. "Welcome children. Are we not blessed with another day to serve Him?"

All the Angels but Amy and Megan respond immediately. "Yes, Mother!"

"I want you to welcome two new Angels who have joined our flock." The Mother points to Amy and Megan. "Autumn and Spring."

The others in the room applaud. They all smile except Petal.

Megan glares at them, but they don't seem to notice or care. *Why are they so happy we've been abducted? What's happened to them?*

The applause ends, and four new people show up in brown jumpsuits, carrying food and drink.

Mother ignores them and starts preaching, her face a combination of certainty and passion. "God has made each of us in his own image. That makes each one of us equal in His eyes, yet the world has been poisoned. Some have so much, while most of us have so little. It's the work of the Devil. The Devil has punctured people's hearts and perverted them. Has He told the same to any of you?"

Ten Angels eagerly lift their hands and grin.

God has spoken to them?

Mother smiles and nods. "I thought so."

A brown-robed woman places a plate of food in front of Megan, and a man hands her a large plastic cup. Condensation covers the outside of the cup and it feels cool to the touch. Grilled squash, chicken, and rice fill the plate. It smells good and looks fresh. The squash and chicken are probably grown and raised on the farm.

Mother continues preaching about their mission. "We will spread His world across the globe. As we speak, Angels fly to every continent, ready to be called upon."

On the metal plate rests a metal fork and knife. The knife is a dull butter knife, but it's still a knife. Megan decides to keep it after the meal is over.

Mother tells the Angels to partake in their bounty. Everyone starts eating and drinking. Megan pauses. The food smells good and she's dehydrated, but...Buck was right. Starving herself is stupid. She'll need strength to escape.

She drinks from the cup—fruit punch. Sweet, but not too sweet and thirst quenching. The food tastes completely different from anything she's eaten. She's had chicken, squash, and rice before, but they've always been so processed and bland, like eating cardboard. This food explodes across her tongue and shocks her system. Taste buds she didn't know existed awake from a long hibernation.

She eats the entire plate with gusto, and a man refills her cup. Buck smiles at her. He's not eating, and neither are the other guards, which seems weird.

Megan focuses on Mother. She seems to glow in the light and her words start to twist as they float toward her. "We are the Sower of seeds. We..."

It's hard to concentrate on exactly what she's saying, but Megan's sure Mother is right. She's sure God has touched Ivy. The other Angels repeat a response as Megan takes another large gulp and drains the rest of the punch from her cup.

Maybe she's been hasty. Maybe she needs to give this place a chance, like Buck said. She feels content and lightheaded. Thoughts of her own mother force their way into her mind. She must be sick with worry. She needs to find her, but then, those thoughts fade.

Megan drains her cup a second time. When she looks at the knife still clutched in her hand, her head swims.

Why am I holding this?

CHAPTER 15

Kate and I walk in a familiar pattern. She leads, and I follow. Most of the time while we dated, I found myself following her. She always seemed to know where we were going, and I went along for the ride. I'm not sure she wanted that responsibility back then, but she was so confident — much more so than I was — that it just felt natural. That's probably one of the reasons she took it hard when I left. She never saw it coming. I can't blame her. She didn't know about the demons or the changes I was going through. I kept that part hidden from her because I didn't understand them, and that frightened me. All these years later, I still don't understand, and that scares me even more than it did back then.

We stop outside a familiar place — an old diner called Grandma's Pie Shop. We used to eat here back in the day, when we had a little scratch to spend. It can't be a coincidence that she's led me here now. There has to be a dozen other places she could have taken me. We passed an entire street of food stalls packed with cheese steak vendors, artificial sushi stalls, and noodle shops. Grandma's isn't even on our way back to her apartment.

I was never great at reading her mind, but maybe she's telling me something. Is it too much to hope that she missed me, or that she might give me another chance?

I hold the door open for her. "Are the pies still terrible?"

"The worst."

The place looks the same as it did sixteen years ago. Same cracked black and white tile floor, long wooden counter, a dozen tables and booths throughout. Not a small place, but not large either. An ancient woman sits behind a cash register by the door. It's hard to believe that Grandma is still alive, but there she is, eyes as sharp and clear as ever. It might be my imagination, but she seems to look through me and isn't happy at what she sees. Why would she be?

A youngish, dark-skinned woman, with a full Afro, a pretty round face and an athletic body greets us with a smile. She wears a yellow apron that covers a blue, collared shirt, and faded jeans. "Just you two?"

"Just us," Kate answers in a voice that makes it clear we're not on a date.

The waitress grabs two menus and walks us to a booth along the far wall. We settle into our seats and order coffees. It's a dead time for the diner, between breakfast and lunch. Only one other customer sits in a booth along the front windows.

I check out the guy's reflection in the mirror. He's wearing a navy, Italian-made suit, crisp, white, cotton shirt, and a blue, silk tie. He's in his thirties, has a light complexion, and a round face. Ridiculous blond frosted tips highlight his short brown hair. It's feathered back in an expensive cut that, undoubtedly, cost him a bundle. Even his eyebrows have blond tips. An overpriced barber fleeced him and probably called it a "hair styling." A trace amount of makeup conceals dark circles under his eyes.

He looks up from the tablet he's studying, and his eyes settle on Kate. An arrogant smile crosses his face as he winks at her.

Kate rolls her eyes, and I grin. Funny how it doesn't bother me when she's rolling her eyes at someone else, but I suspect Mr. Frosty doesn't even notice. He's oblivious to others. Especially the lower classes. Not all rich people are like that, but he's full on arrogant.

Mr. Frosty tells me everything I need to know without saying a word: the flashy clothes, the arrogant body language, the rude gesture to Kate. Hate bubbles out of me. What's he doing here anyway? He probably has a business deal in the lower district and stopped here to wait until he found the poor sap he's about to rip off. He's well built, but it's a gym body with fake muscles. I'm sure he goes to an expensive gym where he meets a personal trainer named Vick. Frosty Hair thinks Vick's his friend even though he doesn't tip Vick well, but in reality, Vick would smash a barbell into his frosty hair until it turned red if he could get away with it. I'm rooting for Vick.

I tear my eyes from the creep. Kate should be my sole focus. Neither of us looks at the menu. We don't have to. We always order the same things at Grandma's. When we were dating, we'd check out the other couples in the place and make up stories about them. They'd be doctors who got lost and came to the wrong district, or a wife cheating on her husband, or a husband who was a serial killer, or...whatever.

Some of our imaginary couples were in love, but none as much as we were. Kate's stories were always the best. Her imagination had no end. We were sure we'd stay together forever, until one day we didn't. I started training for the special operations unit with Caesar, and the voices started.

The waitress returns with our coffees and a pleasant smile. When she places the mugs on the table, we order. A cheese omelet, white toast with butter, and bacon for Kate. And a pizza burger, medium rare, with fries for me. The perfect combination of my two favorite foods. The waitress scribbles our order on her handheld device and leaves.

On her way to the kitchen, Frosty snaps his fingers and waves at her. From his obnoxious body gestures, he wants more coffee. The waitress smiles at him, turns, and mutters a curse when he can't see her face.

"Medium rare." Kate smiles. "Why do you bother?"

It's a running joke. I always order the burger medium rare and it comes back well done. Once, I tried rare, and it came back well. Grandma's grill, while not bad, always makes the burgers well.

"You never know. Some things change." I'm not exactly sure if I mean the burgers at Grandma's, or me. Maybe I can change, drive away the demons to be with Kate? But that's silly. I made that choice already. She's putting up with me so she can get Megan back. After that, I'll slink away, and she'll be happy to be rid of me.

"Do you really think I'm getting my Megan back?"

"We have some strong leads. And whoever took her went to a lot of trouble to pick her out. That's not something someone does lightly. This is bigger than just a run of the mill snatch. We'll get to the bottom of it."

Kate looks into her coffee and stirs it slowly, as if it's essential that the milk and sugar perfectly blend together. "What do you think...?"

I know what she's going to ask, and it's a train wreck. Imagining what Megan's going through will lead to complete catastrophe, twisted metal, broken pieces of track, dead bodies littered all over the place.

I change the subject and cut her off before the train crashes. "So, what have you been up to?"

Kate knows what I did, so she smirks. "Really? We're going to play the catch-up game after all these years."

"We have time."

"Do you really want to know what my life was like with Ethan? How in love we were and what our favorite places were."

I do. I hope they were happy, full of love. And part of me wonders what it would have been like if I was braver and made a different decision, but Ethan's a trap. A milder form of the what ifs that plague Kate, but still the same fundamental quagmire.

My life with Kate wouldn't have been the same as the one she shared with Ethan. We were explosive together. Incredible heat that often burned out of control. That life wouldn't have produced Megan. Maybe another child, but not Megan. A child damaged by my genes, who might hear voices and see demons and have a thing for knives.

I clear my head and start down another path. "How about we try something easy? What do you do for a living? Did you continue with your art?"

"Art didn't pay the bills. I used the money you left behind to become a nurse."

"A nurse. I can see that." She's probably a good nurse. She's good at reading people, and she's more than smart enough. She could have been a doctor if she'd gotten a chance.

"What about you? Did you find someone special, get married, have kids?" She leans forward, pupils dilated, breath shallow.

She wants to know, which is something, I guess. "I never got married, and I don't have children. In my line of work those...entanglements are dangerous."

"Right," Kate wrinkles her face and her lips bunch together in a cute way that means she's not buying it. It's the same face she'd make when we first met and she was angry at something I said or did, back when we were eight.

"What's with the face?"

"You didn't answer all my questions. So, by your non-answer, I can assume you did find someone special. Maybe not someone you married, but special anyway."

It's foolish for me to think I can hide anything from her. She still sees through me like I'm a piece of Saran Wrap.

"There was one woman."

Thankfully, the waitress brings our food. It's hot and real, which is way better than the cheap vending stores and food stalls I've been eating at lately. Before she leaves, Frosty snaps his fingers again.

I ask her, "What's the deal with that creep?"

"You mean my favorite customer. He's a real peach, that one. His daddy owns half the buildings around here, so he comes slumming once or twice a month. He always orders the blackberry pie and drinks a boatload of coffee. Never tips."

"He actually likes the pie?" asks Kate.

The waitress shrugs. "Hard to believe, huh? Grandma's used the same recipe for better than fifty years and none of us can talk her out of it. I had better go find out what the prince wants. He won't get any nicer if he has to wait."

I bite into the pizza burger and it's pink inside. I show it to Kate, who grins.

"I guess people can change," she says. "There's hope for you and me yet."

Hope is more than I can ask for; it's more than I deserve. We give each other a little space while we eat. The pizza burger tastes damn good. Almost as good as when we were kids.

My phone rings. It's Mary. "What's up?"

"Brad Drudge is dirty. I hacked into the school databases. That's easy. No one pays for top of the line encryption for schools. I found Drudge's file, looked up his direct deposit bank account and hacked in from there. He has received a bunch of money lately."

"Let me guess. Five large deposits this school year."

"Close," says Mary. "Four deposits of $30K each."

"Can you trace the source of the funds? Who paid this asshole off?"

"It's impossible to trace the wires. They come from a bank in the Caymans. That's a dead end, but I've done some additional digging on Drudge. He's recently divorced, no children. And he just bought a car."

My hand aches from clutching the phone so hard. "What bridge does this troll live under? He's about to get some unexpected company."

"He just moved to a high-security building. It won't be easy for you to get at him. I'll send the address to your phone."

"Thanks, Mary. I don't need easy. Consider me forewarned."

"I'm still looking up the other info for you. I'll let you know when the facial rec hits, or when I know more about the van. Be safe."

Kate's heard enough to know the gist of the conversation. She stabs the last forkful of eggs with murderous intent. "So that prick sold out Megan and the others?"

"Looks that way."

She shovels eggs into her mouth, and for a moment, her eyes focus over my shoulder.

A weird look crosses her face, like she's seeing a naked man with a long beard and a cane walking across the street, so I glance at the mirror and see Frosty lick his spoon suggestively and point toward the men's room. He gets up and strolls in that direction. Before he turns the corner, he glances at Kate and smiles.

Kate's knuckles are practically white from the pressure she's using to choke out the fork. The slick suit-wearing, frosty-haired jackass has only made her angrier.

"What do we do now?" She won't tell me about Frosty. She knows I won't take it well.

"We visit Brad tonight. Mary said he's moved to a new high-security building, which causes some problems. They have armed guards and sophisticated security software, but I'm working on a plan."

Kate rips into a piece of bacon, and I excuse myself. Grandma's has a single bathroom for men, around back, out of the way, toward the kitchen. No one watches me as I move toward the back. I knock softly against the door.

Frosty opens it with a sly smile on his face, which turns into a scowl when he sees me instead of Kate.

"Expecting someone else, ass face?" I shove the door with my shoulder and bash it against his nose. He stumbles backward, and I push my way in and lock the door behind me. The bathroom is just big enough for both of us.

"What the fuck are you doing?" he snaps. He flexes his arms and puffs out his chest in a primitive attempt to make him appear bigger than normal.

I'm not impressed. His breathing is shallow, and his eyes look petrified. He's probably never been in a real fight and doesn't know what to do or expect. Unfortunately for him, I do. I punch him in the stomach. I put my weight behind the punch so that it takes all the air out of him, bending him over. Since I don't want him screaming, I swing my elbow into his nose, hard enough to snap his head back. I can practically see the birds flying in front of his eyes.

He moans and lifts his hands in the air in surrender. All the fake muscles he's spent hours creating at the gym are lost on him now. He'll probably fire Vick and never go back. I feel badly for Vick. Not that he lost a client, but he'll never get the chance to smash Frosty's head in with the barbell. Oh well, he had his chance. I'm sure he's got other clients who deserve an equal fate.

Frosty wheezes and sputters. "I-I-I have...money."

"This isn't about money. Not everything is about money." I slap him across the face. It's the most disrespectful thing I can do to the punk besides spitting. And I hate spitting on people. It's oddly intimate. I don't want my spit on Frosty's face, so I settle for a nice, hard slap.

He touches his face and tears brim his eyes. "What do you want?"

"Do you think it's polite to make lewd gestures at a woman? She doesn't need to deal with your shit. She's got problems of her own to worry about."

"I didn't mean anything. I was just fooling around."

"Right." I slap him twice this time. Two hard quick shots to his left cheek. "And what about me? Did you think about me? How do you think that makes me feel that you're hitting on my friend?"

He shrugs.

"Say something." I lift my hand to slap him again and he cowers.

"Bad."

"That's right, you arrogant, self-entitled twat. Now I'm going to hurt you. You've left me no choice. This is on you."

An energy in my head growls. Not Caesar this time. Something darker and nastier that I can't name. It wants blood, so I pull the knife from my jacket pocket and lift it toward his face.

"You're cr-crazy, man."

"There you go, being rude again. You don't even know me." I press the tip of the blade against his cheek and pierce his flesh. "But you're right this time. I'm nuts. I guess even a worthless, walking vagina like you can be right once in a while. My faith in humanity has been restored."

I flick the blade against his cheek and the blood trickles down his face and onto his white shirt. For the first time, I'm hoping the blood will be black and sludge-like. If Frosty is a demon, I'll have no choice but to kill him. It's red. He's too much of a creep even for demons.

I yank Frosty by the hair to the toilet. "Can you swim?"

"Su-sure."

"Good." I whip his head into the toilet and hold it down. He tries to push himself up, but I have all the leverage. I count to twenty before I let him up.

He shakes his head and gasps for air. His perfect haircut is ruined, toilet water soaking his hair and his suit.

I dunk him again. This time I count to thirty before I pull him up. When I do, I lean close to him and whisper. "Try to take your head from your ass and see people for who they really are. Be a better person, you self-absorbed meathead."

He blabbers. "Got it. You're good. I should have known."

I slap him across the face with the back of my left hand. "Keep up, Frosty. I'm crazy. You got that right originally. It's probably the only thing you've ever gotten right in your miserable little life, but my friend is good."

"Whatever you say."

"I'm going to be watching you, and if you act like an ass again, I'm going to cut off your pecker and stuff it in one of Grandma's pies. Let's call it the secret ingredient. It's probably useless where it is anyway. Understand?"

He nods.

"Good. Ready for one last dunk?"

Frosty holds his breath.

I intend on dunking him one last time, I really do. But when I push his head down, the energy inside me takes over, changes my direction, and I bash his head against the side of the porcelain toilet bowl instead. I lift it and do it again. I let go, and he topples to the side of the toilet and onto the tile floor. He's got a nasty gash on his forehead and he's not moving.

Shit. Is he dead?

I didn't mean to kill him. I just wanted to scare him, but the demon inside took over. I'd have to check his pulse to know if he's dead or just knocked out, and what's the point? I don't want to touch him, and if he's dead I can't help him anyway. I note the time on my phone. If I'm not going to check his pulse, I have to assume he's dead. At least I made it beyond three weeks. I'd like to try for four, although I suspect things are going to get real nasty to get Megan back.

When I shut the bathroom door behind me, the waitress shoots me a quizzical look.

"Some people can't hold their coffee," I say. "Caffeine makes them sick."

"Sure," she says.

I hand her a fifty-dollar bill. "Better not go into the bathroom anytime soon. And if anyone asks, you've never seen us."

She smiles. "What? Two eighty-year olds. You were such a cute couple, I'm sure to remember you."

"That'll be fine."

Kate stands when I approach the table, a scowl on her face. I drop a twenty next to my plate for the food.

After we leave, she stops me on the sidewalk. "Was that necessary?"

"What?" I say, although I'm sure she's busted me.

"You know what. Did you have to beat that guy up in the bathroom?"

"The bathroom?" Sometimes it works to play really dumb. I make it sound like I've never even heard of a bathroom before, but that doesn't work on Kate.

"There's blood on your hand, Steven."

She's right. Some of Frosty's blood must have rubbed off when I slapped him.

"In my defense, not only was he rude, but he had a horrible haircut. Frosted hair on a guy over thirty. Come on. It's ridiculous."

"Did you kill him?"

"Fifty-fifty."

"Seriously?"

"Maybe 75 percent dead and 25 percent just knocked out. I got a little carried away. I admit it. That's on me."

"Great."

"Either way, I did Vick a favor."

"Who's Vick?" she asks.

"Long story." Getting into my fertile imagination and discussing the fictional trainer named Vick is probably a bad idea at the moment.

"I guess you can't change." She rolls her eyes, turns her back on me, and marches to her apartment.

Man, I hate it when she rolls her eyes at me.

CHAPTER 16

I'm not going to apologize for what happened to Mr. Frosty. I may have overreacted a touch, but he's not blameless. He's undoubtedly insulted scores of women and treated everyone else like shit. Some people move through life as if their actions don't have consequences. Fuck that. Someone has to remind guys like Mr. Frosty of the basic moral code. He's not above common decency. No one is.

Kate and I have been in this place before. When we were a couple, crap like this would happen all the time. Some guy would hit on her (she's gorgeous and way out of my league) and I'd react. I'd break the guy's nose or bash in his teeth. I killed two brothers who pulled knives on me. They flashed the blades but didn't really know how to use them. A stupid mistake.

Afterward, Kate would yell at me, and I'd apologize, but not this time. Mr. Frosty knew what he was doing, and he should have known that in a decent society someone would eventually kick his ass.

It takes two and a half blocks for Kate to cool down, which isn't bad. In the past it would have taken an entire day, but Megan's kidnapping changes everything. Time has morphed into the enemy. Every minute for her has become a what-if filled eternity.

When we cross a street and head for her apartment building, she asks, "So, you said you had a plan to get to Drudge?"

"Working on one. Mary sent me Drudge's address. He's moved to a Klendall apartment. They're a new outfit that specializes in high security for their tenants. I guess scumbags that sell young kids to kidnappers can't be too careful these days. I'd like to spend some time alone with him in his apartment. We'll have some privacy, and that's the best place to get him to talk."

"But his apartment has all that security," says Kate. "What did you call it, a Klondike?"

"A Klendall, but there's always a way to get at a target. We have to think outside the box. How do you feel about online dating?"

"I'm more of a traditional girl. Get drunk, find what seems like a decent guy in a bar, suck face, and regret everything the next morning. Rinse and repeat four months later."

"What about all those doctors at the hospital? Aren't they pestering you?"

"Only the married ones. The single ones look down on a girl from District 12."

"That's disappointing. I'd like to think more of our medical professionals."

"Doctors are mostly dicks. I'd date a nurse or a PA over a doctor every time."

"Good to know. We can try to snatch Brad on his way home, but that's complicated. There are too many variables for a carjacking, and now that he has a flat, he'll call a car service to fix it. We can stake out his place, but we don't have time. He might stay in tonight and then we've lost an entire night. That leaves us with two options. Either I break in, which is hard, but possible and probably messy, or he lets us in. And—"

"And you saw those notes on the Eros online dating site in his car," she says.

"Right. Looks like he's just joined. His username is Sam Steele. From my initial look on the website, the company boasts about hooking up 'successful' men with high quality women from lower districts."

"So, it's a prostitution ring?"

"Not that I can tell. I think women from lower districts try to hook up with guys in the upper districts. Maybe they hope to get married or something like that."

"Sounds shitty," she says as we reach the stoop of her apartment building. "Deal me in. I'm your girl."

"I knew I could count on you."

We trudge up the stairs, and Kate unlocks the door to her apartment.

Tina, Kate's oldest and best friend, rushes forward and swallows her in a full body embrace. Words gush from her mouth, toppling over a linguistic waterfall, "I can't believe this. We're going to get Megan back. Don't you worry about that. We'll get her back."

I shut the door and curse my rotten luck. *Tina*. Couldn't she get hit by a bus or die from the plague or something?

Tina disentangles from Kate and makes a show of sniffing the air. "I smell cow shit." She looks up and glares at me. "Oh, Steven. I should have recognized the stink. I heard you crawled out from underneath a rock."

"Nice to see you too, Tina."

She ignores me and focuses on Kate. "Any word yet?"

"We have a lead," Kate explains what we know about Brad Drudge and the other missing kids.

Tina's short, just over five feet tall, pretty in a haphazard way. Long, curly, chestnut hair falls to her shoulders, and her well-developed chest looks like it might break free from her white blouse at any moment. She's mostly tucked the blouse into a pair of jeans with a rip on one knee.

Tina loves Kate and hates me. Officially, she's always said I was bad for Kate, and she has plenty of proof to back that up. But unofficially, I suspect she doesn't just love Kate, but is *in love* with her. She probably hated Ethan too.

It's been sixteen years since I last saw her. That's a long time to hold onto those types of feelings and keep them secret. I wonder if she's ever told Kate how she really feels.

She looks at me as if she's just smelled rotten meat. "I'd say you look good, but that would be a lie. The beard is awful. You look like cow shit that's been baked in the sun."

Welcome to Tina World.

CHAPTER 17

I use Kate's tablet to look up Eros and study the dating site in more detail. "It costs $500 for women to join and there's a per hookup fee of fifty. Oh, and there's a premium membership. I guess there's always a premium membership these days. Everyone wants to be treated better than the other guy.

"The premium membership costs $2,000 and guarantees date requests go to the head of the line," I say. "Guys have to pay $5,000 to join, and there's no fee for dates."

Tina whistles. "That's a lot of dough for a dating site. The ones I use are free."

"This one is *discriminating*."

"Hey, eat monkey-shit pie, Steven. I could join that site. They'd be lucky to have me."

"I'm sure. We'll get a premium membership. What name do you want to use? We can't use your real one in case Brad recognizes it from school."

"Something sexy," says Tina. "How about Emanuel Estrange?"

"I don't want a hooker name. How about Emma Sykes?"

"Emma Sykes it is," I say. "Now what about your occupation?"

"What's wrong with nursing?" Kate says.

"It sounds a little dull," says Tina. "Let's do dancer."

"Nurses are hot," I say, and not just because it pulls a small smile from Kate. "Brad just signed up. He might not be ready to start dating exotic dancers just yet. He might want to start out a little slower."

"We'll compromise then," says Tina. "Part-time nurse and part-time dance instructor. That way we cover all the bases."

"Done," Kate says.

"I'll fill in the rest of the information, but we'll need some photos."

Tina grabs Kate's hand. "We're on it. That douchebag won't be able to resist her." She pulls Kate to the bedroom. "I know the exact dress we should use."

I'm sure Tina's got an outfit in mind. Hopefully, Brad has the same taste as Tina. I'm a little worried Kate will come out dressed in leather, riding whip in hand.

I list Kate as thirty-one instead of thirty-five, and list her hobbies as reading, watching movies, and eating out. My goal, to attract a somewhat shy new user. If I knew Brad, I could tailor this thing to make sure he'd bite, but I've only uncovered a few things about him online. He's flabby and likes fancy restaurants. Undoubtedly, there's more to him than that, but he's not a prolific social media poster. Either he doesn't feel the need to show off, or he doesn't have anything to show off. I'd bet on the latter.

The rest of the touches on Kate's fake profile doesn't take long. I'm done when she comes out of the bedroom, and my heart stops cold as if it's submerged in ice and quick-frozen. She's wearing a short, sleeveless, black cocktail dress with a low, swooping V-neck. She's braless, but the outfit's still tasteful.

She's a complete knockout. Even more attractive than when she was twenty and, until this second, I thought the twenty-year-old Kate was as close to perfection as I've ever seen.

Her cheeks turn pink. "Well, what do you think?"

"Oh, Steven's a fan. His tongue is practically on the ground," says Tina. "Get a grip caveman, we've got work to do."

I ignore Tina, although she's right. My tongue has hit the floor and flops around on the tiles like a fish out of water. "You look fabulous."

"Really?" she asks, her voice velvety soft.

"Who cares what Neanderthal man thinks?" asks Tina. "We need to snare ourselves a different shitweasel."

"He'll be interested." I use my phone to snap a few photos of Kate in different poses and add them to her profile. A few seconds later, I buy the premium package and we're ready.

I access Sam Steele's profile. He's edited his picture to make himself look younger and thinner and, under occupation, he's listed educator and talent scout.

"Talent scout," grumbles Kate. "I'd like to..."

No doubt her imagination goes so dark she's embarrassed to use the words. Not to worry. My imagination is way darker than hers, and I don't need words. When I get my hands on this guy, he'll regret his mother ever met his father.

"Let's focus," says Tina. "We need to send him a message. Something that will pique his interest right away."

Kate says, "Why don't we be straightforward and ask if he wants a date tonight?'"

"Oh, honey, that's lame," says Tina. "No wonder you suck at dating. How about, 'I see you're an educator, I'm a willing student?'"

"We don't want him to take out a restraining order on us," I say. "We need something a little more provocative and less forward."

"What does he list as his hobbies?" Kate asks.

"Reading, traveling, cooking, and deep-sea diving." I huff. "Deep-sea diving, my ass! I bet he's never even been to the deep end of a pool."

"I've got it. Ask if he's read *Secrets in the Darkness*," says Tina.

We both shoot her a look.

"What, I read?"

"Was it good?" I ask.

"It's way better than you, Stevo."

"You'll never find out."

"Thank God. I'd rather screw a zombie and have his dick fall off half-way through."

At least Tina World is colorful.

Kate steps between us, "Do you think this will work, Tina?"

"Definitely. It's all the rage in literary circles. He probably hasn't read it, but at least he can search it online. Trust me."

Kate nods at me, and I send the message.

"How long do you think it'll take for him to reply?" asks Kate.

I shrug. "He's working so..."

Kate's tablet pings, and I almost jump. Brad's opened up our invite to chat and seen our message already.

Ten minutes drags past and no response yet. I look at Tina.

"He'll respond. You'll see. Trust me."

I stand and stretch, starting with my legs. By the time I get to my neck, the tablet pings again.

Tina reads the response triumphantly. "'Rebecca Scarlet is one my favorite authors also.' The assclown added a smiley face afterward. Who puts a smiley face in a message like that?" She hands the tablet to Kate and says, "Okay, at least we've got him on the hook. Now we just need to reel him in."

Kate hands her back the tablet, and Tina types the next message. "How about we get together and discuss the book? An intimate book club…"

The response takes half as long this time, and Tina reads it for us. "Sounds fun. How about dinner on Saturday? I know a place near my apartment."

Kate groans.

"We need to see him tonight in his apartment," I say. "We can't wait until Saturday."

Tina grins. "Don't worry, I've got him wriggling on the hook now. Watch and learn, Stevo." She types and talks at the same time. "How about tonight instead? I'm teaching a tango class tomorrow night and can't meet then."

The response, "Tonight works. How about we meet at Carlucci's restaurant at 9:00?"

"Almost there," Tina says, and her fingers go to work. "I'm not usually this forward, but you have sweet eyes. How about we do book club first in your apartment and dinner later? I'll bring a bottle of wine."

Brad responds immediately. I imagine him pounding the keyboard with fat sausage-like fingers, a sick smile stretching across his flabby face. "Nine o'clock at my apartment then. I look forward to it. 325 Spruce Street, Apartment 12B. It's in District 10. Do you have access?"

Kate nods. "The hospital is in District 9, so I can travel through 10 at night."

Tina types the final response, "Access won't be a problem. I teach some of my dancing classes in the poshest places. I'm so looking forward to meeting and reading with you."

She hands the tablet to me.

"Poshest places? Meeting and reading."

Tina smirks. "I thought this pile of festering turds would appreciate the turn of a good phrase. Now that we have Brad on the hook, what's the rest of the plan, Stevo?"

"It's not going to be easy," I say, and I'm not kidding.

CHAPTER 18

Every inch of Megan's body hurts. It isn't a bad hurt, but one born from a long day of clearing rocks from the dirt, a relentless assault that only dented a short stretch of the field. According to the other Angels, rock clearing is only one of a number of tasks they perform on a regular basis, each one physically grueling, yet they don't seem to mind. The chores are necessary. It's how they gain favor with Mother and speak with God.

Megan shakes her head and tries to clear the cobwebs. The day feels foggy. She remembers working in the field, but only has a vague memory of lunch and Mother's sermon. Afterward, they went back to the rocks only to be collected by Buck for dinner. Unlike lunch, dinner was held in a large mess hall.

New jumpsuit colors appeared: blue, orange, and black. She couldn't get an accurate read, but she had counted more than 150 people. And the black jumpsuits carried M18 assault rifles with them. Megan wanted to ask why they needed so many guns, but she had no one to confide in. She'll have to learn on her own. That's okay with her. Most learning is hands-on anyway.

Four musicians played folksongs before dinner. A rather heavyset woman dressed in orange sang with a sweet, clear voice. They played songs she hadn't heard before—songs praising Mother and the Angel's role as champions for God. Mother offered a simple prayer before they served dinner. Nothing as elaborate as lunch. The community responded to a few verbal clues with chants of their own. Not knowing what to say, Megan kept her mouth shut. After dinner, different people offered testimonials. They spoke about their conversations with God and His plans for them. Everyone clapped after each testimonial.

Megan can't remember anyone's specific speech. Her mind still buzzes, and she feels a general sense of contentment. After dinner, Buck led Megan's group of Angels to a plain cabin where they share a room—six beds and six Angels—the same cabin where she started the day. They all changed out of their jumpsuits to simple yellow robes, each robe with a green or purple armband to match the ones on their jumpsuits.

Megan tries to remember the name of the girl who was taken in the van with her, but all she can recall is Autumn, her new name. It's almost as if the other girl, the pre-Angel version, has already been wiped away.

May sits on the edge of her bed and smiles at her. "I know that look. Everyone feels the same way when they first arrive. Mother overwhelms us with her goodness, and God fills this place with serenity and peace. Don't try to fight it. Let it fill your body and soul. Soon you'll adjust and won't be so overwhelmed."

Megan reaches into her mind, through the fog, and pulls out some random thoughts. "My head feels funny. I can't seem to focus on anything."

A different Angel named Violet sits on the bed next to her bed. "It will pass and then you'll see. You'll be happy you're here. We all are."

"Not all of us," says Petal who's standing by the door, her voice singing a cautionary note. "Some Angels never accept it here. They're touched by the Devil, and he turns them."

"What happens to them?" asks Megan.

Petal says, "Depends upon what God tells Mother. Either they're burned or buried alive. Mother won't let demons live among us." Petal's voice sounds unhappy; obviously she's not as content at the others.

Violet touches Megan's arm. "Don't be one of *those* Angels. You have to resist the Devil."

A cold knife carves its way up Megan's spine. They kill Angels who make trouble, and then she remembers her mom, and her groggy thoughts start to focus. To escape she'll have to be careful. Her fingers touch the chain around her neck. First, she'll need to get rid of the pendant.

"It's only her first night," says May. "It's a little early to talk about the Devil. We don't want to scare her."

"It's never to early to warn her about what happens if she disobeys Mother." Petal's voice is darker and even more sober than before.

"What happens now?" asks Autumn who sits on the bed to Megan's left.

Violet claps her hands. "This is the best part. At least for some of us. They'll take us to talk to God in the sanctuary. Only those who've been good and are worthy get to go."

"Do you really talk to God?" Megan asks, her voice breathless.

"Oh, most certainly we do," Violet answers.

"Sometimes we minister to His chosen people," May adds. "We're Angels and must do his bidding. But we always talk to Him first."

A soft knock raps against the door, and when it opens, Buck stands in the doorway. "How are the new Angels making out?" He asks about both of them, yet he only looks at Megan, his deep, blue eyes solemn.

"Oh, they're making out just fine." May adds a lilt to her voice that's clearly meant to flirt.

Buck continues to stare at Megan until she nods to confirm that she hasn't been mistreated.

He then points to May, Violet, and one other Angel to come with him. Violet claps with excitement and the girls leave a step behind him.

"He'll be back later and then maybe I'll be forced to go." Petal doesn't sound particularly happy with the idea. "You probably won't be called tonight. Usually an Angel has to be here a week or so before her first trip to the sanctuary."

The lights go out and Megan stretches onto her bed. The day has been long and exhaustion tugs at her. Sleep comes quickly.

At some point, she wakes to the sound of knocking against the window. May, Violet, and the other Angel haven't returned yet. Megan stretches and walks to the window to investigate.

The knocking continues and Megan peers outside. Her heart skips a beat.

Frankie is standing outside, peeking into the room.

She wants to run, but her feet won't obey her brain.

Frankie blows her a kiss and then she notices that his jumpsuit is unzipped down the center.

She pulls away from the window and jumps back to bed, her heart beating faster than ever.

Petal quietly sneaks over, slides in bed with her, and whispers, "Frankie's going to be trouble. I've noticed the way he looks at you. You'll need to be tough with him."

"Should I tell anyone?"

"No, whatever you do, don't tell anyone. They might suspect the Devil is involved, and you don't want that."

"Okay."

"And that groggy feeling has nothing to do with God. I know it's a cliché, but they drug the punch. Drink as much water before lunch and dinner as you can, but you'll have to try to dump out some of the punch or they'll get suspicious."

"Thanks."

"Oh, and God has nothing to do with what they do here."

Footsteps come from outside, probably Buck and the girls returning to the cabin.

Petal brushes one of her fingertips down the side of Megan's face, and goose bumps form in its wake. She kisses Megan on the cheek and slips out of the bed.

CHAPTER 19

I flee Kate's apartment, a cowardly act, no doubt. But I can only take Tina in small doses, and she made it clear she's hunkering down for the duration. She left me no choice, which is exactly what she wanted. Besides, Tina's been with Kate since the beginning. She didn't go AWOL to join a special operations group.

It was best that I leave, so I did. I said I needed air and started wandering the streets. Without planning it, I've returned to my old neighborhood, my original destination yesterday, and stare at an abandoned apartment building across the street – a building I used to call home. Acid churns in my stomach, my heart jumps, and sweat slicks my palms. I feel foolish. I'm too old to be afraid of ghosts.

A not-so-recent fire has destroyed the roof and charred much of the outside of the seven-story, brick building. All the windows are gone, and the herringbone design in the brick that borders the roof is barely visible beneath the blackened soot left by the fire. It's a shame. That design was the only sign anyone cared about the building or the people who once lived inside. I used to think whoever added that detail thought of us as people rather than useless ghetto scum. I guess it's true. You can't ever return home.

The light-stepping old-timer from last night moves behind me. I don't need to turn to identify him. The smell is enough.

"Sneaking up on me again, old-timer?" I ask, still looking at the apartment building. "Didn't we discuss this last night?"

"You'd be the last person I'd sneak up on after I seen what you did to those Red Dragons. That sure was something. Have you found that woman you were looking for?"

"Not yet. What do you know about this apartment building?"

"That's the Devil's Armpit. That's what we call it, all right. It's haunted and smells bad, like rotten eggs. You can feel the ghosts and evil spirits coming from it, right? I can. It's creepy even to me, and I've seen my share of creepy in this world."

"Why do you say it's haunted?"

The man shrugs. "I've lived in this neighborhood a long time and I know all the stories. A while back," the man pauses for effect, and then continues in a quieter voice, as if he's sharing a secret, "maybe twenty years or so, the killings started. Each victim stabbed to death in the most gruesome manner. I seen one myself. He was stabbed a dozen times at least. His skin shredded to a messy pulp. No one could figure out who done it. We called the killer the Seventh Street Stabber, which I always thought was weird being this here Devil's Armpit is on Eighth Street. I reckon you could hear the screams from Seventh Street, and it sounded catchy so… Whatever you want to call him, he sure killed lots of folks."

"He?"

"We always figured the Seventh Street Stabber for a guy. No one caught him or even seen him or nothing like that. But no woman could've done it. That's for sure. The Stabber could've been a ghost, a monster, or the devil himself, for all we knew. We sure didn't want to find out. No one wanted to be alone with the Stabber.

"The killings always happened in spurts. Three or four at a time and then nothing — just long enough for people to think the haunting had stopped, and then it all started again. Same thing all over again, more stabbings, and then a pause, as if the devil had his fill of the living and went back to hell for a bit of rest."

"When was the last killing?"

He shrugs again, which barely shifts his trench coat. "Could be five years or more. Hard to say."

"And then they stopped? No one ever caught the killer?"

The man frowns. "Nope, but the fire happened three years ago. I remember that clearly. Burned like a son of a bitch in the dead of the night. Quite a blaze, that one. They said it was arson. A dozen people died. Someone locked them in the top apartments. I remember their screams. You could hear them all over the ghetto that night. Seventh Street and beyond. A thing like that, a man don't forget."

"Let me guess. No one caught the arsonist."

"Nope. I'd say it was the same devil as before. Must have been the Stabber. The insurance company sent some guys to investigate, but the owner burned in the building. I guess they had to pay something either way, so they didn't give a damn. It's a haunted building, that one is. The Devil's Armpit. I don't think it's done yet. I think it's just waiting for another chance to kill again."

Somehow the Fates are working their magic again, and that story sounds too familiar to be a coincidence. I hand a fifty to the old-timer. "You should move along now."

The old-timer takes the bill and moves away. After two steps, he pauses and looks over his shoulder and back at me. "You'd best leave that building alone. It's trouble, I tell you. Some nights I hear ghosts from inside, and I feel a chill every time I walk past it."

The old man offers good advice. Sucks that I can't take it. "It's out of my hands, old-timer. The Fates want what they want."

The front door has been replaced by plywood. I splinter it with a simple front kick and rip broken pieces of wood away with my hands until the newly created hole is large enough to fit through. I could have found a quieter way into the abandoned building. Perhaps pried off one of the boards that blocked the windows or go around to the alley and sneak in some way. But this used to be my home, and I want to go through the front door.

The place reeks of smoke and filth. I click on my phone's flashlight and sweep the beam across the lobby in a slow, long loop. Chunks of wood, plaster, and glass shards litter the floor. The light also reveals signs of life: a dozen empty tequila bottles stacked in a corner, fast-food bags scattered across the floor, and someone has painted dragon symbols with names sprawled underneath them on the walls.

The staircase looks sound, so I climb up. At the sixth floor, I trudge onto the hall. Despite the charred walls, the plaster scattered about, and the mold that infests everything, it still feels familiar. It feels the same as when I was fifteen.

Three apartments down, Number 66, I stand frozen in the doorway. The fear that shook me outside intensifies and sounds like a waterfall crashing in my head. The flood of memories throws me back in time where I don't want to go.

My mother wasn't always afflicted by demons. Well, it's hard for me to be certain of that. I didn't notice any signs of demons at first, but I was young back then. The demons seemed to come upon her slowly. At first, she started going to church daily, spending hours in the pews praying. Grace became long, complicated rituals at every meal. And then came the demons.

She saw them everywhere and worried they'd drag her to hell. My father did his best, but he traveled a lot for work. He loved her, but his best wasn't good enough. Not even close.

One night, when I was eleven, I cowered in my room while my mother raged at my father. "You're a demon. You won't take me!" she screamed over and over again. He tried to calm her, but she wouldn't have it. Furniture flew around the small apartment, wood splintered, metal pans crashed against walls.

I curled myself into a ball and shook. A tornado touched down inside my apartment. My mother's rage penetrated through the walls, explosive. I made myself smaller, hoping it would pass like the other times. I even prayed.

And then came a long silence that bit into my bone like a winter frost. I sat with my ear pressed to the door, hoping to hear sounds of life, hoping to hear my father's voice. It could have been ten minutes or two hours. Finally, I summoned enough courage to open my door. My mother squatted over my father's body, muttering, bloody scissors clutched in her hands. She had stabbed him so many times in his chest and throat that it looked as if he'd been run through a grinder.

I stared at her, but words never came. What could I say?

She didn't move for a long time, but finally, around dawn, she snapped from her trance and looked at me. "I had no choice, Stevie. He was a demon. He wanted to take me and then he'd come for you. I had to protect you."

She sounded lucid, normal even, as if she was explaining a simple concept, something I should have already known. She cleaned up most of the blood and called the police.

Back then the police made believe they had an interest in investigating crimes in the ghetto. But they really didn't care what happened in the North Philly Badlands. My father was just one less ghetto scum for them to deal with, and my mother could be convincing when she wanted. She painted a picture of the poor wife, defending herself against a drug-crazed, abusive husband. They fell for her story because she looked the part and they wanted to believe it. Less work for them, so they simply collected the body and wrote it off as self-defense.

I was such a coward. If I'd left my bedroom earlier, if I'd helped my father, if, if, if...

The incident seemed to purge the demons from my mother. For years, she reverted back to her old self. We never discussed that night. I almost forgot about it, but who could really forget such a thing? And then, the demons returned without warning. They came back in force and my mother turned her focus on me.

I was bad. Demons lived inside of me. I needed to be cleansed.

I always assumed my mother was wrong, that she murdered my father in a fit of insanity. I couldn't see demons myself back then. I had no way of knowing they were real.

I've only recently started seeing them myself, my first encounter three years ago. Now I can't help but wonder if my mother had been right. Was my father a demon?

I suck in a deep breath and enter the two-bedroom apartment. Nothing remains. No furniture, even the kitchen fixtures have been stripped away. Still, my mother's presence hangs in the air.

I stare at the corner of what had been the kitchen and see my father's mutilated body lying there, my mother screaming about demons. Light glints off the scissors in her hand, and a dangerous fire burns in her gaze. She looks up and smiles at me. "Hello, Stevie."

"Mother, what happened to you?" I ask. "Did you become the Seventh Street Stabber? Did you conquer the demons inside you? Are you still alive?"

"What do you think, Stevie?"

"I wouldn't have come back if I knew. Come on, I could use a little help here. For once, just a plain answer."

"You already know." Her eyes burn brighter. "You have demons inside you, boy. I'll cut them out of you, just like your demon father." She raises her bloody shears and laughs.

"Don't expect a Mother's Day card this year," I say, and the image vanishes.

I walk through the apartment and look for signs of my mother, anything that'll provide a clue as to her fate. Although unlikely, it's possible she's still alive, which is why I'm here, searching through the wreckage for one last chance to find out what happened to her. By knowing her fate, I hope to make sense of my own.

I sweep my bedroom door with light. Gouges remain in the wood where my mother clawed at the door, begging me to let her in. Each night, I pushed my dresser against the door, but sometimes, that wasn't enough. Some nights, I had to brace my arms against the dresser and push with my legs, so she couldn't get in.

The apartment looks different, and it takes me second before I figure out what's off. Someone hung wallpaper on the walls and even the ceiling: a pine green background with small golden stars. It's charred now, peeling away from the plaster. Why would someone go to the expense of wallpapering such a crappy apartment? I rip down a long strip from the wall.

Rows of blood-red crosses, uneven in size and shape, cover the wall. I rip another strip. My mother painted crosses on every inch of every wall and the ceiling.

My legs turn to jelly, and I fall to the floor. Memories whipsaw through me. Most are terrifying, but a few good ones mingle with the bad: a picnic by the river, a baseball game with my dad.

The crosses and the wallpaper reveal two important clues. One, my mother's behavior grew more extreme after I left. Not good. And two, she moved out of the Devil's Armpit before the fire. The landlord must have hung the wallpaper to get a new tenant. That's even worse. There's really nowhere shoddier to go, and I can't picture my mother moving to a better place. Not in her condition, which means I should start checking the city mortuary records.

Whatever secrets I hoped she might tell me are buried with her. I should feel something—sadness, happiness, angry—something. Instead, I feel numb.

CHAPTER 20

I leave the Devil's Armpit with no answers, only nagging questions that shake me. When I return to Kate's neighborhood, I spot two unsavory types following me. They wear long trench coats, have broad shoulders and beards, and stink like demons. I use all the reflective surfaces I pass to check out their eyes. I catch a glimpse in a car's side mirror, another in a window, and a particularly clear one on a street sign. That reflection bothers me. Red sparks flicker in both sets of eyes.

All of my... let's call them interactions... with demons so far were one on one. I started to doubt whether they work together, but these two are following me. They don't seem to be in a rush to intercept me, but plans like that can change, and I don't love my chances against two demons at once.

I'm looking for a way to ditch them when I spot an old stone church. It looks familiar. Probably a place my mother took me sporadically, so I duck inside and hope the hallowed ground will keep the demons at bay. The place enjoys a simple beauty—tall cathedral ceilings, stained glass windows, a large organ, rows of empty pews, and a mahogany altar.

I find a priest, or really, he finds me. A youngish man with a slight build and short black hair steps from behind the altar and asks if he can help me. He's wearing black and a priest's white collar. He has welcoming black eyes and a soft voice.

I turn my head toward the door and wonder if the two demons will barge in and tear this place apart. Since they haven't yet, they probably won't.

The priest touches my arm and says, "Sit with me."

"I'm not sure I'm the type to spend time in church."

He grins. "You're the perfect type. If not you, who? This place was built for people just like you. Consider it your house."

Can he see through me and recognize the changes raging inside? Can he tell that I'm turning into a demon, that the voices inside are winning, or is this just his way of being nice to a troubled person? Either way, I'm in no rush to go back outside with the demons or to go to Kate's apartment for another installment of Tina World, so I take him up on his invitation.

He sits beside me and doesn't say anything. He waits for me to talk about whatever is on my mind. There's a lot of stuff crammed in there, most of it bad, but thoughts of my mother are festering at the top. Maybe he knew her before she died? I show him the artist rendering on my phone. "Have you ever seen this woman?"

He shakes his head. "I'm new at this church. Maybe Father Detomaso might know her, but he won't be back until later this week."

When I turn to get up, he touches my arm and asks if I'd like to say a confession. I almost laugh. What would he think if I confessed my sins? Would he race from the church screeching? I don't want to add to his nightmares. "Maybe next time."

He takes my refusal in stride, as if he knew I'd decline. "Well, then how about a chat? You'd be doing me a favor. It gets lonely in here during the day."

I doubt he'd think I'm doing him much of a favor if those two demons burst inside, but they would've come in by now if they could. At least I've learned that churches are safe places. I guess I owe him something.

"My name is Paul, but my friends call me Paulie," he says.

I never thought about priests having friends before. Why shouldn't they? "Nice to meet you, Father Paul."

"What shall we talk about? You must have stepped inside for a reason."

I can't tell him that I'm running from demons and thought the church would be a good place to hide, and I do have questions. Lots of questions. And he seems as good as anyone to ask.

"Are there sins that can't be redeemed, or is the whole thing some type of cosmic scale? If I do enough good deeds, can I tip the scale in my favor? Can I still be saved?"

He thinks about that for a while. He probably didn't expect me to ask such a serious question off the bat. Finally, he says, "Neither."

"Neither? I don't understand."

"Sins are not redeemed. People are redeemed. God doesn't keep score in a ledger. It's what's in our souls that count."

My voice raises a touch. "But how can those who commit bad acts be redeemed?"

He smiles, which disarms me. "Those who believe in God, who have goodness in their souls, act that way. The two line up over time."

"Which comes first?" I ask. "Good deeds or belief in God?'

"The old chicken or the egg question. They didn't cover that in seminary." He laughs, and that pulls one out of me.

He rests a hand on my arm. "You must see this as good news. God's not worried about your past. He's worried about your present and your future. He's worried about your soul and your heart. We can all be redeemed. It doesn't matter what we've done in the past."

After that we chat about lighter topics, just two guys talking. He likes football, but he's not an Eagles fan. He grew up in New York, so he favors the Giants, but he can't tell people around here that. They'd run him from town in an instant if his secret got out.

I ask him why he trusts me with such a sensitive secret, and he says I look like a trustworthy person. His phone buzzes, and he has to leave. He has an appointment with a sick person in his congregation who needs his company.

We stand, and he puts his hand out to shake. "I hope to see you again."

"You will, Father Paul." I say and I mean it. I have more questions, important ones about demons that maybe he can help me solve.

He grins again, a natural expression that comes easily for him. "Next time call me Paulie." His eyes sparkle with a light in them. "There's a door behind the altar that leads to an alley behind the church, if you'd rather not go out the front door."

Does he know I'm running from demons, or was it just a lucky guess? I want to ask him, but he's already gone.

I stay in the pew. I've never met anyone like Father Paul before, a true believer. So now I have new thoughts to mull over. Perhaps if I do good deeds, belief in God will follow. Perhaps I can stave off the demons inside and keep my blood from turning black. It might not be too late for me.

I'd like to believe in God, but I don't know how, and I suspect it won't be easy to start now. The demons have their claws in me.

CHAPTER 21

I stay in that church for hours. My life has been filled with so many bad things, but there's been some good. If I focus on the good, if I'm called to do that, maybe there's hope for me. Hope is more than I started the day with, probably more than I deserve. I'll come back and talk to Father Paul again after these thoughts settle in my mind.

I find the door in the back and crack it open. The alley is empty. I leave, make sure no one follows me, and return to Kate's apartment.

Tina opens the door and lets me in without a word. She has that look on her face—part pit bull and part wiseass. She insists she's joining our mission. Apparently, she's worn down Kate because Kate just nods along.

I try to talk them out of it, but they present a wall of opposition so sturdy I can't break it with an ice pick. When women stick together, there's nothing men can do to change their minds. I'd have a better chance climbing Mount Everest naked.

We leave at eight, so we'll have plenty of time. I steal a beaten up Japanese sedan parked three blocks away. Getting into the car isn't a problem. My wireless key scrambler blitzes the car's CPU with enough code variations that the doors click open in two minutes. Not bad. More expensive cars take a lot longer, but this one is about eight years old and didn't cost much new.

Once inside, I re-wire the circuit panel, and the car starts. Luckily, it has half a tank of gas, more than enough. I drive with Kate sitting next to me and Tina in the backseat.

Tina doesn't have access to District 10, so she volunteered to ride in the trunk. I was tempted to take her up on the offer. The roads can be bumpy, and she's already rubbed my nerves raw, but I have a fake ID with access all the way to District 8 she can use. The picture isn't a perfect match, but the hair color and face look basically the same. We add a mole on her cheek that matches the ID with some makeup. Besides, Homeland doesn't check IDs all that closely until someone wants into District 7.

Homeland really only cares about Districts 1 through 5. They use Districts 7 and 6 as buffer zones. To gain access into District 7 or lower, the process involves DNA scans and more highly trained officers. She wouldn't pass that level of inspection.

When we approach the checkpoint into District 10, the guards look bored and barely check our IDs before they scan them. And just like that, we're waved in. I cruise to Brad's street and find a spot a half-block away facing the apartment building.

Kate's wearing the short black dress she used for the photos. It's hard for me to concentrate with her in that dress and so close, but we need to go over the plan one more time.

"Kate, you'll approach security and ask for Sam Steele. Obviously, they'll know Brad is using a false name and they should be expecting you. You won't have a problem getting buzzed inside. Not in that dress."

"Right," says Kate. "And then when the bastard opens the door I blast him with this taser thing you gave me." She shows me a tiny taser that fits in the palm of her hand.

"Wait for him to close the door before you zap him. You don't need to rush."

"Except that I'll want to puke at the sight of him," Kate says. "That might cause complications."

"Try not to throw up. Afterward you..." I wait for her to continue because this is her part of the plan. She needs to know it cold.

"I get him to read the note we wrote," Kate says. "That way, security will let you up."

"Right. Make sure he reads it word for word. The apartment building probably has a safe word for security in case of trouble. Remember to keep the taser at his throat. If he needs persuading—"

"I'll happily blast him in the throat."

"Roast the fucker," adds Tina.

"He has to think we're going to rob him," I say. "That's important. Don't let on that you're Megan's mom or he'll be more desperate and less likely to go along with the note. If he thinks we're going to rob him, he'll hope he'll get through this okay."

Kate grinds her jaw and Tina reaches over the seat, rubs her neck, and encourages her. "You've got this. The dumbass will know something important and then we'll get Megan back."

I check my phone. It's 8:55. "You ready?"

She nods. "Just don't take too long to come up. I might kill him before you get there."

"I'll be there in a flash. In the meantime, we can communicate through the coms. I'll hear everything that's going on, and I'll be that voice in your head."

"Great, that's what I always wanted." She squeezes my hand, grabs her purse, a bottle of wine, and leaves the car.

Tina jumps from the backseat and settles next to me. "We've got to talk, Jarhead."

"One, I was never a Marine. And two, now's not a good time. With any luck, there will never be a good time."

"You're an asshole."

"I know. Good talk."

A security guard, armed with an AK-47, meets Kate at the entrance to the building.

Kate smiles at him and says, "I'm here to meet Sam Steele."

The guard acts professionally. "State your name and look into the camera."

Kate says, "Emma Sykes."

The guard says something into a microphone, presses a buzzer, and lets Kate in. At least this part of our plan works.

"Steele's in Apartment 408," the guard says. "Take the elevator."

Kate disappears from view. She must have entered the elevator because she whispers. "Going up."

A bell rings. A few seconds later, Kate knocks, and a door opens.

"Sam?" her voice forms a question mark.

"In the flesh. Come in, Emma, my literary friend." The door shuts. "You look exactly like the photo on your profile. You hear so many stories these days about people photo-morphing their profile, but not you. Gorgeous."

I don't know about Kate, but I want to vomit.

"What's going on?" asks Tina, and I shake her off with turn of my head.

"You look even...better in person," says Kate. "I really like the mustache."

She should have zapped him already. My heart's beating fast. I wish I had a camera on her so I could see what's going on.

"Thanks for the wine," Brad says. "I've taken the liberty of opening a red to give it a chance to breathe. It's from France. I find that book clubs always go better with a little vino. Don't you agree?"

"Yes, certainly. Sometimes, the more wine, the better."

Wine splashes into the glasses. I imagine the snake lifting one to hand it to her.

What's she waiting for? Blast him already.

"Thank you," says Kate.

A second later a glass crashes to the floor followed by a hum. Brad's toppled to the floor, 60,000 volts racing through him. It sounds like he's thrashing his legs and making gurgling sounds.

"I've tased him," says Kate.

"Excellent," I say.

"He's foaming at the mouth."

"Try the wine."

I hear spitting sounds and stifle a laugh.

"That's not from France. It tastes like vinegar. I'm very disappointed in you, Sam."

Brad grumbles a couple of incoherent sounds.

"Time to get to work, Kate," I say. "Remember, he has to think we're just going to rob him. That way he'll cooperate."

"Got it," says Kate. "Okay, Sam. I'm sorry that hurt so much. I needed to get your attention. I have a change in plans for us this evening. Book club is canceled."

"Y-y-you're not Emma?"

"That's really special, Sam. I'm as much Emma as you are Sam. I need you to let my friend up."

"Wh-wh-why."

"We're going to rob you, of course. Once we're done, you'll be able to entertain lots of other women with book clubs or whatever. Although, I recommend you shave the mustache. It looks like a snake died on your lip."

"I don't have anything to steal." Brad's voice sounds almost normal now, the effects of the electrical charge having worn off a bit.

"Oh, come now, Sam. An important talent scout like you? I'm sure we'll find something."

"Show him the note and the taser," I suggest.

"In a second, the security guard is going to call. You're about to have another guest. Read this note exactly as it's written. Don't be a bad boy and deviate by one word, or I'll tase you again. And Sam, I'm a little worried about your heart. I can imagine it bursting. If I might be frank, you're not in the best shape. All the pumping it must do to keep the blood flowing in that big body of yours. You never know."

"I-I have a few hundred dollars. You can take that and go."

"That's not nice. Do you think I look cheap? Is that what you're telling me?"

"No. Keep that thing away from me."

"I'm on my way," I tell Kate. "Just get him to read the note when the security guard calls up."

I grab my backpack and open the door.

Tina calls out, "Don't fuck up."

"Thanks," I mutter as I head to the apartment building. When I reach the door, I smile my friendliest grin.

The security guard approaches warily and talks into a microphone that broadcasts outside the door. "What do you want?"

He's a lot less friendly to me then he was to Kate. I can't blame him. "I'm here to visit Brad Drudge. He's waiting for me."

The guard shoots me a quizzical look. "You're not on the list."

"He must have forgotten. You know Brad. He can be a bit of a flake."

The guard snorts, lifts a phone, and dials a number.

Brad's phone rings in my ear.

Kate says, "Remember, just read the note, Sam."

Brad answers the phone. "Can you let my friend Steve in? I'm sorry I didn't tell you about him before. I must have forgotten."

The guard calls out to me, "Look at the camera."

I shrug and smile.

"Yep, that's him," says Brad. "Thanks."

The guard opens the door and gives me the once over. "Apartment 408. Take the elevator."

"Do you have stairs?"

He points toward the staircase. "Suit yourself."

Kate tells Brad to sit in a chair as I bound up the stairs two at a time. When I reach the fourth floor, a stitch stings my side. I should be in better shape. I enter the hall and speed walk to the apartment.

I knock, and when the door opens, I realize something is horribly wrong.

"You've really fucked up this time, Trainee," Caesar gleefully tells me.

I'd argue with him, but he's right.

CHAPTER 22

Brad is duct-taped to a chair like we planned, but Kate didn't tape his hands to the arms. The worm managed to hit a silent alarm under a table. I should've warned Kate about silent alarms. I'm used to working with pros who would've known. Obviously, Kate didn't and that's on me. It's my screw-up that I have to fix somehow.

I drop the backpack on the floor. "Brad, that wasn't a smart thing to do. Hitting the alarm? How long do they claim is their response time?"

He smiles a slick grin as if he's thwarted us somehow. He's thirty pounds heavier than his profile picture on Eros, and an awful pencil-thin mustache slithered across his lip. His long, bloated face comes to a point at his chin that makes him look like a fat rat. He's wearing a high-collar black shirt and tan slacks. The shirt stretches tightly against his stomach, as if it'll give up any moment.

"Two minutes," he says. "You better leave now."

He's lying, of course, but they'll be here soon. I turn to Kate. "We have five minutes, maybe a little more before the Klendall response team shows up."

"And I thought the date was going so well, Brad," says Kate, but real worry lurks underneath the snarky tone in her voice. She's not concerned so much about herself, but about Megan. If we don't get out of here and learn something important, we won't save her daughter.

"Hey, how do you know my real name?" A touch of indignity floats in Brad's voice.

I remove my knife from my jacket. His eyes lock onto the blade like a laser. "We know a lot about you, Brad. We want some information about your work as a *talent scout*."

He shakes a bit. "I'm just a teacher. I made that up for the profile. I wanted to impress women. That's all."

I slowly twist the blade a few inches from his face. It still has a streak of Mr. Frosty's blood on it. "We don't have time for the bullshit, Brad. If you hadn't pulled the alarm, we'd have all night, but you did. And that's on you. So now we're going to have to speed things up a bit. We know you've sold students at the high school to someone. We want to know who and where the kids go."

Brad visibly shakes. "I don't know what you're talking about."

"Wrong answer. I thought we got this out of the way already. Don't be so slow. We don't have time for the back and forth, you sniveling twat."

I duct tape his wrists to the arms of the chair. When I finish, I press the point of the blade against the joint where his pinkie connects to his right hand and carve it off. It takes about five seconds. I would have had a more difficult time carving a turkey leg. Normally, I'd take my time, add more flair to the situation, but time is of the essence.

He yelps.

I shrug. "That's your fault. It's on you, Brad. Start talking or more body parts are coming off and it's going to hurt a lot more. Who's paying you?"

All resistance breaks down. Somewhere in Brad's peanut-sized brain, he knows his life is in jeopardy, so his survival instinct kicks in. I've seen it dozens of times, but it won't help him in the end.

"I-I don't know any names."

"What do you know, Brad?"

"After my divorce became final, two guys met me in a bar near where I lived. They said they worked at a farm. That they needed young people to work for them." Brad's eyes light up as if he just now realizes how shitty this sounds. "It's not bad. Really. They said the young people become enlightened and end up with rich families around the world. They have better lives that way. That's what they said. I believed them."

Kate slaps him across the face.

"That's what they said." She mimics his voice and then continues in her own. "You've sold four girls to these people like they were cattle. You miserable pile of donkey shit."

"Three girls and one guy, but they've promised me that they're all doing well. That they're better off this way."

Five students have gone missing from the school. One must have disappeared for some other reason besides Brad, which sounds about right. He only received four payments.

"Better off?" snaps Kate. "You self-absorbed bloated bag of pus." She slaps him again.

Normally, I'd let Kate blow off some steam, but we're in a crunch for time, so I move between Kate and Brad.

A handprint appears on his cheek. He tries to defend himself. "What chance did they have coming from District 12? This way, they might hook up with someone rich. They're probably thanking me right now."

"Stop making believe you care about these kids, Brad. It's really pissing me off. Give us a name."

"I don't have one."

I shake my head. "I don't think you're hearing me." I grab his chin in my left hand, so he can't wiggle, and saw through his right ear, taking it clean off. Good thing the blade is sharp. The gap left behind gushes blood.

"Oh, shoot," I say. "That's probably not going to help."

He bucks at the tape, but it holds. His yelp lasts longer this time than with the pinkie, like one long screech.

"You see what happens when you piss me off. I make mistakes and you lose body parts." I hold his ear in front of his face. "That's on you again, Brad. You're making bad decisions, and we don't have time for them. Where do they take the kids?"

"I don't know...a farm. They said they go to *The Farm*. That's exactly what they call it."

"How do they contact you? And the answer had better not be you don't know, or you're going to look like a Picasso painting."

He's yelling now. "There's a chat room on swapping used crap! Their username is The Farm. They ask for a certain bike. It's all code. Female version, age, good for off-roading. I have a file on my tablet with all the info. My username is Sam Steele, like for the profile."

Blood oozes down the right side of his face, runs down his neck, and onto his collar.

Kate grabs a computer from a table in the living room. "Is this your tablet?"

He nods. "You don't understand. My wife took everything in the divorce. And she makes more money than I do. They pay shit at the school. I would have had to move into the ghetto. I wouldn't do well in the ghetto."

"Love sucks," I say, but I understand. He was trying to survive and to do it, he sold out the kids—a totally despicable thing to do, but he's right, he wouldn't have made it long in the ghetto. I almost feel sorry for him. Almost, but this is Kate's daughter we're talking about.

Kate's phone rings, and she answers it. She looks up at me with worry in her eyes. "Tina says two black SUVs have arrived. Eight armed guys have piled out and gone into the building."

I had hoped we had another couple of minutes more. "How do we get onto your tablet, Brad? What's the password?"

"No password. It uses a retinal scan."

I remove a nylon cord from the backpack and hand it to Kate. "Fasten this to something sturdy. We're going out the window."

"Seriously? I know you're afraid of elevators, but there's got to be a better way."

"Sorry. With the response team here, we've got no other choice."

Brad bucks in the chair. "You'll have to take me with you to use the tablet. Killing me won't help you."

"Wrong again, Brad. This is just not your day. I don't need you. I just need one of your eyes."

He squirms as I approach. "No, don't take an eye. I'll do anything. I need to see."

"That's precious, Brad. I didn't realize you were such an optimist. Do you really think I'm going to let you live? I just can't do it. You'll find a way to tell The Farm or whoever, and they'll know we're after them. No can do, Brad. You're headed to hell. No chance at redemption for you. The Fates have just cut your string and you don't know it yet."

"You're crazy."

"Why does everyone keep saying that?" I slice the knife across Brad's throat. Blood spurts for a few seconds with the last of his heartbeats, and his eyes lock on mine. I think deep down he's happy. I've done him a favor. Eventually his crimes would have consumed him. He was already eating himself to death—every pound a cry for help. I've shortened the torture for him. Maybe he made good with God in that last moment. I can't imagine it would be enough to redeem him, but Father Paul said it's what's in your soul that counts. Maybe his soul was redeemed at that last moment...or maybe he's headed to hell and I'll see him again. Next time, I won't be in a rush to finish him off.

"How are you making out with that cord?" I ask Kate.

She finishes tying a knot around the base of a sturdy looking bar that's bolted into the floor. It'll probably hold.

"Done," she says. When she looks up, she's not in shock or even upset at what I've done to Brad. She's angry, which is the best I could've hoped for.

I remove a small palm-sized explosive out of the backpack, set the timer to thirty seconds, and slide it to the door. It'll cause havoc with the response team and buy us time to escape.

"Better not look at this part," I tell Kate and go back to work with my knife. "This will get gruesome."

This is the third time I've taken someone's eye. Once, the person was alive when I carved it out. We needed information from him. We had intel that a new terrorist group was going to attack one of our bases. He wouldn't willingly give up the information. My orders were clear. Use any means to get him to talk, and he talked in the end. The terrorists were only in the beginning stages of planning the attack, but they had an inside man. We got him before he could run.

Was it worth it? Would I do it again? Could I have found another way?

I'm wasting time we don't have, so I shake my head and clear it. I make quick work of removing Brad's eye, slip it into a small plastic container and slide that into my pocket. We still need to escape through the window, but this one doesn't open—probably an air quality thing. I fire three shots from the Smith and Wesson into the window facing the street. Glass explodes everywhere.

Fifteen seconds have elapsed since I set the explosive. I grab the cord at roughly forty feet of length and tie it around my left hand. I wrap my right arm around Kate's waist.

Ten seconds left.

The security guards have reached Brad's door. They don't really care about Brad's safety, but if we escape alive, it'll be bad for business. They sell these buildings as ultra-high security. The brass won't want a news story about a successful robbery or murder.

They bang on the door. "Open up and give yourselves up!"

"The door is wired to blow! You've got ten seconds!" They're only doing their job. They deserve some warning. What they do with it is on them.

"We run for it," I tell Kate.

"Shit," she says.

I pull her toward the windows at a sprint. When we reach them, I leap with my shoulder toward the glass and break what's left of it. It sounds like an explosion.

We're free falling.

Kate's wrapped both her arms around me. The asphalt rushes up to meet us at an alarming speed.

"I hope you didn't fuck up the measurements or you're road kill," says Caesar.

The slack in the cord disappears and we jerk to a stop. Our combined weight wrenches my hand and shoulder. It feels as if someone's ripped my arm out of its socket. Luckily, Kate doesn't weigh that much, and I keep my grip.

We're hanging six feet from the ground. Not bad.

The explosive detonates, and a fireball erupts from Brad's window. The cord comes free and we fall the rest of the way.

I help Kate up and we run for the sedan. Tina's got the car running. I jump in front and Kate dives into the back.

One member of the response team bursts from the lobby and opens fire.

Tina pulls away from the curb and glares at me. "Good work, genius. I thought you did shit like this for a living."

"Sometimes you have to improvise."

"Is that blood yours?" she asks.

"No."

"Too bad."

CHAPTER 23

Tina parks the car on a quiet street. "What in holy hell happened? Do we know where to find Megan?"

Kate starts to tell her the story. I don't need to relive it, so I go outside, peel off my jacket, and wince at the pain. The sudden stop dislocated my shoulder. I reach behind my head, cross my hand to the opposite shoulder and shove it back into place. A groan slips through my lips, and tears brim my eyes, but the shove pops my shoulder back into the socket. It's sore, but at least it works.

I grab a new T-shirt from my backpack and change. There's too much blood on the old one, and I don't want Homeland asking questions at a checkpoint. Blood always spurs questions. It's a natural response. One I'd like to avoid.

Kate must have finished telling Tina the story because Kate and Tina leave the car and both lean against the vehicle next to me.

"You really cut that guy's ear off?" asks Tina.

"He wouldn't listen to me."

"Funny," says Tina.

"He had to die either way. We couldn't take him with us as a hostage until we got Megan back. Too many variables, and if he escaped, our chances of getting Megan back would have dropped."

Kate asks, "Do you think that chat room will help us find this...Farm and get Megan back?"

"It's a clue. Depends how frequently they monitor it. We've also learned other clues. Every new bit of information helps. It's hard to know what will pay off, but something will."

"Yes," says Kate. "Megan's been taken by some type of cult that calls themselves The Farm, and they promised Brad she'd have a better life. It's not much to go on."

"At least we have a name," says Tina. "That's more than we had this morning."

I touch Kate's arm. In desperate situations like this, a simple touch helps people stay grounded, reminds them they have help. "Let's go back to your apartment and see what we can find out on that chat room. If we're dealing with a cult, we probably have a few days before they move her. They'll want to initiate her first."

"Initiate her?" Kate shudders. "I wonder what that means."

Tina grabs her hand. "Megan's a strong kid. We both know how hard it is to get her to change her mind after she's made it up. She'll hold out just fine."

"You think?"

"I do," says Tina. "I only wish you'd have let Brad live."

"Why?" I ask.

"So, I could've killed that shithead myself."

No one from Homeland bothers to check our IDs as we drive back to Kate's neighborhood. We're going to lower, less secure districts, so they just wave us on, and we park the sedan back in the spot where we took it. I leave a twenty on the front seat for the gas and the mess. That's on us.

At Kate's apartment, I use Brad's eyeball to access his tablet. This is the only crack we'll get at it. The eyeball will deteriorate to the point it won't fool the retina scan again.

Tina takes control of the tablet. She's always been into computers and works for a social media marketing firm. It's good for her to feel useful, but I hover over her shoulder to make sure she doesn't miss anything. We can't afford mistakes.

"Brad said he used a code with The Farm to know what type of young person they wanted," I say. "He told us that he had a file on his tablet somewhere with the info on it. Look for that first."

Tina types on the screen and pulls up some documents. One is marked "Talent Scout," so she clicks that one. Pay dirt. The Farm asks for a used bicycle and adds a bunch of other info that spells out the attributes they're looking for in the young adult they want Brad to identify. The age of the bike refers to the age of the target. A one-year-old bike translates into a kid who's fourteen. Two- and three-year-old bikes mean fifteen and sixteen-year olds. The colors refer to ethnicity. Even some of the features mean different skills. A twenty-speed bike means someone who's athletic. Sixteen-speeds indicate someone with a science aptitude, while twelve-speeds mean a person who is adventurous by nature. Other items get very specific like eye color, height, and nationality.

It's enough to make my head hurt. These Farm people treat kids like widgets they can buy with different options.

"Now that we have the code, we need to find the chat site," says Tina. "Which one did Brad say he used?"

Kate bites her lower lip. "He didn't say exactly. He said it was a site that sells junk."

"That could be hundreds of places," says Tina. "Good thing you have me. Let's look at Brad's search history." She presses a few keys and whistles. "Brad's been a naughty boy. He certainly liked porn sites."

"We can safely exclude them," I say. "Look at something a week old. The abduction team would have needed at least a week to pick the best spot to grab Megan."

Tina calls out names of obvious porn sites as she sorts through Brad's search history. "Women who love tubby men, Penislandia, Pussy Parade, wait...here's something, Swap Market. Could be another porn place, but let's check it out."

She clicks on the link and it's a generic site with general categories of used stuff that's for sale or available for barter.

"Bingo," says Tina.

Kate points to the screen. "They have transportation. Maybe bikes are covered there?"

Tina works some magic, and we find an entry from a user named The Farm. The message is different from what I expected. Instead of using the code we found, it simply says, "Looking for a special bike we've had our eye on for years."

Tina clicks on the conversation and finds Sam Steele's response. "I have what you want." He attached a file to his message.

"What the fuck?" Tina says, when she opens the file. Megan's picture pops up, plus general information about her: her schedule, her best friends, the apartment address, work schedule, grade transcripts, IQ test, etc. "Brad's been watching her."

"Makes sense," I say. "He'd need to give these people some basic info for them to start surveillance, but—"

Kate says, "But why does the message ask for a *special bike*? There's nothing in the code about a *special bike*. How did Brad know they wanted Megan?"

The truth hits me hard. From the looks on Tina and Kate's faces they realize the same thing, but I'm the one to verbalize it. "Megan must be special to them. They must have known about her for some time. Tina, go back, and let's see any other communications between Brad and The Farm."

The site keeps all the communications for six months. After that, they delete them. We find three other messages between Brad as Sam Steele and the mysterious cult named The Farm. All the others use the code.

Everything looks predictable, with Brad sending The Farm a file just a few days after their first inquiry. Megan's file is the only outlier. It can't be a coincidence. This puzzle becomes more complicated. More pieces are in play than I thought.

"Let's post a message on the site for The Farm," I suggest. "We need something they might respond to so we can set up a meeting."

"I've got it." Tina types a simple post. "I've just discovered that one of the bicycles I've sent to The Farm has faulty brakes. Please respond, so I can fix them."

"That should get their attention," I say. "Hopefully, they'll answer using the chat site. It's worth a try."

Kate nods, and Tina sends it as Sam Steele.

We stare at the screen for a few minutes hoping for an immediate reply, which is silly. It's late and who knows how frequently they monitor the website? They might not look at it unless they want a new girl, which means we'll be shit out of luck.

After a long stretch, Tina starts to rifle through the computer, which lasts hours. She finds nothing else of value. My eyes hurt when she finishes. She copies whatever looks remotely interesting on a flash drive and we shut down the tablet.

Kate looks wiped, and I'm exhausted. I haven't slept in two days and the voices in my head are growing more numerous and louder. They want me to go out, prowl the streets, look for sinners to punish. It's stupid. I need to take some of my pills to quiet them and get a few hours of shuteye.

Tina suggests that we stop for the night and re-group in the morning.

I'm grateful she said it and try to end the night on a positive note "We've got some leads. I'll see if Mary can find a file on this Farm in the morning. A few hours' rest will do us good."

Kate and Tina disappear into Kate's bedroom. Megan's room is open, but I don't go in. That's her room. So, I take three of my sleeping pills and curl up on the couch, hoping for a little sleep. The doc told me never to take more than two, but two won't stop my racing mind tonight.

I lie quietly and wait for the darkness. Eventually it takes me. Unfortunately, I start to dream. Dreams never work out for me. Happy endings don't exist in my subconscious.

This one starts out in Brad's apartment. He screams when I saw off his ear and then his face morphs into that of Father Paul. The priest looks disappointed, and I bolt upward, breathing heavy, sweat coating my shirt.

It's still dark out. I check my watch. I got three hours of sleep, which isn't bad for me. Kate's tablet is on the table, so I open it and check the swap site for a response from The Farm.

Nothing yet.

I look over Megan's file Brad sent to The Farm. She's clearly an exceptional girl. When I leaf through her personal records, my heart skips a beat. Under father, they list Ethan, yet there's no other information about him. Just the first name.

It's probably not important, but shouldn't the school have his last name on file?

CHAPTER 24

Ivy forces herself to regulate her breathing. At least no one else is in her office with her. She twists her hand on the ultra-thin phone and does her best to keep her voice even, although her patience is stretched to the breaking point. Trevor is a dope, but she needs him for a while longer and can't cross him just yet. "I know this is a setback. The process isn't foolproof. We've lost candidates before. You know that. It can't be helped. Sometimes the process doesn't take."

"We have one week! Our most important client is waiting. I've assured him we're on track. I can't go back and delay him now. The consequences will be catastrophic."

"We have to stay flexible. I'll talk to him and smooth it over."

"That's the last thing I want. You're not to contact him. You know how he feels about you. He'll kill us both."

Trevor has a point. This client has no imagination and a quick temper. Ivy races through all the possible options and finds nothing appealing. She's left with only one, and a most disagreeable one at that.

She sighs. "I've identified a promising new candidate. One week will be tight to work her through the system. I'll have to expedite everything, and it might not take. If you give me another two weeks, I can make sure we follow the best protocols and it'll be safer for her, and us. The extra time will—"

"We don't have more time. Wait, let me clarify that—*you* don't have more time! We're making this delivery in one week, or I'll replace you *permanently*. Am I clear? I can find another *Mother* for my Angels. This is your screw up. Get it done!" He disconnects the call.

Idiot! Just a few months more and she can do away with him. She'll stab him in the heart and send him to a fire-filled pit where demons will claw at his body for eternity. She's seen the vision. Trevor's future isn't bright, but she still needs more time to change the world forever. Change it for the better. Change it the way He demands.

Ivy reluctantly reviews Megan's file on her tablet. She has big plans for the girl, and now this mess will delay them. She'll personally supervise the girl's initiation. Even then, the risks are great. If there was another way, she'd take it, but she can't remove Trevor yet. She'll have to make certain sacrifices for His plan, and besides, it'll be a short-term loan only. Once she starts her plan, she'll find a way to recall Megan—two months tops.

Someone knocks on her office door. "Enter!"

Buck and Frankie stroll into the room. Frankie has proven himself capable, but Buck is a born leader. Although he only joined her flock three months ago, she installed him as head of security, an easy decision.

"We have June locked in a confessional," says Buck.

Ivy removes the pendant from inside her jumpsuit and gently presses it against her lips. She makes a show of it, so Buck and Frankie mimic her.

"Such a pity the Dark One corrupted our fair June. She was an innocent, spoiled by his evil intentions. More proof that we must stay ever observant. We are at war. Good and evil, fighting among us. Only through vigilance will we prevail."

Both acolytes speak at the same time. "Yes, Mother. Vigilance in all matters!"

"Where did you find her?" asks Ivy.

"She had slipped through the cow pasture and was headed to the highway," says Frankie. "We grabbed her before she reached the road. No one noticed."

"Well, gentlemen. You know what we do with those who become corrupted by the Devil."

Buck asks, "Shall we do it now?"

The sky outside her window has lightened from its darkest moment, and dawn is just about to break. "Not now. Build the cross and get the pyre ready during the day. I want everyone to watch her burn. The whole community needs to see what happens if someone turns from the light. It's regrettable, but June's screams will serve as a reminder for everyone."

CHAPTER 25

I run through some simple stretching exercises to keep my muscles loose and responsive, as the light spills over the horizon. Extensive internet searches didn't reveal anything useful on a cult named The Farm. At least the pendant symbol with the cross makes more sense now. Cults like symbols, and the cross in a star seems like something a cult might use. It feels like an important piece to the puzzle. I just don't know why yet or how it'll lead me to Megan.

Kate's bedroom door opens, and Tina steps out. She looks like a lioness, hair a crazy tangle behind her as she stalks toward me. She crosses her arms over her chest, and her eyes burn with the anticipation of an easy kill. I've faced more than my share of terrifying people in the past, but she scares me.

"Expecting someone else, Stevo?"

"Hoping is more like it."

"Let's talk."

I'd rather stick red-hot needles in my eyes than talk to Tina right now, but I have no choice. She isn't going anywhere, and neither am I. At least, not until we find Megan. Eventually she'll corner me, so now's as good a time as any to talk.

"Listen, Tina, I just don't like you that way. You're sweet in a prickly way, but we can only be friends. I hope you're not too upset." Starting off snarky might rattle her a little. I don't need her repeating some pre-programed speech.

"I'd rather fuck a banana."

"There are laws against that sort of thing. I think they call it cruelty to fruit."

"Don't be a wiseass. You're not funny."

I shrug and decide to just get on with it. She doesn't want me around and I understand why. No sense delaying the inevitable. "You're right. There's nothing funny about this situation. I get it. You want to protect Kate from me. You think I'm bad for her. That I'll just hurt her again. You're wrong about that. I won't hurt her, but I'm no good. So, you're right there. I'm bad. Bad for her, for Megan, for everyone. When we get Megan back I should leave them alone."

"Yes, you should, but I see how you look at her," Tina says. "It's not an innocent, friendly, I'll be leaving soon look. You still love her, don't you?"

I grind my jaw. "Yes. No. Maybe. I don't know. It's complicated. What more do you want from me? I'll leave when this is done."

Tina touches my arm. It's a warm gesture that takes me by surprise, not the kick in the balls I was expecting. "When you left last time, she was devastated. She could barely function. It took a long time before she was herself again."

"Couldn't have been that long," I say with surprising hostility in my voice. "Ethan showed up on the scene in a month and they hit it off rather well. Megan is evidence of that."

"Ethan, yes, well, he helped fill the hole, but he never replaced you. I just don't want Kate to go through that wreckage again. It might be more than she can take this time. I don't want her hurt."

"And neither do I," I say. And I don't.

"So, we're agreed," says Tina.

I nod. Tina should know I'm unreliable in this area. I intend to leave. That's as good as I can muster right now. If things turn out otherwise, she'll have to deal with it. Besides, she's not revealing all of her true motives. Sure, she doesn't want Kate to be hurt, but she also wants Kate for herself. She'd rather the competition—in this case me—mosey out of town. I wonder how far their relationship has progressed since Ethan died. Does Kate know the depth of Tina's affection for her?

Tina breaks my train of thought. "Kate said you were back in town when she reached out. Why did you come back?"

"I had a hankering for a good cheese-steak and it had been a long while." I'm not going to tell Tina the real reason—that I needed to know what had become of my mother. Or rather, what she had become. My demons, my mother's demons, are none of Tina's concern. They're for me to worry about alone.

Kate wanders from her bedroom, rubbing sleep from her eyes. "I don't see any blood. Have you two been behaving?"

"We're the best of friends," I say. "Tina was just telling me how much she likes bananas."

"Bananas?" asks Kate.

"Yep, my favorite fruit," answers Tina.

"I don't think I've ever seen you eat one." Kate stumbles a few steps forward. "Any word from The Farm yet?"

Tina checks the tablet. "No response yet. I guess the cult leader likes to sleep in."

My phone rings. "Good morning, Mary. Awfully early for you, no?"

"I know you never sleep Steven, and I'm conditioning my body to need as little sleep as possible. I'm down to four hours a night. It's amazing how much time that frees up for more productive purposes. Anyway, I got a hit on the facial recognition program and thought you'd want to know right away. Only one of the photos had enough detail to pull a match. The guy's name is Frankie "The Boner" Batson. He got himself dishonorably discharged from the Army for multiple sexual assaults. He's not a very nice dude."

"Great. Do you have a file on him?"

"I'm sending it to your phone now. His last known address is in Philadelphia."

"It seems as if we're dealing with a cult. Have you ever heard of an outfit called The Farm?" Mary has a photographic memory, so if she's seen anything on them, she'd remember.

"No, it doesn't ring any bells. I'll ask Gabriel."

"Gabriel?"

"Oh, that's right, you've been out of the loop for a while. Sheppard's appointed Gabriel to Homeland. He's a special agent now."

"The same Gabriel who was a gang leader a few months ago?"

"Yep. To change the system, it's important to get the right people inside. We need to pull from the outside, and push from the inside. Gabriel's an agent of change now. He'll be working inside, doing a lot of the pushing."

"That's awesome. No one will be better at pushing than him. Thanks for the help."

"Don't mention it. I'll call Gabriel a little later. He's more of a night owl than an early bird. I doubt he's into the sleep deprivation kick like me."

Mary disconnects and my phone pings—the file on Frankie.

I send the information to Kate's tablet so we can look at it together. It's not good news. Mary wasn't kidding when she said Frankie was a bad dude.

Kate turns green as we rifle through the information. At age sixteen, the cops arrested Frankie for his first sexual assault. He joined the military when he turned eighteen. Committed his first sexual assault inside the Army when he was twenty. The Army gave him a pass and then he got caught two years later. Those two were the only instances where he'd been caught. He probably committed dozens where victims never filed complaints. He spent three years overseas and saw combat. Handled himself reasonably well. Even earned a purple heart.

On the domestic front, he married a local girl while still in the Army at age twenty. She had a baby girl six months later. He lives with his wife in an apartment in District Eleven, close by. The file contains no recent information. They don't have a current employer or anything like that.

Kate reaches for a trashcan and wretches. She pauses, vomits again, and straightens up. "This guy captured Megan?" Her voice wavers, as if she'll need another go at the can.

"There are a lot of Frankies in the country now, people who can't find purchase anywhere," I say. "This guy is worse than most, but it's hard for the government to watch them all. They probably think he's not important enough to worry about. He's dangerous, but he's poor, and as long as they have their checkpoints and restricted neighborhoods, they can keep him out of the Upper Districts."

"Let's make sure he's our bad guy," I add.

Frankie's military identification picture from the file matches the creep in our video. "It's him, but he's working for someone else. This Farm cult. They know Megan's special. They want her for a reason." I leave it there. I can't say Frankie hasn't touched Megan or won't harm her. A guy like that with a girl like Megan spells trouble.

Tina says, "This is good news, Kate. It's a lead. When we find Frankie, we'll find Megan." Tina encourages me with her eyes to say more, to focus Kate on the positives.

It's a good idea to keep her from the looming world of what ifs, so I follow Tina's lead. "When I get my hands on him, he'll tell us everything we need to know. I promise."

That's an easy promise to make. Frankie will wish he were never born. Looks like the Fates have woven one of Frankie's strings into my loom.

Too bad for Frankie.

They screwed him big time.

CHAPTER 26

Tina and I drag Kate to the common kitchen, a large open space with half a dozen refrigerators, three large stovetops and ovens, a dozen microwaves, and plenty of sinks and counter space. Everything is well marked. All the appliances and counters have apartment numbers listed on them, so it's clear who's supposed to use what.

Tina uses Kate's card key to swipe open a cabinet with Kate's apartment number on it. I grab the mugs and the coffee pods from her and make coffee for us. Tina adds hot water to three bowls of oatmeal. We sit at one of the long tables and drink the coffee. It's bitter and hot and burns on the way down. The burn feels good. I add more sugar and milk.

Sitting here with Kate and Tina, I slip into an alternate universe— one where I chose a different path. If I quit the military after serving my first tour of duty, I could have come home, gotten a job in security. Not a job like my last one. A simple one, for a company or a business. The type of position where I could come home for dinner, eat with my wife and daughter, talk about their days, be a part of a family. I could have spent every night with Kate. Megan wouldn't have been our daughter, but we could have had a different girl, probably a good student who acted sassy most of the time but had a big heart like Kate. With any luck, she'd look like Kate.

Dozens of families probably crowd into this kitchen at dinnertime. Kate would cook most nights, but I'd take over on the weekends. I can make Italian food. With years of experience, I might even have been half decent at it. We'd have our own special spot on this table at the end, and we'd laugh if someone else accidently took our place for a dinner. Life would have been full, good maybe.

As the image takes hold, I see my mother among the crowd. She's sitting with Caesar at the end of the table; he wraps his arm around her shoulders and winks at me. The illusion breaks.

Who am I kidding? That type of life would never have worked for me.

Tina forces Kate to shovel in a few bites of oatmeal. Four other sleepy people join us in the kitchen with coffee mugs in hand. They smile pleasantly at Tina and Kate, then cast a suspicious look my way. They know Tina and Kate and must be wondering what I'm doing with them—am I a friend or an unwanted visitor? Perhaps I'm a family member here to mooch off Kate, or maybe an old friend running from the government.

Kate looks up from her coffee mug and smiles at me. "Welcome to communal living. It sucks, doesn't it?"

"I don't know," I say. "If you run out of sugar, you don't have to go anywhere to ask your neighbor for some."

"True. I used to worry that one of my neighbors might be dangerous for Megan. There's no way to know who's living on the same floor and we live so close together. Now—"

"Now, nothing," Tina interrupts. She glances at the others in the kitchen and lowers her voice. "We're making progress. We have a name."

Kate frowns and the sadness in her eyes makes me look away. "But that Frankie's a monster."

I bend the metal spoon in my hand. "Well, let's pay him a visit then. He'll learn what a real monster can do."

We finish the coffee and clean up after ourselves. Back at Kate's apartment, we dress for the day. I stuff my backpack with an assortment of weapons and gadgets that might come in handy once I get my hands on Frankie. Afterward, I hide my duffel in Megan's closet. I don't want it out in the open just in case someone breaks into Kate's apartment.

We need a car, so we borrow a beaten-up white Ford sedan. Duct tape holds down the trunk and secures a side mirror to the door. It's perfect for District 11, battered and well worn. We pass a checkpoint and park on the opposite side of the street to Frankie's apartment building: a white, plaster, five-story walk-up with no doorman or fancy security. It's not in bad shape and looks better than the others on the block.

I face Kate and Tina. "Okay. I'm going to pick the front lock and sneak into Frankie's apartment. Hopefully, he's home and then I'll get answers out of him. If not, we'll figure out what to do next."

"I'm coming with you," says Kate.

Not to be outdone, Tina adds, "I'm not waiting in the car, if that's what you think."

They mean well, but things will go better without them. They won't intentionally do anything to hinder me, but just their presence will constrain me. I don't want any restrictions when meeting this guy, and they shouldn't have to see what I plan to do. The nightmares will keep them awake at night.

"Don't even think about going without me. Megan's my daughter." Kate won't back down. We've been down this road before, and it's long and nasty. We don't have time for another trip. I need to be smarter than I was when we were young, so I try to make a deal and avoid another all-consuming death match between us.

"Okay, Kate comes with me. I can use an extra set of eyes, but if I say you have to leave, you leave. Deal?"

She relents. "Fine."

"What about me?" says Tina. "I want to come too."

"Absolutely not. You've got to stay in the car. We don't have eyes on Frankie yet. He might not be in the apartment. Maybe he's out, and we can't have him surprise us if he returns to the apartment. You know what he looks like. If you see him, send us a message right away." And then I speak slowly and loudly, so Tina knows I'm serious. "Don't confront him."

Tina would like to force her way into the apartment, but she understands the logic behind the plan. "I'll play lookout, but don't fuck this up like you did with Brad, Stevo."

"Thanks for the vote of confidence."

Kate and I cross the street. The ancient lock on the front door is a twenty-year-old pin and tumbler – easy. I grab my lock picking tools from the backpack, size-up the best ones and go to work. In thirty seconds, the lock clicks and we're inside.

Mary's file listed Frankie's apartment as 307, so we march up the stairs. "Kate, stay behind me until we've cleared the apartment. Don't try to be a hero. Leave the physical stuff to me."

"Yes, dear." Kate says, which partially ticks me off, but I know better than to get into it with her now. She's too fired up about Frankie. One spark and she'll explode. I get it.

We enter the third floor. It's still early, so no one's in the hallway. I could kick in the door and make a big, loud show of it to scare the shit out of this creep. The more scared he is, the better chance he'll cooperate right away. But that would be noisy, and one of the neighbors might react. We don't need a neighbor to get in the way. The lock to his apartment is the same type as the one on the front door. I slip the two metal picks from my pocket and twist.

The lock opens. I replace the picks in my pocket, remove the Smith and Wesson from my holster, and switch off the safety. I place my finger to my lips to tell Kate we're going in quietly.

When she nods, I open the door to a short hallway that leads to a living room. The living room is a mess: children's toys are scattered about, a dress and a blouse are tossed on a chair, a bra hangs from the end of the couch, and a pizza box sits on a metal cocktail table. A newish holographic projector hangs on the wall. It's on standby mode, so an image of a roll of parchment that's meant to be the Constitution, with the words "Originalists for a Greater America" underneath it floats in the air, revolving slowly. I carefully work my way around the room, avoiding anything that might squeak or crunch under my feet. Luckily, there's no sign of a dog.

A pass-through kitchen is on the left. Dishes are piled up in the sink, and the kitchen smells rank, like the garbage should have been taken out a day or two earlier. No sign of life yet. We pass the kitchen and enter a hallway to the right that leads to two bedrooms.

Kate nervously stalks behind me and shrugs her shoulders.

I don't like what I'm seeing. A few photos are hung in the hallway, of an attractive woman and a toddler with brown hair and big eyes. Unless Frankie cross-dresses none of the clothes are his, and I can't find any signs that he lives here. In a messy apartment like this one, I should see some of his clothes or at least a picture or two.

I creep down the hallway and slowly nudge open one of the bedroom doors with the barrel of my gun. A little girl is sleeping in a bed, half a dozen stuffed animals scattered around her. On her dresser sits a picture of Frankie in fatigues. The first sign of her father.

"Fuck," I whisper to myself and turn to face the master bedroom. I twist the doorknob. More chaos in the form of mess: clothes and dishes, an empty bottle of cheap white wine on the bedside table.

Only one person sleeps in the bed: Frankie's wife, Darleen. She's curled her leg around the blanket and hugs a pillow. She's nude.

I move like a shadow and check out the attached bathroom. No one else is home. Only one toothbrush sits on the sink. No shaving stuff or anything that might belong to a man.

I motion for Kate to shut the bedroom door. She does, and Darleen stirs. I move to the side of her bed and nudge her ass with the barrel of the gun.

She twists on her back and says, "Go back to sleep, Cindy."

"I'm not Cindy."

She bolts upward and pulls her blanket over her chest. A feral look frightens her eyes. "Who the fuck are you?"

I keep the gun trained on her face. "We're looking for Frankie."

"You've come to the wrong place. That impotent, limp dick isn't here."

"Where can I find him?"

"Beats me. What's that prick done now?" Darleen looks at Kate for the first time. "Did that good-for-nothing ass-wipe assault you?"

Kate shakes her head.

"I didn't think so. No offense, honey, you're not his type."

"He's taken my daughter," Kate says.

Darleen frowns. "Oh shit, that sounds right."

I lower the gun and sit on the edge of her bed. "How do you contact Frankie? We'd like to chat with him."

"Contact Frankie," she huffs. "Why would I do that? We're better off without him."

"You married him and that's his daughter in the other room."

"Worst mistake I ever made, that's for sure." She turns to Kate. "Listen, I'm real sorry about your girl. I'd help if I could, but I haven't seen him in six months. I don't have any way to contact him. He usually stops in on Christmas with a few presents for Cindy, but that's all we see of him. And that's too much, if you ask me."

"What's he doing?" I ask. "Who's he working for?"

"After Frankie got his stupid ass discharged from the Army, he started working for the Red Dragons, selling drugs, doing bullshit crimes. He'd do a robbery now and then, and enforcement stuff for them. Some shop owner failed to make a payment and Frankie would crack a few skulls. All that stopped a little over a year ago. He hooked up with some new group and said he was getting religion."

Religion. "What did he call them?"

"He didn't use names. Said something about a farm. They have cows and shit. He cut his hair back to the way it was in the military and acted stuck up. Like he was holy and better than everyone else. Frankie didn't know anything about religion, so it was weird to hear him talk about God and stuff."

"Did he say what he did for these people?" I ask.

"Fuck if I know. Probably no good. What else can Frankie do? He's not too bright."

She sounds sincere. Kate and I share a look and it's obvious Kate believes her also. But the demons inside me growl. They're not so certain, and then the door opens.

Cindy wanders into the room, half asleep her footsteps tentative. She holds a pink stuffed rabbit by an ear and looks at us with sleepy eyes. "Mommy, who are these people?"

She's so close.

Caesar barks in my mind, "Take her, numbnuts! Take the girl and the floozy in the bed will have no choice but to tell you everything. Don't go soft on me. You'll have to hurt the girl to show that you're serious, but after that, the tramp will do whatever you say. Get it done! Your girlfriend will thank you later."

One of the Fates put Cindy in the doorway, but which one? The witch who controls her fate or mine? Whose tapestry is in play?

CHAPTER 27

Sweat trickles down Megan's forehead and into her eyes. She wipes it away with the back of her hand and goes back to work, swinging a long wooden pole in a somewhat successful effort to capture the last few ripe apples from the highest branches in the trees. She traps about half of her attempts in the wicker basket at the end of the pole. The rest fall to the ground.

The other Angels score a much better success rate. Under the circumstances, she should care less. But she's competitive by nature and hates sucking at anything. Even though it's mad-cow crazy, she's still peeved at sucking. Her arms and shoulders ache from the effort, but the other Angels wield their poles with no sign of letting up, so she continues and tries to do better.

An electric cart pulls up to the patch of trees and Frankie steps out. A cat-ate-the-canary grin stretches across the pervert's face. "Spring, you're to come with me. Mother wants to speak with you."

The cart is empty. She'll be alone with Frankie, and he's holding one of the electric prods. Another guard in a red jumpsuit wanders over in their direction. She could run, but she'll never outrun them. Plus, the pendant swings around her neck like a noose. They'd know exactly where she is. She has no choice but to go with Frankie.

At least she can act like she's not afraid. She drops her pole, straightens her back, fixes a stoic expression on her face, and steps forward. Just as she takes her first step, behind her, someone screams.

Petal topples to the ground, flings her apple-picking pole in the air, and holds her ankle, groaning. "I've twisted it on one of the fallen apples."

Frankie scowls at her. "Shake it off and go back to work."

Petal stands but she can't put any weight on her injured ankle. She hops over to Megan and loops her arm over Megan's shoulder. "Take me to the doctor. She's on your way."

Frankie's eyes darken. "I'm just supposed to take Spring."

May and Violet stop working and lean against their poles. "She's hurt," May says. "Take her with you."

The other two Angels with them stop and watch. The Angels have power. They won't go back to work unless Frankie takes Petal. He has no real excuse to leave her behind, and he'll have a hard time explaining why the entire group stopped working.

Megan can almost see the thoughts run through the rickety wheel in his demented head. He wants to be alone with her, but he doesn't want to get in trouble either. He doesn't want to lose another patch on his jumpsuit.

Finally, the wheel stops. He slaps the prod against his hand and sighs. "Okay, both of you in the cart. I don't have all day."

When Frankie turns around, Petal winks at Megan, and leans on her as they three-leg walk and hop to the cart. When they reach the cart, Megan scoots into the back first and Petal slides next to her.

Frankie grumbles a few choice curse words involving a donkey and a sex act from the front and takes off.

Petal leans in close and whispers, her breath brushing against Megan's ear like soft bristles from a paintbrush. She smells like fresh apples. "You should be okay. There are always people around in the main courtyard. Run to Mother's office as soon as possible."

"Won't you get in trouble when the doctor realizes you haven't really twisted your ankle."

"I'll fake it. If she suspects anything, she'll think I'm just being lazy, so she'll make me do some extra chores. I'll survive. Better than the alternative." Petal nods toward Frankie in the front seat who drives aggressively, turning the cart roughly onto a dirt road that leads to the courtyard.

Megan suspects Petal could get in substantially more trouble than she has let on. Petal is sacrificing herself for her even though they're virtually strangers. Unsure what to say, she settles on a throaty, "Thank you."

The dark-skin girl leans in closer. "We have to stick together." She brushes her lips against Megan's cheek. They feel soft and warm.

Petal laces her fingers between Megan's, and Megan squeezes her back.

A few minutes later, Frankie pulls the cart in front of the medical building next to Mother's office. He grabs Petal by the shoulders and yanks her roughly out of the cart.

"You had better be careful or that clumsiness will get you in trouble."

"Oh, I'll be fine," she says and then she turns to Megan and points to the next building. "Mother's office is in that building. You can be on your way."

Megan bolts out of the cart and runs for the door. Frankie races after her, but he's too late to grab her. She opens the door to the building two steps in front of him. Once inside, she knocks on the first door to the left, the same one Buck knocked on the other day.

Ivy calls from inside the office for her to enter.

She opens the door and breathes deeply. Thanks to Petal, she's escaped Frankie, at least for now.

Ivy stands by the windows, wearing the same multi-colored jumpsuit she wore yesterday. It shimmers in the early afternoon light.

She smiles at Megan. "Thank you for coming so quickly."

"Did I have a choice?"

"No, I guess not." Ivy turns to Frankie who steps into the room behind Megan and dismisses him.

When Frankie leaves and shuts the door, Ivy says, "I saw you run from the cart. Is there anything you want to tell me?"

Megan's instinct tells her to stay quiet about Frankie. She doesn't know how Ivy will react, and she assumes anything she tells Ivy will get back to Frankie and that will only make the situation worse. Plus, Petal warned her against telling. She said Ivy would suspect the Devil was involved and that would be bad.

"Nothing. I was just anxious to see you."

"Right," says Ivy. "I'm taking over your education personally. We start now."

Ivy strolls past Megan and through the doorway. "Well, come on. God is waiting."

CHAPTER 28

Megan feels like she's about to take a test in a class she hasn't attended. A pit the size of a watermelon grows in her stomach. What does Ivy's cryptic statement mean, and does she really want to find out?

She hesitates. "I think you're wasting your time with me. God doesn't want to talk to me. Just send me home, and you can work with some more deserving girls."

Ivy smirks. "A fine idea, but none are more deserving than you. You just don't know it yet. Come with me. Otherwise, I'll call Frankie, and he'll help you join me. And we don't want to involve him in our little discussions, do we?"

Ivy leaves the office and Megan follows after her helplessly. She certainly doesn't want to see Frankie again. Not now. Not ever.

When they leave the office and enter the courtyard, Ivy points out different buildings and what they use them for. When she finishes, she says, "You're probably wondering how we got this land in the first place."

"I figure God must have given it to you." Megan says with a touch of snark in her voice.

Ivy ignores her tone. "I guess you could say that. I'm sure He had a hand in it. On a more practical level, we have a wealthy benefactor who provided it to us. He's been with us since the beginning."

"Who?"

"You'll learn, but only later when we reach the End of Days." Ivy continues along the side of her white office building away from the courtyard.

"What do you mean by the End of Days?" asks Megan. "I didn't know our days were running out."

"Oh, but they are," says Ivy. "We see signs everywhere. Floods, earthquakes, diseases, great heat waves. Even the coming revolution here in America is a sign. The poor will rise up against the foolish Originalists. Blood will run in our streets."

Once Ivy passes the building, she starts along a paved road that cuts through a hemp field. The plants have already been harvested, so it looks barren and somewhat desolate.

Megan's mind spins logical reasons for the problems Ivy mentioned. "Global warming accounts for most of those changes and the revolution can be avoided. The new president can—"

"The causes aren't important, and it's too late for the new president to change our path. We are headed for the End of Days. You don't understand yet, but I don't expect you to. It's not a bad thing, the End of Days. It's good, and we have such an important role to play."

The end of the world is a good thing? If Ivy didn't sound so sure of herself, she'd seem nuts, but confidence fills her voice with certainty, and she looks like she's glittering with forbidden knowledge as the sun sparkles off the silver flecks in her jumpsuit.

"How is any of this good?"

Ivy pauses and stares at Megan. She uses her eyes like a crowbar and wrenches open the girl's heart.

"The End of Days is inevitable. It's been written down for thousands of years. We have nothing to fear. When the apocalypse happens, we will be given places of honor in the next life. We will have earned that honor. Our time on Earth is nothing but a speck of sand in a vast desert. What happens next is what truly matters."

"Everyone will die?" Megan asks.

"Maybe. If He wins, some will survive and populate Earth. And those He favors will live on in glory. We are the chosen ones. We will live on until He calls us home." Ivy starts walking again, leaving Megan no choice but to follow.

"If He wins?"

"Yes. The End of Days is the final war between light and darkness. We are to help bring it about. We are here to help Him win and in so doing we will be lifted above all others. You'll see."

"Where are we going?"

"To the cathedral." Ivy points ahead at a massive steel industrial building. Soaring windows mark the entrance. Two men in black jumpsuits guard the front door. Both hold assault rifles, and another shadow lurks on the side of the building.

"Black jumpsuits," says Megan. "What do they mean?"

"They're my angels of death."

A shudder ripples though Megan's body. *Why would Ivy need angels of death when she has Frankie and Buck and all those others with red jumpsuits and electric sticks? And why would black-clad Angels guard a cathedral?*

Her blood turns to ice, and so much fear ripples through her, she can hardly breathe. It feels as if someone's put a plastic bag over her head.

CHAPTER 29

If I interrogated Darleen alone, I would've grabbed Cindy and forced more information out of her. Caesar wanted me to do it. He thought she knew more than she was saying, and he's almost always right. But Kate stood between Cindy and me like an impenetrable wall of motherhood. She wouldn't let me harm the girl, even just a little bit to scare Darleen. Luckily for Cindy, the Fates tied some of Kate's threads through mine.

When Kate and I return to the Ford, Tina starts asking questions before we even get inside. "I don't see any blood or body parts, and there's no explosion this time. Is that good news or bad?"

"Not good," I say. "Frankie's not in the apartment. Apparently, he's estranged from his wife. She says she hasn't seen him in six months. She did confirm that Frankie's working for a cult, and that he's an all-around snake in the grass."

"So, we got camel spit," says Tina.

"Basically," I say. "But I think Darleen was holding something back. She's a single mom, so how can she afford that apartment in District 11? It's the nicest building on the block and there's plenty of space for her and her young daughter."

Kate nods. "And her clothes were nicer than anything I can afford. The holographic TV looked expensive too."

Tina glares at me. "So, Darleen isn't so estranged after all. Why didn't you wring more information out of her? Use your medieval talents? As far as I can tell, that's about all you're good for."

"There were some…complications. She has a young daughter who interrupted us. There are other ways to get information. Let's stake out the apartment. Maybe Frankie will show up or she'll lead us to him. If she's in contact with the creep, she'll likely tell him we came calling. I can always grab her later, when she's alone, if we want to go down that road."

"A stakeout," says Tina. "I've never been on one of those. What shall we talk about?"

"Oh, this will be a boatload of fun," I say.

When it comes to stakeouts, there are two types of people. Those who don't mind silence, who look inward and pass the time thinking. That's me. Stakeouts give me a chance to think, run down probabilities in my head, come up with possibilities that hadn't occurred to me before.

Then there's the second type. They treat silence as an enemy they must vanquish at all costs. Nothing is worse than being stuck with one of those people. They think silence is some negative pronouncement on their own self-worth. They make it all about themselves, as if no one cares enough about them to engage.

I once spent ten hours with a guy who wouldn't shut up. He was determined to set a record for mindless chatter. Around hour nine, my entire body turned tense like a coiled spring. The sound of his voice felt like needles jabbing into my brain. I couldn't take it and knocked him out with a right cross. I had no choice. It was self-defense. It was that, or my head would have exploded and sent little bits of skull and brain spraying all over the car. Our subject appeared within minutes after I clocked Mr. Annoying. Obviously, the Fates set up a test for me. I'm not sure if I passed.

Kate has never had a problem with quiet, but Tina can't stand it. Within seconds, she starts talking about random topics, stupid things to pass the time like favorite foods, or places we've visited, or weird people we've come across.

I try ignoring her, but she pokes me in the back every time I don't answer one of her idiotic questions, like "If I had one type of food to eat on a deserted island, what would it be?" Pizza is apparently a bad answer. Or, "What super power would you have if you could only have one?" Making people shut their traps was met with another poke.

At least her babbling conversation keeps Kate occupied, so she doesn't fully retreat into the land of what ifs. Unfortunately, last week Tina watched a documentary on aliens who visited the planet in ancient times, and she begins sharing. She starts a long dissertation about ancient aliens, rambling on for forty-five minutes about all the times aliens already visited Earth. She finishes explaining how the ancient Egyptian Gods with animal heads and human bodies were really alien visitors.

I hope that will end the topic on a low note, but when she continues on about Mexico and pyramids, I almost lose my shit. It's not that I don't believe in alien visitors. Sure, why the hell not? Some things can't be explained otherwise, but what's the point in discussing ancient pyramids? If aliens helped build them, awesome, but it has nothing to do with me, and I hope they never come back.

Humans have enough problems dealing with the mess we've made of the planet. Add an advanced society capable of space travel into the mix, and we're screwed. All of a sudden, we're second on the food chain, and there's a good chance we're slaves or on the menu for some advanced species. We'd probably taste like chicken to them. After fifty-eight minutes about aliens, I grind my teeth until my jaw aches.

Kate puts her hand on my knee and smiles at me, which settles me down. "So, what do you think about those pyramids in Mexico?" she asks me. "Are they evidence of alien life or just piles of well-placed stone?"

I sigh and roll my eyes.

That's not good enough for Tina. She pokes me in the back for the eighth time. One more bloody poke and I'll break her finger. I know there'll be hell to pay, but sometimes you've got to act and damn the consequences.

She barks, "Well, Stevo, what do you think?"

"I didn't know there were pyramids in Mexico," I grumble, but that's not true. Once, I spent three weeks with a Mexican operative name Marissa. She had the longest legs, which she used like a vice in the sack. She showed me pictures of the Mayan pyramids and explained much about them when we weren't screwing. Most operations are boring. We had to do something to relieve the tedium, and there was nothing tedious about sex with Marissa.

I wonder where she is now.

Tina cuts my revelry short when she pokes me again and says, "He's just a Neanderthal. No sense asking him what he thinks."

I check the rearview mirror and map out my path to her obnoxious poking digit when Kate jumps to my defense.

"Steven has traveled all over the world. Where have you been—New Jersey?"

Tina's not about to let that go without a fight. She needs to prove she's better than me in everything. "If you travel and don't observe the culture around you, it doesn't count. You know I watch the Travel Station all the..."

I tune her out. After two hours and fifty-three minutes of virtual hell, Darleen leaves the apartment building with Cindy in tow.

"There's our target," I say, interrupting Tina's yammering mid-sentence.

Darleen and Cindy jump into an old green coupe and speed away from the curb. We follow behind in the Ford. She doesn't go far. Only about seven blocks and pulls into a spot. I park a block away and wait.

A moment later she's carrying Cindy and opens the door to a place called Otherworldly Experiences, one of those virtual reality shops. She flips on the lights, shuts the door, and locks it behind her.

"Looks like she works there," says Tina. "Probably cleaning up before it opens."

"How much do you think a place like that pays?" I ask. "Enough to pay rent for the apartment and buy nice clothes?"

"No way," says Kate. "A friend of mine works at a VR place that's owned by a different outfit, but she makes two-thirds of what I do. Maybe the manager would make enough, but she doesn't strike me as the managerial type."

"Interesting," I say.

When Darleen doesn't show any signs she's about to leave, I turn to Kate. "I'd like to return to Darleen's apartment and search it. Maybe we'll find something that will lead us to Frankie. If we see any evidence that he's been there recently or that Darleen can contact him, then we know Darleen is keeping secrets from us. We'll have to get more aggressive with her."

"Sounds right," says Kate.

"But, we should keep eyes on her here. That way, we'll know if Frankie shows at the shop or if she leaves to head back home." I cock my head at Tina and Kate grins.

"You want me to stay here and watch the store while you go back," says Tina. "Why shouldn't Kate and I go to the apartment and you waste your time here by yourself?"

I tick the reasons off with my fingers. "First, you don't know how to pick the locks to get into the apartment. Second, I know how to conduct a proper search. And third, if you and I went together, only one of us would survive."

Kate interrupts Tina mid-huff with a hand on her shoulder. "Keep watch here. We'll call you if we find anything helpful. Once we're done, we'll be right back. Promise."

Tina opens the door without looking at me and steps out. "I'll let you know if Frankie shows or if Darleen leaves."

I lower my window. "And keep an eye out for aliens," I say, which is totally unnecessary but makes me feel good. She deserves something for torturing me for almost three hours, and she's lucky her obnoxious poking finger is still intact.

Tina flips me the bird, and I drive away, heading back to where the day started.

"Was that necessary?" asks Kate, but her voice sounds light, not at all like when she's angry.

"Better than running her over."

She chuckles. Her laugh sounds like music. It's the best sound I've ever heard. I'm getting Megan back and she'll laugh again. A real laugh, even if I'm not with her to hear it.

CHAPTER 30

The sun blares off the cathedral's steel and glass shell, and the light burns Megan's eyes. "It's so large."

Ivy doesn't break her stride. "We're growing, and this is only one farm." She strolls through the door, which open automatically.

Helpless, Megan follows without hesitation. She doesn't want to appear weak or reveal the rubber that's replaced the muscle in her legs.

"One farm?" she asks.

"Oh, yes," Ivy says. "We have another one nearby that's even larger. The cathedral serves both."

Even larger? How big are they, and what does she have planned for me?

Ivy pauses in the entrance. A large oak cross, the height of three people, suspended by thick rope, hangs from the ceiling in the center of the open space. A star, also made of oak, circles the cross. Megan touches her pendant; the symbol is the same.

Under the cross is a raised platform large enough for a dozen people. The ceiling shoots up five stories high. The high ceilings, the massive windows and the empty space makes the place feel otherworldly, similar to the church Megan goes to on holidays.

"This is our cathedral," says Ivy. "We gather here once a week and for special occasions. He hears us here. He's listening now. This place acts as a special portal to Him. Nothing happens inside these sacred walls that He doesn't know about."

"I thought God is always watching us?"

"Yes, but this place is special. The distance between Him and us here is as thin as a razor blade. It makes it easier for us to communicate with Him."

Megan frowns. Although the gathering space is large, it's not nearly as big as the outside of the structure. "What about the rest of the place?"

Ivy smiles. "The rest are enclaves where we preach to individuals or small groups. And then there's the sanctuary where we communicate directly with Him. You'll see that soon enough. Come, we're headed to one of the enclaves."

They walk around the cross and through another automatic door on the far side of the room. A long hallway stretches out before them, the tiles and walls white, the doors black. Each door has a letter on it. A woman steps out from a door marked B. She's wearing a multi-color jumpsuit similar to Ivy's but not quite as beautiful, and there are no silver sparkles to catch the light.

Upon seeing Ivy, she stops and bows her head in a short nod. "Mother," she says.

"Megan, this is one of my priestesses. Her name is Rachel. She's busy preaching to a small group, so we don't want to interrupt her. On your way."

"Yes, Mother," says the priestess before she turns and strides purposefully down the hallway.

Ivy opens a door marked M and holds it open.

Inside the room, half a dozen chairs form a circle. One is twice the size of the others and looks like a throne. The only adornment in the room, a poster of the cross and star symbol on the wall behind the throne chair.

Ivy sits in the large chair, and points to a simple one across from her. Light streams through the one window and reflects off Ivy's jumpsuit, engulfing her in a surreal glow—a halo of light.

Ivy lights the candle that sits on a small wooden table in the center of the circle of chairs. The smoke swirls around the room and gives off an earthy bouquet.

"This is a place and a time to open your heart," says Ivy. "We're here so you can be closer to God. Haven't you ever felt something is missing from your life?"

"Yes." The word slips from Megan's lips. She breathes in the scented air and feels lightheaded.

"That's because you lacked purpose, and those around you lost contact with God." Ivy smiles and her face is bathed in white light. She looks like an angel. "Do you want that to change?"

Megan focuses all her concentration to follow Ivy's words, but they're hazy, like they turn to smoke and are hard to grab.

"Yes, Mother," she says without knowing what she's doing.

CHAPTER 31

It's harder to search a messy room than a neat one. Especially if you don't want the subject to know. Some people see through the mess and will know instinctively if something's moved and out of place. Darleen's apartment offers challenges, but we work our way through the chaos.

To conduct a proper search, we break up the apartment into a grid. Picking the most obvious spots will only waste time in the end. We search sections and cross them off when we finish. We start in the kitchen and check the cabinets, and the fridge. Find nothing and move on to the living room. After that, we go through the bedrooms.

Her clothes are too good for her job and circumstances, and Kate finds half a dozen new, unworn dresses stuffed in the closet. Either Darleen's a thief or she's getting help paying the bills.

After more than two hours, we find only one sign of Frankie other than the photo on Cindy's night side table—a wrinkled picture of Frankie in uniform stuffed in the bottom drawer. Someone has crumpled it in a ball and then straightened it out later.

Kate looks dejected. "Nothing. No sign of that pervert. Maybe Darleen was honest. We should have found something if they stay in contact."

She's right, but I still haven't eliminated the idea of snatching Cindy and leaning on Darleen.

My phone buzzes. The number is unfamiliar, but I answer it anyway. "Hello."

Eddie's voice sounds uncertain. "Is this the guy who's helping us get Megan back?"

Denise says, "His name is Steven."

"Okay, I forgot. You know how I get when I'm nervous."

"Yes, everyone knows—"

I interrupt because it's obvious this back and forth could go on for a while. "This is Steven. Did someone respond to your posters?"

"No," says Eddie. "Not yet anyway. We just put them up. Maybe someone will call us today. If we—"

"He doesn't care about the stupid flyers, Eddie," says Denise. "Tell him why you're calling."

"Oh, yeah. Sometimes I ramble when—"

"When you get nervous," I say. "No worries, just focus on whatever you want to say."

"Sure. It's that funky symbol on that pendant. The one with a cross and the star. I knew I'd seen it before. I just needed a little time to relax. And—"

"Tell him where you saw it," says Denise.

"It might mean nothing. But I saw it at one of those new VR shops. They're popping up everywhere."

Denise says, "Like an idiot, Eddie went to one and spent all his money on an *experience*. If he had told me what he was up to, I would have stopped him."

"Good thing I didn't tell you then. Otherwise, I wouldn't have found the clue. Do you think it's significant?"

"Where did you see the symbol? Was it out in the open like part of the store name or something?"

"No," says Eddie. "That's why it took me a while to remember. It was on a poster in the back."

"Did you ask about it?"

"Yes. The manager said it was a private club that was way too expensive for me to even think about joining. The poster read *Total Otherworldly Extreme*. He said that club's located in the District 3 store. He shouldn't even have the poster, but he worked in that place for a few weeks and took one."

"Now you don't have any money at all," says Denise. "I don't understand why you would spend your money at a virtual reality place."

"Everyone talks about those places. I just wanted—"

I ask even though I know the answer. Better to be sure. "The place you went to was an Otherworldly Experience place, right?"

"Yep, just like in the name of the club."

"Thanks guys," I say. "You've been a big help. Don't go investigating anything without me, and let me know if you remember anything else."

I tell Kate about Eddie's experience with the symbol and Otherworldly Experience.

"It can't be a coincidence. Frankie got Darleen a job with that company," I say. "And they're paying her extra so she can afford this apartment and new clothes and stuff. I'm sure of it. Looks like I'm going to experience some virtual reality magic. I hear the experiences are better than real life. I can't wait."

"You'll have to wait, because they open for business at sundown," says Kate. "That's part of the marketing gimmick—from dusk until dawn. What's the connection between a place like that and Megan?"

"I don't know, but we're sure as hell going to find out."

Kate pulls her phone from her pocket.

"What are you doing?" I ask her.

"Calling Tina. We don't need her staking out the store anymore. Frankie's not showing up there."

I groan. "Can't we wait and pick her up later? Maybe tomorrow or the next day or in a month?"

"Tina's my best friend. She's always been there for me."

Kate turns that last statement into an accusation. What she's really saying is unlike me, Tina never ran out on her. I want to remind her that I answered her message right away and came to help. Gratefully, I eat those words. They sound lame in my head, and the truth is that she's right. Tina's always been there for her, and I haven't.

After we pick up Tina, we go back to Kate's apartment. Tina stakes out the internet as her domain. She's sure she can drum up information about The Farm and Otherworldly Experiences. She's positive a connection must exist, and since everything is on the internet, it must be there somewhere. It's a good idea.

She plays techno-modern music on her phone. She can't really like that music. Music should be played by musicians on instruments, not manufactured by technicians on computers. The notes sound sharp and disjointed and there's no soul. The vocals scratch along without meaning or emotion.

Tina has always professed love of techno music to prove her uniqueness. She thinks being different means the same thing as being special. It's silly. The two aren't the same. She should have learned that by now.

For all of our conflict, I know Tina is special, but she doesn't see it. Assholes like Mr. Frosty believe they're important when they're not, but Tina needs techno music or ancient alien invaders to feel good about herself. It makes no sense. She shouldn't need outside validation to prove she's worthwhile, but she does.

Kate's the opposite. She doesn't worry about being different. She just *is*. Put her in any situation, and she seizes the moment. She makes playlists of songs she likes, not some genre. It's too bad that Kate hasn't rubbed off more on Tina, but it's hard to change, and who am I too judge? My problems make hers seem like a speed bump.

Kate sits next to Tina and the two form a team—a sleuthing-the-internet-for-clues team. I'm clearly the third wheel, and the walls close in again. I tell them I've got a few errands to run and will return before nightfall.

Kate says she'll call me if they turn up anything useful and looks at me with soulful eyes. She'd rather I stay but understands why I can't.

CHAPTER32

Ivy smiles, lifts her face to the sun, and breathes in fresh air. Even though she'd been living on The Farm for more than two years now, she still marvels at the fresh scent: the trace of apples and freshly mowed grass, a hint of hemp and earthy tones from the pastures. She can't imagine living in the city again and breathing that poison. She'd rather die than be subject to that again.

She takes another deep breath to help clear her head. She designed the enclaves with air circulators that swirl the smoke away from the throne chair. Of course, none of the Angels ever suspect a thing, but all the priestesses know. Angels need the help provided by the drugs. The priestesses don't. They need their wits.

Even though the circulators prove effective, long sessions like the one with Megan are problematic. She breathes deeply to clean her lungs. The smoke makes the Angels receptive to new ideas and thoughts. It opens their minds and hearts, and that's what Ivy needs for her plan to work—open minds and hearts she can manipulate.

She always selects the smartest young people to become Angels. Trevor doesn't understand why it's so important. The fool would lower the standards and pay less for candidates. He boils everything down to profit and loss. A true fool, but she can't fault him... completely. Unaware of her true plans, he doesn't know why she needs exceptional Angels, but she does.

The smartest Angels respond the quickest to the treatments. That's what she tells Trevor. And it's true. Their minds, subtle and flexible, like the limbs of ballerinas, absorb the drugs and the lessons quickly and fully. They realize the truth behind the sermons and submit to their powerful, coercive force.

Once the process takes hold, the Angels become permanent converts, willing to do whatever she requires. Megan's mind works more like a gymnast than a dancer. She advanced in one session more quickly than any previous Angel. So quickly, Ivy is sure she'll be ready in time for the dreaded delivery next week.

The girl already knew on an intuitive level the unsustainability of the current system. The Originalist government hoards all the wealth and opportunities, leaving virtually nothing behind for 99 percent of the rest of the country. They rig voting, weighing it on income, disenfranchising most of the country.

People are angry and losing hope. The divide between the top 1 percent and everyone else has become a yawning expanse, too wide to imagine crossing it. Megan feels the unrest brewing and violence growing, and it frightens her. She needs a way to make sense of it all, and Ivy provides that—a simple plan that appeals to her logical mind.

The story, simple and compelling, immediately resonated with Megan. God wants the chaos, the suffering, the hatred. He wants to bring about the End of Days. Only through the misery can a new life, a new path for humanity unfold—one that's better and more just. One Megan can believe in. Once Megan fully commits to that essential truth, Ivy will have her.

The girl understands the logic in it. She also knows that time is running out on the Originalists. The ghettos and lower districts are rising up. They're arming and organizing themselves. It is foreseeable. A simple glance at any history book shows other examples of great societies succumbing to the greed of the few. America is no exception.

Ivy knows it too. She counts on it. The more hate and violence in the world, the more powerful she'll become, and the more quickly she'll bring about the End of Days. She can hardly wait. She wants it so badly she can taste it, and it tastes sweet.

Ivy, lost in her visions of the future, almost fails to notice when her phone buzzes. Trevor's name appears on the screen with the word urgent beside it. He always designates his calls as urgent, as if his time is worth infinitely more than hers. A selfish child, he will soon receive the punishment he deserves.

If she doesn't answer, he'll send over his Reapers to find her. "Yes, Trevor."

His voice sounds amped up, always a bad sign. "Brad Drudge is dead!"

"From the tone in your voice, I'm going to guess he didn't die of natural causes. No heart attack then?"

"I wish he had. He was murdered in his apartment last night. The initial reports assumed it was a robbery gone bad, but I reviewed the videotapes from the lobby in his apartment building. They tell a different story. I'm sending them to you now."

Ivy places the call on hold and opens the file. Megan's mom appears in the video.

She takes Trevor off hold. "That's unfortunate."

"No kidding," says Trevor. "Our operation depends upon secrecy. We can't tolerate any leaks. I don't know who the man is yet."

"Man?"

"You didn't watch the entire video? Fast forward a few minutes and he'll show up. He never looks at the camera, so we can't identify him."

Ivy speeds through the video, until a man shows up, who carefully keeps his face averted from the camera. Her stomach twists, but she keeps her voice calm. She expected Megan's mom to ask for help, but she didn't think they'd find the connection to Drudge so quickly.

"Don't worry about the man, Trevor. Let me focus on the woman. Once we have her, we'll find out what the guy knows. He's probably insignificant. Maybe a friend who's helping her out. I'm sure he doesn't know anything. What can either one really know?"

"They found Drudge, so they must know something. And they didn't just kill Drudge, they blew up the fucking apartment! I don't like loose ends. I'm sending over some of my Reapers to coordinate with you and deal with this immediately. I pay them plenty to handle problems like these. I want it done today."

Ivy frowns. Is this a test? A divine test of her loyalty after all these years. He demands complete loyalty from her. He always has. She can't dismiss the possibility of a test. If that's the case, she'll pass. The end is so close. She'll do whatever He desires. There is no alternative.

She'll make sure Luke handles this. He's Trevor's most skilled Reaper. Besides being a skilled killer, he's a true believer. He'll take direction from her. He won't fuck this up.

She glances back at the cathedral. If this is a test, it means she has to speed up Megan's indoctrination even faster. She breathes in the air again, but this time she smells cow shit.

CHAPTER 33

I walk the city streets, relieved to be free from the apartment and Tina. The weather has turned sour, which matches my mood. Gray clouds have invaded the blue sky, and rain falls in short spurts. It feels like the Fates are spitting on me. Fine, I deserve it. I can take it.

Without a destination, my wandering spins me back into the Badlands. I pass the Devil's Armpit. Someone's fixed the plywood front door. No doubt the Red Dragons would rather keep the rest of the ghetto out of their hangout. It seems like an invite-only place.

I continue my wandering and stop at the edge of a small park. I'm surprised it's still here. I guess land in the ghetto isn't worth all that much. The city used to mow it back in the day, and a functioning swing set stood at the far end. Now it's a collection of weeds and trash, minus the swing set. Pity. The deeper inside a city, the more important swaths of green space become. The Upper Districts still have them, but the neighbors pay for the maintenance of those parks, and only those with special identifications and memberships can use them. Clearly, no one has money to maintain this park.

Kate, Tina, and I used to hang out here. We'd spend lazy summer days talking about everything or nothing depending upon the day or the moment. Kate and I kissed for the first time by the swing set.

We were thirteen and had been best friends for three years. Tina had just stomped away. The time late, she had to go home for dinner. Her family situation was better than ours. They ate dinners together.

Neither Kate nor I wanted to go home, but the sun dipped, and night would soon blanket the area. Walking the streets after dark was dangerous, even back then. My mom's affiliation with the Monarchs only provided me a small touch of protection and did nothing for Kate.

I said something stupid. I can't remember what exactly, but it made Kate laugh. When I turned to face her, her eyes had grown wide and full of life and promise. She leaned into me and kissed me softly on the lips. I had wanted to kiss her for a year but couldn't summon the courage. She's always had courage. More than me. Still does.

I'll never forget that first kiss. It was perfect with so much wrapped in it—love, even if it was just puppy love, friendship, and a promise of a future. We didn't talk about the kiss afterward, although it lingered on my mind for months. Finally, I gathered up the nerve to make the first move, which was really the second move, and kissed her. Same park, different season.

That was a clumsy kiss, still sweet, but not nearly as perfect. Kate smiled and even chuckled. She told me it was about time. I apologized for bumping into her nose, and she grinned and kissed me again. Longer that time and deeper. When we separated she said we'd have plenty of time to work on it. We could have had a lifetime I suppose, but reality got in the way. Eventually, it always does.

The sun has dropped. It's late afternoon, and everything is different. The swing set is gone, and Kate and I no longer have a future. I turn my back on Kissing Park and head back to her apartment. At least the walk has helped me sort through some threads.

An obscure cult called The Farm has abducted Megan. Frankie's working for them. Frankie got Darleen a job at Otherworldly Experiences where she makes more than she should. That means the cult and the virtual reality company are connected. Plus, Eddie spotted the cult's symbol at the Otherworldly shop he went to a few months ago, which isn't a coincidence. That's all I know about who's involved. It's not enough yet, but I'm getting close.

The why seems more straightforward. The cult targets teenagers. Smart, beautiful, young people, which makes my stomach crawl. I don't know why exactly they want these kids yet, but it smells bad. They paid Brad a lot for the targets, which means the cult values the best kids.

That's the only positive I've unearthed so far. The cult pays top dollar for these girls, so it'll be hard for Frankie to hurt Megan. They won't want that. And the cult has had its eyes on Megan for a while. She's special to them. More than the other girls for some reason. I need to find the connection between The Farm and Otherworldly. All I need is an address and then...

I turn a corner. Kate leans against a building on the next block. She's wearing the black dress she had on when we went to see Brad, and she's braided her hair the way I like. She smiles and waves me over.

I check my phone, just to make sure I hadn't missed any important messages from her or Tina. Nothing. I cross the street and close in. She winks at me.

"What are you doing here? I thought you'd be back at the apartment with Tina."

"Tina doesn't have what I want." She backs away from me, stepping into the alley, a come-hither look on her face.

I don't have any idea what to say to that, so I keep my mouth shut and step after her. My heart starts pounding and sweat coats the hollow in my back.

She takes one more step, farther into the shadows. "I'm not mad at you. I forgive you for everything." She leans against a brick wall, lifts her skirt, and reveals the top of her thighs. "It's been a long time."

I freeze two steps away from her. Every fiber of my body wants to feel her next to me, to take her in this alley, but my blasted mind trips me up. "Wasn't that dress ruined when we jumped from Brad's window?"

Kate lifts the hem even higher.

Glimpses of blonde hair appear between her legs.

"I own a second one."

She grabs my hand and pulls it under her dress. My fingers touch her thigh and she lifts it higher. She kisses my neck and my hand reaches between her legs. She's wet. Her fingers unbuckle my belt.

She breathes into my ear and says. "Fuck me, Stevie. Right here."

And that's it. It's possible to want something so badly you'll believe almost anything. I know what that feels like. You see it all the time in get-rich schemes. People fall for the most ridiculous fantasies, but there comes a time when you know it's too good to be real. You know it's a fantasy. Like now.

I pull my hand from underneath her skirt and grab her throat. "Stevie? Kate never calls me that. What the fuck are you?"

It frowns at me and suddenly morphs into Marissa, the Mexican operative I had a fling with years ago. "Is this better? Marissa liked it rough."

I squeeze its throat tighter. "I'm only going to ask you one more time. What the fuck are you?"

It pries my fingers from its throat as if I'm a child. Whatever it is, it's way stronger than me.

"You can call me Raven, and I'm so disappointed in you. Another minute and Little Stevie would have been inside of me. That would have been better. Easier for everyone. Oh well."

I step back and the thing changes. Wings form on its back. Razor-sharp talons extend from the hands. The skin turns scaly and red. I can still see a bit of Marissa in the face and it still wears the dress, which looks ridiculous.

"Want to fuck me now?" It lifts the hem of the dress to its waist and laughs. "Raven still has a place for your little thing, Stevie. Once you've had a fallen angel, you'll never go back."

I grab my Smith and Wesson and stumble back a step. "What do you want?"

"You. We want you. You're almost complete now, Stevie. Let yourself turn, and our master will reward you forever. He'll give you Kate and so much more. You know it's the right thing to do. Stop fighting."

The gun shakes in my hand, but my voice sounds confident. "I'm sorry to disappoint you, but you can't have me. I'm on the human team."

The creature smiles and the last bit of Marissa vanishes from its face. The head stretches longer, the features sharper. Hellfire burns in its eyes. "Not for long, Stevie. We're in your blood. Why fool yourself when you know better."

The monster's eyes blaze hot and it pulls me. Not in a sexual way, but it's rich with power. Part of me craves that power. Another minute and I'll be some demon's bitch, so I aim where its heart should be and fire.

The demon moves impossibly fast. It jumps in the air, using its claws to push off the wall and lands on its feet in the alley. The bullet bounces off the brick building behind it.

"That's not nice, Stevie." It says. "Don't be so stubborn, Loverboy. I promise you'll like it. I've never had any complaints. It will be an adventure."

"What can I say? I'm in a mood."

"You're such a prude. Next time, I won't be so nice."

"There won't be a next time." I level the gun and blast away. Three shots in a triangular pattern. At least one should have hit it, but there's no sign any of them actually does.

The demon races down the alley, and I go after it. With each step, it fades, until finally it morphs into black smoke and disappears.

I stop. No sign of it. It's as if the demon was never really here in the first place.

Bullets couldn't kill that thing, so I need to find out what can.

The alley is deserted. It's gone.

What does it want with me? If it wanted to kill me, I'd be dead. It let me live, and that scares me almost as much as seeing the monster in the first place.

I need a safe space to think. The alley looks familiar. There's a door with a cross carved into the brick above it.

A sign below the cross reads St. Thomas.

CHAPTER 34

The door is unlocked, so I step inside the old church. Considerably darker than outside, only a few candles add to the small traces of natural light filtering through the windows. I pause and soak in the sanctuary, absorbing the smell of the wooden pews, the vaulted gothic ceiling, the artistry in the windows, and the sanctity of the altar. This place feels special, as if it's connected to another realm. Perhaps it's the echo of all the prayers spoken in this building, or the flickering candles, or that it's empty.

It's apparently not completely empty. Father Paul steps from behind a pew and into the center aisle. He smiles at me like we're old friends and waves me over. I'm in his place. To refuse would be rude, and besides, he seems genuinely happy to see me. How many people really want to see me? I can count them on one hand. I tuck the Smith and Wesson back into the holster at the small of my back, and stroll to him.

When I stop a few feet away, he grins and says, "So good of you to stop in and visit once more. I'd been hoping we'd see each other again."

What can I say? That I came close to screwing a freaky-looking demon in the alley and found this door by accident? Probably not my best option, so I settle for the easy. Sometimes easy is best. "I thought we might talk. I have some questions I'm hoping you can help me with, Father Paul."

He crosses his arms against his chest and frowns at me. "You really disappoint me."

What does he mean? I've done a lot to disappoint a priest. Does he know about the demon gang member whose head I smashed to oblivion, or Mr. Frosty, or Brad, or the thing named Raven in the alley, or Cindy, whom I would have hurt if Kate hadn't been with me in Darleen's apartment? With so many bad acts to choose from, I don't know what to confess to, so I add befuddlement to my voice and wait for the verdict.

"Disappointed?"

He smiles, and I know he's not going to bust me for any of my recent sins. "I thought we'd become friends, and my friends call me Paulie. Father Paul sounds so stuffy."

I breathe easier. Why do I care what the priest thinks of me?

"Come," says the affable young man. "Let's sit and I'll make up as many answers to your questions as I can."

He sits in the first-row pew, and I settle next to him. "So, what's on your mind this time?"

I need to talk to someone about my rising demon problem. It's not going away on its own. "What do you know about demons?"

Father Paul looks at me for a short while; the silence thick between us, a grim expression creases his face. Finally, he says, "There are all types of demons. Personal ones we fight, and then others."

Leaning forward, I ask, "It's the other ones I'm interested in. Real demons, sent from hell."

Father Paul tents his hands together and presses his fingertips against his lips. "The Bible talks about demons. As Christians, we can't pick and choose what we believe. Demons are as real as angels. I don't think you can have one without the other."

I don't want a lecture on the Bible. I need practical advice, and it seems Paul knows more than he's saying. "Here's the thing. I've seen real demons. They've taken an interest in me. I need to know why and how I can defeat them. I'll understand if you think I'm nuts and want me to leave. I'll go, but I could really use your help."

Father Paul looks over his shoulder and surveys the empty church. When he looks back at me, it seems as if his eyes shine. "I don't think you're nuts. We don't learn much about demons in seminary, but there was one priest, Father McInerney, who's an expert. He's a bit odd and some people find him creepy. The novices mostly stay away from him, but I spent time walking with him. He told me some interesting stories about demons. Are you sure you want to know?"

"Well, since one tried to screw me in the alley, it's not a question of what I want. I need to know."

"It tried to have sex with you?"

"It's a long story. I'll save it for another time."

The priest cocks his head as if to examine me before he speaks. He lowers his voice, so I can barely hear him. "You must understand that these are only his ideas. I can't be certain they're true. He wasn't even certain."

"I got it. You're offering no guarantee."

He nods. "Just so we understand each other. McInerney said two types of demons live among us. One form, the less dangerous type, is a human who succumbs to the Devil. He or she embraces evil, and the Devil uses a dark version of the Holy Spirit to inhabit the person. Call it an Unholy Spirit. While this form is far less dangerous than the other type of demon, it's still highly lethal. It can possess extraordinary strength and is hard to kill. Usually a blow to—"

"To the head is needed to kill the thing. Right?"

"Not just a knock on the head, but a total destruction of the skull. Or, a blade that's been properly blessed, that would do the trick. A knife washed with holy water for example."

"Interesting," I say, "And what about the other type. The more dangerous ones."

"They're even more of a challenge. When God cast Satan from heaven, Satan didn't go alone. A number of angels took his side."

"How many?"

He shrugs. "No one knows. A good number, but less than half. When they fell to hell, they changed in appearance. Their feathers burned into their flesh and became leathery. They took on a reddish color. And—"

"And their nails turned to talons and their faces grew longer and sharper looking."

"That sounds about right. On Earth, these demons have similar powers to angels."

"Can they change their appearances?"

"Certainly. Among other traits."

"Great," I say. "And how can I kill them?"

"With great difficulty," he touches my hand. "Look, these are only stories. I don't know if they're real or not."

"Oh, they're real." I don't want to freak out the priest and tell him the frequency in which I'm seeing these demons. It's not his problem, and I don't want to weigh him down with it. Still there's another way he can help me. I remove my phone from my pocket and retrieve the symbol of the cult from Frankie's pendant. "Have you ever seen anything like that?"

He makes the sign of the cross. "That's a dark symbol."

"It isn't a Christian symbol? I figure it was since it has a cross in the center."

"Yes, however the star has five points, so it's a pentagram, and the cross is enclosed inside the star. That changes the meaning completely. This suggests the power of God is limited and can be overcome. It foretells that Satan will eventually prevail in the Great Struggle."

"The Great Struggle?"

"Yes, at the End of Days."

"Great," I mutter. "Do you know any group that uses this symbol? A cult called The Farm?"

Paul shakes his head. "It's an ancient symbol. I had hoped it was long forgotten."

I stand. "Nothing is ever forgotten. Shit just gets recycled and comes back in new and worse forms."

The lack of light streaming though the window means that dusk has fallen. I need to return to Kate's apartment, see if they've uncovered anything useful, and make plans to visit Otherworldly's shop in District 3. Talking about demons and the Great Struggle won't rescue Megan. After that, I don't know.

I lift my hand toward the priest. "Thanks for the help, Father Paul."

He shakes it with a firm grip. "Next time, it's Paulie."

"Deal," I say and move down the aisle toward the main door.

Before I reach the exit, Father Paul calls out to me. "Steven."

I turn, and he says, "When you've decided, come back to see me."

A bluish light sparkles in his eyes before he turns and disappears behind the altar.

Decide what?

I reach the door, and a chill runs through me. I don't recall ever telling Father Paul my name.

A bowl of holy water sits by the door on a pedestal I hadn't noticed before. I wash the blade of my knife before leaving. Better safe than sorry.

CHAPTER35

Megan hoists the tip of her apple-picking pole toward a ripe target on the top branch and can't quite reach it. Her head, still buzzing from the smoke in the enclave, only gets in the way. Her depth perception is way off, her arms shake, and the pole droops to the ground.

Petal steps in front of her. "What did they do to you?"

They had drifted from the others, far enough that no one else can see or hear them among the trees, a rare moment of privacy.

Megan speaks slower than normal. "I...spoke to the Mother...alone in one of the special rooms. There was this...smoke, and...."

Petal bites her lower lip. "You've only been here a couple of days. They never drag someone into the enclaves until they've been here at least a week. They like to break us down physically first. I don't get it. Why the rush?"

Megan shrugs. All her thoughts spin in wild directions, like fireflies she can't catch.

Petal grabs her by the shoulders. "You can't believe what she told you. The smoke is a drug. It affects you, makes you compliant."

"I don't know what to believe. She made a lot of sense. She's—"

"Very persuasive. I know." Petal moves close to Megan so they breathe the same air. She smells like ripe apples. "My name is Felicity Sanders. I live in District 12 and have a younger brother and sister. What's your name?"

"Spring."

Petal brushes a loose hair from Megan's face and strokes her cheek. "What's your name?"

The touch of Kate's fingers helps her concentrate. "Megan Smith. I also live in District 12 with my mom. Her name is Kate."

Petal leans her head against Megan's shoulder. "Tonight. We escape tonight. We can't wait any longer."

"How?"

"They're having a burning tonight. Everyone's required to attend. We'll slip away in the darkness."

Megan lifts her pendant. "What do we do with these?"

"Don't worry about that. I have a plan. They take them off when we go into the sanctuary. It interferes with their process. I know the password for the computers. Trust me. And don't drink the punch at dinner. I'll sit next to you, and I'll switch cups."

"Won't it bother you?"

"My chemical make-up is different from most. The punch and smoke doesn't affect me much."

"Why me?" asks Megan. "Why are you helping me?"

Petal smiles. "I've met you once before. Well, not really. I went to the science fair last year and saw your presentation."

Megan's face flushes hot. "You competed at the fair? I don't remember seeing you."

Petal smirks. "No. I'm not a science type. I'm more of a literature person, but I watched your presentation on faster-than-light travel. You explained wormholes and created a model to twist time and space. That girl, the one who's going to explore space, isn't going to get stuck in some fucking farm in the middle of nowhere."

"I feel useless. You'd be better off without me."

"I'm not leaving without you." Petal leans closer to her, her emerald eyes blazing. "You're smart and strong. I need your help or I'll never get away. And I know it sounds silly, but I like you a lot, so there's that."

Petal kisses Megan, and Megan's lips melt into Petal's. Heat runs down her body from her lips right through her toes. She feels a longing she's never felt before and wants more from this brave girl with emerald eyes and brown skin who smells like apples. She can't believe they just met yesterday.

When they separate, Petal says, "I'm Felicity Sanders and you're Megan Smith. They can't take that away from us. Say it."

"You're Felicity Sanders and I'm Megan Smith."

"Damn right. Promise me you won't forget it."

"I promise."

May approaches, her basket full of apples in one hand, swinging her pole over her shoulder with the other, driving away their moment of privacy.

"Tonight," Petal whispers. Then she grabs her pole and speaks in a loud voice, "You've got to hold it this way," she says as if she had been simply instructing Megan on the best technique to pick apples.

"Got it," says Megan and then she smiles. She thinks about Eddie and Denise and how she wants to tell them about her first kiss. Eddie will want to know all about Petal, and Denise will want every detail of the kiss itself. She'll have a problem getting any of her own words in and it'll take forever to describe. She's sure it's the weirdest first kiss under the oddest circumstances ever. And she's sure her friends will like Petal when they meet her.

She has one more question to ask Petal, but the moment is gone.
What's a burning?

CHAPTER 36

I trek back to Kate's apartment, trying hard to flush thoughts of demons and Father Paul from my mind. Finding Megan requires my full attention, and I can't picture how demons are involved in the girl's kidnapping. Once Tina opens the door to Kate's apartment, a gloomy mood hits me like a gust of bad news.

Kate sits on the couch with teary, red-rimmed eyes, and Tina's body language sucks. Her shoulders slope downward and she doesn't look me in the eyes. The only positive: Tina has stopped playing the techno-modern crap. Once she got rid of me, she probably shut it off. Job well done.

"How did your *errands* work out?" Tina asks, a trace of bitterness in her voice. She makes it sound as if I left to avoid helping with her social media searches, just another example of me deserting Kate when she needs me. Of course, she chased me away, so she has no reason to feel bitter, but that's Tina. She'll blame others when shit happens, even if it's her own fault. Some people are like that.

"Fine. Did you guys learn much?" I have to ask, even though the answer is obvious. Not to ask would be bad. It would mean I didn't have confidence in them, or that I didn't care what they were doing.

"A few things," says Kate. She's acting as a bridge between Tina and me to avoid the predictable car crash. "We found only two threads on social media about the Otherworldly Experience's private club. Both were basic questions, but no one seems to know much about it, except that it's exclusive."

"That's weird right there." Tina perks up. "Usually a place like Otherworldly would want some buzz about an expensive private club, but it seems like it's the opposite. As if they want to keep it a secret."

"Did you find out who owns Otherworldly?" I ask.

"No," says Tina. "That's even weirder. Usually some pompous windbag takes credit for a success like Otherworldly, but there's nothing. Even their website doesn't say who owns them. And they don't advertise. All of their growth is organic through word of mouth."

"And their business model makes no sense," says Kate. "Tina mapped out where they have places. Take a look."

Tina twists the tablet so I can see it. "They're a new company. Just three years old. They started here in Philadelphia and they've expanded fast, but look where."

The pattern jumps out at me immediately. "They're in ghettos and Lower Districts and a few of the exclusive Upper Districts around the country. They're not in any of the Middle Districts where they should be able to make a good deal of money."

"Right," says Tina. "They could charge more in the Middle Districts than the Lower ones and there should be demand. Other virtual reality places have shops in those districts, but not Otherworldly. And it's weird how they have one or two stores in an Upper District at each of the big cities."

"And," Kate adds, "they've expanded internationally. Just a few places, but each one is in a major city."

Tina ticks them off her fingers. "London, Hong Kong, Tokyo, Rome, Berlin, Moscow, Tehran, and New Delhi."

Another piece to the puzzle falls in place. "Mary said the van The Farm used to abduct Megan was owned by a shell company. I bet it's connected to Otherworldly. I thought it was probably stolen, but now it doesn't look like it. Otherworldly is involved somehow. These kids must be part of their plans. And their plans must involve more than just entertainment."

"But what?" says Tina.

"And why would a virtual reality company want kids?" asks Kate.

I can think of a few reasons, and all of them bad. It won't help to guess. Tina keeps her mouth shut also, even though the look on her face confirms that her ideas on the subject track along the same lines.

"We'll find out," I say. "Did you discover anything about The Farm on the net?"

"Nothing," says Tina.

"I have a contact inside Homeland who's looking into The Farm. He'll track them down if the government knows anything." Mary said she'd involve Gabriel, and he'd move a mountain for me if it needs moving. I don't tell them what Father Paul said about the symbol. Keeping it secret feels like a lie, but I can shoulder it. A satanic symbol might be too much for Kate to take right now, and I don't see how that'll help us get Megan back.

Kate stares at Tina until Tina huffs. Tina pinches her face together angrily and says, "I'm going out to grab us some food. I'll be back in a few minutes." Before she reaches the door, she shoots one last glare at me. She doesn't say anything, but she's reminding me of our last conversation, the one where I promised that I was here only temporarily and would leave after we brought Megan home.

I shrug.

And she's gone.

Kate and I are alone and the past barrels down on me like a big rig on an open highway. Sixteen years ago, when I was twenty, I left her without an explanation. I gave her a number she could use to text me if she ever needed me and walked out. Over the years, I've regretted that moment. I'm not sure what I could have said or done, but surely walking out without explaining myself was wrong. And now that original sin is coming home to roost. Kate deserved more back then, and she deserves more than I can give her now.

She stands beside me. "I need to know."

Four fucking words, yet they might as well be a full-length novel. "It was a long time ago, Kate."

"Bullshit. It feels like yesterday. What did I do? Why wasn't I good enough for you? Weren't we good together? Tell me."

Her voice drips with pain. Pain I've caused her, and my heart twists. I look to the door, but I can't run out now. Not now that I'm older, and with Megan missing. I've got to make some sense out of this for her, so she knows it wasn't her fault. She has no blame in this. It's all me.

"You were always out of my league. From that first kiss when we were thirteen until now."

"Then why? Why did you run out on me? I know it wasn't another woman. You would never have done that to me."

It all comes back to me in a rush. The pain and confusion that tormented me back then. The power and sense of destiny I felt when I joined the secret special operations group. All those emotions swirled inside me. A toxic stew of part dark and part light. I feared what I was becoming, yet I wanted to explore it, seep into it, be free to experience it.

"I had started in a new group. You remember, I told you about it. Special operations."

She nods.

"It was more than that. It wasn't an official government agency. It's what they call dark ops. We were off the grid and could employ whatever extreme measures we needed to fulfill our missions. And we had important objectives. At least they seemed important back then."

"So, you left me to join this group?" Kate asks. "Why couldn't we still be together? I wouldn't have asked about your missions or any of that. I didn't care about what you were doing."

Lying would be easy. I can just say they watched me, and they needed me unattached at home. I can say my schedule was going to be crazy, and I would be on assignment for months at a time with no way to contact her. All that would be true, but that's not the reason I left Kate, and she'd see through the excuse. She deserves the truth, even if it's harder to believe and harder for her to take.

I swallow my cowardice and say, "It wasn't the job. Not really. It was me."

"You?"

"I'm no good, Kate. During the training for the group, I realized I'm bad. I have demons inside me. I did things."

She grabs my hand. "I'm sure you did things you had to do to complete your missions. Every soldier grapples with that. I could have helped."

"It's different with me. Yes, I was ordered to do some rotten things, but there were others I did just because I wanted to. I enjoyed it. And I couldn't give it up. Not then, so I couldn't trust myself around you. I needed to leave."

"What types of things did you do?"

What a simple question. I wish she hadn't asked it because now I'm stuck. For her to fully understand, she needs to know the monster I've become. "I killed people. And I tortured some before I killed them. What I did to Brad was nothing compared to some others. And that's not the worst thing." I sigh. "I liked it, Kate. God help me, but I like hurting people. I'm a monster, and it's not getting better. I'm worried my mother was right. I'm turning into a demon."

Kate releases my hand. She should slap me or walk away, but she doesn't. She looks at me for long moment. Her beautiful blue eyes shine on me. "Steven Cabbott, I've known you a long time. I know you better than you know yourself, and there's good in you. You may have done bad things, and even enjoyed it, but there's good in your heart. You can't convince me otherwise. You're no demon, and you'll never be one if I have anything to say about it."

"I don't know. I want to change. That's why I came back. I was hoping to find out what happened to my mother. Maybe... if she changed, I can change."

"Your mother was a drug-dealing psycho. You're nothing like her." She brushes her fingers against the rough stubble on my chin. "Thank you for being honest. I know it was hard."

"Do you forgive me?"

She kisses me. It's nothing like our first one at Kissing Park. Love is here, in this kiss also. It fuses along the contours of her lips and mouth, but none of the promise of our first kiss comes along with it. This doesn't feel like the start of something. It feels more like the end of a long road.

Kate says, "Yes, I forgive you. We were just kids. I forgave you long ago. I just needed to know why." She frowns at me. "But I can't forgive you for the other stuff. You'll have to do that yourself. Put the past behind you. Give yourself a chance to change. Let the good come out."

"You really think I've got good in me?" I ask, hoping she still sees the real me, the one underneath the messy exterior.

She kisses me again. Longer and harder this time. She slides her tongue inside my mouth, and I push my body against hers. She feels familiar and different at the same time. My hand moves under her shirt. My body aches for her.

I hear a commotion outside as if someone is fumbling with a set of keys and a foot kicks the bottom of the door.

Kate pushes me away and smiles. "Tina's back."

"And great timing," I say. "That's the fastest food run in history."

The door opens and Tina walks in holding a pizza box.

I'm neither upset nor disappointed. I've had one more moment with Kate than I deserve, than I thought I'd ever have, so I thank the Fates for that. When good things happen, they deserve the gratitude. Their antics can take you up or down. Today, I'm fortunate.

Tomorrow, well, I'll have to burn that bridge when I get to it.

CHAPTER37

"Who's hungry?" Tina places the pizza on the table in front of the couch. "I got half Neanderthal style for Stevo. Meatballs, pepperoni, and sausage, although God knows what lab they got the meat stuff from. And the other half for us civilized folk, with mushrooms."

At least Tina remembered my favorite pizza toppings. She throws me a curious look, and I give her nothing, just a bland smile in return. She doesn't need to know what's going on between Kate and me. At least she won't get that from me. Kate can do as she pleases.

"I'll take one of each," says Kate. "I like a combination of caveman and civilization."

While we eat, I explain my plan. "I'll go into District 3 and visit the Otherworldly Experience place. My identification card will let me in, and I'll inquire about a membership to their exclusive club. While I'm there, I'll sneak around and see if I can find an address for The Farm, or some other clue as to where they're located."

"I thought this club is exclusive. How are you going to get in?" asks Tina. "No offense Stevo, but you're never going to pass for a rich guy."

"My identification card says I'm working as a private bodyguard for a rich billionaire named Samuel Jeffries. Jeffries doesn't really exist, but if they check him out, they'll find a fictitious pharmaceutical man whose family goes back for generations. The cover will hold up. It always does."

"What about us?" asks Kate. "How do we get in?"

"You can't. There's no way I can get you guys into Districts 1 through 5. The Green Zone is off limits for you. The security at those checkpoints is too tight. And if I managed to smuggle you in somehow, you'll get thrown in jail as suspected terrorists if they catch you. You'll do at least seven years hard labor, if not more. It's not worth the risk. Besides, I'll be better at snooping on my own."

"I don't like it," Kate says.

"Neither do I, but we're going to have to trust Steven on this one," Tina says. "We can't help Megan if we're stuck in a work camp for the next decade."

With the matter decided, I go into Megan's room, retrieve my duffel, remove a pair of black slacks, a plain white dress shirt, and a black blazer. Made from the most advanced wrinkle free fabric, the clothes look finely pressed. I can keep my Smith and Wesson because I have a carry permit, but that's the only weapon I'll bring, except the tab of explosives in the heel of my boot and my ceramic throwing knife in my belt. They won't detect those at the checkpoint, but they will my knife. The knife has to stay behind. I can't give them an excuse to detain me.

When I enter the living room, Kate smiles.

Tina chuckles. "Yesterday, I said you look like shit. I take it back. You don't look half bad. Only partially shitty."

"Thanks," I say. "Really touching."

Kate places her hand on my chest. "I think he looks handsome. He's filled out in all the right places." She kisses me on the cheek. "Be safe and come back soon."

I hit the streets. It will take me hours to walk to District 3. Each checkpoint will take progressively longer, and I don't want to waste the time. I find a cab and whistle him over.

When he pulls over, I talk to the driver through his open window. "I need to go to District 3."

The cabbie twists his head. "Do I look like I have clearance for the fucking Green Zone? This isn't a limo. The best I can do is drop you off the highway next to the checkpoint. After that you're on your own."

"Good enough." I open the backseat and slide across the vinyl seats. It's dirty, with a candy wrapper on the floor and the smell of cigarette smoke in the air. The cabbie drives west and merges onto the highway that loops the city.

The checkpoints only start when a car exits the highway, so he can exit in District 3, turn around, and pull back on the main road without running afoul of Homeland.

The cabbie looks forward as he talks. "You'll need clearance to get into District 3. If you don't have it, they'll arrest you just for showing up at the checkpoint."

"Don't worry about it. It's none of your concern."

We pass a gigantic screen off the highway. A large eyeball moves around on it in a disturbing way with the words "Report UnAmerican Activity. Rewards Paid." Underneath that the Originalist logo appears in white.

"Fucking Originalists. My son died overseas defending our country for *this* shit. I remember when we didn't have any checkpoints. You could drive anywhere you wanted in the city. Now they pen us in like animals. It won't last long though." The cabbie's eyes search mine in the rearview mirror. "If you know what I mean."

Cabbies like to talk. I call it 'cabersations.' I guess it's a byproduct of an otherwise lonely job. They spend a lot of time by themselves looking for customers. When they take in a live body, they want to connect. Part of the human condition.

I indulge him, since cabbies have a way of knowing things. "Have you ever been to a place called Otherworldly Experiences?"

"Me, no," he flashes his eyes at me again in the rearview mirror, "but I've picked up people who have. I hear some crazy shit goes on in those places. People get addicted and hooked on it like a drug."

"What type of experiences are we talking about?"

"All kinds. Adventures to far-reaching places. One guy told me about a fantasy game where he fought like a knight. Sounded stupid to me, but he was jazzed by it. Said he could feel his sword slice into someone's chest like he was carving a turkey. And of course, there's always sex. These things always include sex."

"Sex?"

"Yeah. Those virtual reality places are driving hookers out of business. I don't get it. Maybe I'm an old-fashioned guy, but I want to feel real flesh. You know what I'm saying?"

I nod, and he continues, "Still, some of these guys say the sex is mind blowing. The technology hooks into the pleasure centers in the brain and makes them go nuts. They spend all their money at these places."

I grind my jaw. Mind-blowing sex and The Farm's collecting beautiful young people. I may not be a genius, but the connection seems obvious.

The cabbie must have misread my tense expression because he says. "You don't work for one of those joints, do you? I'm sorry if I offended you. Like I said, I've never been to one of them. I've only heard stories from other people."

"No offense taken. I've never been to one either. I'm just curious."

The cab pulls off the highway and stops behind a limo. "This is as far as I can go. You're on your own from here."

The meter says I owe him twenty-five dollars, but I give him a fifty. "I'm sorry about your son. I knew a lot of good people who died overseas."

I approach the checkpoint on foot. Spotlights brighten the area like it's daytime. A heavy, metal bar blocks cars from coming through, and sharp spikes in the road will rip through the toughest tires. Booths made of bulletproof glass block both sides of the barrier. I count eight Homeland officers at the checkpoint. Each wears body armor and is heavily armed with an M18 assault rifle as well as a handgun holstered at the hip.

The metal barrier lifts, and the limo slides through and disappears. I walk toward the checkpoint with both my hands lifted over my head, palms out, my identification card held in the open so they can see it. Violence has escalated lately, and I don't need a nervous Homeland goon blowing a hole in my head.

Six of the eight guns point at me. Two from inside the bulletproof booths. The barrels of those guns stick out through narrow slits. The six officers on the street spread out in groups of two. A good formation. Tight. It offers me only two easy shots. By the time I tried to take out the third officer one of the gunmen in a booth would put a bullet in my chest, another would aim for my head, in case I'm wearing Kevlar under my shirt.

"I come in peace," I say with a smile. "I have access to District 3."

"Sure," says an older officer, with gray hair that flows past his helmet. "You look like a high roller. Do you have any guns on you?"

"I have a carry permit for a handgun. It's holstered on my back."

"Don't move a muscle. I'm not in the mood," he says warily. He squints and works his jaw hard. He's on edge.

He nods to one officer on his left and one on his right. "Pat him down. Take the gun and the ID card. If he moves or even blinks weird, shoot him in the face."

The officers stalk forward, carefully, both guns trained on me. They pat me down, remove my Smith and Wesson, and take my identification card. The older officer, in charge of the group, takes the card and swipes it through his handheld device. A moment later, he visibly relaxes.

"Okay, Steven," he says. "Place your hand on the reader so we can do a DNA validation. Blink at me too fast and you're a goner."

I try not to blink, place my hand against the glass screen, and wait five seconds until it flashes green.

The leader smiles and hands me back my identification card. The other officer returns the Smith and Wesson.

"I'm sorry for all the security, Mr. Cabbott, but terrorists have been very active lately. We lost an entire checkpoint last week when it was overrun by ghetto scum. We can't be too careful."

"I understand." They're stuck in a rotten place. The last gatekeepers between the wealthy few and the unwashed masses.

"You can enter," he says.

It's odd, but I feel like I'm entering a prison instead of a rich section of the city. It shouldn't be that way, but things have gotten turned inside out. What did the cabbie say? "Things won't last like this for long."

He's right.

Something will give, and the streets will run red, but whose blood will be spilled?

CHAPTER 38

Megan shuffles out of the mess hall with the rest of the Angels from her cabin. The food has restored a small measure of her energy. The testimonials during dinner were all about the Devil and how God challenged them to turn their backs on the Dark One. The dark theme seemed clear. It wasn't a coincidence. The message must be connected to the *burning* that Petal had mentioned in the apple orchard.

Petal keeps close to her side as they move outside. She switched cups with Megan and drank her punch during dinner, so Megan's mind is mostly clear, and she feels more like her usual self.

When the Angels break away from the group to follow Frankie to their cabin, Buck stands in their way. They stop as the two talk. Frankie smiles and then Buck approaches Megan. His eyes search out hers. He wants to take her away. Petal must sense it because she grabs Megan's hand.

Buck stops two paces from Megan. "Good news, Spring. Mother is waiting for you at the sanctuary."

"It must be a mistake," says Petal. "She's only been here for a couple of days. No one talks to God so quickly."

"Jealousy is a sin, Petal. Don't tell me you're jealous." Buck steps toward Megan and Petal moves to block him.

"It must be a mistake, that's all," says Petal. "You should check on it."

Buck arches his eyebrows, and he removes the electric prod from a pocket on his jumpsuit. "Is there a problem here, Petal?"

Megan nudges Petal out of the way with a small hip check. She doesn't want to go to the sanctuary. She wants to escape with Petal, but she doesn't want her friend to get hurt, and she's afraid Buck will use that prod on both of them. He won't have a choice. He can't let an Angel challenge him so openly.

"No problem," Megan says. "The other Angels all said I wouldn't get to go to the sanctuary for a week at least, so this is a surprise." Megan shoots Petal a cautionary look. She tries to tell her not to intercede with her eyes. That she doesn't want her to get hurt. "I must be lucky."

"Yes, you are," says Buck. "Let's go." He grabs her elbow and pulls her off the path and toward the cathedral in the distance. Megan doesn't turn around, but she feels Petal's eyes burn her back.

"You and your friend need to be careful," Buck says.

"Careful about what?" Megan plays it stupid. What could he know about their plans?

"I saw Petal switch cups with you at dinner. She's messing with fire. You both are."

Megan sneaks a sideways glance at Buck. He looks sincerely worried. He's not using this information to hold over her or for some other hidden purpose. "Are you going to report us?"

Buck increases his pace toward the cathedral, now visible in the distance. "No, but I won't cover for you if others notice. Frankie keeps a close eye on you."

"Why don't you report us?"

Buck stops. "I like your spunk. You've got courage. When you see Mother, don't let her know you haven't drunk the punch. You need to act as if you had."

"Why are you here? You seem different. Not at all like Frankie."

"When I finished my tour with the Army, I came back to a country that didn't give a shit about me. All I can do is security, and this gig seemed better than most."

Megan smirks. "So, you're not a true believer?"

"I didn't say that. Come on. Mother is waiting." Buck takes crisp, long strides toward the Cathedral, making it clear their discussion is over.

Once inside, Buck walks Megan behind the altar and pauses at the door to the enclaves. "Remember what I told you." He doesn't wait for her to answer and steps through the automatic doors.

Megan moves inside and is greeted by Ivy, a smile on the older woman's face. "Are you ready for the next step? Are you ready to talk to God?"

Megan swallows the lump that's formed in her throat. She's not sure what to say, but Buck nudges her foot. She has to say something, so she says simply, "Yes," and tries to add a measure of breathless wonder into her voice for affect.

Ivy glances at Buck. "Thank you. I'll take over from here."

"Of course." He shoots Megan a stern look before he turns and leaves.

"Are you nervous?" Ivy asks Megan.

Megan is nervous, completely scared out of her mind really, but she'd feel differently if she had drunk the punch. She lies and says what Ivy wants to hear. "I'm excited. I hope I'm worthy of this gift."

That seems to satisfy Ivy because she smiles back at Megan and leads her down the hallway. At the end of the corridor, there's a black door with "Sanctuary" in white letters at eye level.

Ivy opens the door and reveals a vast, open space with tall ceilings. It feels like a warehouse divided by five-foot tall screens that make private spaces. Megan catches a flash of yellow in the distance. An Angel who looks to be in her mid-twenties slips behind a screen.

"Welcome to the sanctuary. We have almost one hundred chapels here. We use the chapels to communicate directly with God." Ivy points to a series of glass offices that ring the open space on the second floor like a balcony that oversees the entire operation. "My priestesses use those workstations to make sure everything functions smoothly."

Ivy grabs Megan's elbow and leads her inside one of the screened-in spaces. Inside is a steel tube slightly larger than a coffin. She says, "This is a chapel."

She presses a button on the side of the tube, and the top opens on a hinge. "Inside is a gelatin-like substance. We call it God's Tears. You'll go inside, and it will help you talk to God. It blocks out all Earthly distractions so you can communicate with Him directly."

Megan's stomach twists. "We have to go in there? Why can't we just pray or something like that?"

Ivy chuckles. "I can communicate with Him that way, but it's taken me a lifetime of training and prayer to accomplish. This is a shortcut. He needs your help and can't wait so long. Don't worry. It's safe and comfortable really. Take off your jumpsuit."

"Why?"

"We don't want anything between you and God. It interferes with His ability to communicate with you."

Megan still hesitates with her hand on the zipper.

"Now isn't the time to be shy," Ivy says. "This is the only way for you to talk directly with Him."

Megan glances at the offices that ring the warehouse space.

Ivy chuckles. "Don't worry about the priestesses. They're only doing their part."

She can't delay any longer, otherwise Ivy might suspect she didn't drink any of the punch. She unzips her suit and steps out of it. The chilly air sends goosebumps across her naked body.

"Good." Ivy unfolds a tablet from her pocket and slides her hand along the screen. The pendant around Megan's neck vibrates.

Ivy's breath brushes against Megan's neck. She touches the clasp on the chain, it opens, and she removes the necklace.

Megan says, "I thought the chain couldn't be removed."

"Only when you talk directly to God in the chapel." Ivy grabs a small mask from a hook on one of the screens.

"What's that?"

Ivy points to the tube. "God's Tears will totally surround you and support you. It automatically adjusts to your body temperature, so you'll be more comfortable than when you were a baby in the womb. Still, we need the mask to send you oxygen and keep your breathing clear. This mask will cover your eyes, nose, and mouth."

Ivy slips the mask over Megan's face and adjusts the straps so it's secure. "It's time now."

A small plastic step stool with three steps leads upward into the steel tube. Megan fights hard against the impulse to run. She uses all her willpower to climb those stairs and slip into the chapel.

She sinks into the gelatin substance. She's not sure what to expect, but a rather pleasant sensation washes over her and she shuts her eyes. The oxygen flows, and she breathes easily.

Ivy closes the cover on the tube and Megan opens her eyes.

She's in a meadow filled with wildflowers. A warm breeze blows through her hair. The blue sky smiles at her and the golden sun caresses her face. Even without the punch, she doesn't feel scared at all. She feels content and wonders what will happen next.

She forces two names into her head, Felicity Sanders and Megan Smith, but after a few seconds, they float away on a gentle breeze.

Ivy settles in a chair beside Lily. "Well doctor, how's she doing?"

Lily points to a set of readings, "Her heart rate is a little fast, but look at her brain functions. It's lighting up like a Christmas tree. She's very advanced."

Ivy smiles as she looks at the computer screen. It allows her to see and hear everything Megan does. It taps into her brain to project the images and the sounds. This program lets the subjects create their own environment. It makes the experience feel real, as if God is exactly who they expect Him to be all along. "I like the wildflowers. She's a bit of an artist."

"Yes, she is. Look." Lily points to the scene as it develops around Megan. Animals appear, a stream, an orchard, butterflies. "She's already building a complex environment. So soon. It's remarkable. Which protocol shall we use?"

"I just want to introduce her to God. Nothing else yet. And maximize the pleasure and addictive portions of the brain."

"That's a lot for her to absorb on the first session," says Lily. "It could damage her brain function."

"Do as I say."

The world develops more fully, and a presence walks into view. It's Megan's version of God, and the image surprises Ivy. Her idea of a holy presence is a young, dark-skinned woman. It reminds Ivy of one of her Angels but she can't recall which one.

"Odd," says Lily. "I've never seen one of the Angels imagine a god-like figure like that before. Most are old and male with long white hair."

"Odd indeed," says Ivy.

CHAPTER 39

The pavement in District 3 shines like polished silver. No potholes or cracks diminish its luster and no trash swirls about. The buildings — modern glass structures, sparkle like gemstones. All the lampposts work, and the lights from restaurants and stores brighten the streets, transforming night into dusk. Shadows lurk in the nooks and crannies, but they're nothing like the sinister ones in the ghetto. I wonder if the old-timer from the ghetto could move unseen in these parts? Probably not.

People walk the streets, but the neighborhood feels like a ghost town. Only a few residents stroll out and about and at least two bodyguards trail each one. A few paces in front of me, an aged woman, dressed in a fine purple overcoat and a pink hat, glides on a personal walker as she holds the leash of a small dog. Two bodyguards trail close behind her.

Her perfume, a heavy floral scent, follows her like a train on a long dress. She must have bathed in it the way old people sometimes do. Either they can't smell as well as they used to, or they've grown so accustomed to the fragrance they drench themselves with an overwhelming amount so it registers. She strikes me as a person who likes to register.

A pristine park has an immaculate lawn, benches, and a fountain. It's so different from Kissing Park, the two can't reasonably be placed in the same category. An electric fence surrounds this park and a private guard blocks the gate to restrict access. Only dues-paying neighbors can enter, but it's empty: no kids, no lovers, no old, married couples. No pigeons. No sense hanging out in the park where people don't eat. They'd starve. All in all, I prefer my version of Kissing Park when we were young. Everyone and anyone could use it.

A few vehicles zip past me on the street. They're all secure, black SUVs built to military specifications. Bulletproof glass. Reinforced panels. Run flat tires. It looks like District 3 is preparing for an invasion, but in reality, they're living through a siege. They might not know it, but those walls they're building, those armed checkpoints, are keeping them in as much as they're keeping others out.

It's been a few months since I've been in one of the posh districts, and this one strikes me as more desperate than those in New York City. But maybe that's a function of time and space. Small, granular changes can become major sandstorms if ignored long enough. That's how the country got in this mess. The divide between rich and poor inched wider until it caved the ground out from the middle class and created a yawning chasm. Inevitable political changes followed the economic ones, which only made the chasm wider.

Fancy restaurants and shops take up much of the street level. Most of the shops are closed. The restaurants are open but not crowded. It's early, so diners might stroll in later, but I doubt it. These people don't feel safe to go out any more. They have private chefs to cook for them. Most of the bodyguards gather by the doors in unorganized knots, vaping and leaning against buildings, wasting time. A few check me out as I walk past them, but they see a kindred soul in me. The smart ones know by my posture, by my stride, that I'm one of them.

I wonder which side they'll take when a revolution starts. Will they defend their rich patrons, or will they side with their own? It's a hard call. Most hate those they call boss. I can see them turning on their masters, but only if they think the other side can win.

A few Homeland SUVs, filled with heavily armed agents, roll past me. Neither Homeland nor the regular police bother to patrol the district on foot. They leave that work to the private police hired by the residents. Homeland is here to respond to "terrorists," an ever-increasing category filled with those who can't abide with the status quo any longer. The word has practically lost all meaning and is now used to describe anyone who disagrees with the Originalists.

Luckily, my walking tour of District 3 is a brief one. Otherworldly Experience is only a few blocks from the checkpoint. I turn right down a main drag and see life ahead of me. A gaggle of four young men strut down the street. Six bodyguards trail them and two lead the way. An inefficient formation. With that many guards, a few should flank them, but their protectors are going through the motions. Either they're not worried about threats or they don't care. I'm betting on the latter.

A half-dozen SUVs are parked in front of the virtual reality shop, which is brightly lit. It stands out in the otherwise sedate neighborhood. An old-fashioned, blue, neon sign reads "Otherworldly Experiences."

I've got to be smart. I need a lead, an address. Megan's a smart, tough young woman, but these Farm people are well organized and funded. They'll know how to break a girl like Megan. They'd have lots of practice doing it, so she can't hold out for long.

Otherworldly stretches for an entire city block. Two guards, armed with M18s, flank the entrance to the store. The four young men stroll past them without hesitation, and the guards don't bother questioning them. They'll treat me differently.

The bodyguards go inside a different door. One that's not lit. That door, the one for bodyguards, is manned only by a single armed guard. A waiting area. An option for me.

I'm not sure which door to use when I spot another armed sentry, who guards a plain-looking door at the end of the street. I meander toward him. Above that entrance is The Farm's symbol blazed in gold. A wooden sign below it reads, "Total Otherworldly Extreme, a Private Club." Bingo.

The guard is in his early forties and heavyset. His body borders that murky area where fat and muscle merge. Back in the day, people called that hard fat. He's wearing all black with body armor and a baseball cap with Otherworldly Security in white block lettering.

His sharp eyes assess me as I approach. His legs tense as he drops the assault rifle to chest height and speaks in a low grumble. He sounds how I imagine a grizzly bear would sound, if it could speak.

"I think you're lost, friend. The main door is back that way." He nudges the barrel of his gun toward the lit entrance. "This is for private clients only."

I lift my hands out to my side to put him at ease. "I'm looking for the private club. My employer would like to join."

"So would I, but it doesn't work like that, friend. Only those with appointments get in, and the main office vets them carefully. He'll have to contact them and set it up."

I can take this guard out. It won't be easy. He's a mountain and he holds the gun steady at my chest with an easy confidence, which means he's used it, or one like it, before. I'd need a quick diversion to move his eyes off me and then I'd chop him in the throat. I'd have to get my weight behind it to crush his larynx. I couldn't take any chances that he'd be able to shake it off.

Reaching for the Smith and Wesson would take too much time but disabling him won't get me what I want. Even after I incapacitate him, I'd still have a problem getting in the club. The steel door behind him is undoubtedly locked from the inside and no one's likely to just let me wander inside while the big man is on the ground. A video camera will record the entire incident. Armed guards will flood the area in less than a minute.

Brute force isn't going to work, so I smile and try a different angle. "I just do what my boss tells me. He wants me to check out the place first. If I don't, he'll fire me. He's that type."

The big guy shrugs. "I know that type, but there's not much I can do for you, friend. Tell him it's great. They don't have a problem attracting the richest this town has to offer. I've never heard any complaints."

"How about an incentive?" I pull a roll of money from my pocket and peel off a hundred-dollar bill. "After all, we're all capitalists."

He doesn't move, but his eyes lock on to the bill in my hand. He's tempted, but one hundred is not enough for him to rankle his boss.

I peel off another hundred. "I'm desperate. What do you say?"

He takes the bills with his left hand, careful to keep the assault rifle pointed at me with his right. "I'll take your money, friend, but all I can do is call over the manager. You can press him, but he ain't gonna let you in. Pocket change won't work with him, unless you've got a suitcase somewhere. Even then, he's the prickly sort."

"Thanks. It's worth a shot."

The mountain talks into a radio, and a few minutes later the door opens. A thin, well-dressed man stands in the doorway. He's wearing a navy pinstripe, three-piece suit, white shirt, with a gold tie and matching handkerchief in his front breast pocket. Highly polished black shoes and a gold watch complete the ensemble.

He's in his thirties. He'd like people to think he has money, but he doesn't. The gold watch is a good fake, but it's still fake, and all that polish on his loafers can't hide that they're at least a few years old. He looks annoyed and peers down at me past a pointy nose.

He speaks with a muddled European accent. It's also fake. He's mixing up an English accent with an Australian one. He's probably never left the country.

"What's the problem, Robert?" he asks the guard primly.

"I'm sorry to bother you, sir, but this *gentleman* insists he needs to see you. He says he represents a significant Originalist who wants to inquire about joining."

The manager frowns. "This is highly irregular. No one gets in without an appointment. Let me see your identification card. I'll let you know if your employer should bother to call and set up an appointment."

I hand him my card, and he swipes it through a reader. A few seconds later, his demeanor changes, and he looks at me with fresh eyes. "You're in luck, Mr. Cabbott. We can make an exception for your boss." The manager opens the door and clears space for me to walk past him. The security guard lowers his rifle and looks confused.

The inside appears like someone's mixed modern technology with an old-fashioned country club. A lush, burgundy-colored carpet covers the floor, and mahogany paneling stretches halfway up the walls. It's reminiscent of a library in an old university club one of my former employers frequented, but modern flat panels adorn the top half of the walls.

Even though the place must have cost a fortune to decorate, it feels like a whorehouse. Underneath all that polish and wood and technology is a sleazy layer you'd find in a ghetto brothel. The place reeks of it. I wonder if I should say anything, maybe stuff a note into a comment box somewhere.

Images of exotic scenes like mountaintops, underwater reefs, and ancient ruins flash across the screens. The image of a beautiful young woman catches my attention. A large glass cross, enclosed in a star, spins on a mirrored table. Only the star spins. The symbol of The Farm in motion. I'm in the right place.

The fake quasi-European prick speaks in a smooth, well-practiced voice. "My name is Decker Kirkland, and I'm the manager of this establishment. Welcome to Otherworldly Extreme, a private club like no other in the world." He points at a metal detector and says, "I'm sorry about the inconvenience, but a necessary precaution in today's troubling times."

An attractive young brunette with long legs operates the machine. She smiles sweetly and hands me a small plastic tray. Another armed guard stands behind her, his eyes fixed on me, his hand resting on the grip of an automatic handgun. He must be the brother of the mountain who guards the door. They share the same body type and look, which could only be the result of the same genes. He's a few years younger than his brother and he looks meaner, which hardly seems possible. This one likes to fight.

I reluctantly drop the Smith and Wesson in the tray.

"And your phone also," says the brunette.

I glance at Kirkland and he says, "We'll keep those items here and give them back to you when you leave. We never allow phones or anything that can record images inside the club."

When I pass through the metal detector, Kirkland plays tour guide. "We have our experience chambers down that hallway." He points to his left but walks to his right. "That's where we have our conference rooms and my office. Otherworldly Extreme is the most exclusive private club in the world. It costs one million dollars to join and each experience costs twenty thousand – U.S.," he says, as if we are somewhere the currency would be something else. "I hope those numbers won't scare away Mr. Jeffries."

Those numbers should scare away everyone, but I play along. "He's willing to pay for the best," I say. "Money is just a means to an end for him." I'm not sure what that means but I heard a wealthy person say it once, and other rich people nodded in agreement, like it made a lot of sense.

"Of course," says Kirkland. "Well put." He opens the door to one of the conference rooms. Same décor as the lobby but smaller, with a cherry wood table in the center and a full-sized glass refrigerator along one of the walls.

He points to the fridge. "Help yourself to some refreshments. We have an exclusive brand of organic apple cider that's outrageously good. Locally grown and fresh."

"Maybe later," I say. "Why is the private club so much more expensive than the regular service?" I know this club is an important puzzle piece, but I need to understand what they do here and how it might relate to the cult and Megan.

Kirkland smiles. "The two aren't close to the same. Imagine the difference between riding a bicycle and driving a Ferrari."

"Quite a difference."

"That's about right. The regular virtual reality experience is truly remarkable. The guests use full-sized helmets that immerse them into the virtual world. We even use well-placed electrodes to stimulate realistic experiences on the chest and other areas. Those experiences feel as lifelike as we can make them. In many cases, more intense than real life, but they depend on computer simulations, and that's limited. Plus, we can only stimulate so many nerves with the helmet and the electrodes."

Kirkland touches a button on a screen and a sleek, stainless steel tube appears. "For *extreme experiences*, we fully submerge our guests into a special substance inside these experience chambers. This truly enhances the experience. The guests literally feel more connected to the virtual world than the real one."

"So, the connectivity is better?" I ask.

"Not just that." Kirkland smiles before he continues. A well-practiced expression to make sure his target listens to what he says next. "We offer *real* experiences. These experience chambers are connected to real people, so we avoid computer simulations. No two experiences are the same. Every experience is unique. It's more real than real life."

More real than real life? They connect to real people? I'm beginning to understand The Farm's connection, and I don't like it. "So, if my boss wanted sexual experiences, he could, in effect, have sex with a real person virtually."

"Oh, yes. And the sex will be better than anything he's ever experienced. Our Angels are specially trained, and our technology touches upon all his nerves. I guarantee that it will blow his mind." Kirkland beams a bright smile, and I resist the urge to rip out his throat.

"And what if my employer's tastes tend to the younger side?"

"No worries. Any desire can be filled."

A more sinister idea pops into my mind. "What if my employer likes to hurt people?"

"Oh, certainly. The Angel on the other end will experience everything as if they were together in person. Once the experience ends, the Angel won't suffer any lasting injuries. Only vague memories."

"And if he wants to experience killing someone."

Kirkland grins. "That can be arranged – for an extra charge. In those cases, the Angels actually die. Their brains believe the injuries are real and what the brain believes, is reality, no? But there's more."

"More?"

"Yes. The client can alter his avatar. In this way, he can appear and feel young again." Kirkland's eyes light up. This is his clincher—the final argument he uses to sell clients. Every good sales pitch has one. "We can adjust the avatar based upon the client's wishes, so he can be both younger and stronger. Thinner. Taller. Whatever he wishes. How much is that worth? To go back in time and practically make yourself a god?"

It's a good question, and I see why he uses this last pitch as his clincher. Who wouldn't want to be younger, or stronger, or better looking? Even if it's just for an hour in a virtual reality? The wealthy would pay dearly for a reality that allows them to become gods.

"How will he know if it works the way you say?"

"Oh, we offer a free experience to prove our claims." He makes a show of looking at his watch. "I need to step out for a second. We can discuss other details when I return." He leaves and shuts the door behind him.

I need to find a connection between this place and The Farm. I need an address. A keyboard sits on the table, so I attack it. There's not much functionality, but one of the options leads me to a screen with more information about Otherworldly Extreme. Lists of locations. Typical experiences. Costs.

Nothing about The Farm or who owns the place. I search the program, but it doesn't give away any secrets. I'll have to wring the information out of Kirkland, which makes me smile. He's no innocent in this. I'll enjoy giving him an experience that's more real than real life.

I spot the refrigerator. *What did Kirkland say again? Something about locally grown apple cider.*

I open the door and remove a glass jug with a label on it: Organically produced apple cider for Otherworldly Extreme. Bottled at The Farm in Walden, PA.

Walden, Pennsylvania? That's only a few hours away from the city. And they used a capital T for The and F for Farm, which means it's a name. They're too cute.

I replace the bottle and grin. I have a town at least and that's more than good enough. There's no need to waste time here. I want to tell Kate and get moving.

I try the door and it's locked. Locked from the outside. The hair on the back of my neck stands up.

Caesar's voice barks in my head, "What a clusterfuck you've created here, Trainee. This is worse than the Dubai debacle. You acted like a pimply kid at prom. So overeager, you missed all the signs. It's enough to make me hurl my lunch."

The guard didn't think I would get in. The manager was about to dismiss me until he scanned my card. The fake Samuel Jeffries shouldn't have made that big of an impression on him. He couldn't have recognized the name since it's not real. Why did he turn so accommodating?

He saw my name and then he changed. Oh, for fuck's sake! I was so intent on getting inside, I ignored the obvious signs that something was screwed up. These Farm people must know I'm looking for them. I try the door again, and it's bolted shut. Reinforced by steel, the wood frame won't splinter if I throw my shoulder into it.

"Trapped by a slippery talking, good-for-nothing-snake-oil-salesman," says Caesar. "You'd better move quickly or that broad of yours is a goner. If they know about you..."

The Fates are screwing with me again, and now they're after Kate.

Two things are certain. I need to escape from here and fast. And I'm going to kill that prick Kirkland. He doesn't know it yet – but he's already dead.

CHAPTER 40

Every investigation has a turning point—the moment when the target realizes he's being hunted. Usually it happens right before I achieve my objective: an instant before I put a bullet in someone's skull, or kidnap my target, or steal a valuable piece of intel. On rare occasions, the turning point happens sooner, before the end of my investigation, like now. I won't lie about it. It makes everything more difficult.

The Farm knows I'm after them, but how? I can think of only three likely possibilities. One, Mr. Peterson grabbed a photo of me off his surveillance system and sent it to the cult. Possible, yet highly unlikely. Even if Peterson knows how to contact these people, a coward like him wouldn't want to get involved so directly. Second, Darleen could have told Frankie. Another unlikely choice. She truly hates him, and she'd only have a vague description to tell him about me. That would be useless. They'd never identify me that way. I'm hard to find.

So that leaves only one possibility left, and it's the worst. They know Brad is dead, and they've reviewed the surveillance video from the apartment building. I thought I looked away at all the right times, but I could've missed a camera. No one's perfect, least of all me. Somehow, they got their hands on that tape, which means they've got government connections. They have money and now they have connections. They're becoming more formidable by the minute.

I reach for my phone, but they took it from me when I entered the club. I need to contact Kate right away. If they know about me, they probably know about her. She's in danger, but there's nothing I can do about that until later. First, I need a way out of here. When in crisis mode, always prioritize and handle the immediate crisis first. Wasting time worrying about next steps is a sure way to get killed.

I grab a chair, swing it over my head and smash it into the video camera attached to the ceiling. I don't need them watching me. Next, I tap on the windows. Four-inch bulletproof glass. Even if I heave a chair into it, it'll hold.

There has to be a way out. The ceiling vents are too small to fit through. Another dead end.

I've only one play left. The small tab of plastic explosives concealed in my boot. I pop open the heel and remove the tab. It's powerful stuff. Too powerful for this, but I'm desperate. I can blow the windows or the door. The windows are the better option. The mountainous security guards are probably behind the door and the street looks clear.

I flip the cherry table on its side and secure the tab to the glass window. I activate the detonator, which gives me ten seconds, and jump behind the table. The explosion shatters the glass and much of the wall. Shards pound the table and the building rocks.

The table holds. At least it's made from real wood. Score one for the bad guys. For a million dollars to join the club, at least they didn't cheap out with crap furniture.

I toss the table to the side and jump through the gaping hole that used to be the windows. Freedom. I hit the ground running, away from the main street and the entrance to the club.

An SUV screeches to a halt in front of me, blocking the side street. Three private security guys jump out. They're armed to the teeth, and all I have is a small, ceramic throwing knife concealed in my belt. It's not worth pulling out.

I run back the other way. Maybe the club's security guards won't leave the shop. I could use a break, but I don't get one. Two giant shadows step into the street directly in front of me.

Kirkland stands behind them, points and shouts, "That's him! Take him alive."

I glance over my shoulder and the three private security guards move in on me in a classic triangle formation, guns trained on me. I'm no longer worried about the guns, though. Kirkland screwed up. Now I know they won't fire. They want to take me alive. Good luck with that.

The two giant-sized guards block my way out. Robert, who guarded the door, hands his assault rifle to his brother, who then hands both to Kirkland.

Robert talks in a calm, sure voice that floats toward me in a confident wave. "Listen, friend, this isn't going to work out well for you. Get on your knees, turn around, and let me cuff you. Otherwise, you leave me with no choice. I'm going to have to pound you into next week."

His brother snickers and says, "Let's pound him anyway."

"Shut up, Joey. We don't need to hurt the little guy." I'm no little guy, but to these two, I might as well be a toddler.

Robert acts as if he's in control, thinking he has every advantage. I've got to flip the table, and quickly.

I stalk toward him. "You know what they do here. Your brother is too stupid to understand, but you know. It's not right. They have to be stopped."

The big fellow shrugs. "It's not my concern, friend. On your knees or you'll wake up tomorrow after I give you a beating."

I'm within a step of him now. He's massive. I don't have a lot of choices. Punching or kicking him in the body would be mostly useless. Too much fat and muscle for me to cause him any real pain. I've got to hit him in a sensitive spot like the face or neck or knee, yet he's moved into a competent defensive position, hands around his head. He doesn't care if I punch him anywhere else. All he has to do is protect his face and get his hands on me.

"If you put it that way. I'd rather not spend the night in the hospital." I lower my hands and move forward. He subconsciously lowers his in response. He's used to people giving up at the sight of his bulk, so this is what he expects.

I shift my weight as if I'm about to get on my knees, but instead I pull my head back and snap it forward, bashing it into his nose with all the force I can muster. I've caught him by surprise. Everyone expects a punch or a kick, but no one anticipates a head butt. The skull is like a club with thick bones, strong neck and core muscles. A fine weapon.

I connect hard and shatter his nose. He wobbles backward and falls on his ass.

I know how he feels. His nose felt like a brick, and I'm momentarily dazed.

His brother curses. "What the fuck!" He rushes me before I can focus, grabbing me by the shoulders, and slamming me against the building. His face twists angrily. "I'm going to kill you."

He's serious as he circles his ham-like hands around my neck—vices that shut off my oxygen.

I jam the heel of my palm into his chin as hard as I can. I don't have much leverage, but I snap back his blockhead. He loosens his grip for a second, which lets me gasp some air.

He spits blood and a chunk of his tongue, but that doesn't lessen his resolve. He grips my throat tighter this time. Lights burst in front of my eyes and his face twists. I reach for his sausage-sized fingers to break one, but the world goes fuzzy and gray.

He's going to kill me. I'm not afraid to die. I lost that fear a long time ago. Part of me embraces the idea, but to be killed by an idiot like Joey is beyond embarrassing. It disrespects all the better people who have tried over the years.

I find his pinkie and yank upward with all my strength. It snaps. I've broken it, but he still holds on.

A light shines in the distance. Bright. Piercing. It's coming closer or I'm going to it. I can't tell if it's real or a hallucination created by my oxygen-deprived brain.

Joey turns and squints. His grip loosens, and he growls, "What the fuck is that?"

A Homeland SUV barrels down on us. It drives right over Robert like he's a speed bump and skids sideways, plowing into two members of the extraction team who had closed in on us from the alley. The driver door opens, and a massive shadow jumps out. An M18 fires in short bursts and blows apart the extraction team.

Joey is so confused he's mostly forgotten about me. I jam my right thumb into his eye and press hard. He claws at my hand. My thumb stabs into his eye and blood streams down his face. When I pull, I yank out his eyeball. He'll never use it again, and I let go.

"I can't see," he says as he stumbles around, hands clutched to his face.

The driver of the Homeland SUV steps forward and bashes Joey in the head with the butt of his assault rifle. The blow knocks the big guy out.

My savior smiles at me. He's truly a giant—a full head taller than me and eighty pounds heavier. A red afro and curly beard contrasts with black skin. A black T-shirt strains to cover his chiseled body. He's as large as the two brothers, but there's no fat on him. On the shirt, white lettering says, "Homeland Security – Special Agent. Deal with it."

"Thanks, Gabriel," I say.

"I was in the neighborhood, so I thought I'd drop by."

"Hey, now that you're a special agent for Homeland, aren't you supposed to warn people before you start shooting?"

He grins. "I'm new. I missed orientation."

Everyone is disabled but Kirkland. He lifts his hands in the air and whimpers with his back pressed to the building. The assault rifles lie at his feet, useless.

I step over to the weasel. "What's The Farm? Where are they?"

His terrified eyes flicker between Gabriel and me, unsure who frightens him more.

"Tell me about The Farm."

He pisses his pants and his voice loses the fake European accent. "I don't know much. I overheard some of the bosses talking. They provide the Angels for the experiences."

"Are they in Walden? The same place as the apple orchard."

He nods. "Don't tell them I said anything."

I glance at Gabriel. "Let me borrow your handgun."

"Sure." He tosses me a Glock.

"D-Don't shoot," sweat is pouring out of Kirkland now like a freakin' geyser. He's practically drowning himself.

I point the gun at his forehead. "Do you know anything else about them?"

"N-n-no. They'll kill me if they know I've told you this much. Don't shoot me."

"It's too late for that," I say.

"Why?"

"You're already dead." I pull the trigger and he's gone.

I toss the gun back to Gabriel.

"A friend of yours?" he asks.

"He pimped out teenagers as sex toys. He got off easy."

We both get in the SUV.

"We need to go to District 12," I say. "My friend's in danger."

Gabriel blasts down the street.

"Let me use your phone." Gabriel hands it to me and I call Kate, but the call goes straight to voicemail.

I force my mind away from what ifs and ask Gabriel how he found me.

He grins. "I'm a special agent at Homeland now, right? I know stuff. Oh, there are two farms in Walden. Both operated by a cult we don't know that much about."

"You could have called and told me."

"And then I figured you would've gone off on your own. Even the Lone Ranger needed Tonto. This way I get to tag along, right? How else am I going to pay your sorry ass back for saving my butt?"

And now I owe Gabriel.

I only hope we get to Kate before The Farm does.

CHAPTER 41

Gabriel skids the SUV to a stop in front of Kate's building. I jump from the passenger door before the vehicle fully stops. Someone's leaving the building as I reach the door, so I hold it open for Gabriel and he hands me his Glock.

We bound up the stairs and race to Kate's apartment. It's ajar, and my heart backflips in my chest. Not a good sign. I shoulder my way in and swing the gun in an arch that covers the empty living room. No one's in sight. I check Megan's room first, Gabriel behind me. Nothing.

Next, I open the door to Kate's bedroom and stop in the doorway. No one's here, but I'm frozen in place. The room is identical in size and shape to Megan's, but Kate has hung a dozen paintings on the wall. All watercolors she painted. A version of me, over the years, appears in each painting. One has me as a teenager in Kissing Park and another, a close proximity to what I look like today, sans beard.

The paintings are more than just random scenes with me in them. They tell a story of what could have been, from our first kiss to who we could have been as a couple together. Emotions jump off the canvases: longing, love, passion. They imagine a possible version of me, of us together, but it's a fantasy. It's not real. They don't show the demons inside me. The part of me that likes to hurt people. The part that's bad, that would have poisoned any chance of happiness Kate and I could have had together.

Gabriel says, "Your friend has real talent, but who's the ugly guy in the paintings? He ruins them."

"Funny," I say.

"She'd sell them if she changed muses. I'll volunteer to sit for her. I figure that'll make all the difference."

"Let's get her back first." I tear myself away from the paintings and go back to the living room. A splatter of blood dots the floor by the edge of the couch. It's not much, just a few drops, probably from a bloody lip or a scratch. The couch is twisted out of place, the coffee table is tossed away from the couch and the throw pillows are scattered about the place.

I picture what happened. The extraction team picked the lock and surprised Tina and Kate. The team had at least four members: three who snuck into the room and one who waited with the SUV out front. Tina scratched one of the goons who came for them, and Kate threw a punch and maybe a kick or two. The extraction team would have been professionals. They would've had no problem taking the two women.

At least The Farm wants Kate unharmed. If they wanted to kill her, she'd be dead, and they would have left the body. They must have plans for her. That's good. It buys me time to get her back. At least a day and probably two.

I sink onto the couch, and everything catches up to me like a sudden typhoon. I've screwed up and now Kate's missing. I've fucked up before, but never like this. I've lived through more than my share of low points, but I feel shattered as if my heart has exploded into a million tiny pieces. If I could trade my life for Kate's, I'd sign on the dotted line without hesitation.

Gabriel points to Kate's tablet on the cocktail table. "Looks like there's a message."

A notice flashes on the home screen. Tina set up an automatic notification to alert us if The Farm responded to the message we sent them on the swap site. I click on it and read the response.

We've taken her. Stop investigating and we won't harm Kate or Megan. It's better this way. Make the right choice, Stevie. Otherwise...

"Get back in the game, Cupcake," barks Caesar. "Now's not the time to feel sorry for yourself. You've got work to do."

He's right.

I hand the tablet to Gabriel whose red eyebrows scrunch up. "I thought you went by Steven, right? Who calls you Stevie?"

"Good question, and what happened to Tina?"

A noise comes from Megan's room and my blood jolts. We open the closet and find Tina. Duct tape covers her mouth and binds her hands and feet.

I cut her loose and she's all fire and vinegar. "Those bastards took Kate. I tried to stop them, but there were too many — three of them and they were armed."

A nasty bruise that will soon turn purple and black darkens her left eye.

I introduce Tina to Gabriel and walk her to the living room where I hand her the tablet.

Tina's voice turns acidic. "So, this is your fault. They found out you were after them and they came for Kate."

I could argue with her, but she's right. They recognized us at Brad's apartment. I should have found a way to destroy the surveillance system first.

"Where did they take them?" asks Tina. "Tell me you know where these dick wads are located."

"A small town called Walden."

Tina steps toward the door. "Let's go."

I grab her arm. "Not yet. We all need to be on the same page. We can't afford another mistake."

I tell Gabriel everything I've learned, starting with Megan's abduction, Frankie, Otherworldly Experience, the organic apple cider. Everything.

He takes it all in. He's sharp and thoughtful. It doesn't take long before he wraps his mind around what we're dealing with.

When I finish, I ask him, "So now it's your turn, big man. How come you said the cult owns two farms?"

"The government pays close attention to cults and militia groups. They're worried that some of these groups might take up with rebels in the ghettos to initiate an uprising."

"The enemy of my enemy is my friend type of thing," I say.

"It's a reasonable concern, but I doubt we have that much to worry about, right? I mean most of these militias are white nationalists and want nothing more than their own little white nirvana. Still, not all of them feel that way. And if they combined with the ghettos, the government would have a hard time with a war on two fronts — the cities and the rural areas. Now if we add in some of the industrial sectors, the Originalists have real problems. Those meat packers are jammed with angry people, and they're more likely to join with the ghettos, right?"

I nod, and he continues.

"Anyway, The Farm appeared on their radar two years ago. They couldn't find out much about them, just rumors. Homeland caught its first break a few months ago and placed an asset inside the cult. So far, they haven't figured out who's behind the operation, although you're right about Otherworldly. They do provide Angels for their experiences. And even worse, they sell some of these Angels to wealthy business people around the world as sex slaves. We're talking about bad people."

"What the fuck!" says Tina. "Why hasn't Homeland shut these assholes down?"

"Sex trafficking is a huge business—over 35 billion dollars. We're looking into it, but more than two and a half million people, mostly woman and girls, are sucked up in it. We used to be an importer of these women. Now we export."

"With that much money in play, some wealthy folks must be making a ton off of it," I say. "It won't be easy to shut it down."

"Bingo," says Gabriel.

"But this is going on right here," says Tina. "And we know about it."

Gabriel shrugs. "I've just joined Homeland and I don't think Sheppard even knows about this group. It's bad, but it's small potatoes in the grand scheme of things, right? There are so many risks in the country, this one is a low priority. Plus, we want to know who controls the group first. Shutting down a farm or two might make us feel better, but it won't do much if the head guy starts up a new operation in a month in another state."

It sucks but it makes sense. Sheppard and Gabriel have to prioritize their efforts, and the ghettos represent a bigger threat than a cult like The Farm.

Tina looks at me, a light-bulb-just-came-on look in her eyes. "Wait a second. Sheppard? You know the president?"

She shoots me a look like I'm a traitor for not telling her, but I'm not going to fall for it. "Yeah, maybe I know the president-elect. So what?"

Tina says, "I thought he had more sense than to hang out with a guy like you. That's all."

Gabriel snickers.

"Gabriel, you said they have two locations in Walden."

"They operate two different farms, both in Walden. The farms are a front for the cult."

"Do we know which one they're using to hold Megan?" I ask.

He shakes his head. "We communicate with our asset infrequently and I just read the file a few hours ago. Our asset has a satellite phone hidden on location somewhere. We sent the asset a communication today with Megan's picture. Hopefully, we'll get a response tonight."

"We can't wait around for a hopefully," says Tina.

I feel the impulse also. It pulls at me to do something bold, but years of experience and training hold me steady. "We can't go to the wrong farm. We're only going to get one shot at this. We need to know."

Tina jabs her finger into my chest. "You screwed up and got Kate kidnapped. Now you had better fix this train wreck."

Gabriel grins at me. I know what he's thinking. He likes Tina. In spite of myself, I like her too.

"I'll get them both back," I say.

"We'll get them both back," Gabriel says. "And I have a team on standby when we need them."

"Well, let's get going," says Tina as she marches toward the door. "This circle jerk isn't getting us anywhere. And I don't have all the equipment to play along."

She's right. We have to go to Walden, but not yet. I have one stop to make first.

CHAPTER 42

Megan's thoughts churn in wild circles as she returns to the cabin where the other Angels wait for her. She wrestles with her experience in the chapel and what it means. Nothing in her life prepared her for this, yet here she is. She has to find a way to sort things out or they'll overwhelm her.

May greets her at the door, her voice breathless. "You went to the sanctuary and spoke to God?"

Megan isn't sure what to say. She was in the sanctuary, but did she actually speak to God? Maybe. It certainly felt that way. She never experienced anything like it before, but the entire vision felt surreal. One thing she's certain of — she wants to do it again. It's all she can think about.

Unable to put her thoughts into words, she just nods her head.

May hugs her. "It's amazing, isn't it?"

When May steps back, Megan searches for Petal who stands at the far end of the room, her arms crossed against her chest. She looks angry and doesn't say anything. Megan wants to tell her that God looks a lot like her, but she can't say that in front of the other Angels, who have all spoken to God before. How does God appear to them? Does everyone see Him the same way, or does a different version of Him exist for each person?

Before she can ask, Frankie opens the door, a torch in his hand. "Come on, Angels. We have a burning tonight. Everyone out." He speaks to everyone, but his eyes stick on Megan.

A fire burns in those eyes — hotter than the torch, and it scares her. She tries to avoid looking at him as she falls in line with the others and goes outside, but she sneaks a look anyway and doesn't like the satisfied grin on his face.

Outside, she smells moisture. It clings heavily to the cool night air and feels like the sky might open up at any minute. Frankie's torch blazes against a nearly complete black backdrop as he leads them through the hemp field. Men in red jumpsuits, holding torches, accompany other Angels marching with them, the atmosphere charged, as if they're headed to a concert.

Megan had been to only one concert in her life. Last year Eddie had to see the Goldfish. He fell in love with the two lead guitarists and singers, a brother-sister duo. They dye their entire bodies gold and perform naked. Eddie won't say which one he prefers, but he certainly wasn't alone. The large crowd felt electric.

They had tickets for the standing section and danced the entire night. By the end of the concert, she couldn't hear anymore, but she didn't mind. It was cool, a moment of fun that stands out in her childhood like an oasis in the desert.

The concert was in District 8, so their ticket included a bus ride. They boarded the bus at a checkpoint in their district and got off when they reached the venue. Afterward, they boarded the same bus, which took them back to District 12. The bus's windows were darkened, so Megan and her friends couldn't see much of the better districts. She managed to scrape away a tiny strip of paint. It looked clean and the air didn't smell rank, like spoiled food.

Megan searches out Petal and walks beside her. They have no privacy here, so they can't talk. She wants to tell Petal everything before she forgets it all. As it is, the details are starting to fade like a vivid dream she can't hang on to, leaving behind only echoes of the real thing and the need to do it again, right now. A maddening itch.

When they clear the hemp field she sees a round clearing on top of small hill. A half dozen priestesses in multi-colored jumpsuits form a circle, each with a lit torch. Others fill in the circle behind them. Megan can't count them in the darkness, but there must be over two hundred gathered together. At least a hundred Angels in yellow, many of whom look older than those Megan has seen so far. Most have purple armbands. They probably bused them in from the other farm.

Besides the Angels, all of the other color jumpsuits mingle here, creating a chaotic rainbow. Those in black, who send a shiver up Megan's spine, patrol the outside of the gathering.

Petal gently pulls on Megan's jumpsuit, stopping their progress and letting others stream past them. They end up along the outer rim of onlookers. The air smells like the incense from the enclaves. A bonfire burns in the center of the priestesses. Random crackles and pops fill the clearing and the smoke swirls above the crowd.

Music starts playing, a choir with three guitarists. They play a sweet song. When the second verse to the song starts, the crowd joins their voices to the choir and the night bursts with song.

Megan knows the second song, or at least the beginning of it. The choir leads the crowd through "Amazing Grace." Everyone sings and when the song ends, Ivy stands in the middle of the circle of priestesses, standing six-feet above the crowd on a pedestal. She wears a robe instead of her jumpsuit. It 's multicolored like her jumpsuit and glints in the firelight. She reminds Megan of the Goldfish. She has the same presence, one that demands to be seen and watched.

Her voice projects across the clearing, enhanced by a microphone and hidden speakers. "Close your eyes and breathe Him in." She closes her eyes.

Megan checks those around her and everyone has closed their eyes. Everyone except Petal, who scans the outside of the clearing.

After a long pause, Ivy opens her eyes. "Who can feel Him with us?"

An Angel to Megan's right, shouts, "I can."

Other people cry out. Do they speak out because they truly feel His presence or do they want to be special? Soon, the entire clearing rings with shouts, a desperate voice, all wanting to be heard. All agreeing with Ivy, their leader. In a weird way, Megan thinks she feels a presence also.

Ivy grins and lifts her arms. "I feel Him. He is here."

The crowd cheers.

"Once again, the Dark One tests us, and we answer that test. He wants to weaken our resolve. He..."

Megan loses track of Ivy's speech and scans the faces lit by torchlight. While most look rapt, as if they're looking upon God, a few seem scared. Megan wonders if the believers really believe, or just want to believe so badly, they've fooled themselves. She's not even sure what she believes at this point.

Ivy presses on, "We will not weaken. We will prevail! We will bring about the End of Days."

Those gathered around the clearing chant, "End of Days! End of Days! End of Days!"

The energy and passion in their collective voice explodes in the night air. Megan resists the urge to chant herself.

Two men, dressed in black, wheel in a naked young woman tied to a cross. The woman has blonde hair and resembles Megan. She's probably the same age, the same height, the same eye color. The men stop when they reach Ivy.

The girl struggles, the sluggish actions of someone subdued, someone drugged.

Ivy lifts her hands and the crowd silences. "The Dark One possessed our fair Angel. He tried to turn her against us, but he will not win. We are vigilant. What are we to do with our fallen angel?"

The crowd shouts as one, "Burn her! Burn her! Burn her!"

Ivy nods to her priestesses who bring their torches forward.

The crowd continues to chant, "Burn her!"

Megan wants to look away, but she can't. The energy, the chanting, the torches keep her eyes fixed forward.

One of the priestesses hands a torch to Ivy, who holds it above her head.

The chanting continues. "Burn her!"

Ivy lifts her head to the sky, as if she's talking to God.

"Burn her!"

"So be it!" She tosses the torch onto a small pile of kindling at the young girl's feet. The priestesses do the same, and red flames engulf the girl. Not ordinary flames, but darker and redder flames that look like they come from hell.

Megan gasps, still unable to look away.

The girl screams, and a shape rises behind her—a dark crimson creature with horns. It screams a defiant yell and vanishes.

Petal pulls at Megan's jumpsuit. "We've got to go now while everyone is distracted."

"Was that the Devil?"

"What do you think?"

"I don't know what to think?"

Petal frowns, "That's the incense in the air. It's effecting your ability to think. You're a science person. If you wanted to make flames that red, how would you do it?"

A small ray of clarity burns through the fog in Megan's brain. "I can think of a few chemicals that burn red."

"Right, and if you wanted to create a devil?"

"Maybe a small projector. The smoke would work like a screen. But it seemed so real. Are you sure?"

"I have no proof either way. All I know is that Mother is the Devil. Come on, we've got to go." Petal pulls Megan from the gathering. "We'll go to the apple orchard and cut through the hemp field. It's the fastest way to the cathedral and the sanctuary. We've got to get there before the crowd disperses. This way we can remove these pendants and escape. With any luck, we can reach the main road and hitchhike."

Petal grabs Megan's hand and pulls her faster. Small plants scrape against her legs.

Once they reach the apple trees, Petal sighs. She looks over her shoulder and says, "Good. No one's come after us. With a little luck, we'll make it."

Megan yanks Petal to a stop. Their luck has just run out.

CHAPTER 43

I point to an open space on the curb, and Gabriel pulls the SUV over.

"What are we doing here?" asks Tina.

"I have to see a priest about something important," I say.

"Since when did you get religion?"

"I'm not." I climb out of the car.

"We'll wait for you right here, as long as it takes," says Gabriel.

He doesn't know why I'm headed inside St. Thomas. Heck, I'm not totally sure, but the message from The Farm said I had to "make the right choice." The language seems odd under the circumstances and sounds a lot like what Father Paul told me early today. It could be a coincidence, but I'm not a big fan of coincidences.

I don't know how my growing demon problem relates to Kate and Megan, but my gut says they're twisted together, and I'm not going to ignore that feeling. Not now.

I open the heavy, wooden door, stand in the doorway, and let my eyes adjust to the dim light. A few wall sconces and a dozen candles by the altar offer just enough brightness to see the general contours of the old, dusty place. Without the sun streaming through the windows, it feels even emptier and hollower than earlier in the day.

A priest kneels at the altar, praying.

I head to him. Halfway there I call out, "Father Paul, I need to talk to you."

The priest stands and turns. He's thin with short dark hair, but he's thirty years older than Father Paul. He looks confused as he squints, "Excuse me, young man. Have we met?"

"I'm sorry. I'm looking for Father Paul." I look around the church and find no one else.

The aging priest frowns. "I'm sorry but you have the wrong church. There's no one named Father Paul here."

I grab his arm. "Listen, I've been here the last few days and met a young priest, about your height. Black hair, young, sharp eyes, he's new to the parish. Maybe you don't know him."

"You must have the wrong church. Some of these old buildings look the same. This one has been closed all week. I only just opened it an hour ago. This Sunday they're shutting it down for good. It's a shame, but attendance," he shrugs his thin shoulders, "isn't what it used to be."

He's telling me the truth, so I let go of his arm. If Father Paul isn't really a priest, then what is he, and how did he know who I am? This puzzle only gets more complicated.

I hear laughter. It's high-pitched and mocking—the blasted Fates, screwing with me.

"Do you hear that?" I ask the priest.

He raises his bushy eyebrows. "I don't hear anything. Just you and me in this old place. Do you want to tell me your confession my son? Confession can do wonders to settle a worried mind."

"I'm afraid my confession would take too long and would keep you up tonight, Father." I turn my back on the priest. I don't like being jerked around and I feel like a tennis ball in the middle of a sick match.

I slam the door on my way outside, and the skies open up, cold rain pelting me.

Perfect.

CHAPTER 44

Megan blinks and wipes the sweat from her face. She hopes her eyes are playing tricks on her, but no such luck. Deep down, she always knew this would happen. Monsters don't just disappear; they have to be destroyed.

Frankie stands a few steps in front of them, an electric prod in his hand, fire burning in his gaze. "Where are you birds flying off to?"

"We're headed back to the cabins," says Petal. "We just got a bit turned around."

"Right. Looks like you two are trying to run away. That's not going to happen."

Megan figures she has two options. She can run, but Frankie will eventually find her. He's obsessed with her and a fixation like that only grows stronger; it won't fade away. Or she can take a stand. Frankie expects her to run, so she charges forward instead.

Frankie grins. He outweighs her by a hundred pounds, so she can't try to tackle him. That would be foolish.

When she reaches him, he swipes the prod at her head in a wide arc. She ducks under and kicks his left knee. Her foot lands hard and he buckles. She spins to deliver a roundhouse kick to his ugly face. She's good at roundhouse kicks in the gym, but this isn't a gym, and she slips on a rotten apple. Thrown off by the fruit, she misses badly and twists to the ground.

He laughs and smacks her in the leg with the electric prod. Excruciating pain surges through her body. Her leg feels like it's about to explode, and blinding light erupts in front of her. She'd scream except her mouth is clamped shut in a death clench. The pain is twice as bad as her first encounter with the electrified stick.

She tries to get to her feet, but her body convulses. She's lost all control. Angry, fat rain drops fall from the sky in a torrent of water.

Frankie curses and a blur of yellow launches itself at him. Petal shouts and they both tumble to the ground. Megan uses one hand to prop herself up, but it slips on the wet ground. It's useless. Rubber. She desperately tries to see what's happening, but she only glimpses a few desperate images through the rain: Petal scratching Frankie's face, Frankie grabbing hair, a fist swinging.

Frankie must have thrown Petal off him because two shapes move in the darkness.

Small functions return to Megan's body. She pushes up on rubbery arms. Her legs are still wooden. Useless when she needs them most. She has to help Petal, but she still can't even stand. Panic flares up inside her.

Petal charges Frankie again. This time he flips her over his shoulder. She hits the ground and, when she struggles to get up, he kicks her in the head. The blow makes a sickening thud. It snaps her head back and her body bends backward onto the mud awkwardly.

"No!" Megan's anger combats her pain and brings life back to her legs. She stands shakily, her balance unsteady.

Frankie sneers at her. "It's time for you and me to get to know each other better. Petal can't interfere now. It's just us."

Petal moans and rolls onto her side.

Frankie unzips his jumpsuit to his waist. He's no longer holding the electrified prod. It's useless in the rain.

"You can't touch me," cries Megan. "I have a green armband. Mother will know and she'll—"

"I don't care. Your time has come, Bitch."

Megan staggers backward into a tree.

Frankie lashes out, slaps her across the face. The force of the blow spins her backward. "You've been nothing but problems. Teasing me from the moment you arrived. Now you're going to get yours."

Megan spits blood from her mouth, and with the last of her energy twists and throws a wild right hook at Frankie's face.

He blocks the punch with his elbow and hits Megan in the stomach.

Megan crumples to the ground. She gasps for air, desperate to breathe again.

Frankie falls on her like a vulture and flashes a small two-inch blade in his hand. "I like it if you struggle, but don't fight too much, or I'll cut your throat and leave you here to die."

Megan sucks in air but it's spoiled by him. Foul. Sour. Rank. The apple tree shields much of the rain, so she can see him clearly. Small details pop. His face contorts into a rage-filled mask. Dark blood drips from a cut on his cheek and his eyes look as if they're on fire, red sparks burn inside of them. He smells awful, as if his sick excitement cloaks him in pus.

She struggles to throw him off her, but his weight anchors her to the wet ground and she has no leverage. He grabs the zipper of her suit and she goes for his eyes. She knows he's holding a knife, but she doesn't care. She'll take her chances, but he slaps her across the face. The blow numbs her thoughts as pain buzzes through her head.

He unzips her jumpsuit all the way down to the crotch and holds the knife near her face now. She can't struggle, or the blade will cut her. She's forced to breathe his air, rancid, fetid, hateful.

"Don't do this. You don't need to do this." She pushes her heels against the ground, but they slip, and his weight keeps her planted.

"Oh, yes I do." He cuts away her bra with the edge of the knife, the steel sliding along her flesh. His rough fingers scrape against her skin. She resists the urge to vomit. A bolt of lightning tears into the sky, and thunder rips through the night.

A discarded, apple-picking pole leans against a tree, just outside of her reach.

Frankie circles her throat with his hand and licks her cheek. Disgusting slime from his mouth slobbers against her skin, his tongue slithering across her neck like a snake, working its way downward.

She reaches for the pole, but it's a few inches away. His disgusting paw reaches down her body. Rage rips through her.

An apple bounces off the brute's head with a clunk. He twists his body off her for a moment and looks away.

Petal still lies on her side, but she reaches for another apple on the ground.

He sneers at her. "Are you jealous? Don't worry, I haven't forgotten about you. I'll have plenty left to satisfy you."

With Frankie's attention distracted, Megan reaches the pole, and brings it down on the creep's head. The wood snaps in two across the monster's skull.

He grins at her. "Nice try. Now, where were we?" He squirms further out of his jumpsuit.

"You won't be needing that little thing where you're headed."

"What?"

Megan kept her grip on the split pole and rams the jagged end into Frankie's eye with all her strength. The wood sinks in and he screams.

She shoves him off, and he strings together an incoherent slew of curses. Megan finds another pole, this one solid.

Frankie pulls the splintered wood from his eye, blood streaming down his face.

"This might leave a mark," Megan says right before she swings the pole down with all her strength against Frankie's head. This time it connects, and the wood doesn't break.

Frankie falls face first into the mud.

Megan tosses the pole to the side and zips her suit up with shaky hands. Her entire body trembles. Air comes in gulps. She'd probably stay there for hours if it weren't for Petal. She staggers to her and falls to her knees in front of her friend.

Blood darkens Petal's head where Frankie's boot cut her. Megan's stomach clenches. "Are you okay?"

Petal nods. "A little woozy, but I'll live." She looks in the distance towards the cathedral and then back at Megan with sorrowful eyes. "We don't have time now. They'll be back at the cathedral."

"We'll try again tomorrow," Megan says even though there's no conviction in her voice. She helps Petal to unsteady feet.

Petal's eyes grow wide and she falls backward to the ground.

Megan spins.

Frankie stands like a monster bathed in darkness, one shattered eye hanging from the socket, sludge like blood seeping down his face. He wobbles forward, the small knife held in his hand. "I'm not supposed to kill you. He won't like that, but now you have to die."

"Shouldn't you be dead by now?" asks Megan with as much false bravado as she can muster. Fear courses through her veins, chilling her blood. She edges away from Petal, who's too dizzy to run. She's hemmed in by another apple tree only a few feet away.

"You're going to beg me to kill you before you die."

Megan frantically searches for some advantage before Frankie closes in on her. She sees nothing but a low hanging branch. Desperately, she grabs it and tries to pull herself up, but the wood is slippery from the rain and she's exhausted from fear. Her arms are only weak impressions of her real ones.

Frankie's voice transforms into a young tone, high-pitched and totally frightening. "No where to hide, little Angel."

Megan's hands slip again from the slick wood and this time she turns to face her attacker. If she's going to die, she won't go meekly. She'll hurt him as much as she can.

She readies herself to lunge at him and go for his throat. An explosion rips through the air and a large chunk of Frankie's skull bursts from his head. For a moment he looks confused, as if he doesn't realize he's already dead, and then he falls to the mud, head first.

Buck marches toward them. "Are you all right?" he asks Megan.

Megan's not sure. She'll live but Frankie will also live on, in her memories, tormenting her in quiet moments. She can't find the words to express those thoughts even if she wants to, so she nods. And kicks Frankie's dead body a half-dozen times before she stops.

Buck helps Petal to her feet. "You guys are a mess. Get back to the cabins before you're missed. Let the rain wash away the blood and tell them you slipped into one of the sinkholes by the hemp field we use for drainage. Get May to cover for you because they'll notice something's wrong when they see you. You'll need a witness, or they'll suspect the truth."

Megan says, "Thank you. Without you..."

Buck shrugs. "I should have killed Frankie months ago."

Petal says, "What are you going to tell Mother about us?"

"All I know is that I found Frankie near the main road. He tried to take off his pendant, and well, the explosives are real. He was a stupid creep, so she'll probably believe me. Without any evidence to the contrary, it'll be my word versus that of a dead psychopath. Don't do anything else stupid. I don't need another burning tomorrow."

He bends down and picks Frankie up fireman style, throws him across his shoulders, and stalks off.

Megan loops an arm around Petal's shoulders and helps her head back to the cabin. One thought sticks in her mind.

At least now I'll get to go back into one of the chapels and talk to God again.

CHAPTER 45

One part of the puzzle is clearer—this mess with Megan and Kate is partly my fault, and I'll find a way to fix it. I'm not sure why, but too many coincidences involving me are piling up, like cars in a wreck on a highway.

Tina has wormed her way into the front beside Gabriel. That's good with me. I can use a little space to think, so I jump in the backseat and shake the rain from my hair.

Gabriel asks, "Learn anything new?"

"Just an empty, dusty, old building."

Tina sighs, "What have you done? Who are these Farm assholes, and why do they know you?"

"I don't know. I've never heard of them before."

"Right, but they know you," says Tina. "We know they thought Megan was special. Maybe they targeted her because they knew you had a relationship with Kate. Maybe Megan and Kate would've been fine if it wasn't for you. You're the turd in the middle of the toilet clogging up all the pipes."

"Maybe." I can't argue with her, but I don't see how they could have connected me to Kate. I hadn't seen her for sixteen years. Even if someone knew about our prior relationship, it would take a huge leap to assume she'd contact me to help. And how could they have identified me so easily from the surveillance video? My file is a ghost in the system. The only possibilities left are my identification card and my alias as a bodyguard for Samuel Jeffries, and that ID is specifically set up as a dark piece of info in the system. It can't be accessed any other way except through the ID card.

"That's all you've got to say," Tina huffs. "Maybe."

Gabriel starts the SUV. "Arguing about the why won't help us. The Farm people are the bad guys in this. We need to focus on how we're going to take them down and get Kate and Megan back. That's our priority, right?"

He doesn't wait for an answer and pulls from the curb. "Let's go to Walden. That way, when we get the intel from my asset in the cult, we'll be in position to move quickly."

"Let's stay in a town outside of Walden," I suggest. "Walden's a small place and we're not going to blend in well. I don't want anyone to warn them we're on our way. As far as the cult knows, we have no idea how to find them. We have the element of surprise."

"Great idea," says Gabriel.

"How about Gochen?" Tina hands me her phone with a map on the screen. "It's ten miles away from Walden and there's a motel right off the highway."

The stretch between Gochen and Walden consists of mostly empty space. Must be farm country, but Gochen looks far enough away from Walden that we should be all right. At least for a day. Any more than that, and someone will ask us questions. Besides, I'll go out of my mind worrying about Kate if we're stuck more than a day.

"Looks good," I say.

Gabriel navigates onto the highway and heads for the country. No checkpoints slow traffic on the big highways. Originalists use checkpoints only for the cities and suburbs. The rich rely upon massive gates, and their private police in rural areas, to keep away unwanted vehicles or visitors.

Gabriel drives fast, swerving around the few cars on the road.

Tina tosses out random questions about my past that explode in her mind like firecrackers. "How many enemies have you made over the years?"

"Too many to count. Most are overseas."

"Makes sense. You're a prickly person."

I agree and add that it takes one to know one. Gabriel chuckles, but that does little to slow Tina down.

"How many people in the country would like to kill you?"

"Including you?"

"You bet your skinny ass," she says.

Gabriel laughs a full body laugh at that one.

I sigh. "At least a dozen, but none of them know about my history with Kate. I haven't told anyone about her, and I haven't seen her in a long time. I also can't imagine any of them involved with a cult. It's a dead end. Believe me. I've wracked my brain about it."

Tina eventually slows her verbal assault. When she's out of ammo, she points out the window and asks, "What the fuck is that?"

"Terrafarm." I felt the same way the first time I saw one. The massive farm sticks out like a spaceship. The greenhouse is three stories tall, made of a new composite material to regulate heat and keep moisture inside the building. Spotlights reflect off specially designed mirrored surfaces that provide light to the first two tiers, enabling low-light plants to grow.

"I've heard about them, but I've never seen one," says Tina.

"The government doesn't like to publicize them, but there aren't many old-fashioned farms left. The land is too polluted, and the hotter weather makes most of them useless."

"That's where we get our food?" asks Tina.

"If you can call it that," grumbles Gabriel.

I add, "Most of the foodstuff they generate gets ground down and shipped to labs where they shape it and add chemicals to make it taste like real food."

"What about animals? Is it true that they have six-foot tall chickens and pigs as big as cars?" asks Tina.

"You don't want to know," I say. "Best not to think about it or you'll never eat again."

"How do you know so much about it anyway?" huffs Tina.

"I used to work for a guy who ran a large food consortium."

"Maybe he's the one who's connected to this?"

"No chance. He's dead."

Tina sighs, "Does everyone die around you?"

"Not everyone," says Gabriel. "I mean, I came close a couple of times, but I'm still kicking."

"Great," mutters Tina.

I can't blame her. People die around me. It's only one of the reasons I never tried to find Kate.

Gabriel's phone pings with a new message from Mary. She's sent him satellite surveillance of the two farms in Walden. We'll study them later.

Twenty minutes pass, and Tina asks, "What's wrong with us?"

Gabriel answers, "I'm just about perfect, but we can talk all day about Steven's issues."

"No kidding," I say. "And you're not perfect either."

Tina sounds dispirited. "I didn't mean us as in the three of us. I meant us as in the human race. We've dry humped the planet so much we can't grow real food anymore, and people would rather spend time in virtual reality pods than with real people. I hope the ancient aliens come back and take over. It can't be worse."

"Ancient aliens?" asks Gabriel.

"Not again," I say. "Please, I'm begging you."

Luckily, Tina doesn't start in on aliens again and lets the conversation die. She's right though. We've totally screwed things up.

After another thirty minutes in silence, we see signs for Gochen. Gabriel turns off the highway and pulls into a motel parking lot. It's part of a national chain. Old, but bright, and in decent shape. The parking lot is filled with big rigs and old pickup trucks used by farmers.

We pile out. I grab my duffel, and it feels good to stretch.

Gabriel leads the way to the manager's office to rent a few rooms for the night. The small, well-lit office has a TV hung on one wall and a long counter on the other side of the room. Dingy gray tiles cover the floor, some cracked.

Gabriel pings the old-fashioned bell on the counter, and the manager emerges.

My heart skips a beat.

Father Paul smiles at me.

CHAPTER46

I resist the almost titanic urge to jump over the counter and strangle Father Paul.

He plays it cool and pretends he doesn't know me. "How can I help you? One king room for all three?" He winks at Tina.

"Over my dead body," she says.

"We'll need three rooms on the second floor, facing the parking lot." Gabriel places a Homeland ID on the counter and a Homeland credit card.

Paul scoops up both, taps the credit card against a reader, and hands them back to Gabriel. "Anything to help Uncle Sam. My name is Paul, but my friends call me Paulie. Let me know if you need anything else."

He says that last bit while looking at me and then hands Gabriel three card keys. "Rooms 215, 216, and 217. My best."

Gabriel grunts and walks out. We go up the stairs and find our rooms. Gabriel hands me the key to room 217 and the one to 216 to Tina.

I say, "Let's meet up in Gabriel's room in an hour. I need to take a shower and think."

The others agree, and I unlock my door. Standard motel room. Just enough space for a double bed, small flat screen television hung on one wall, and a dresser with three drawers. The bathroom looks clean. I toss my duffel under the bed and retrace my steps back to the manager's office.

The office is empty. I bang on the bell with three sharp jabs.

The door behind the counter opens and Paul steps through. "I hope the room is up to your standards."

"Moonlighting as a motel manager. Seems like an odd job for a priest."

"It's not so odd, if you think about it. I offer shelter to weary travelers and listen to their stories. I even offer advice when they're willing to listen."

"I went back to St. Thomas and met a *real* priest there. He's never heard of you. He said the church is being shut down for good this Sunday. That the place has been closed all week."

"It's truly a shame they've decided to close that church. They could do such good from it, but they don't see it. Pity."

I ball my hands into fists. "I don't want to talk about churches. I want answers! Why are these demons after me?"

"That's the wrong question to ask for now. Who cares why? All that matters is they want you."

I vault over the counter to his side, penning him in. "Why do they want Kate and Megan? Does that have anything to do with me?"

He shrugs. "Certain things I can't see or know. Again, it's the wrong question for now."

I grab his neck with both of my hands and squeeze. "Well, maybe this is the right question—which farm are they holding them at? I need to know."

I squeeze his throat in a tight Fort Knox grip, yet he calmly pries my fingers away. His eyes flash a strange blue, a light from within. I remove my knife from my jacket pocket and press the point against his chest.

"I've washed this in holy water like you suggested. Now answer my question."

He grins. "I'm happy you listened to me, Steven, but that knife won't hurt me. Holy water is like vitamin water to me. You'd have to burn the steel in hellfire for it to harm me. Hopefully, you don't have any of that handy. Hellfire stinks. You can't get the reek out of your clothes. It's worse than being stuck by a campfire all day. Might as well burn them."

My hands shake. I'm not sure what to believe. Either way, I can't stab him. If the knife works, he'll die and that'll do me no good. If it doesn't, I've made the wrong enemy, so I slip it back into my jacket.

He touches my arm. "You can't force me tell you what you want to know." He glances upward and then smiles a wry grin at me. "All I can say is that He's provided you enough information to figure it out. To figure everything out. And even that could get me in trouble. Trust your instincts, go back to Gabriel, and look closely at what he has to show you."

"And this choice I have to make. The one you mentioned in the church."

He puts both of his hands on my shoulders. "I really like you, Steven. I'm rooting for you. I know you're special and will be important in the days to come. I'd much rather have you as an ally than an adversary. You will be presented with a choice. We all are, but yours is imminent. It won't be an easy choice to make. You must decide. Are you working for angels or demons? You can't straddle the fence. Dedicating yourself to God is a difficult path. It takes faith."

"And this has something to do with the Great Struggle you mentioned before?"

"Everything."

"You don't understand. I'm a killer. What use could God have for me?"

"Every war involves killing. It's regrettable, yet unavoidable. And the Great Struggle is the biggest of all wars. God has a place for you in his army. If you're willing to accept it." He releases me. "I have other business to attend to."

"Like what?"

"For starters, I should wake up the manager. Man, that guy can drink. Give him a free bottle of tequila, salt and limes, and he's as happy as a fish in a coral reef. I'll be seeing you."

Paul opens the door behind him and disappears.

I can't just let him leave. I want more answers, so I storm after him, but when I open the door, he's gone. A middle-aged fat man sits on a bed in a drunken stupor. Two empty tequila bottles lie on the floor amid dozens of used lime slices. The room stinks of alcohol and sweat.

He looks up at me and slurs his words. "Who are...you?"

"Good question."

I shut the door.

Paul left me alone once again, and one strange thought bullies aside all the others in my mind. For some reason, I have a harder time believing in angels than demons.

Why the hell is that?

CHAPTER47

Darkness, complete and heavy, wraps around Kate and threatens to smother her. She feels as if she's suspended in space. A cold and miserable space, without any stars or planets to brighten the suffocating blackness. It doesn't help that the monsters who took her chained her hands to a rafter above her, so she can't sit or move.

She's unsure how long she's been strung up like this. Her arms and back hurt. The prick who punched her in the stomach at her apartment surely cracked one or two of her ribs. Each breath hurts.

The door opens, and a shape steps inside. She carries a small, digital lantern that shrouds her in light, as if she's actually wearing a cloak made of energy. At first, Kate squints at the light and it burns her eyes, but she quickly adjusts. The light dances off the woman's multicolored robe, glimmering off silver sequins like glittering stars.

Kate tries to focus on the woman's face; something about her looks familiar, but the sudden light in the darkness blurs her features. "Where's my daughter? What have you done to her?"

"Megan is fine. More than fine. She's an Angel now."

Kate struggles against the chains. "An Angel? Let me see her!"

"That's not going to happen anytime soon."

The voice.

Kate knows that voice, and an arctic blast freezes her. It's amazing how appearances change over time, yet voices stay the same as if it comes from inside a person, comprising more of a person's essence than his or her appearance.

"You're Steven's mom, aren't you?"

The woman moves forward and the light around her shifts.

Kate sees her face and now she's certain. Healthy and confident, this woman looks different than the one Kate remembers. Almost as if she's been cured from a soul-sucking illness, given an unexpected reprieve from a terminal disease.

Ivy steps closer to Kate. "At first, I didn't know what Steven saw in you. You're beautiful, but other than that, I thought you were — ordinary. Now I know better. I've been watching you the last few years, and you are special. Strong. Smart. Capable."

"Unchain me and I'll show you how capable I am."

"Yes, I see it now." Ivy smiles. "I would have realized it earlier, but I wasn't myself back then. Pity. We could have made a great team. The three of us. You, me, and Steven."

"A team? Steven despises you."

Ivy shrugs. "I wasn't the best mother. I'll grant you that."

"Not the best mother? You killed his father and you tried to kill him. You terrorized your own son."

"Let's not argue over trifles. I wasn't a good mother. That's my fault and I own it. Back then, I didn't understand. I do now. Once I explain things to him, he'll change his mind about me. We're going to be a team. Now we can add Megan. She's an extraordinary young woman. And maybe you. That part will be up to you."

"Why do you need Megan? The last I heard you were selling drugs for a gang."

"Things change. I've moved up in the world, become an entrepreneur. We provide experiences that are even better than real life, and if we make them addictive in the process, can you really blame us? Others did it before us. Coke initially used real cocaine in the formula, cigarette companies altered the amount of nicotine to create cravings, and technology companies design apps to make them addictive. We've just improved on that process. We can addict millions immediately, or slowly over time, depending upon our desires." Ivy smiles smugly. "I've come a long way from selling drugs on the street corner. I've perfected capitalism."

Kate imagines a world of zombies all storming to Otherworldly shops, but that doesn't explain why she's stealing girls? "You don't need Megan or any of the other girls for that."

"I'm not going to sugarcoat it—sex sells. And some depraved men like young girls. They want to feel young again even if they suck it out of someone else. Sick, weak people really." She frowns. "Sadly, there are limits to my control over the operation. As profitable as we have become, delivering Angels to rich men across the world provides record profit margins."

Kate strains against her chains. "You're selling my Megan to a rich foreigner?"

"We don't like to say *sell*. Sounds negative. We call it *marry*, but in reality, it's the same thing. The client can use the Angel for whatever purpose he wants. But don't worry. Megan's marriage will only be for a short time. I'll recall her in a few months when I'm ready for Phase 2."

"Phase 2?"

"Don't worry about that, my dear. We have time for that later."

"Some things don't change. You're still nuttier than a fruit bar. Unchain me and let me see Megan!"

She shakes her head. "I can't do that. You're useful right where you are."

The truth dawns on Kate. "You knew I'd message Steven when you took Megan."

"Know is a touch strong. I thought you might. Who else would you contact?"

"Kidnapping Megan was an elaborate ruse, so Steven would come, and you'd see him again."

Ivy purses her lips together. "Not a total ruse. Megan is extraordinary. I want her as one of my Angels. So, if Steven didn't come, I'd still be ahead. It's the best form of capitalism—a win-win for me. And this way, he'll think it's fate that he found his mother again."

"All for what?"

A flash of the old madness returns to Ivy's eyes. "Steven can help me bring about *His* vision. *He* thinks Steven's important! *He* wants Steven!" She pauses and composes herself. "That's more than you need to know. I'll give Steven your regards when I see him. He should be here soon, I'd expect."

"God wants Steven?"

"God. Who said anything about God?" Ivy grins.

"Let me have Megan! You don't need her. Please, you're a mother. You must understand. She's innocent."

"I have good news and bad news about Megan. I'll start with the bad news. One more session in a chapel and she'll never be the same. Sadly, we've had to speed up her education, so we've increased the addictive nature of the visions. Later tonight, she'll have another dose, and she'll be fully addicted. Just like a heroin addict. Cut her off from chapel, and she'll go crazy. The good news is you've been a great mother. She's extraordinarily smart. Her mind grasps new ideas so easily. It's what makes her so susceptible to the chapel visions. You've done a phenomenal job raising her. You should be very proud."

Ivy turns and leaves the small hut, taking the only light with her.

Kate screams, a desperate cry from a mother facing only darkness. But the darkness doesn't respond.

CHAPTER 48

After undressing in my motel room, I wash the grime from my body. Father Paul said I had to listen to Gabriel and trust my instinct. He didn't leave me much choice.

Ten minutes later, I knock on Gabriel's door. Tina hears my knocking and joins me in the hallway, not wanting to be left out. Gabriel opens the door, and we both stroll inside.

He holds his tablet.

"Have you heard from the asset at The Farm yet?" I try unsuccessfully to keep the anxiety from my voice. We're close now, Walden only a few miles away. I can almost feel Kate nearby, but we might as well be on different planets if I can't figure out which farm they're holding her. Guessing isn't an option. Fifty-fifty odds don't work for me.

"Not yet." Gabriel projects the images from his tablet onto the wall. "I have the satellite surveillance photos Mary sent. They were taken earlier today. We know the cult operates both farms. They're probably keeping Kate and Megan at one of them."

I've studied photos like these hundreds of times. Things look different from space. It takes imagination to understand what's in the photos and how they relate to each other. Gabriel is clever, but he doesn't have training or experience in something like this, so the heavy lifting falls on me.

I study the larger farm first. A half dozen of those massive terrafarm greenhouses run alongside the nearest main road.

"They use the greenhouses as a camouflage for the other activities at the farm. Anyone driving by on the main road would think it's nothing more than a typical foodstuff manufacturing plant. They can't see beyond the greenhouses." I point past the large glass structures. "If this were a true terrafarm, they'd have greenhouses on all the open space. Instead, after the greenhouses, they have what looks like a few organic crops. Probably wheat and corn that ring the outside portion of the property. Toward the center of the farm, they have these buildings. From the shape of them, they're long bunkhouses. This one in the center is different. It looks like a gathering place, most likely a mess hall, and this one looks like a church of some sort."

We study the farm for the next thirty minutes. I call out structures like the depot for cars and trucks, a firing range, and a plain building in the center of the bunkhouses that's probably administrative offices. The roof has satellite dishes for communication.

Gabriel whistles. "Looks like a big operation. They must have three hundred people on the compound."

"Probably more," I say. "They'll use the residents to farm the greenhouses and the fields. They wouldn't want strangers to come on property."

"Why would a cult go through all that work to actually create foodstuff?" asks Tina.

"Two reasons. They'll want a cover for the local population. And they probably use the physical labor to break down the inductees. Exhausted people are susceptible to brainwashing. It's an old Army trick." I touch the tab for the second farm and a new set of photos pop on the wall. "Let's see what this one looks like."

Half the size of the first farm, the second one sits a good distance from a highway, connected to the main street by a private road that dead-ends into a security hut and a roadblock. Guards patrol the roadblock and limit entrance. No greenhouses appear in the photos. It's an old-fashioned farm with neat, well-maintain crops.

Tina points to a massive building in the northwestern portion of the property. "Is that another greenhouse?"

"No," I say. "Those are solar panels on the roof. It looks like a giant warehouse."

"That uses a lot of juice." Gabriel hovers a thick finger over one side of the building. "Those are pretty big generators. It could fire up an entire city block. Why do they need all that electricity?"

The answer hits me like a ton of bricks. "Kirkland, the manager at Otherworldly, told me they use real people for the *extreme* experiences. That way the sex is real or the violence or whatever the rich pervert wants to experience. If that's true, they'd need a place to store all those pod things. This could be the place."

"Fuck me," says Tina. "How many people are we talking about?"

"Should be room for a hundred or more?" Gabriel says.

I do the math in my head and say, "One hundred experiences at twenty thousand a pop would generate 2 million dollars. Assume they can turn that over three times a day and they'd make 6 million a day, easy."

Tina adds, "They have private club locations all over the place now, including foreign cities, so that's very doable. I'd be surprised if they don't do twice that much business."

I study the rest of the photos while Gabriel and Tina discuss economics. I look for small details and find a few. They have a dozen little huts in the eastern portion of the property with a utility road that connects the huts to the main administration buildings. I zoom in briefly and find a few armed guards, carrying M18 assault rifles.

When I zoom out, I notice the apple orchard, dozens of trees lined in neat rows and a juice press off to the side. That's where they make the organic apple cider for the private club. I've seen enough and hand the tablet to Gabriel.

"You said you have an operational team nearby that can help?" I ask.

He nods, "It's a four-member group. One helicopter and an armored SUV. That's all I could commandeer in such a short notice. They're at a Homeland base twenty minutes away."

"Does Sheppard know you've commandeered them?"

Gabriel smiles. "He's a busy man. He can't be bothered with every operation."

"I'll take that as a no." He's taken a risk helping me out like this. Sheppard will protect him, but even that protection has limits. If this operation goes south, he'll catch hell for it.

"Do you know the team?" I ask.

"I've never met them, but they look good on paper. Well trained. Successful."

Tina tosses the tablet on the bed. "What are you thinking? I can almost see the rocks tumbling in your Neanderthal like brain."

"I'm not certain yet. We need to know for sure which farm they're holding Kate and Megan. They warned me about investigating. We have to assume they'll follow through with that threat. If we choose the wrong one, they'll kill them. We can't guess."

Gabriel checks his phone. "No word yet from our asset. We should hear something by the end of the night."

I need an excuse to leave. "I saw some vending machines by the manager's office. I'll get us some water. It's best if we stay hydrated."

I don't wait for them to reply and stalk out of the room. I run through the two sets of surveillance photos in my mind.

Where would I stash high-value assets or captives?

These cult people have plenty of resources, and the layouts are well designed. They'd organize their compounds in a logical way. The larger farm holds the majority of the members of the cult, but it's less secure. To keep up their cover, they'd have to load trucks and send them out on a daily basis. Plus, it's closer to the main road and there's more property, which means more borders for people to escape.

The smaller farm is hidden away. The entrance to the only road in and out is manned. More armed guards patrol the place. And that's where they have the main operation. The bunkhouses are cheap to build, but that warehouse with those experience chambers probably cost a bundle.

If it were me, I'd keep the new members at the small farm and any captives I want to keep secure. Still, my analysis is flimsy. Normally, good reconnaissance relies upon patience, detail, and time. A three-legged stool. Unfortunately, I don't have time to make furniture. Each minute might be hell for Kate and Megan.

I reach the vending machine, use cash to buy three large bottles of water, and remember what Father Paul said. I have to trust my instinct. When I saw the apple orchard, my heart jumped. Normally, I'm not a superstitious guy, but I can't deny the obvious. Demons and angels are involved somehow in this, so I can't rule out signs or my gut.

My mind calculates the odds at 80 percent that the cult is holding Kate and Megan at the smaller farm, but my heart is absolutely sure. Those odds, I can't ignore.

Caesar's reflection, off the vending machine, stares at me. "You're not dumb enough to go in alone. Call in Gabriel's team. I taught you to use every resource to your advantage."

"I can't ask Gabriel and Tina to risk their lives on my intuition. Besides, you also taught me never to trust someone else if I don't know them. I'm not trusting Kate and Megan's lives to a Homeland team I've never met."

Caesar smirks. "It's the broad then. You're pussy whipped. She shacked up with some other guy the moment you left, and you'll still do anything, risk anything to save her. Even us?"

"Yes."

"I hope you know what you're doing cowboy, or this is our last rodeo." Caesar frowns and disappears.

I remove the bottle of sleeping pills from my jacket pocket, pop it open and crush eight of them in my hand. I slip the powder inside two bottles. More for the bottle I'll give to Gabriel, and less for Tina.

I'm going tonight and I'm not coming back without Kate and Megan.

CHAPTER 49

Ivy sits behind her desk; Lily, the doctor, stands beside her. Luke, the Reaper who abducted Kate, leans against the door. Lily just finished updating her on Spring's and Petal's conditions. Apparently, both fell in a drainage ditch on the way back from the burning. Lily can't be certain, but both might have suffered concussions. She cautions against subjecting them to the chapel for a few days. The visions might be dangerous for them.

Ivy smiles blandly at her, but her heart rate ticks up. This is not good news, not the sort of thing she wants to hear tonight.

Buck knocks, and she calls for him to enter.

"You found Frankie?" Ivy asks.

"Yep. I found his body at the edge of the apple orchard, near the press. He must have tried to pry off the pendant because his head is gone. Either that, or it went off in some type of freak accident."

"Why would he take off the pendant?" asks Ivy. "He wasn't the brightest bulb, but he knew what would have happened if he broke the chain."

Buck shrugs. "He didn't seem happy the last few days. Maybe he missed his wife and daughter."

"Maybe. Or maybe there's another reason." Ivy removes a .38 caliber semi-automatic Berretta from a drawer and places it on her desk.

All eyes in the room focus on the gun.

Buck shifts uneasily at the sight of the weapon.

"What we do here is based upon trust," says Ivy. "Without trust we can't implement His plans. If we fail, we lose our rightful place. We won't be chosen anymore. I can't let that happen. You understand, right? I need to protect the interests of everyone. All the Angels we've married, and the ones who work on both farms. Not to mention you and the Reapers."

Buck stands taller. "Of course. You can trust me."

"Can I? I have some bad news. We have a traitor among us. I found this phone hidden on the edge of the cow pasture by the fence." She places a satellite phone next to the handgun. Regular cellular phones don't work on The Farm. Their frequencies have all been jammed, but a satellite one would work.

"Someone has been communicating with Homeland for months. I suspected as much, but we couldn't gather proof. We intercepted a quick signal now and then. But, it could have been a fault in the system. A ghost in the machine as they say. But today, Homeland has been very active. Apparently, they want some information desperately. They've left three different messages. Enough for me to track the signal and find the phone. I'm very disappointed that a Judas resides among my flock. And usually, I feel so good after a burning."

"Whose phone is it?" asks Lily.

Ivy ignores her and lifts the device from the table so everyone can see it. "Luckily, one of the techs hacked into it. We could only retrieve today's messages. The ones that haven't been answered yet. They really want to know where we're keeping Spring and her mother. I've given them a location on the bigger farm, our sister property. It will make for an easy trap. Most of the Reapers are already on the way there to spring it when Homeland shows up."

Ivy sighs. "Oh, well. He has a way of delivering for us. No doubt He led me to the phone for that very purpose."

Luke snickers as he levels his assault rifle at Buck's chest. He's always so eager to kill. He feeds on it.

Buck's face remains stoic, except for the eyes. They flicker between the phone and the gun. "Surely you don't suspect me?"

"Oh, I know the identity of the traitor. How could I not?" Ivy smiles. "Only two people are possibilities. Both started here about three months ago and both would have the freedom to hide a phone. I can safely rule out any of my Angels, so that leaves me with only two people."

Ivy lifts the Beretta and points it at Buck's chest. "When did you start working for me?"

"Three months ago. But I have nothing to do with this phone. You can trust me."

Ivy flips the safety off. "I know who I can trust." She swings the gun from Buck and points it at Lily's head.

"No! I—"

She pulls the trigger and blasts a hole in Lily's forehead. Blood splatters on the desk as Lily topples to the floor.

"It's a shame, really. Doctors are hard to find."

"What about Homeland?" asks Buck. "Are you worried they're about to crack down on us?"

"No. According to Trevor, they're not planning anything big against us. He'd know. I suspect someone is calling in a favor for our Spring. We can deal with it and not worry about a larger response from Homeland. They'll write it off as a rogue agent. Trevor will make sure of it."

She cocks her head toward Buck. "Bury this traitor in the mass grave next to Frankie. That will really piss her off. She hated Frankie. Diagnosed him as a psychopathic pedophile. She was a traitor, but she knew her medicine. When you're done, bring me Spring and Petal. I'm personally going to supervise their visions in the chapel tonight. I think it's time they both see His full glory."

If Lily hadn't tried to get me to keep them away from the sanctuary, I might not have realized she was the Judas. Such a small tell, but in the end, the details are always what trip people up.

"Some good news, at least," says Ivy. "Blood mixes well with the purple on Lily's jumpsuit. It makes a nice combination."

CHAPTER 50

Gabriel and Tina would have puzzled out the truth between the two farms if I had not drugged them. They started asking the right questions and saw the two compounds the right way. They're too smart not to get it. I tried to play it cool and gave them half answers to their questions, but I was just delaying the inevitable.

Luckily, the drug in the water kicked in hard before I had to start lying. Tina slurs her words and can't keep her eyes open. I practically carry her to her room and drop her on the bed. She looks oddly beautiful sprawled out on the comforter, her face unlined by stress. One thing I'll say about her, she's devoted to Kate and Megan. That type of devotion can't be faked.

By the time I get back to Gabriel's room, he's drained his water bottle and sits dazed in a chair. I'm not sure he suspects the water was drugged before he passes out. He probably does, and he'll make me pay for it when he gets his hands on me.

It's a risk I'll take. I need to do this on my own. Gabriel's Homeland team would make things safer for me, but they'd increase the risk that Kate and Megan wouldn't make it out alive. That's unacceptable, so I steal Gabriel's thumbprint with sticky tape and swab his cheek for DNA with a Q-Tip. I slide out of the motel room, plod down the staircase, and head for the Homeland SUV.

The tape works; Gabriel's thumbprint opens the door and starts the vehicle. I ease it out of the parking lot. I've already memorized the satellite photos. I shut off the headlights and switch on stealth mode. The windshield brightens with night vision. The chrome portions of the car and the windows blacken. The gas engine shuts off and the car relies solely upon the electric engine. The car won't go quite as fast at top speed, but that doesn't bother me. I fight the urge to rush. I need to arrive unseen. I need patience.

I drive along a country road that leads to the farm. A pickup truck whips toward me. The windshield flares for a second and then adjusts to the headlights. The night vision isn't perfect yet, but it works well enough. The pickup speeds past, oblivious to the SUV.

At times like this, I wonder if I'm still me, or if I've become something else. The demons inside me growl, the pressure in my mind building. They know what's coming. Killing. A lot of killing. A dark part inside of me looks forward to it. Not Caesar or the normal voices I often hear, but something darker and more powerful. Troubling.

My immediate problem — gaining entrance to the farm. A fence rings the property. I'll bet my last dollar it's supplemented with advanced motion detector technology. The kind they use at the borders now. If I had time, I could find a way around it. There's always a dead spot or I could tunnel in, but that would take time, and time isn't something I have.

In an odd twist, the only way into the farm where I can avoid the motion detectors is the main entrance. They won't use the detectors at the guardhouse. Why bother? That's patrolled by armed men. That's my way in, so long as I kill all the guards before they raise an alarm.

I pull the SUV onto the shoulder of the road, three hundred yards from the entrance to the private road to the farm, and hop out. The rain comes down in a steady downpour. I open the SUV's hatch. It looks like a plain, empty storage space, but a Homeland vehicle like this one will be loaded for bear. I push the back seats forward, grab the Q-Tip with Gabriel's DNA on it, find the reader in the corner, and press the cotton against the screen. It flashes green and the false floor pops open. Hello, traveling arsenal.

Gabriel didn't mess around. I take an M18 with a silencer. That'll come in handy. A small baton, a pair of brass knuckles that fits really well, three hand grenades, and one laser knife. I find a tube of night makeup. I smear the black grease on my exposed skin and streak my army jacket. I look at my reflection in the side mirror. A reasonable job. The night is dark, and the pounding rain will mask the sound of the SUV's tires on the packed dirt road leading to the security gate.

I grab the remote control for the SUV and ease the car onto the country road. Jogging behind, I find a sign that says, "Private Road

Keep Out." No guards patrol the turnoff. That would be noticeable from the road and might spur questions. Instead, guards man the roadblock at the entrance to the farm—I figure at least three of them, all armed with assault rifles.

I'll need a diversion, so I can kill the guards at the roadblock before they radio in to headquarters. Surprise is an important ally, one to treat with a healthy respect. I turn the SUV down the private country road. In stealth mode and the pouring rain, I can get within one hundred yards before the guards will notice anything, maybe even fifty, but I don't need to be that close.

The M18 is a good weapon. Even with the silencer, it's more than accurate from one hundred yards away, and I'm a good shot. Not an expert marksman, but capable, better than most.

One hundred yards from the roadblock, I stop the SUV, and use the scope. A small hut with a glass window sits to the left of the metal gate that blocks the entrance to the compound. Two guys dressed in red jumpsuits survey the road from inside the hut. Two other guys hang outside in the rain getting drenched and looking miserable. They stand off to the side, far away from the hut, on the other end of the metal barrier. They're hard to see clearly, but one of them smokes. A nasty habit that's more dangerous than he realizes. With each puff, the tip glows orange, and helps me sight both men.

The two in the hut are my biggest concern. They're most likely to radio for help. I should be able to take both out within four seconds. One breath between shots. That way they won't have time to radio anyone, but during that interval, the two guards outside will likely scatter. I'll get one of them for sure and possibly the second, but the odds of success start to drop. One is likely to raise an alarm. I need a diversion to draw their attention. Luckily, I have the car.

I find a nice spot on the side of the road, behind an oak tree, that offers a clean shot inside the hut and a straight line of sight for the two guys outside. I flip the safety off the rifle, and make sure the laser sight is off. The laser in this darkness will give me away, and they're close enough I don't need it.

The scope zooms in on the two inside the hut. They look bored. The taller of the two is talking about something—probably sports or nonsense to pass the time. I check on the two outside. They haven't moved. They're standing under the cover of a thick branch of an oak. It doesn't do much to keep the rain off them, but it's better than nothing. I'm convinced the Fates want me to succeed. At least in this.

I ease the SUV forward. It's seventy-five yards away now. The closer it gets before I start shooting the better. The tall guy in the hut stops talking. He leans forward and squints. He can't be certain in the dark and the storm, but he thinks he's seen a shape in the distance moving toward him…

I focus my shot on his heart. At this distance, the heavy caliber bullet will shatter the glass and make a mess out of his insides. When the SUV gets a little closer, the tall guy taps his buddy on the arm. He sees the vehicle now.

I switch stealth mode off. The SUV's lights come on, and the engine purrs to life as it inches forward.

Speed is critical now. I breathe smoothly through my nose and squeeze the trigger. Glass shatters, and the tall guard is thrown backward. Before the other guy in the hut reacts, I nail him in the head.

The two guards outside aim their M18s at the SUV. They don't know where the shooting is coming from and the big vehicle makes such an easy target. It's an automatic response. The smoker fires at the SUV, which will do him no good.

I blast him in the chest. His companion lowers his assault rifle and turns to run, but he's too late. He should have fled right away. Big mistake. I cut him down with a shot through his back. Using the scope, I make sure all four are still down. The smoker struggles to get back up, so I plug him with another round, this time to the head. No sense prolonging his pain, and this way he won't grab a radio.

I switch the SUV back to stealth mode, and sprint to the gatehouse, hop over the rail, and confirm that everyone's dead. I'm not happy the smoker got off a few rounds before I took him out. I don't know if anyone's heard the gunshots.

I listen for the sounds of alarm but hear nothing but the steady pounding of the rain. No shouts or sirens or anything that worries me. That could change in a heartbeat, but at least I'm still the hunter for a while longer.

The scent of blood mixes with the rain in the air, and it makes me smile. An energy rumbles inside me. I'm back to doing what I'm good at—hunting and killing. If that makes me a demon, so be it. I'll do whatever needs doing to save Kate and Megan.

CHAPTER 51

Simple plans make the best plans. Can't get too clever when your life is on the line, and my plan is as simple as they come: find and free Kate and Megan, and then get our asses back to the SUV before the cult realizes they're gone. After that, drive to the motel and reconnect with Gabriel and his team. He won't be in a good mood after I've drugged him, but he'll come around and together we'll rain hell down on everyone else at The Farm. Although simple, it's as thin as tissue paper. It's more of an aspiration than a real plan.

For starters, I only have a few pieces of helpful information. Based on my reading of the surveillance photos, they're probably keeping Kate in one of the small huts on the southeastern portion of property. I can't be certain, but that's where I'd stash a prisoner. Out of the way and guarded. After that, everything falls apart. Megan is most likely with the other girls. No reason to separate her, so she's probably in one of the cabins. Probably. Maybe. Possibly. Not good words to use when making a proper plan.

I'll worry about Megan later. First, I need Kate. I can't march through the compound, up a main path and search the huts. That's a sure way to get dead. I stay out of the way, keeping to the lightly wooded forest that rings the outside of the farm.

The rain makes for slick footing, and the dark night doesn't provide much visibility. I can't use a flashlight, so I move slower than I'd like. Breaking an ankle won't do Kate and Megan any good. The forest is mostly made up of pines, oaks, and tall grasses that cover the ground. Not a bad combination for me. I scrape my way through, careful to keep quiet, picking my way around pine trees and ducking under oak branches.

I have to stop twice when I hear other people. I'm not far from the paths they use, and they trod past me, splashing through puddles. No one is talking. They likely want out of the rain, and to get wherever they're headed as quickly as possible. I can't blame them.

After an hour and twenty minutes, I see the first hut in the distance—a black cone-like shape, blacker than the forest around it. There are six huts in total. If I'm right, there's got to be at least one guard, possibly two to make sure no one escapes.

I move within ten feet of the hut and squat low. The rain has slowed to sporadic bursts now. Small soaking gusts after little stretches of nothing. I hear the guard before I see him. He's limping slightly, favoring his left leg. I know that gait. He's one of the men who abducted Megan, the one who punched her in the stomach.

He steps beyond the hut and into view. A wind gust brings cold, fat raindrops like bombs dropped from above. The guard looks up to the heavens, no doubt wondering if the rain is meant for him, and whether he's pissed off the Fates.

He's right to wonder. The Fates are pissed at him and they sent me here to make it right. I could shoot him with the M18 and the bullet would make such a mess of his skull no one would be able to identify him, but that won't do. I want to talk to him, so I ease out from my hiding spot, keep low, and sneak up on him. I keep my weight balanced and carefully place my feet on solid ground. The wet pine needles help muffle any noise my boots would otherwise make.

Within two steps, I can hear him breathing, the rub of the rifle's strap against his shoulder, the curse he mutters under his breath. He turns to march toward the rest of the huts, and he moves away from me.

I slide behind him, clamp my hand across his mouth, and press the blade of my long knife against his neck. At first, he tries to jerk away, but I hold him steady and whisper in his ear. "If you move or cry out, I'll slice your throat. Be cool and answer my questions."

He nods.

"Where are you holding the woman you took tonight? Which hut?"

"I don't know what you're talking about."

"Bad answer." I stab his neck with the tip of the knife, making sure the blade doesn't cut his carotid artery. "Next time I'll cut you so bad, you'll bleed out in less than a minute."

He's shaking now. "Okay, okay. She's in the next hut over."

"Anyone else on patrol?"

"Not now. Someone will relieve me in an hour. Let me go."

"Did you think we had some type of deal? That's my bad. I didn't explain the rules—I don't make deals with thugs who hurt young women and kidnap them." I rip the blade across his throat. It's harder to slice a throat than they show in the movies. It takes two cuts to do the job properly.

When all life drains from his body, I drop him to the ground. He's dressed in all black and blends in with the grasses, so I leave him where he falls. No need wasting time and energy dragging him into the woods. Someone would have to trip over him to notice the guy.

My heart pounds when I reach the second hut. When we learned that Kate was taken, I didn't know if I'd ever see her again. I thought my mistakes got her killed. Now, the Fates gave me a second chance to make things right. I fling open the door and find her standing upright, her arms stretched above her by long chains hung over a wooden beam.

"Kate." I drop the M18 to the hard-packed dirt floor and dart forward. "Are you hurt?"

She doesn't answer me. Her eyes go wide as if she doesn't believe I'm here. I cut through both of the chains with the laser knife and catch her when she slumps forward.

"You shouldn't have come," she says.

"I thought you'd be happy to see me. It's not every day I get to save a damsel in distress."

She speaks in one breathless burst. "It's a trap. Your crazy psycho bitch of a mother is the leader of the cult. She set you up. She knows you're coming."

The world stops spinning, and everything freezes. I guess a small part of me had already figured out my mother could be involved in this mess. I wasn't certain she was dead, and she used to call me Stevie. That message on the website sounded like her, but I refused to believe it. I didn't want to believe it. The mind is strong that way. We can deny all types of things if we try.

Other shapes burst into the hut. Six armed men. Four of them point M18s at Kate, and the other two point them at me. They must have been watching the hut from the forest. I should have waited longer after killing the first guard. But I rushed, too anxious to see Kate and play the hero.

I run through a million different scenarios in my mind, and Kate doesn't survive any of them. I have a ten percent chance to make it out alive, but she has zero.

The assault team spreads out along the hut's outer wall, further reducing my odds. The leader snickers. "Get on your knees and lift your hands behind your head. Do it and maybe I won't kill you both."

"You're making a mistake," I say. "An entire Homeland battalion is headed here. Let us go, and I'll put in a good word for you. Maybe they won't send you to one of their black site interrogation holes. We can strike a deal."

One of the henchmen calls out to the leader. "He'd like to make a deal, Luke. He thinks he has something to trade."

"He's sadly mistaken." Luke's eyes burn red. He's not human. Maybe he was at one point, but not anymore. "We know about your Homeland buddies. We have a special surprise for them."

He nods to two of his men, who roughly strip my jacket from me, toss it to the side of the hut, and pat me down. An efficient job. They find whatever they need and toss it by the jacket.

Luke grins and says, "I want both of them strung up."

Someone brings new chains, locks them on both of our wrists, loops them over the rafters, and lifts us up. My arms stretch to the limit, so I need to balance on my toes. At least they're kinder to Kate. She can stand flat-footed.

"I appreciate the effort, but I don't think I'll get any taller. Stretching me like this won't help."

The leader orders everyone else out of the room.

He stalks forward. "You don't look special to me."

"Take me down and we'll find out."

"I have a better idea."

His idea of better is not going to work out for me. He grabs one of the old chains I cut off Kate and whips it at me. He must be amazingly strong to flip it so casually. It cuts through my T-shirt and slashes my chest.

My skin is like leather, having taken multiple beatings over the years, but the chains slash into me and the force feels like I've been hit with a concussion grenade. I groan, but I don't cry. I come close, but he's not going to see me cry. "Is that the best you can do?"

He whips me again, this time closer to my throat and hits me high on the chest. Now that I know what to expect, I take it stoically.

He tosses the chain to the floor. "You'd be wise to think about your future. You wouldn't want me to do that to your friend and maybe that sweet thing she calls her daughter."

"Touch her and I'll kill you slowly," I say.

He sizes me up, grins, and moves close. The links from the chain have cut into my chest. He touches the wound, rubs the blood between his fingers, and brings it to his nose. He sniffs and chuckles.

I swing my head at him, hoping to catch him off guard with a head butt, but he's too fast and sidesteps me. He leans close to my ear and whispers so only I can hear him. "Welcome to the club."

Luke, who may have been human once but is now clearly a demon, turns and stalks out.

"That was weird," says Kate.

"You have no idea."

So much for simple plans.

CHAPTER 52

Megan watches the rain fall outside her window and it deepens her dour mood. She's on the verge of tears and her eyes sting. She's usually a positive person by nature, but her mind sticks on all the many reasons she should cry until she feels like she's buried alive: she misses her mother and her friends; Petal is hurt; they blew their best chance at escaping. Each time her mind completes a circuit, it feels like another shovel full of dirt is tossed on top of her. The weight and the darkness suffocate her.

Strangely, of all the many reasons she has for feeling sad, one dominates her thoughts more than the others — the doctor said she couldn't go to the chapel for a few days — a few days without talking to God. How will she survive without slipping into one of the steel chambers and feeling the comforting warmth of God's Tears for a few days? It doesn't seem fair. She just experienced it for the first time today, and she's not sure if she can wait until morning, never mind a few days.

Someone knocks on the door. It opens before anyone moves to get it, and Buck stands in the doorway, the edges of his lips turned downward. He points to Megan and Petal and says, "You two. Time to go to the cathedral."

The weight burying Megan lifts. Light comes back into the world. She practically jumps off her bed, giddy at her reprieve. She won't have to wait after all.

Petal's response is the opposite. She crosses her arms over her chest and scowls at Buck. "There must be a mistake. The doctor said it would be dangerous for us to go into a chapel. We might have concussions from the...fall."

"No mistake. Mother herself will meet both of you at the cathedral. Let's go. We don't have all night. Tonight's been long enough for me as it is."

Megan skips forward and grabs Petal's arm. She doesn't understand Petal's reluctance. She's never experienced anything as wonderful as the chapel, and this is their chance to go again. So soon. Right now. "Come on."

Petal shakes her off, her voice desperate. "This isn't right, Buck. Look at her. They're pushing her too hard. She's not…"

Megan doesn't bother listening. She skips out of the cabin and into the driving rain. She barely notices the cold water as it drenches her. All thoughts about Petal, her mom, friends, and her desire to escape flee from her mind.

Instead, she focuses on one thing, like a child who sees an ice cream truck. *I'm going back to chapel. I'm going to talk to God again. I hope I can stay there for… forever!*

CHAPTER 53

Kate and I are alone in the hut they call a *confessional*. At least one guard must be stationed outside, but for now, we're no threat to anyone. They've locked us in chains. Why leave someone inside to watch us?

I turn to Kate. "So how is mommy dearest? Looking well?"

"I didn't recognize her at first. She looks like a new person. Healthy in a way I've never seen before, but her voice is the same and the crazy gave her away. She can't hide the crazy."

"It's nice to know some things haven't changed." I glance up at the beam that holds the chains, and it triggers an idea.

"She wouldn't let me see Megan. She said something about marrying these girls to rich guys. If anyone touches Megan, I'm going to kill her."

"We'll see Megan soon. We're making great progress. We're together and Megan must be nearby. All we need to do now is grab her and go. Shouldn't be all that hard."

"Not so hard?" She shakes her chains. "If you hadn't noticed, we're not exactly killing it. I wouldn't say we're on track or anything like that."

"Oh, ye of little faith. The hard part was finding out who took Megan quickly enough for us to get her back. We can check that off the list. Then we had to infiltrate their operation. Another item off the list. Once we free ourselves from these chains, the rest of our plan will be easier."

I swing from side to side and use the momentum to climb up the chain. With each swing, I slide my hand six inches up the chain. First right, then left, back to right again, and so forth. The strain rips through me. To keep from focusing on the pain, I talk to Kate.

"What are you going to do when you get Megan back?"

"Lock her in the apartment, which will last exactly five minutes before she'll find a way out."

I've made it up more than three feet. "When I returned to the apartment, I found Tina tied up in Megan's closet. I thought about leaving her there. The tape over her mouth was the first time she's ever been quiet. When I took it off…"

"She cursed like a sailor. I can only imagine."

Five feet up now. "I can't believe I'm saying this, but she's not so bad. She grows on you."

"You've only known her for twenty-five years."

"A slow growth, like a cactus maybe. Prickly with all those needles, but if you look at it right, you see the flowers too."

Six feet. The beam is only three feet above me. The ache in my shoulders sends a shudder down my spine. My right shoulder, the one that dislocated when we fell from the apartment starts to seize up on me.

Kate says, "Your mother is certainly anxious to see you. She said He thinks you're important, but she didn't tell me who *He* is."

"I've been trying to figure that out myself. I'm not positive, but I have the feeling she means the Devil."

"I'm not surprised. Crazy is crazy."

I can tell Kate about the demons and Father Paul now. That door is open, but I don't. She'll only think I've inherited the crazy gene from my mother, and I'd rather lose an arm than have her think that.

The beam is only one foot above me now. With most of my strength drained, I swing a little farther than before and grab the wooden beam with my right hand, pull myself up, and snatch it with my left. I have enough energy left to do one last pull up and sit on the beam. I'm breathing heavily. "At least I didn't pull my arms out of my sockets."

"Don't expect me to climb up there with you. That looked hard."

"Come on. The view up here is great. You can really see the spider webs."

"Screw the spiders. I hate them."

"Everyone hates them. It's universal."

Before they chained me to the beam, they searched me and took everything they thought would be problematic, but they didn't take my belt. No reason to worry about a belt. They didn't know about the buckle. Attached to the buckle is an expandable needle. It comes in handy as a tool or a weapon. It'll take an eye out, which isn't particularly applicable right now, but I can also use it to unlock the chains. A few twists and the cuffs fall off me.

"Neat trick," says Kate.

"All that training in the Army didn't go completely to waste." I climb down from the beam using the chains like a rope. When my feet hit the ground, I unlock the cuffs off Kate's wrists.

She wraps her arms around me and kisses me hard. It surprises me and steals the wind from my lungs. After a few heart-stopping moments, we separate.

"Just because," she says. "Don't read anything else into it."

"You know me. Reading has never been my strong suit."

I grab my jacket, which they left in a pile against the wall. They took the guns and anything else that's useful, but for some reason, they left my knife in the pocket. At least I have that. And my belt buckle.

I study the confessional one last time. There's only one way in or out. "You stay here, and I'll go outside and chat with the guard."

Kate shakes her head. "You're crazier than your mother if you think I'm staying in here while you go outside. No offense but if that guy who whipped you with the chain is out there, you'll need my help. He's a monster. Without me, you'll get your ass kicked. It'll be like Tommy Tubs in seventh grade all over again."

I roll my neck. "A lot has changed since Tommy Tubs, and I would have beaten his ass if you hadn't stepped in."

"Right. I'm just saying."

I can't really argue with her. Luke is a monster. She only knows a small part of it. "Okay, stay behind me. And don't do anything stupid. Leave the stupid to me. They have guns, and we don't."

"No kidding."

With any luck, the guard will be looking away from the door. There's no reason for him to watch the hut. As far as he knows, we're chained to the beam. The danger would come from outside—an ill-conceived rescue mission by someone.

I turn the latch on the door, and it clicks. Sounds loud like a bullet firing from a gun, and I cringe. I listen but don't hear anything, so I inch it open so slowly you'd need a time-elapse camera to notice anything. Eventually it's open enough to see outside.

The rain has stopped. It looks like only one guy stands guard, although I can't be certain. He's ten feet in front of the door. He's not the demon who whipped me with the chains. He's shorter and heavier. His shoulders are slumped, and the assault rifle hangs limply on the straps. He's bored. That boredom every guard who thinks he's on a pointless mission suffers. I know how he feels.

I slip the knife back into my jacket. I need him alive so we can find out where they're holding Megan. Killing him too quickly would be a mistake, and I'm done making mistakes.

Kate tugs on my jacket, so I signal that only one guard is outside, slide out of the hut, and move within arm's length. He shifts on his feet, trying to stay warm and loose.

I tap him on the shoulder. He twists, and I clothesline him, sweeping his legs out from underneath him at the same time. He lands on his back. I don't give him a chance to stand. I stomp on his head with my boot, then I drop one knee on his chest, pinning him to the ground with my weight, my right hand clutched around his throat. I squeeze hard and he gasps for air.

"Listen up. I need some information."

The hair on the back of my head stands on end, and I realize someone else is out here with us. I reach for my knife with my left hand and a voice says, "I wouldn't do that if I were you."

Another guard stares down at me. He's dressed in a red jumpsuit and holds an automatic handgun in a perfect shooter's stance.

I squeeze the throat of the guard harder and the man whimpers.

"Put down the gun and I won't kill him," I say.

"Kill him if you'd like. I don't care. Are you really with Homeland?"

"Of course I am."

He lowers his gun.

"You're the asset on the inside," I say. "You're the guy they've been trying to reach."

"My name is Buck." He nods at the guard underneath me. "You can let him go now. Looks like you've already killed him."

Damn it. I've crushed his windpipe.

He holds out a hand and helps me up, then introduces himself to Kate.

"You must be Spring's mom?" Buck says. "She looks just like you."

"You've seen my Megan?" says Kate. "How is she? Is she okay?"

Buck shrugs. "She's not hurt physically."

"Where are they holding her?" I say. "We need to snatch her and go."

"She's in the cathedral. Mother wanted to handle her experiences personally."

"The cathedral," says Kate. "What is that witch doing to her?"

"The chapels are in the cathedral. That's where Angels believe they talk with God. It's really a virtual reality cylinder, using advanced technology to trick them into believing they're really talking to God. They have the ability to shape the event anyway they want. Usually, they give the girls certain messages to brainwash them. Later, they hook the girls up to rich clients on the outside so they can share experiences. The Angels think they're doing God's bidding, but..." He doesn't finish. He must have thought better of it with Kate hanging onto each word.

"That twisted bitch!" mutters Kate.

"And that's not the worst part," says Buck.

"What's that?" I ask. Someone had to.

"For some reason Mother is pushing things with Megan. They can make the experience addicting, and they're cranking that up with her. By the time she finishes with Megan tonight, she'll be completely hooked. I'm afraid it won't be reversible."

CHAPTER 54

Megan can't understand Petal's frosty mood. Sure, their plan to escape got derailed, and they had to kill Frankie, but Frankie deserved it. She's tried, but she can't manufacture any sympathy for the dead pervert. He needed to die, and they were in the cathedral and would soon use the chapels. They'd soon talk to God, and that was the best feeling in the world! She starts sweating in anticipation.

They've changed out of their jumpsuits and into simple silk robes while they wait for Ivy to join them. A guard watches them, electric prod in hand. He's here so they won't try to escape, which Megan thinks is foolish.

Why would we want to escape? We're going to talk to God.

Petal touches Megan's hand, her voice rough and raw. "Try to resist the vision. Remember that it's not real. It's…"

Ivy arrives and smiles at Petal. "It's what, Petal?"

Petal looks at her feet. "It's better than reality. It's otherworldly."

"Yes, exactly. For a minute there, I was worried you were off track, but that's exactly right. It's heavenly." Ivy points to two chambers ready to receive the girls. "I have a surprise in store for both of you. God would like to talk to you together. You might not remember the experience the same way, but you will stay connected throughout. I sense a closeness between you, and this will only serve to deepen it and your connection with God. You want that, don't you, Petal?"

"Of course, Mother."

"Good. You will help Spring grow closer with God. It's your mission. Don't fail."

"She won't," Megan adds, worried about the threatening tone in Ivy's voice.

"I'm sure you're right, Spring." Ivy touches the screen on her tablet and unclasps both Megan and Petal's pendants. "Time to begin."

Megan and Petal slip out of their robes, letting them fall to the floor, and step to the chapels in unison.

Megan grins at Petal, her lips stretched so wide they practically hurt her face. What could be better? She gets to talk to God with Petal. Won't Petal be surprised when she sees that God looks just like her?

CHAPTER 55

While I change into the dead guard's black jumpsuit, we work out a plan. At least I have two proper weapons now. The M18 feels good in my hands, and my knife fits snuggly in a pocket on the leg of the jumpsuit.

We head toward the cabins, Buck in the lead, Kate in the middle, and me bringing up the rear. We look like we're escorting Kate at gunpoint, our cover story if anyone stops us. We pass only one other person, a guy in a red jumpsuit. Buck knows him and tells him we're bringing the prisoner to the cathedral, so Mother can interrogate her personally. The story works well enough. The guy doesn't ask too many questions. He has somewhere else he needs to be.

When we reach the edge of the cabins, Kate and I hide in the woods while Buck goes inside to retrieve a yellow jumpsuit. We need Kate dressed like an Angel if all three of us are going to enter the cathedral unchallenged.

According to Buck, the cathedral is mostly empty. They just had a burning and my mother likes to leave some time for contemplation after a gathering like that.

A burning? I don't ask him what it means. Why bother? The name tells me all I need to know. My mother is even crazier now than when she wanted to cut the demons out of me.

Kate is jittery, fidgeting in place next to me while we wait for Buck. "We need to hurry. Your nutjob mother said Megan will be addicted to her chapels like a heroin addict if she has another one of those virtual reality sessions. A heroin addict! I don't want to think what something like that can do to a person."

Of course, that's exactly what she's thinking about. It's natural. Any mother would act the same way.

"Megan is a strong young woman," I remind her. "My mother doesn't know her. Megan will surprise her. We can't blunder ahead without a plan. This is the only way. People see what they expect, and it's dark. If we're in these jumpsuits we should get in the cathedral at least. After that, we'll improvise."

"Do you trust Buck?" she asks.

It's a good question. "I know the type. He's Army trained. He could have shot us back at the huts, and he didn't. He'll come in handy when we need him."

He reminds me a little of myself back when I was young. Capable. Well-trained. Dedicated.

Buck returns and hands a yellow jumpsuit to Kate. She breaks a speed record for changing.

We follow Buck to the cathedral. "We still should have an hour or so before they start visions with the other Angels if we hurry."

We travel the narrow path to the cathedral in single file, using the same order as before: Buck in the lead, Kate behind him, and me bringing up the rear. We move at a brisk pace, just short of a jog. Running would attract unwanted attention, but it's hard on Kate. She desperately wants to sprint. Buck slows her down by blocking the path in front and keeping a measured pace.

We emerge from a hemp field to find the cathedral in the near distance. The building looks like a church swallowed a warehouse. The front windows resemble a place of worship, but the back stretches on, all warehouse. It's built from steel. Cheap construction put up quickly, no doubt.

Two guards in black jumpsuits patrol the front glass doors. Buck keeps his pace consistent as we approach, but I sense trouble. The guard on the left has a close-cut, mostly gray beard. He stares at Kate with a sly smile. The one on the right has a long nose and nervous eyes.

Gray Hair whispers something to his younger partner, and they both stand taller and look more alert. They aren't going to let us inside. Once we get within three strides, Buck is forced to slow down as Gray Hair signals for us to halt with his hand.

His voice sounds weary. "Hey Buck, where are you headed, and who are they? I haven't seen this Angel around here before, nor the Reaper."

The younger guard looks at a screen in his hand. "Nothing on the schedule."

"She's one of our Angels," says Buck. "This is her first time here and," he nods his head toward me, "he's new. I'm surprised you hadn't seen him before. Must be a Trevor thing."

I grunt at Gray Hair, my best impersonation of a new guy who'd like to avoid trouble.

The guy ignores me. Instead, he touches Kate's chin. "She's pretty, but isn't she a tad bit old?" He taps the guard next to him. "I guess we cater to all tastes, but this is a first."

"Old?" Fire consumes Kate's voice. She's strung tightly, and this might be too much for her to take right now.

"Yeah?" says Gray Hair, curious at her response. He's probably not used to Angels talking back to him.

"Bite me!" Kate kicks him in the nuts. Gray Hair bends at the waist, his hands clutching his groin. Kate connects an elbow to his head that drops him to the ground. Without hesitation, she kicks him in the skull and knocks him out.

If I weren't already in love with her, I would fall for her at this very moment. She's fucking awesome.

The younger guy drops the screen he's holding. Having anticipated Kate's response, I'm two moves ahead of him. I swing the butt of my assault rifle into the guy's stomach, knocking the air out of him. Then, I hammer the stock into his forehead. He crumples to the ground.

Kate kicks Gray Hair in the stomach even though he's out cold. "Old, my ass."

Buck looks at me with raised eyebrows.

"Never talk about a woman's age." I shrug. "They weren't letting us in anyway. Come on, let's get them inside so anyone passing by won't notice."

He grabs Gray Hair and I sling the younger guard over my shoulder. Kate opens the doors. We walk inside and drop both on the floor.

It takes a moment for my eyes to adjust in the dim light. Candles flicker in sconces against the walls, and a spotlight brightens the large oak cross suspended from the ceiling. Plenty of room for shadows, and the skin on my face tingles. We're not alone.

Buck points behind the cross and says, "The chapels are that way. Let's go."

He starts in that direction, with Kate at his heels. I move after them warily until a high-pitched voice freezes me. "Oh, Stevie, have you come to play with me?"

Oh, shit. It's Raven – the demon from the alley behind the church - and she stands between the door to the chapels and us.

I send Kate a silent message with my eyes. She understands. Megan is more important than me. Whatever happens here, she needs to save her daughter.

"Play isn't exactly the word I'd use." I sprint to my right and open fire at the monster. The spray from the assault rifle would have ripped apart a normal person, but Raven isn't normal. She's a demon and moves faster than should be possible.

She's a blur as she leaps upward, kicks her feet off the wall, flips in the air, and does a somersault on the ground. It's a freaky thing to see. Every Olympic judge would give her a ten, but it makes my skin crawl. No human can move like that.

Buck runs at her.

"Don't!" I shout. He doesn't understand what we're dealing with, but it's too late.

He swings an electric prod at her head.

Raven ducks under the swipe and punches him in the stomach. The force of the blow lifts Buck off the ground. She must have cracked half of his ribs. When he hits the tiled floor, he rolls onto his side.

I level the M18 again, but before I pull the trigger, Raven throws a chair at me. It's a bone-crunching missile. I dive out of its path at the last second, and it shatters against the wall behind me.

By the time I jump back to my feet, Raven has grabbed Buck's electric prod and jams it into his mouth. The young man's body convulses. She grins a wicked smile. After it dispenses its full charge, she tosses it away and Buck folds flat on the floor.

He could be dead or fried unconscious. I can't tell.

Raven smirks at me. "Just you and me now, Stevie. Have you reconsidered my earlier proposal?" She transforms before my eyes. Battered, black wings sprout from her back, and her jumpsuit melts away, replaced by scaly, reddish black skin. Her hands and feet turn to talons; her eyes become red slits and her mouth stretches into a snout. She retains only a bit of her human-like appearance. "Do you want little Stevie to come and play with me?"

Kate's gone. She went to fetch her daughter, and I smile. "It's an attractive offer, but I'm an old-fashioned guy. I need some courting. Maybe flowers and a movie?"

CHAPTER 56

My blood races and my inner demon growls. Not Caesar or any of the voices I sometimes hear, but that darker force, that energy that scares me, the one that made me bash Mr. Frosty's head against the toilet. Instead of fighting it, I embrace it, and my senses scream as if they've woken from a long slumber. My eyesight sharpens to where I can see all the folds of scaly skin on Raven's body. They glisten as if Vaseline has been rubbed on them. I smell the scent of burned flesh from Buck's throat and hear him breathing, and the flickering sound of the flames in the candles. Strength and quickness flow through my body like I've never felt before. It's as if I've shed my human skin, and transformed into something else, something stronger, and faster, and darker.

I'm still holding the M18, but before I can aim and fire, Raven bats her wings, and darts forward at terrific speed. It's almost as if she's hovering a foot over the ground. She grabs the gun, twists it from my grip, and bends the metal.

"I was just borrowing that gun. I'm not going to pay for that damage. That's on you."

She chuckles. "Ready to join us, halfling."

"Halfling?"

"Oh, didn't Mommy tell you? Your father was one of us. That's why He wants you. It's very unusual that one of us can mate with a lower species like humans."

For a heartbeat, time seems to stop. "My father was a demon?" The words sound ridiculous as they slip between my lips, yet it makes sense. I thought my mother was crazy all this time, but she was right. About my father. About me.

Raven grabs my throat in one of her talons. Her nails dig into my neck. "Who said anything about demons? Your father was an angel. Like me."

"You mean a fallen angel."

"A minor setback in the scope of things. We will rise again. Our beauty will be restored, and our reign will last forever."

"Have you considered a makeover? It's amazing what they can do with concealer."

"Yes, you must feel it now. The hellfire is burning in your eyes. I can see the sparks." Her tongue whips out like a lizard's and scrapes against my cheek. "I can taste your father in you. We were lovers once."

"Gross. I don't know where that tongue's been." I need to break free, and this is my best chance. I punch Raven in the stomach, a hard right with all my weight behind it. It should have crippled her, but it feels as if I've smashed my fist against a brick wall. I've never punched anything that hard before.

She groans and releases me. I hammer her head with a left cross, and then a right. The force of the two blows staggers her backward. When she steadies herself, she spits black demon blood from her mouth and bares her fangs.

"Now I'm going to drag you to hell myself."

She grabs my shoulders and tosses me in the air. I slam face first on the tile floor. I pull my knife and manage to stand.

She laughs. "What are you going to do with that?"

"My best." I lunge forward, stabbing the knife at her chest. She catches my wrist and twists. The pain burns up my arm and into my skull.

The knife clanks on the floor.

She kicks it away. "Fool. Your human weapons can't kill me."

She whips me in a circle by my arm and flings me against a wall. At least one rib is broken, and my head swims.

Raven mutters under her breath and waves her arms. A circle of flames burst beside her. Not normal flames, but darker and richer in color as if they've come from my worst nightmares. They hover a few feet above the floor.

She grins, or at least it looks that way to me. It's hard to know for sure because the snout distorts her face.

"Ready for a road trip?" she asks. "I've created a portal just for us."

"I think it's a little too early for that. We've only just met. You're rushing the relationship."

"Either you come with me now, or I'll snap your skinny neck and you'll go to hell a different way. A lot less desirable, if you ask me."

Neither sounds all that appealing. I need a weapon and spot my knife a foot away. She must have kicked it here. I grab it and gamble with my soul. "You're not going to kill me. You can't do it. You like me too much. And besides, you're weak. You're no angel at all. You're barely a demon."

Her face contorts angrily. It's the reaction I'm hoping for. She's a vain creature, not used to being challenged.

She screams, and it sounds like hundreds of children being tortured. The muscles in her wings twitch, and I thrust out the point of the knife, making one last gamble.

She flies toward me like before. She moves so fast, she can't stop before the knife plunges into her chest.

A sick grin spreads across her face. "Didn't I tell you that human weapons can't kill me? It feels like a bee sting."

"Yes, but this one has been doused in holy water."

Her eyes go wide.

"I know this changes things between us, but I just don't think we were developing the right type of chemistry." I twist the knife. "In this case, I'd have to say it's you, not me."

A river of black sludge pours from her chest. It stinks like sulfur. She twists, spins, and transforms into a black cloud. The cloud screams one last time and gets sucked into the portal she had created. The flames disappear, and my knife falls to the floor.

I'm breathing hard, positive I've crossed that invisible line from sane to insane. I doubt I'll cross back now. When I retrieve the knife, I scrape the black sludge off the blade against the side of a chair.

There's no time to contemplate Raven or the portal to hell or what she told me about my father. Kate's on the other side of the door, somewhere deeper inside the building where she needs my help.

Willing myself forward, I ignore my ribs and run through the door that leads to the chapels. I stumble through a hallway with closed doors on both sides. This isn't right. Where are the metal tubes?

I push through the door at the end of the hallway and enter the massive warehouse space. A field of chapels spreads out before me with half-wall dividers separating them.

Someone screams, "No!" Another shot of adrenaline surges through me. I lock onto where the shout came from and weave my way through the dividers until I see Luke, the black-clad guard who whipped me with the chains, holding an M18. He's outside of the divider, down a narrow hallway.

I take off toward him, sprinting faster than I've run before. He sees me, levels the gun, and fires.

The bullet spins at me, and I twist out of the way without slowing my momentum. He fires again, and this time I leap over the bullet, land on him and drive my fist into the top of his forehead. He falls to the floor, and I snap his neck like a twig. He never had a chance.

I freeze.

Megan's wearing a robe and pointing a gun at Kate. Another young woman stands near Kate, her skin ashen. My eyes skim over them and find my mother. She's dressed in a multi-colored jumpsuit, holding a tablet.

She looks at me, her gaze intense. "My son. It's about time."

My stomach twists, and all my strength leaves me. I can barely stand. I'm a teenager who barricaded the door as his mother scratched her nails into it, promising to cut the demons out of him.

Did I make a mistake? Maybe I should have gone with Raven to hell? Could it be worse than meeting my mother again?

The Fates are cruel puppet masters.

CHAPTER 57

Megan remembers a tropical island, a giant waterfall that ended in a ten-story statue of an angel. The statue stood, her arms stretched wide, the water cascading from both hands. Megan touched pools of clear warm water, stepped on smooth sand, and waded into a calm ocean that lapped against her skin. An eagle circled overhead, and Petal accompanied her everywhere. She looked beautiful, with the sun sparkling in her eyes and caressing her hair.

Megan kissed her in the ocean and she tasted happiness on her lips. Although unable to swim, Megan kept wandering deeper into the blue sea, wanting more. She had never swum before, never even stepped on a beach prior to this. Petal kept a firm grip on her hand, always tugging her back when the water reached her neck.

Tears flowed down Petal's cheeks when they kissed. At first, Megan thought they matched her feelings, tears of unbelievable delight, but no joy lit her eyes. Sadness clung to them and clouded their gem-like beauty. It made Megan hollow like a husk of corn after all the kernels were gone.

God spoke to them on that island. He didn't appear in physical form, like he had during Megan's first experience in the chapel, but she heard His voice in her head – certain, knowledgeable, stern. Over time, it sounded more like Ivy's voice until she couldn't tell the two apart. God wanted unwavering loyalty, to Him and to Ivy.

Harsh white lights burned her eyes. Her vision ended, and the lid opened. She stepped out, got dressed in a robe, and waited as Petal did the same. Still dazed by her vision, Megan wasn't sure what to believe.

Her experience had been so euphoric, so otherworldly, and now this, stark brightness. She wanted to go back into the chapel, experience the paradise island again, with Petal, longer this time.

Ivy clasps the pendants around Petal and Megan's necks and then hands a gun to Megan. "Spring, a demon is coming for us. She's birthed from the fires in hell. She's here to kill me. She has horns, wings, and her skin is blood red. A long tail swoops behind her. You believe me, right?"

Megan nods. She believes every word. God told her to believe Ivy. She has to trust in Ivy, that's the only way back into a chapel.

A monster stalks forward. She's on the other side of the partition, ten feet away. Megan points the gun at it. "Stay away, demon."

The demon stops. "Megan, it's me. Your mom!"

Megan squints. The voice sounds familiar, like her mom's voice, yet that can't be right. Ivy said it was a demon. God said she must trust Ivy. The creature has horns and a tail, and looks like a demon, just like Ivy described. Megan holds the gun steady.

Gunfire sounds from the hallway. A figure moves in a blur, and then appears at the partition. It's a man, dressed in a black jumpsuit, fire burning in his eyes.

Ivy looks at the intruder. "My son. It's about time."

The man says, "What are you doing? What have you done to Megan?"

"She's one of my Angels now." Ivy touches Megan on the shoulder. "Child, if I tell you to pull the trigger and slay that demon, will you?"

"Gladly, Mother."

CHAPTER 58

I've seen brainwashed people before. To some extent, everyone is brainwashed. They might want things they don't need, or be hooked on gambling, drugs, or virtual reality. Those who suffer the most can be convinced of almost anything: that black is white, up is down, bad is good. We all know people like that, but cults take it to the extreme. They perfect the art of brainwashing so much they wipe away a person's self-control. They wipe away a person's identity.

It's only been a few days, but my mother has that level of control over Megan. So much control she trusts the girl with a gun. I want to rush forward, disarm Megan, save Kate, and confront my mother, but if I make any sudden movements, Megan might shoot Kate—a risk I can't take. It's unlikely, maybe only a thirty percent chance, but that's way too high.

My mother waves for me to come closer. "Come here, Stevie. It's been too long. We need to catch up." She backs into another divided space, separate from the one with Megan, Kate, and the other young woman. Before she disappears, she says, "Spring, if the demon speaks, shoot it."

"Yes, Mother." The girl calls out.

My mother disappears behind the partition and I have no choice but to follow her. I have to deal with her. I don't want to hurt Megan or risk Kate's life.

My mother stands behind one of the stainless-steel tubes, holding a tablet.

I move cautiously. My heart pounds, every beat thumping in my head. Kate was right about my mother. She looks healthier than I remember, more confident, more alive.

From this spot, we can see Megan and Kate through the opening in the partition wall. "Let Kate and Megan go," I say. "You don't need them anymore. You've gotten your wish. I'm here now."

"We'll worry about Kate later. Let's talk, son. It's been so long."

I need answers. This is why I came back home, and this is my best chance to get them, possibly my only choice. "Is it true about my father? Was he a... demon?"

"He was a fallen angel, my dear. Don't let Raven hear you call him a demon. She's very touchy about the difference. Demons are ordinary people who Lucifer possess. Fallen Angels are practically immortal and willingly followed Lucifer in his fight against the Cursed One."

"Raven's no longer a problem."

My mother smiles. "You found a way to kill Raven? Like mother, like son, they say."

"No one says that."

"They should. I never liked her. She held a grudge against me because your father preferred me to her. Can you blame him? The smell alone is enough to drive someone crazy." My mother washes her eyes over me, measuring me. I wonder what she sees.

"I'm proud of you, son. You were such a weak child."

"Weak? You were trying to kill me when I was a teenager!"

"That's the problem with your generation—always ducking responsibility for your own failings. I might not have been perfect, but it's hard to be a single mother. Now you've grown strong. Good genes, I'd say."

"Good genes?" I shake my head. We're off track, so I try to bring us back to something useful. "You were right about Dad and me. You've been right all along."

"I told you he was a demon when I killed him, which was almost right. You should have listened to me. But I was only right about some things. I should never have killed your father. Or fought the demon inside me for so long. It was a silly thing to do. I didn't understand."

"Understand what?" I'm holding my breath. Does she know some truth that will save me?

"Lucifer isn't bad, after all. Sure, he lost that pesky confrontation with God, but that was only one battle in a long war. Now, he will rise again. He will win. He will defeat the Cursed One with our help."

"In the Great Struggle. Is that what this is about?"

"Yes, the End of Days is coming. All the hate and violence in the world strengthens Lucifer, his fallen angels, and their demons. They ready for war while God is nowhere to be seen. I mean, where is He? In the ghettos? Stopping the endless conflicts that plague mankind? No, but Lucifer and his followers are there. And they will win with our help."

"What does this have to do with me?"

"You're a Nephilim, a child born between an angel and human. Not many like you exist. You're way more powerful than a normal demon. Practically as strong as an angel. Lucifer wants you to do his bidding."

"What if I don't want to?"

"Of course you want to. I can see the flames in your eyes. You must feel the power surging through your body. You don't have to repress who you are. Lucifer loves you for it. He will glorify you for your strength. Besides, you've practically turned already. You feel how good it is! That power, that sense of being alive! You can't turn back now."

I clench my hands into fists. She's right. I do feel alive, and it feels damn good. If I turn to her, I can live my life the way I'm hardwired. Free to let my inner demon hunt. Free to hurt and punish those I want. Isn't that what I'm made for?

She chuckles. "I have good news and bad news for you, Stevie."

"You know how I hate when you do that."

"The bad news is that God will never take you in. You've committed too many sins. You're not pure enough for him. The good news is that Lucifer will welcome you, and his side is so much more fun. You will launch both of us to the highest levels. We will help rule over mankind. Mother and son together. We can bring humankind back to its true nature. The strong should rule over the weak. Not the wealthy. Us!"

She speaks with such certainty, such authority, that it all sounds reasonable. I see why she succumbed to it. We can be important. The current system leads to such pain. Wouldn't a new system be better? One based upon strength. How could it be worse?

She grins. "You can have Kate and Megan and whoever else you want. Lucifer can be a generous master. He knows how to reward his followers."

I glance at Kate and Megan. Megan still aims the gun at her mother.

"We are the same," my mother's voice turns into a throaty whisper. "Join us and free yourself."

The world crashes around me, as if I'm in the center of an earthquake and skyscrapers fall everywhere and shakes the ground. Am I like my mother? Should I join her, and be free to be myself, stop fighting the demon inside? I can do it. One word, but I'll never be able to go back. Lucifer will claim me as his own. Once I have that power, I'll never give it up.

I'm moving toward my mother, each inch drawing me closer to her world. I stop and think of Buck. I used to be like him. I used to fight for those who couldn't. Can I turn my back on people like him?

I've been doing this all wrong from the beginning. I've been looking to others to find out who I am. I came to Philadelphia to find my mother, hoping she'd have the answer. I even looked to Kate and Father Paul, wanting them to tell me what I should do, who I should be. In an odd way, my mother and Raven helped me realize the truth. No one else can decide for me. They want me to turn to the Devil, which means I haven't turned yet. I still have a choice. Free will even. It's up to me. The Fates haven't woven that part of my tapestry yet.

I can still be saved. It's not what I've done that defines me. It's what's in my heart, and what I will do next that matters. I can still do good. It'll be a harder path, less likely of success, the odds lower, but harder doesn't mean worse.

I'm not my mother's son. I stand taller and release my fists.

"Let Kate go, and I won't hurt you."

My mother nods. "You still need persuading. You need a demonstration. You've always been stubborn. Now you'll see Lucifer's strength. You'll see that any other path is foolish."

She turns and shouts to Megan, "Spring, shoot that demon!"

Fuck, I didn't expect that.

CHAPTER 59

Ivy's command pulls Megan to action. She aims for the demon's chest, but before she pulls the trigger, Petal jumps in front of the creature, her voice pleading.

"Don't do it. It's not really a demon. It is your mom!"

Megan squints, and the image of the demon flickers. For a moment, it looks like her mom. The moment lasts a second and disappears, the demon returning, smoke rising from the horns on its head. "Get out of the way. I have to kill it."

Petal steps toward her. "Your name is Megan Smith. What's my name?"

"Petal."

Petal's eyes mist over, and they plead with Megan. "What's my real name? Please Megan, you promised not to forget it. Remember."

Ivy calls from the other room, her voice fused with the authority of God. "Spring, honey, we don't have all day. Kill that demon or you'll never go in a chapel again. You'll never talk to God again or feel his presence. He demands loyalty, and that demon has to die."

A shiver runs through Megan's body. She needs the chapel. She can't imagine living without it. The demon says something, but she can't hear it. Her finger tightens on the trigger, but Petal won't get out of her way.

Megan focuses on her friend again, remembering the feel of her lips, the touch of her fingertips, the grace in her smile.

She recalls her first vision and how strange it was that God looked like Petal. And then she remembers. "Your name is Felicity Sanders and I'm Megan Smith. I want to explore space."

"Yes, you do," says Petal, relief in her voice. "And one day you will."

The gun shakes in Megan's hands, she blinks, and the demon transforms into her mother. Ivy's lying to her. She's been lying all along. That voice in her head isn't God, it's Ivy spewing venom.

Megan turns and points the gun at Ivy. "I have good and bad news for you. I'm going to start with the bad."

She pulls the trigger, but nothing happens.

CHAPTER 60

I glare at my mother.

"What? Did you really think I was going to hand that girl a loaded gun? I know what you're thinking, that I'm helpless, but you're wrong." She presses the screen on her tablet.

Megan screams. Petal has fallen to her knees, clutching the necklace, which has tightened to the point of choking her.

"Mother, stop it. The girl has done nothing wrong."

"Her life is in my hands." My mother backs away from me. "Here's the situation, Stevie. I control all the pendants from this tablet. All of them—966 Angels across the globe. One touch from me and they all die. Each pendant has an explosive built into it. It will get messy. If I die, they *all* die. It's a failsafe I've built into the system. My heart stops beating, and so do theirs. It's controlled from my pendant." She lifts her necklace to show me her charm. "Don't do anything stupid."

I lift my hands over my head. "Give me the tablet, and you can go."

"Go? This is my place. A dozen Reapers will be here in a few minutes, plus my guards. You're surrounded. You have no way out."

Helicopter blades thump over the building, and I grin. "That's Homeland. The tables have turned, Mother."

"But I did away with the traitor." My mother's face turns red. "I sent a message to Homeland about the other farm."

"Yes, a tragic mistake. Buck was really the traitor, that's the bad news. Oh, and I guess there's more bad news. He told them the truth."

The fire in my mother's eyes burns even hotter than before. She swipes the tablet and places it on top of the stainless tube before her. "I've started a countdown sequence. You have five minutes. You'll have to hack my password and disable it. If you don't, Megan and all the Angels will die. Their heads will explode, and that's on you."

"What's the password?"

"You'll have to hack it."

"How?"

"That's up to you." She hesitates before she runs off. "I offered you everything. It's a shame you couldn't see it."

She runs and she's gone, into the maze.

I grab the tablet. The countdown clock reads four minutes and forty seconds, and it's running.

CHAPTER 61

I bring the tablet to Kate, Megan, and Felicity. Kate and Megan are crying, and Felicity's sitting with tears trickling down her face. The chain chokes her neck, but there's just enough room for her to suck in air.

Gabriel and Tina barrel to us. They're wearing Homeland Kevlar vests and helmets. Gabriel swings the M18 in an aggressive loop before he lowers the weapon.

Tina crashes in on Megan and Kate's hug.

"What's the situation?" asks Gabriel. "Any hostiles about?"

"I don't think so."

"Why that look on your face then?" asks Gabriel.

I speak loudly so everyone hears me. "We have a problem. My crazy mother has rigged the pendants that all the Angels wear to explode when this countdown reaches zero. We have three minutes and twenty seconds left. If I can't come up with the password by then, they will all die."

"Why don't we rip them off?" Kate reaches for Megan's chain, but the girl pushes her hand away.

"You can't break the chain! If the connection is broken, the explosive will detonate."

"What a total bitch," says Tina. "Where is she? We'll ring the password out of that whackjob."

"She took off. I couldn't waste time chasing after her."

3 minutes left.

"Start typing, dipshit," says Tina.

"Thanks."

I don't know what to use, so I eliminate the obvious possibilities: my name, my father's name, The Farm, the town we're in, Otherworldly Experiences, and Lucifer.

Kate's holding on to Megan and Felicity in a death grip. She should back off in case I can't figure out the password, but she won't.

Felicity wheezes something I can't here.

Megan calls out, "Felicity says the password is seven."

I type in seven and it doesn't work. It's too simple. I shake my head at the others.

1 minute 55 seconds left.

I close my eyes. Father Paul said I needed faith, so I pray. I pray that God will deliver me, and that in return, I'll dedicate my life to do His will. Father Paul said I knew everything I needed. Somewhere in my thick skull, I must know the answer, if only it will come to me.

My mother is a complete narcissist. She believes the world revolves around her. What password would she use?

I fall deeper into a meditative state. I'm standing outside my old apartment building. The old-timer is talking to me. His eyes burn with a blue light. I hadn't noticed that the first time we met. The first time I thought his gaze just meant he wanted to live, but there was more to it. The light reminds me of the light in Father Paul's eyes.

Forty seconds left.

What story did he tell me? I reach back, picture his thin, haggard face, and remember the awful smell. Smells bring back memories better than anything else. I see his lips move and then the words spill out. He told me a tale about the Seventh Street Stabber. A person who terrorized my old apartment, stabbing people to death. He thought the murderer had to be a male, but a female demon would work — my mother.

Felicity thought the password was seven. What if she only had part of it?

Fifteen seconds left.

I type "Seventh Street Stabber" press enter and hold my breath.

The tablet vibrates, and the clock stops—*4 seconds.*

Kate releases Megan and Felicity. Gabriel laughs, and Tina slaps him on the back.

I've made a bargain I'll have to keep, but it's worth it.

I fold the tablet, put it into my pocket, and an alarm blares.

Red lights swirl.

What now?

Gabriel points to the corners of the warehouse space. "Explosives. The place is wired to go. We've got to get out of here."

He grabs Tina and pushes her toward the door. Kate, Megan, and Felicity follow him.

It's the best way out, the shortest route to safety. I freeze. Buck's alive, and he's the other way. I can't leave him. He risked his life for us.

I take off in the other direction, and blood surges through me. I'm back in that enhanced state, senses popping, strength ripping through me.

I shoulder my way through the door and into the cathedral. Buck's on his knees, and he can't stand. I reach him at a full run, grab him with one arm, and sling him over my shoulder while still running forward. An explosion rips through the warehouse portion of the building. The floor rocks. I sprint for the glass doors. A second explosion, under the cross, follows the first. It's all meant to be simultaneous, but the half-second delay is all I need.

I crash straight through the glass doors, shards raining everywhere. Another explosion. And then another.

Two steps later, the shaking ground topples me into the mud. I face plant and Buck falls forward. All I can do is cover my head.

Another explosion detonates. Shrapnel flies past me. A chunk of the oak cross skewers the ground an inch from my head, but nothing hits me. I crawl to Buck, who's safe and alive.

The cathedral and the warehouse are gone—twisted metal, burning. Everything inside is toast. A chopper beats in the air, and I wave. Gabriel and the others are on board. Tina flips me the bird.

Something buzzes in my pocket. I pull out my mother's tablet. There's a message for me.

It's strange how Megan has six toes on her right foot. Isn't that a genetic condition?

CHAPTER 62

December 12th, 2041, 8:45 PM

Five days have passed since we saved Megan and blew up the cathedral in the process. Gabriel, with the support of President-elect Charles Sheppard, assembled a massive Homeland team that descended upon both farms like a plague of locusts. As part of the team, Sheppard sent some of the best hackers in the government. They found a redundant computer system at the larger farm, successfully hacked in, and released the chains that held all the pendants. The Angels are free from that threat at least.

Homeland shut down all the Otherworldly Experience shops. They're still searching for the mastermind behind the enterprise, but they haven't found him. The only name that keeps coming up is Trevor, an obvious alias. Even Buck has no idea who Trevor is. He'd been searching for his identity before we blew the top off the operation.

Homeland renamed the farms the "Devil's Den," and is treating the entire situation as a giant sex-slave ring. I understand why. That's certainly part of the story, the easiest part to understand, but it's not the whole thing. My mother was using these Angels to further her desires and push us toward the End of Days. She had more in store for these girls than sex for profit, but I can't explain my suspicions to anyone. Not even Gabriel. I don't have any proof that demons or angels exist, whether fallen or not. Who would believe me? At times, I doubt myself.

We might never know exactly what my mother and this Trevor had planned, but Gabriel uncovered a list of all the sold girls and Homeland is trying to retrieve them. Some might be hard to get because they're overseas, but they'll try. Gabriel is still a little sore about my drugging him. It'll take time for him to forgive me, but he's doing good here, and that takes a lot of the sting out of the situation. Eventually, he'll stop growling at me. I'd like to keep him as a friend. I don't have that many.

Buck survived, even though his throat was badly damaged. He can talk now, but he'll never sound the same. He's been instrumental in helping Gabriel and Homeland clean up the mess. At least he'll live with the knowledge that he helped bring a stop to The Farm and the evil happening there. He knows where many of the bodies are buried, quite literally. Gabriel and I watched as they uncovered two mass graves. At least one hundred souls buried in them.

I've seen my share of evil in the world. Hell, I've participated in more than my share, but that shook me. Bones and decomposing bodies tossed inside in a heap as if worthless. As if they never counted. I can't unsee it now, but I wish I could.

Kate and I are alone in her apartment, sitting on the couch in her living room.

"How was the zoo?" she asks me.

"Amazing. I'm not sure who had the best time."

"Probably Eddie," she grins.

"I'm sure you're right, but Megan and Felicity enjoyed the day, and they could barely pull Denise away from the gorillas."

"What about you?"

"One of the top five days in my life. Megan is remarkable. I know she has work to do to overcome what my mother put her through in those chapels, but she'll make it."

"Yes, she will." Kate touches my hand. "So why the sad face?"

"I know Megan is my daughter. I saw the six toes on her right foot. That's not a coincidence."

"Don't be cross. I made up that story about Ethan so many years ago. I think I actually started to believe it. And when I saw you, I couldn't just dump the fact that Megan was your daughter on you. Not when she was missing. It was too much and—"

I kiss her on the lips, deep, and it's wonderful.

When we pull apart, Kate says, "You're not angry with me?"

"How can I be angry with you? Megan is a miracle. I have a daughter and she's just like you. I couldn't be happier."

Kate touches my face and our lips meld together. It's the second-best kiss in my life, behind only that first one in Kissing Park.

"Why do you look sad then?" Kate asks.

"I can't stay. You won't be safe with me here. My mother will come looking for me and not just her." I explain to Kate the story of my mother and father, and this Great Struggle, which is about to happen between angels and demons.

Kate stands and soaks it in. "You believe it?"

"All of it. I'm not sure what I'm supposed to do next, but once it's over, I'll come back." I stand and take Kate's hand. My heart is shattering into endless pieces, but we can't be together just yet. "I want a life with you and Megan. I just need you to be safe. Once this is settled, we can see how we fit together again."

Kate nods. "Normally I'd have a hard time believing you, but a priest found me in the hospital today. He told me a strange story about a Nephilim. That's what he said the guy was, half human and half angel. I didn't want to believe it, but his eyes shined this blue color and he was convincing. He said this Nephilim was a good person, really. Maybe he'd done some bad things, but his heart was good and might prove to be important in events to come."

"Let me guess. He said his name was Father Paul."

"He told me to call him Paulie."

I've done some difficult things in my life, but leaving Kate in that apartment was one of the hardest.

December 14th, 2041, 12:47 AM

I sit alone in a dark room, my trusty knife in hand. I've carved a half-dozen scars into my forearm over the past few years. Lines I've written into my arm when I needed to check my blood to see if I've turned into a demon. I don't need to do that anymore. I'm in control of my own fate and I've made a promise. I won't become a demon and succumb to the dark side and the terrible power it brings.

I'm on a different path. I keep expecting to find Father Paul waiting for me somewhere. Now, I look over my shoulder for demons and angels. I'm sure I'll see Father Paul again soon. He's not done with me.

Caesar appears next to me, a rare smile on his face. "This is the end of the line for us, Cupcake. You don't need me anymore."

"Why not?"

"My job is done. You've made your decision. You don't need me to fight that demon who was lurking inside of you. You've done it yourself."

"You were protecting me?"

"Someone had to. You're as dumb as a stump. One of the worst trainees I've ever had the displeasure to work with. I—"

"That's enough."

Caesar winks and fades from sight.

Mary did one last favor for me. I sent her my mother's tablet and she hacked into it. I know who Trevor is. He's the governor, and he's not going to get away with what he's done. He's hurt thousands of people, hundreds of girls. He hurt my daughter, and I won't excuse it. Father Paul said God needed warriors on his side. I guess I fit the bill.

The door to the bedroom opens, and the governor walks in. He flips the light switch, and I'm standing before him, my knife fluttering before his eyes. I wonder if his blood will be black like tar.

I can feel the Fates cut his string with their scissors of death. At my heart, I'm a people pleaser. I had better check the time.

---THE END---

Acknowledgements

Many people helped create Devil's Den. Too many to list here, but I appreciate every single one of them. I'd like to highlight Dave Lane (aka Lane Diamond) and Evolved Publishing. Thanks for the confidence and the unwavering support. I'm proud to be associated with such a high-quality publisher and team.

My editors, Kimberly Goebel and Robb Grindstaff, both did wonderful jobs saving me from myself. I really could not ask for two better editors. They tamed my worst impulses and really helped make the final project special. My trusty beta readers, as always, deserve a shout out. Their encouragement and sound advice always see me through the abyss I sometimes dwell in. Finally, my family is my cornerstone. Without them, I'd be nothing.

About the Author

Jeff Altabef lives in New York with his wife, two daughters, and Charlie the dog. He spends time volunteering at the Writing Center in the local community college. After years of being accused of "telling stories," he thought he would make it official. He writes in both the thriller and young adult genres. As an avid Knicks fan, he is prone to long periods of melancholy during hoops season.

Jeff has a column on The Examiner focused on writing and a blog on The Patch designed to encourage writing for those that like telling stories.

For more, please visit Jeff Altabef online at:
Personal Website: www.JeffreyAltabef.com
Publisher Website: www.EvolvedPub.com
Goodreads: Jeff Altabef
Twitter: @JeffALtabef
Facebook: Jeff Altabef Author

More from Jeff Altabef

Jeff Altabef has produced multiple award-winning books and series across multiple genres. Whether you're a fan of fantasy thrillers with strong Native American themes, young adult dystopian fiction, or futuristic crime thrillers with a dystopian edge, you can always count on Jeff Altabef for entertaining stories loaded with great characters.

On the following pages, we'll tell you a little about the first books from each of Jeff's three other series:

1) A Point Thriller
2) Red Death
3) Chosen

We know you're going to love them.

FRACTURE POINT
A Point Thriller – Book 1

An untrained spy and a rebel faction.
A mysterious scarlet-haired jazz singer.
Dangerous secrets guarded by a devious killer.

What could possibly go wrong?

Only everything.

Tom's brilliant, but when it comes to people smarts, he's clueless. When his older brother disappears, Tom opens the door to adventure and terror — and a beautiful red-haired spy. She stands in the doorway and spins a tale so unbelievable it just might be true. What if his carefree brother is not just a tennis instructor, but a spy who has uncovered a secret so explosive it could trigger a bloody revolution?

Tom will do whatever it takes to get his brother back, even if he's completely unprepared for what happens next. He'll need the help of would-be friends and foes, and a whole lot of luck, to outwit the psychopathic killer holding his brother hostage. And maybe, just maybe, he can rescue his brother and keep America from reaching the fracture point, too.

https://evolvedpub.com/APointThriller

This gripping, intriguing glimpse of what America might become will delight fans of thrillers, dystopian fiction, and fast-paced adventures.

RED DEATH

Red Death – Book 1

Danger lurks outside Eden's sturdy walls, in the land of the Soulless – a medieval world filled with witches, warrior kingdoms, and magic.

Seventeen-year-old Aaliss graduated at the top of her class and now protects Eden as a highly trained Guardian. She's sworn to keep Eden safe, for outside the city, a deadly plague reigns over the world. Once infected with the Red Death, no one lives past their early twenties.

Wilky, Aaliss's rather odd younger brother, discovers a cure, but it comes at a cost. The High Priest falsely brands them as traitors, and Aaliss must do what she never expected – run.

Forced to flee the only home they've ever known, they plunge into the land of the Soulless. Captured in the wild new world, Aaliss strikes a deal with the surprisingly charming Prince Eamon – the cure, in exchange for her freedom. Together they search for the ingredients to the cure in a desperate race against time to save the Prince's brother's life.

Aaliss is eager to return home and seek revenge against the High Priest, but when her feelings for Prince Eamon tug her deeper into the world of the Soulless, she questions everything she once believed. Are the Soulless so bad? Will she and Wilky fall victim to the Red Death? Or... might Aaliss finally discover, against all odds, what her heart has yearned for all along?

https://evolvedpub.com/RedDeathSeries

WINNER: Pinnacle Book Achievement Award - Best Science Fiction

INTERNATIONAL FINALIST, UNANIMOUS 5 STARS:
Readers' Favorite Book Reviews and Awards Contest
Young Adult – Fantasy – General

FINALIST: Eric Hoffer Book Awards – Young Adult

WIND CATCHER
Chosen – Book 1

Lies. Betrayal. Destiny. A choice that changes everything.

My name is Juliet Wildfire Stone, and I am special. I see visions and hear voices, and I have no idea what they mean.

When someone murders medicine men in my sleepy Arizona town, I can't help but worry my crazy grandfather is involved. He's a medicine man and more than a just a little eccentric. He likes to tell me stories about the Great Wind Spirit and Coyote, but none of it makes any sense. I thought I knew the truth, but in order to clear his name I dive into his alien world and uncover an ancient secret society formed over two hundred years ago to keep me safe—me! And I can't help but to start to wonder whether there's some truth to those old stories my grandfather has been telling me.

I just want to be an average sixteen-year-old girl, but apparently I've never been average. Could never be average. I didn't know it before, but I'm a Chosen, and those voices I've been hearing... well, they're not just "voices." I've started to develop abilities, but they might not be enough. A powerful entity called a Seeker is hunting me and he's close—really close.

I thought I knew the answers but truth is, I don't. Betrayed by those I love, I must choose to run or risk everything in order to fulfill my destiny. I hope I make the right choice. Don't you?

https://evolvedpub.com/Chosen

GOLD MEDAL WINNER:
Readers' Favorite Book Reviews and Awards Contest
Young Adult – Coming of Age

WINNER: Beverly Hills Book Awards – Young Adult Fiction
Mom's Choice Awards – Young Adult Fantasy, Myths & Legends

More from
Evolved Publishing

We offer great books across multiple genres, featuring hiqh-quality editing (which we believe is second-to-none) and fantastic covers.

As a hybrid small press, your support as loyal readers is so important to us, and we have strived, with tireless dedication and sheer determination, to deliver on the promise of our motto: **QUALITY IS PRIORITY #1!**

Please check out all of our great books,
which you can find at this link:
www.EvolvedPub.com/Catalog/

Thank you!

CPSIA information can be obtained
at www.ICGtesting.com
Printed in the USA
LVHW091912080519
617103LV00006B/888/P